THE BIG EMPTY

Other Books by Loren C. Steffy

George P. Mitchell
Fracking, Sustainability, and an Unorthodox Quest to Save the Planet

The Man Who Thought Like a Ship

Drowning in Oil
BP and the Reckless Pursuit of Profit

The Last Trial of T. Boone Pickens
With Chrysta Castañeda

Deconstructed
An Insider's View of illegal Immigration and the Building Trades
With Stan Marek

THE BIG EMPTY

A NOVEL

LOREN C. STEFFY

STONEY CREEK PUBLISHING
www.stoneycreekpublishing.com

Published by
Stoney Creek Publishing
stoneycreekpublishing.com

Distributed by Texas A&M University Press

ISBN (paperback): 978-1-7340822-9-6
ISBN (hardcover): 978-1-7340822-4-1
ISBN (ebook): 978-1-7340822-5-8
ISBN (audiobook): 978-1-7340822-6-5
Library of Congress: 2020924377

Cover and interior design by TLC Book Design, *TLCBookDesign.com*
Cover: Tamara Dever; Interior: Monica Thomas

Cover images by Deposit Photos:
Cowboy at sunset ©subinpumsom, Techology ©archibald1221

Printed in the United States

Contents

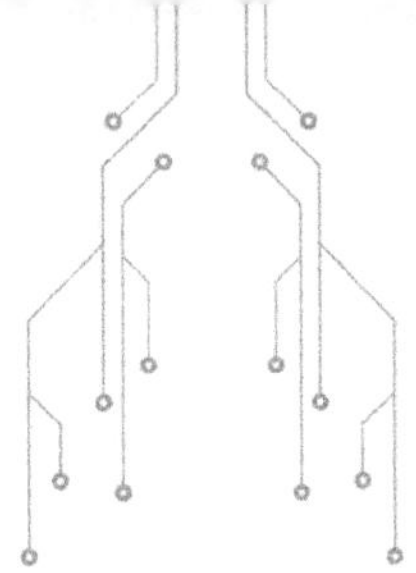

PREFACE

A FROZEN WALL of fear hit Trace Malloy seconds before the oncoming truck. The grille covering the big diesel engine filled his windshield. The horn blew a pneumatic wail that plied his thoughts reluctantly, coaxing him out of his reverie too late to turn away. His right hand shot out instinctively to steady his coffee in the cup holder as he pulled hard with his left on the wheel. Both were futile gestures.

The impact snapped him forward, then back again, as his pickup seemed to hop off the ground and bounce into the bar ditch beside the road. The seat belt snapped hard against his sternum. He heard the big truck's tires lock up behind him as it skidded to a stop. The sound of rubber grinding on asphalt lingered for a moment. Malloy felt his one hundred-sixty-five-pound frame compress into the unforgiving seat, forcing the last bit of air from his lungs. The pickup was suddenly still.

Coffee burned through the leg of his jeans, and his chest felt as if he'd been hit with a two-by-four. He moved hesitantly and was relieved when his body responded with only dull aches. No shooting pains probably meant nothing was broken. He'd likely saved himself the humiliation of explaining what had just happened to Doc Lambeau.

He cursed himself for not paying attention. Looking through the windshield, already cracked before the collision, he tried to orient himself. He felt like a child caught daydreaming in school, his mind racing to catch up with what he'd missed. The bar ditch rolled out in front of him, a partner to the long black line of asphalt on the left, both pulled taut toward the horizon.

He found himself hoping the pickup would still be drivable. He'd managed to swerve enough that the impact must have been a glancing blow. The fact that he was still conscious, still in one piece, seemed to prove that. He'd have to explain how he'd busted up a truck on the open road. The embarrassing truth was he'd just been thinking. Not about anything in particular, he was just letting his mind wander. He'd rolled through his days in Kansas — why they were suddenly in his mind so much he didn't know — and about Colt's accident last summer. By the time the truck hit him, his mind had meandered back to its favorite worry — would he and Darla be better off selling out and moving to town or trying to make it through one more year. And if they made it through that one, what about the next one?

His brain had a way of sidestepping when something was bothering him. Instead of obsessing over a problem as some people's do, his mind tried to distract him by conjuring images from the past. Still, as always, there was a common thread to these random thoughts — Colt's injury, the family farm, his days in Kansas, Luke's death. They all led back to the same problem, one that he couldn't solve. That didn't stop his mind from revisiting it, even if he was driving down the road and should have been thinking about work. His mother, who never believed in stewing over intractable concerns, would have scolded him if she'd seen how distracted he'd been. "Make your peace with the Lord, and you don't have to worry," she'd say. He never found it that easy, peace or no peace. Besides, his mother was usually referring to death. These days she didn't speak of it anymore, of course. Not now that it was almost upon her, now that it had, for all practical purposes, already claimed her. For that matter, she didn't speak of much of anything. And if she did, Malloy wasn't around to hear it.

He tugged on the door handle of the pickup and it opened with its usual hesitation. As he stepped out, he could see the crumpled fender. The headlight was gone, and part of the wheel cover had been pressed down into the tire, puncturing it. He cursed again. Changing it wasn't going to be easy in the ditch.

"Are you okay?" The question came from over his shoulder. He turned around and looked up from under the red brim of his cap. Years of grime and dirt had obscured the hat's patch that said "Possum Kingdom Lake." More than a decade of use had bent the brim of the fishing-trip souvenir into a gentle crescent that cupped his sunglasses. The trip now seemed a lifetime ago, one of the last times he and his brother, Matt, had enjoyed each other's company, pulling up 30-pound catfish from the depths of the lake itself and later plucking small-mouthed bass from the river below the dam.

"I'm fine," Malloy said.

The other man stood on the roadside, hands at his waist with the palms turned upward, as if he couldn't decide whether to shrug or fight. Either way, Malloy wasn't worried. The man wore jeans and a green shirt with a pale plaid pattern and buttons through the collar points. Underneath, a t-shirt was plainly visible. Both shirts — faded cotton — were tucked neatly into the jeans and secured with a webbed belt. He had on wire-rimmed glasses and his swept-back hair made it look as if he had something stored in his cheeks.

"You swerved right into me," the man said, his voice rising sharply in the middle of the sentence and falling at the end. "I couldn't stop. I'm driving that big truck; I couldn't turn fast enough. I was afraid it'd flip over."

"My fault. Sorry," Malloy said, walking up out of the ditch.

He knew he wasn't supposed to say that. Insurance companies said to never admit wrongdoing. More importantly, he knew company policy forbade it. He glanced back at the damaged fender. If he could pull the metal free of the airless tire, he could probably change the flat and get the truck down to Terry Garrison without having to involve the adjuster that the company inevitably would send out. It seemed pointless to argue over something he knew was his fault. "You mess up, you fess up," his mother used to say.

The man stared at him for a moment then went on talking as if he didn't believe Malloy had said anything.

"You were just driving in the middle of the road. I thought you were turning, and as I got closer, you just kept drifting over into my lane. There was nothing I could do."

"It's okay. I was just turning into this road here," Malloy said, pointing to the dirt stretch on the other side of the highway that led to a gate on the Main Ranch. "There's usually not much other traffic out here."

"Well, that's not an excuse..."

"Said I was sorry. Is your truck okay?"

It wasn't his own truck, of course. Malloy could tell just from looking that the man had never driven a truck before in his life. His claim that he couldn't swerve belied his inexperience behind the wheel. The big yellow-and-black markings of the Ryder label clinched the theory.

The truck was idling on the east-bound lane, a few feet from the point of impact. Malloy was no traffic inspector, but he could decipher the tell-tale black skid markings that shot out from the back wheels of the vehicle straight as exclamation marks. The truck hadn't veered from its lane.

The two men walked over to the van's front fender, the big engine rumbling impatiently on the other side of the grille as if annoyed by the inconvenience of the situation. There was a small dent and a couple of scratches, etched white with the paint from the pickup. Malloy had swerved just enough, his instincts asserting themselves over his mental distractions. The pickup, it seemed, had borne the brunt of the impact.

"Oh, man, they're going to charge me for that," the man moaned, looking at the fender. "I knew I shouldn't have tried to do this myself."

"Can't imagine they'll even notice that. They probably get more dents backing them into the lot. Where'd you rent it from?"

"San Jose."

"Don't worry about it."

"Well, I guess we need to exchange license and insurance information."

"Yeah, well, there's a problem there."

"What?" The man looked startled.

"I don't have mine."

"Don't have what?"

"My license. Don't have it with me. Guess there'd be an insurance card in the truck." Malloy walked back down to the ditch.

As he rooted through the glove box, the other man walked around to the front of the pickup and looked at the shattered headlight.

"Looks pretty bad. You've got a flat. And you're going to need a new windshield."

Malloy looked up from under the dash. A crack stretched across the bottom half of the windshield. He chuckled, although the other man couldn't see his smile from under the thick mustache.

"That was there before. Get a lot of rocks thrown up out here. Can't keep windshields. We don't replace 'em until they can't pass inspection anymore."

Malloy slammed the glove box shut.

"Looks like I don't have an insurance card in here either. Have to go back and get it, I guess."

Malloy stepped back out of the truck and closed the driver's side door with the blue-stylized "F" logo of Frye Agricultural Industries Inc. The other man standing in the road, hands on his hips, his posture taking on an impertinence that Malloy instantly found annoying.

"Wait one second," he said. "I'm not about to let you drive off. This was your fault." The man pointed an index finger at him, his brow furrowed in anger and disbelief.

Malloy sighed, looking at the fender biting into the airless tire. Drive off? He glanced at the toes of his boots. The seam that held the uppers to the sole near the toe was fraying. He'd need another pair before midsummer.

"I think we'd better call the police," the man went on.

"Well," Malloy said slowly. "that'd be fine with me, but I don't have a way to do that."

"I've got a cell phone—"

"That probably won't work out here," Malloy interrupted. "And there's only one county sheriff and three part-time deputies to patrol nine hundred square miles, so we may be waiting awhile for one to pass by."

The man pressed his lips together so that they almost disappeared from his face. He threw his head back and looked upward as if he were drinking in the vast expanse of the sky, then exhaled. The wind picked up, blowing hard from the west and working against the mousse that tried to keep the hair against his head.

"Where are you turning the truck in? In town? At Garrison's?" Malloy asked finally.

"I, uh, yes. I'm supposed to have it at a place called—" he fumbled in his pockets until he found a wadded-up receipt in his shirt—"Terry's Auto Repair."

Malloy nodded. "That's Terry Garrison. Tell you what. You tell Terry if there's any problem with the truck, he should settle up with me."

"You've got to be kidding. I don't even know your name."

"Trace Malloy. I've known Terry since we were in diapers. He won't give you any trouble." Malloy extended a hand, and the man stared at the outstretched palm for a few seconds before taking it limply.

"Well, I guess the least I could do is offer you a ride," the man said without telling Malloy his name.

"Appreciate it, but I don't need it," Malloy said. "I'll change the flat, bend the fender out, it'll be fine."

"Uh, okay, but I still don't know that I should be leaving without exchanging information."

Malloy had already started to walk back toward the truck. He stopped and turned, and he could feel the impatience welling up from the soles of his feet. He sucked a deep breath through the cover of his mustache and exhaled before he spoke, hoping to dispel any tone of annoyance. The wind pressed hard against his face.

"Look, I know it's probably not how they do things in San Ho-say, but there ain't that many of us out here. Fact is, even if I tried to hide from you, I couldn't. If I owe anything on the truck, just ask anyone in town, and they can tell you how to find me. I work for the ranch, and they'll back up any damages. You have my word."

"Well," the other man said slowly, "It just doesn't seem proper. What ranch?"

"*The* ranch," Malloy said more sharply than he'd intended. "The Conquistador. You know, the one that the whole town's named after." He stopped short of asking if the man knew where he was. No point in getting off on the wrong foot.

"Oh," the man said. He hesitated. "Of course. Well, uh, I guess it'll be okay, then. But still— "

"I gave you my word," Malloy said bluntly.

"Right. Okay. Well, I guess I'd better get moving."

Malloy watched the man climb back into the big truck, his long legs fumbling to find the proper footholds. Malloy waited, and the man ground the transmission as if he were determined to remove all the teeth from the gears. The clutch finally engaged, and the van lurched forward, stopped, then shuddered down the road, slowly gaining speed as it made for town.

Malloy watched the yellow square of its back door shrink slowly, heading into the burgeoning heat of the late morning sun. He turned back toward the ditch and looked again at the crumpled mess that had been a left front fender. He'd hoped fixing the pickup would be as easy as he made it sound. The truth was, he didn't want some stranger giving him a lift into town. It'd take months before he'd live that down. As it was, he was likely to be the butt of local jokes for weeks.

The bar ditch was flat and wide, designed to handle sudden runoff from downpours that had become disturbingly rare. It was just broad enough for him to change the tire. The ground wasn't terribly level, but it was sufficient for him to jack the truck up and shimmy the wheel off the studs. As he dislodged the spare and rolled it around to the front of the truck, he thought about what would happen at Garrison's as the man rattled through his explanation. He could see Terry standing there, listening to the story like an old sheep dog, handing the man a receipt without saying a word. Then, Terry would calmly walk down to Sam's barber shop. The ranch office would know the whole painful, embarrassing saga by noon and Darla would be waiting for him at their front door by suppertime.

Whoever the man was, he'd be getting a full dose of Conquistador. At the same time, Malloy knew, Conquistador was going to be getting more than its share of soft-handed men in black-and-yellow rental trucks. ✯

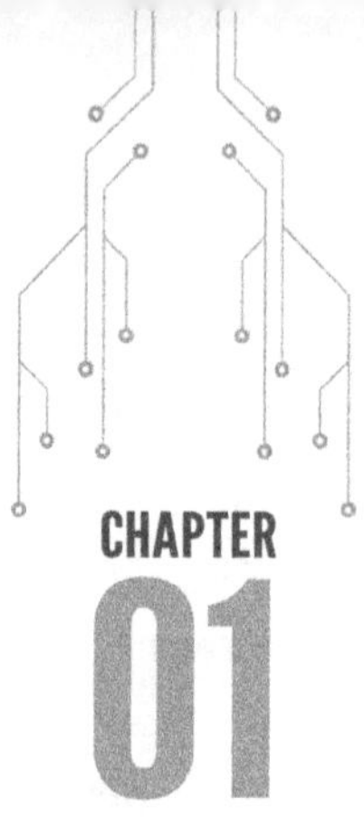

CHAPTER 01

"WHAT HAVE I DONE?" The question echoed in Blaine Witherspoon's head as he surveyed the view from the back patio. "What the hell have I done?"

The patio technically had been his for more than a week, but this was the first time he'd stood on it. Now, as he looked around, the view scared him. He'd never been immersed in a landscape so completely devoid of the vertical. He knew West Texas was flat, everyone knew that. He had been here before, during the original site surveys, and he'd seen the uninterrupted expanse. At the time, it had seemed a curiosity—barren, sure, but nothing that they wouldn't adjust to. After all, the move wasn't about the landscape. It was about money, but it was even more than that. If he was being honest, it was ultimately about prestige, about the chance to distinguish himself by doing what no one thought he could. There'd be plenty of time to nestle into beautiful scenery when he retired, a future made all the more satisfying if this deal worked out.

Now, though, facing immeasurable flatness alone for the first time, he felt as if he were suffocating, drowning in the pervasive nothingness of the place.

He rattled the ice in his half-empty glass of scotch. It was his second. He didn't usually drink alone, but after nearly running over the first local he'd met on the road into town this morning, he'd earned it. Besides, it might help take his mind off the emptiness he felt building inside him as he surveyed the expanse behind his house, a plane broken only by the occasional sage or scrub cedar or thorny mesquite. The land did have a slight slope, as if he were sitting along the edge of a shallow bowl, or perhaps the rim of a dinner plate. There were no boulders or trees or what most people thought of as terrain. The moonscapes he'd seen beamed back from the Apollo missions he'd watched as child seemed more inviting.

Earlier in the day, it hadn't been so bad. He'd had a lot of phone calls to deal with, letting everyone know he'd made it in, touching base with the movers who would bring the rest of their belongings — and Jenna — in a few days. The crews working on nearby houses had created a comforting background noise.

Now, without the builders and the staccato of their nail guns driving back the emptiness, a terrifying loneliness washed over him, like a child at an amusement park experiences when he suddenly turns around to find his parents have disappeared.

The gray blanket of night began to settle, and the silence and vastness overwhelmed him. He found himself gasping.

"What have I done?"

Jenna would be here soon enough, and she'd be furious. Even now, he could almost feel her cold, seething anger seeping into the emptiness that engulfed him, and his dread of the imminent conflict heightened his despair. He'd oversold this move, no question. She hadn't wanted to leave California unless it was to return to her beloved New Jersey. That had been the deal they'd made when they first headed West — no more moves unless it was back to "civilization," as she liked to call it.

They'd spent the first fourteen years of their marriage shuffling from one high-tech boom town to another—Raleigh, Fishkill, Cambridge, Seattle. That last one was tough, a cross-country "relo," as the company called it, with a week's notice. Then the chance to join AzTech opened up in Milpitas and he couldn't turn it down, despite all the Silicon Valley negatives—brutal taxes, stifling human density, freeways clogged as if the whole Peninsula were being evacuated and reclaimed every day. It was the lion's den of high-tech moves, but it came with the chance to run his own plant someday, and it had paid off. A year and a half and they were out—really out. Out here.

Jenna never wanted to move to the Valley in the first place, but she certainly didn't want to leave it for a backwater that to her still meant Indian raids and wagon trains. Even so, he'd managed to make it sound better than the view that now bombarded him from the patio. Sure, he'd said, there would be inconveniences—no chain stores, not even a Wal-Mart close by. Restaurants would be a disappointment after the international fare they'd come to expect in the Bay Area. The schools might not measure up, but Brandon was a smart kid, and they could make up for any shortcomings at home. Besides, the plant would give money to the schools. That was part of the deal. In time, as the factory grew and more people moved in, all of these things would change. The minuses would become pluses, he told her. He would see to that.

They'd had a few arguments, but that was to be expected. Eventually, though, Jenna had given in. He'd promised her it would be for the best, that it would help secure the future she coveted. Once he got the plant up and running, he stood to score a big bonus and then—well, then, he could pretty much write his own ticket, pick any job he wanted. If he could run a successful plant here, he would be the envy of the company, perhaps the whole industry.

"What have I done?"

The reality of the move began to sink in. They didn't belong here—none of them. Dozens, maybe hundreds, of transplants would be following him to what? They would be forced to make a home in a place devoid of everything they knew. The entire retail establishment consisted of a gas station that sold newspapers, candy and coffee, a feed store, and a propane shop. Restaurants? There was a diner that specialized in coffee, eggs, and ham at 4 a.m. and served up chicken-fried steak—a grease-laden gut-bomb—in the evenings. On Thursdays, Fridays, and Saturdays, a part-time rancher sold barbecue from a portable stand just off the town square. Jenna, who'd been a vegetarian most of her adult life, wasn't going to be eating out much. He'd found a grocery store, but he must have driven twenty-five miles, and while the produce was fresh it was lacking in variety—lettuce, tomatoes, cucumbers, cantaloupe, but no arugula or chia seeds.

"What have I done?"

He took some comfort in the thought that more houses would be built soon, and people—his people—would be filling them. He longed to see the wood frames cutting into the unrelenting sky, obscuring his view, adding some desperately needed perpendiculars—anything to hide that insurmountable distance to the horizon.

He wished Jenna had already arrived. Even a good argument would be something to unlock his gaze from the relentless expansiveness. Their arguments weren't the knock-down, drag-out kind. Witherspoon had always prided himself on his control over his temper. He wasn't a violent man, and even in anger, he tried to choose his words well. Jenna's temper was similar to his own, slow to boil over and quick to settle down. Their "fights" didn't simmer, and their grievances weren't harbored in silence. Resolution typically came quickly.

Yes, she would be upset when she saw this place and confronted its big emptiness. When the argument was over, though, holding her close again, he might feel as if he could breathe amid all this nothingness. She would come around, wouldn't she? It would be rough at first, but she wanted the same thing he did. As his wife, she'd have a prominent position in the community they would build, and later, when they moved on — when they could pick where they wanted to go — she would get to choose.

He went inside and closed all the blinds. The need for privacy was purely psychological. He was, essentially, the first one here. Years from now, as he stood in the street sipping a beer with the neighbors, he could claim to have been the first. "I remember when your place went in," he'd be able to say. "They had to pour the slab twice." By then, he would be the old hand telling the greenhorns the way it worked around these parts. He would be the one explaining houses without basements and the peculiar demands that shifting red soil can put on a foundation.

Years — his mind stumbled on the thought. That's what this was all about. It would take years to get this state-of-the-art computer chip factory running seamlessly. It was the one promise about this move he'd be able to keep. "I don't want to keep hopping around the country," Jenna had said when they first talked about it. "Wherever we go, we need to plan to stay there — not just for a year or two. For years and years."

Years and years. They'd say goodbye to one millennium and welcome the next, and then, perhaps settle into middle age here. He huddled inside the house, blinds drawn, trying not to think about the abyss beyond. He felt like a frightened Cub Scout cowering inside a tent, gladly blinded to the terrors outside yet aware that the flimsy barrier wouldn't keep them at bay. In his desperation, he even found himself longing for television, but they hadn't run the cable yet and the place was so desolate an antenna couldn't coax a signal.

He downed another scotch and went to bed early, but he couldn't find sleep amid the clutter of his mind. His brain was soaked in worry about Jenna, about Brandon, about the move, about all the details at the plant that would require his attention, and about the one thing he hadn't anticipated until it barreled out from his subconscious like a runaway coal train: the possibility of failure. He could blow this. He could choke. He could take this great opportunity and screw it up. Then where would they be? He and Jenna and Brandon alone on this desolate plain with no fallback plan.

What were they thinking back in Milpitas? Of all the places on the planet, why expand here? He'd been through all the reasons thousands of times, of course, but what if they were just flat out wrong?

His mind raced through the things that could go awry, a mental laundry list of despair.

"What have I done?"

Cheap labor. What if they couldn't train applicants to the skill level required to make semiconductor wafers? What if, for some reason — cultural or otherwise — the locals didn't want to take jobs at the plant? What if they just couldn't find enough qualified people in this area to get up to full staffing? When they'd made the deal, the county commissioners had promised that drawing workers from nearby towns like Gunyon and Tysonville wouldn't be a problem. Out here, driving an hour for supper was routine, they'd said. Folks would easily do that for a good job. But what if they were wrong? What if that pitch was just economic development blather? The area's desperate hopes for economic salvation underpinned AzTech's deal, and what if, despite all their research, those hopes turned out to be an elected official's fantasy?

What if money saved with all the tax breaks didn't offset the higher overhead of starting up in such a remote place? What if those costs were higher than expected?

Then there was the dust. High tech devices required precision manufacturing. The tiniest dust particle could scrap an entire batch of chips and cost millions. And this factory was surrounded by dust. It was awash in it. The wind would blast across the plains, roiling whole clouds of it like someone sweeping a table clean with his arm. One speck from a cloud like that could cost him his job.

What if the plant didn't operate as efficiently as he said it could? For all the technical precision, making semiconductors was a lot like cooking. Sometimes things just went wrong—"losing the recipe," they called it. Finding it again could take weeks, even months.

What if they couldn't get the power they needed? The company had put up money to run new power lines, but there had been some problems getting the right of way. He was estimating they'd need sixty watts a square foot, far more than anything that had ever been built in this region. What if that number was low? Or what if the infrastructure simply couldn't deliver?

What if the water recycling program didn't work? That could add to the costs, and there didn't seem to be a lot of surplus to draw from. He needed a million gallons a day, and that was assuming he could get the recycling systems working to spec. He wanted the plant to have the best environmental record in the company, if not the industry, but what if it couldn't be done? Even in this land that seemed to abuse all living things until they struck back, he wanted to set an example for treating it kindly.

All of this had been planned and reviewed, of course, but no matter how carefully they'd studied the issues in California, making it work in West Texas was another matter. Things could go wrong. Things *always* went wrong.

And that was just the plant. There was also the house, the surrounding neighborhood, the relations with the community, all of which ultimately were his to worry about, and his to be blamed for if something didn't work out.

He spent the night drifting in and out of his mental sparring match, a fitful sleep of jabbing and covering and shadowboxing with his inner doubts.

With dawn came sanity. He had work to do, both on the house and at the plant. Construction crews filled the freshly poured streets, and the sound of machinery rose from the surrounding lots. He welcomed the noise, the subconscious reminder that he was not alone on some barren planet. At one point, on the phone with the foreman at the plant, he almost found the Tejano rhythms blaring from their radios an annoyance.

He worked through the business of the day, and his confidence increased. There were questions about the blueprints, issues about hooking up to the local power grid, and a half dozen other problems that submerged the fears of the previous night. He pulled the cardboard box containing his dinner from the microwave—spaghetti squash noodles and meatless pasta sauce—the last of a supply he'd brought from California. He sat in the empty living room with his back against the hearth feeling genuinely tired. For a moment, it seemed that sleep, so elusive the night before, might actually make peace with him.

After he ate, he poured himself a scotch. He still couldn't muster the courage to return to the patio, so he opted for the front door instead. As he opened it, he could feel the heat from its metal façade radiating as if it had been pulled from a blast furnace. His attention, though, was captured by a sight so overpowering that the vastness that surrounded him the night before seemed inconsequential.

It was a sunset, yet one unlike any he'd ever seen. The sun was a shimmering copper orb so huge it seemed as if it were pulling the world toward it. Its rays shot across the sky, painting it a scintillating palette of reds, pinks, oranges, and violets. He could see the heat and feel its colors. The sun seemed to flutter as it gradually sank. He stood transfixed, captivated by the blend of light, the smear of hues, and the embrace of warmth. As the sun slipped below the lip of the horizon, he wanted to run to it and beg it not to go.

When Jenna arrived two days later, he waited until the movers had unloaded and left, then he steered her clear of the patio and ushered her to the front door to share his discovery. He stood behind her, her auburn hair tinged with highlights of the sun. He watched her stare in breathless fascination. They stood in silence for half an hour, mesmerized by the descent.

"Okay, there's one thing that's better than Jersey," Jenna said finally, her voice barely above a whisper. The sun peeled away, its retreat leaving a shadow across her face where just moments before the fading rays had flickered. They stared into the approaching twilight as if trying to hang on to the last vestiges of the vanishing beams.

In the final moments of daylight, Jenna close to him, he felt inspiration welling inside him. They could do this. Together, they could embrace this change that he was forcing himself each day to confront. They would prevail. Sure, he'd never set up a plant before, never been in charge of hiring an entire work force from scratch, creating a budget out of thin air, or establishing a production schedule before there was even a production line, but they would make it work. *He* would make it work. He had to.

Brandon would arrive in another week or so. They'd sent him to spend some time with his grandparents while they got through the move. By then, Blaine would barely be aware of another person in the house. There was too much to do, and too much that had to be done perfectly.

Jenna was more a sunrise person, really, though she couldn't deny the beauty of the sunset before her. Growing up in central New Jersey, vacation was always "the Shore"—Cape May, Wildwood, Ocean City, Sea Isle City—her shoes had collected sand from them all.

Even as a teenager she would get up just as the sun was rising, race out of the rented cottage and sit unblinking on a dune, hypnotized by the panorama of the early light washing over the surf.

It was gorgeous, but it couldn't compare with the other-worldly splendor of the sunset she saw now. It became her touchstone, the one thing she would look forward to during the long hot days when Blaine was at work and she was left to herself with only the sound of the central air conditioning to break up the stillness of the house.

As overpowering as the sunsets were, though, they couldn't melt away her list of dislikes that grew daily. It started with the creatures—snakes, mice, bugs, scorpions, and centipedes so large they belonged in a 1950s science fiction movie. She found them all in the course of settling in, which made the whole process, well, unsettling.

One did not generally find snakes—even harmless king snakes—in a garage in Princeton. Nor scorpions. And the centipedes seemed to crawl right out of a childhood nightmare. They were five inches long, blue headed, with a flat green body, and they would rear up and spread their mandibles when they felt threatened.

The land they inhabited seemed every bit as unreal and uninviting as the life forms themselves. She'd never thought of "flat" as an inadequate word, but here, it seemed an understatement. Was there a term to capture the pancake of the terrain? The blazing arc of the sky combined into a sheer, uninterrupted expanse of what? Nothingness? No, that wasn't really right. It wasn't a void; it was full of dirt and scrubby bushes and rocks and cactus and sun and the occasional cloud. It wasn't nothingness, it was the uninterrupted *sameness* that unnerved her. If she walked to the end of the new street, she could choose any direction and the view didn't change: red and tan dirt below, azure sky above.

She missed the closeness of the trees, the narrow windiness of the roads, and the non-threatening wildlife. Back home, in the university town and its bucolic surroundings—not here, this would never be home—her biggest worry was a deer jumping in front of the car as she wound through the lush countryside after dark.

She couldn't get used to the howl of the coyotes, either. Their eerie wails wafted across the plain like wraiths in the night. The second day after she arrived, she and Blaine had seen one near the house as dusk was settling, prancing along the edge of the lengthening shadows. It shot a furtive, hungry glance at them, then picked its way across what someday would be their neighbors' backyards, disappearing into the emptiness beyond. The next morning, Jenna made sure the crew was there to finish the fence.

She stifled her complaints, though. She wasn't happy about the move, but there'd be time for happiness later—the kind she'd agreed to wait for. Blaine was convinced this was their chance to achieve their dreams—move back to New Jersey and perhaps get a weekend home at the Shore. Blaine had even talked about setting up his own consulting business and working from wherever she wanted to live. She could see it in her mind—weekdays, Blaine would work from his office in their Colonial-era saltbox and she could go into the city for shopping or lunch with friends. They'd spend the weekends at the beach. All they had to do was get through however long they had in this desolate hellscape.

In the weeks after she arrived, she busied herself with unpacking and trying to adapt to the strange house. No house they'd had since she left Jersey could compare to the one she grew up in, a stout, well-worn Victorian. That house, with its broad wooden porch and its cozy rooms, always seemed to be a warm bunker against the bitterness of the East Coast winter while the breezy gazebo with its whirring fan kept the summer humidity at bay.

The house she was now moving into was the first new one they'd bought, and she found the freshness and the design—vaulted ceilings and bright, open rooms—strangely antiseptic.

She didn't want to distract Blaine as he tried to adjust to his new job. She recognized the opportunity and did her best to act as if she were adapting. When she sat with him and watched the sunsets, she almost convinced herself. ✯

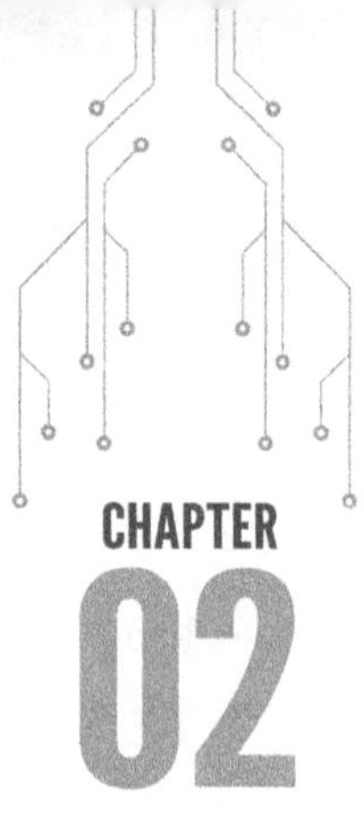

CHAPTER 02

TRACE MALLOY'S FIST landed firmly in the middle of the other man's nose. He could feel the bridge give under the force of his knuckles, and he knew he'd broken it. It wasn't much of a punch, just a quick jab that he pulled back instantly, as if to say he was sorry.

But he wasn't sorry. As the anger and adrenaline coursed through him, Malloy felt no regret for hitting Blaine Witherspoon. God knows, the arrogant son of a bitch had it coming. He *was* sorry, though, about the implications, about the long lectures he'd receive about building bridges or mending fences or whatever other type of psychological construction was supposed to be going on.

Witherspoon lay in a crumpled, whimpering mass on the floor. Several of the other newly transplanted homeowners who'd attended the meeting hovered around him, one or two shooting hateful glances at Malloy. Witherspoon's glasses were shattered, and blood gushed from his nostrils. He tried to cup it with his hand, but it flowed around and through his fingers. His head hung limply on his chest, which heaved as he gasped for air.

One of the homeowners wheeled around, locking his sights on Malloy. He took a step in Malloy's direction. Malloy stood still, looking down at Witherspoon and not saying anything.

"I think you'd better leave," the man said, trying to stare Malloy down. Malloy looked back at him calmly. He could tell the man was scared, and he knew he could send him into the corner with Witherspoon if he had to. Then again, Malloy hadn't come to the meeting looking for a fight, at least not a fistfight.

Others from the group were staring at him now, too, and Malloy rested his eyes on each one. The man in front of him was pasty and fat, about five foot four and wearing the open collared Oxford shirt that the homeowners seemed to favor. Malloy tried to recall his name. Swan? Swail? Swain? Howard, he thought, Howard Swain. He'd met him a half dozen or so times in the months since he'd first collided with Witherspoon and the others had begun arriving in town. He remembered Witherspoon's name, of course, because of the collision. He'd learned it during the insurance settlements. But it was hard to keep the other newcomers straight. The homies—as Malloy had started calling them, largely as an inside joke with himself—pretty much kept to themselves. They didn't come to the feed store or the propane shop or take their cars to Terry Garrison's garage, so most of the townspeople in Conquistador hadn't gotten to know them. They didn't go to church, didn't wave when they drove past you in town, didn't say hello on the street on the rare occasions when they actually came downtown.

Beads of sweat had broken out on Swain's forehead, and Malloy stood motionless, returning the stare. He looked to the others lining up behind Swain. Several were wearing coats and ties, representatives of the developers from Lubbock who were building the housing subdivision at AzTech's request.

Technically, they still controlled the homeowners association, and Malloy had hoped they would understand his concerns.

They understood only money, and right now, the money was coming from Witherspoon and his burgeoning band of geeks. The developers were willing to do whatever Witherspoon wanted, as long as he paid for it. So they now stood with the homies, aligned with the flow of money regardless of whether they understood the issues. The moment hung silent and pregnant between them, Swain pointing toward the door, frozen except for his moistening pores. Malloy had no intention of continuing the confrontation. It had already slipped from his grasp.

"I said, you need to leave," Swain pressed again, finding courage amid the fear that floated up from his corpulent frame, carried on the acrid odor of his perspiration.

"I reckon," Malloy said finally. As he opened the door of the community center, he heard Witherspoon's shaky voice coming after him.

"I'm going to sue you, Malloy. You can't get away with this. You're nothing but a thug, a...a...bully. That's what you are."

If the homeowners had been able to see Malloy's face, they might have spotted the row of white teeth breaking through the bushy overhang of his mustache. He didn't laugh out loud, but he couldn't contain the smile.

A bully? Malloy thought, as he ground the key in the ignition of the pickup. So now he was the bad guy. The homies had gotten everything they wanted, and it still wasn't enough.

He wound the pickup around the carefully paved road leading to the main entrance. To his right, the fountain spurted shamelessly, illuminated by the spotlights planted just under the surface. The flow of its fingers seemed to dance in the light before hitting the sprawling expanse of the surface. After tonight, they might want to call it Lake Nosebleed, Malloy thought, chuckling to himself. He was still too angry to feel bad about what had happened.

The headlights of the pickup settled briefly on the massive limestone sign with "Rolling Ranch Estates" carved into it. He waited for the electric gate to roll back. Yet another annoyance. Most people in Conquistador didn't lock their doors at night. These people were locking their neighborhood. The town didn't even have a full-time policeman. It had never needed one. Yet these people, beholden to their city-spawned fears, felt they had something so precious that even out here it had to be protected, even if it inconvenienced everybody else.

Malloy understood the desire to protect property, but these people weren't interested in what he considered property. They had no land, and they didn't want any. They built huge houses so close together that two people could barely walk between them. Their yards were little bigger than the pools they all had to have. The gate was supposed to keep out undesirables or protect all the fancy stuff inside their slapped-together houses. What thief would come all the way out here for that? And if he did, where would he sell the stuff he stole? The town of Conquistador was protected by the greatest of crime prevention tools—apathy. No one in Conquistador cared what the homies hoarded in their houses, and no one outside of Conquistador thought much about the town or the people in it.

The new chip plant could change that. Hell, if it succeeded, it might even make Conquistador the focus of national attention, of business interest—business *investment.* But it came at a price he was just beginning to understand. Progress meant economic opportunity, but it also meant imported habits, demands, and fears that he hadn't really anticipated.

Malloy suspected that it wasn't just fear of crime that made the transplants pen themselves in. It was just fear. They feared this place that was so vastly different than what they'd left, and they wanted to keep it out, to push back against everything around them and carve out a familiar space. They didn't want to adapt. These weren't people who ever paid much attention to where they lived or where they'd been. They just bounced around the country, moving in, moving out, and moving on. They had no sense of place. They liked houses that all looked the same because it made them feel at home. They didn't care if a house was built to last, because they'd be selling it in a few years. They planted stunted twigs in the front yard and called them trees, hoping to see a few sprigs from the branches before they left.

From the time the first slabs were poured, the big city developers brought in by the homies had controlled everything about the subdivision. Even that term — subdivision — was ludicrous here, yet they clung to it. Malloy realized the homies weren't building, or moving in, they were nesting. They were creating something familiar because in all their moving, they'd never encountered anything like the Big Empty. It wouldn't conform. They were making themselves comfortable the only way they knew how. They were removing this place from itself, and creating an environment they found comfortable, one that was impersonal, prefabricated, and sealed.

As he shook his head, the hypocrisy of his thoughts jabbed at him. Wasn't this progress? The homes behind him were the newest and nicest for a hundred miles or more. Weren't there going to be jobs? Even if he wasn't interested, shouldn't the people of Conquistador be allowed a chance at making a living that didn't involve coming home caked in sweat and dirt and animal shit every night?

Really, Rolling Ranch Estates wasn't any different from the last big wave of progress to hit these parts. Instead of yellow rental trucks and moving vans there were wagon trains filled with foreign investors and wide-eyed Easterners out to make a new life and a fast buck. They tore up the land, changed the very face of it, and fenced it in. They brought in cattle from half a world away, raised crops that had never grown here, and later, punched holes in the ground and pumped out its guts. They talked of "taming the land," with all the pride of a big game hunter who'd just bagged a white lion.

You couldn't tame it. Not this land. It fought back, and it always won. They learned that too, and so would the homies. He was still seething from the altercation, and he almost forgot that he had supported the AzTech plan, at least initially. If he was being honest with himself, he had to acknowledge that everything that made him so angry about the subdivision was at least in part his fault. Recognizing that only made him angrier.

The gate rolled aside enough for him to squeeze the pickup through. It was nicer than anything they had at the ranch, where they actually needed such devices to keep the stock in the appropriate grazing areas. He stopped the truck instinctively after he pulled through. He was about to put it in park and hop out to close the gate when he caught himself.

He turned onto what he still called "the Main Road." He wondered how much longer that name would stick. How long before the homies demanded it be renamed "Rolling Ranch Parkway" because Farm-to-Market Road 3792 just wasn't good enough or wasn't the way they named roads in California or New Jersey.

In Malloy's mind, the Main Road deserved its nickname. It cut through the center of Conquistador and provided a reference for the few visitors who might be unfamiliar with the ranch and its sprawling branches. In the center of town, the Main Road intersected with what locals called "the Gunyon

Road," because, well, that's where it went. The largest portion of the ranch — and the ranch offices — were just off the Gunyon Road, south of Main. The West Fork was on the opposite side of Main, out toward Tysonville. The Tie Bow, sloping pastureland that reached to the horizon, was back toward the east. Even further east, Rolling Ranch Estates, the scene of the evening's dustup, was taking shape across the Main Road from the Tie Bow. Leaving the development, Malloy remembered that the chip plant would be conveniently located for Witherspoon and the other homies just five minutes south — home and workplace strategically linked to minimize contact with the town and its residents. It reminded him of pioneers circling their wagons to fend off the unknown. Driving on the Main Road, Malloy realized that the narrow sliver of blacktop was half as wide as the concrete subdivision streets he'd just left. The night's darkness enveloped him, and he began to brood. He was going to catch hell from Roy in the morning. He'd handled the whole situation poorly.

He understood Roy's efforts to welcome the homies. Malloy had agreed with the reasons, at least at first. AzTech Semiconductor would be good for the town, a chance for a future that otherwise hinged on sentimentality. At some point, Frye International would have to sell the ranch, and then what? What would stop Conquistador from withering like so many other towns, fading into the future, carried away piece by piece by each death until there was nothing.

And yet, the hope for economic prosperity was proving equally unsavory. With each new incursion into his way of life, he found himself growing more resentful. Plant manager Witherspoon personified Malloy's increasing agitation. From his hair gel, to his wire-frame glasses, to his dough-like skin, Malloy found just the sight of Witherspoon an irritant. The newcomer had a superior air about him, and every time Malloy talked to him, he felt as if his own shirt were lined with sandpaper. The punch to the nose was a culmination, a release of frustration that had been building since he first collided with Witherspoon's rented moving van.

They had disagreed early on about plans for a new power line that would cut across the ranch. Roy had given in to the demands of the power company, which were basically the demands of the homies as well. Then the water battles had started. The AzTech plant was going to put a huge drain on the water table, and the minute the ranch had raised concerns, Witherspoon started attacking ranching practices.

He fancied himself an environmentalist, and he'd memorized some statistics about land management, grazing methods, and livestock water usage.

The battle had intensified as more homes were built in the subdivision, and each owner seemed to want—or to think they deserved—a pool. It was the stupid pond, though, that stuck in Malloy's craw. For all Witherspoon's self-proclaimed environmentalism, he didn't seem to appreciate the water situation. It was as if they thought all their statistics and Internet-gathered data meant more than local knowledge. Malloy had tried to explain the interaction between limestone and low water levels and what would happen when the aquifer dropped below a certain point.

Around Conquistador, people his parents' age still talked about the drought in the early Fifties, when the water smelled like sulfur. The aquifer could still hold plenty of water, but once the homies drew the water table down, nobody would want to drink it or swim in it or smell it in their precious little pond. They were coming off of two years of drought and possibly facing a third. Malloy hadn't seen it this dry in years, and the old-timers were talking about the Fifties again half a decade later.

Ranchers, like farmers, don't forget droughts. It was that simple. A drought was a blatant reminder of how little control a cowboy has over his own livelihood. If there's one thing the Big Empty teaches you quickly, it's that you don't make the same mistake twice. When it came to the weather, the land, or the livestock, Malloy had learned to listen to the elders.

Witherspoon's ears were clogged with arrogance, and Malloy had run out of patience. Tonight, he'd allowed the months of exasperation to get the best of him. Still, Witherspoon had that pop coming, and more.

"Smug little asshole," Malloy said out loud.

Trace Malloy never claimed to be a diplomat. He wasn't raised to solve problems with words. What was Roy thinking sending him to a meeting like this, anyway? Roy was the master negotiator, the one who insisted that they get along with the homies. Why hadn't *he* come to this meeting?

Witherspoon, the prissy little bastard, probably *would* try to sue him. Well, good luck hiring a lawyer around here who'd be willing to sue over a bloody nose. In fact, Charlie Weeks was about the only one you could find without burning a tank of gas, and Charlie had bloodied Malloy's nose in the seventh grade. Somehow, that ought to disqualify him from the case, Malloy thought.

None of which solved the real problem. He'd done more to hurt relations with the homies than he'd done to help. No matter how many noses he broke, the situation wasn't going to get any better. As a representative of the town's original—and biggest—employer, the Conquistador Ranch, he needed to work with Witherspoon. Instead, the cowboy in him had won out. He felt torn between his job and his livelihood, two things that had always seemed the same until the first wood frames of Rolling Ranch Estates started appearing on the horizon.

Witherspoon didn't understand that, of course. He couldn't understand it. He couldn't understand Malloy's frustration, his growing feeling of obsolescence. Malloy had felt like the homie was baiting him. The conversation replayed itself in Malloy's mind.

"I think we all understand the need for water," Witherspoon said, in a tone so condescending it immediately reminded Malloy of the first ranch supervisor he'd worked for in Kansas.

"If you understood it, you'd turn off that damn fountain," Malloy had fired back.

"Mr. Malloy, the people here are trying to build homes. We want to build a community. We moved here to get away from the city, the crime. We want our community to be safe and attractive, and our lake is a big part of that."

"Well, first of all, your 'lake' isn't much bigger than a stock tank, and secondly, some of us make our livings out here, and a big part of that depends on water. On a hot day, a cow can drink twenty-five gallons of water, and we've got about twelve thousand of them out there."

Both men had pushed to their feet, staring across the table while the ten or so other board members for the Rolling Ranch Estates Homeowners Association stared in silence.

"Mr. Malloy, we all know how ranchers have misused this land for more than a century. You overgrazed it, you exploited it, and now you want us to feel sorry for you."

"This doesn't have anything to do with grazing practices. It's got to do with the fact that pumping water out of the ground for your little show pond out there, just so it can evaporate, is a huge waste. And that doesn't count all the water you'll need for your swimming pools and lawn sprinklers and God knows what else. If this keeps up, none of us will have enough water to get through the summer."

Malloy flung down the preliminary statistics he'd gotten from the county water district. It wasn't just the lake, of course, the whole subdivision was putting a drain on the water table. The number of houses grew with the developers' ambitions, and now they felt a golf course was a necessity because of the "high caliber" of homeowner they planned to attract. And that was before the factory began production and sopped up hundreds of millions more gallons a year. Malloy never knew computer chips needed so much water — ten times as much as cows.

The lake, though, seemed to make a blatant mockery of it all. It was as if the homies had just moved in and decided to help themselves to all the resources. The lake hadn't been included in the original plans for the subdivision. It had been slipped in later, an "aesthetic enhancement" the developer had called it.

"There is plenty of water. I've studied it myself. These people," Witherspoon said, motioning to the other board members, "will tell you no one is more concerned about environmental issues than I. But I hardly think one lake is going to suck up all the water."

"I don't know how much studying you've done of what, but this isn't some Ivy League class project. Have you considered the evaporation rate for that fountain? We're looking at a third straight year of drought. I've lived here all my life. I can remember my mama not washing clothes so we'd have water for the cows. This isn't something you want to mess with."

By now they were leaning across the table, noses inches apart. Everyone else in the room was frozen. Then he said it. Witherspoon crossed the line.

"Your 'mama's' bad hygiene doesn't have anything to do with us." He bobbed his head derisively to accent the word "mama."

The fist flew before Malloy knew he'd let it go. Or at least that's what he told himself. Truth is, he'd never expected Witherspoon to just stand there and take it. Anyone in Conquistador who'd ever dared to say something like that would have thrown up their guard before they finished talking.

Still fuming, Malloy turned into the gravel drive about a mile and a half from the subdivision and stopped at the unpainted metal gate that marked the entrance to his property. He jumped out of the truck and swung the gate open. He pulled through, got out, and closed it behind him, sliding the rusted chain through the latch and locking it with a padlock. Conquistador might be shrouded in criminal apathy when it came to home burglaries, but it had become an increasingly popular target for cattle thieves.

Rustling was still alive and well all across rural Texas. Conquistador was remote, but it was a lot closer to a livestock auction than an auto chop shop or a pawn dealer. Cattle thieves could pull up, load half your herd, and be gone in a matter of minutes. With little law enforcement in the area, the chances of them being caught were slim. Malloy knew the gate alone wouldn't stop a determined rustler, but he saw it as a deterrent. It was also part of the reason he kept his father's old shotgun loaded above the front door, even though he told himself it was at the ready in case the coyotes came after the cattle.

Tonight, the cows had wandered down toward the fence that lined the southern edge of the property. He didn't have to shoo any away from the truck as he pulled up the drive and parked in front of the tan clapboard siding where the garage used to be. He'd enclosed the garage himself after his father died and his mother got sick. The plan was to keep her there as long as they could, which turned out to be about eight months. Seeing his handiwork reminded him of how long it had been since he'd been to visit her, and he chided himself. This weekend, he promised silently.

He stopped for a moment and scanned the darkness that spilled like ink over the front pasture. He walked up the concrete steps to the small porch that jutted out from the front door of the one-story house. In all, the Malloy property covered about one hundred and fifty acres, mostly in a long narrow strip that went back from the Main Road just across from the western edge of the Tie Bow area of the "big ranch," or the Conky, as Malloy used to call it in his youth. Years ago, Malloy's land had been part of the Conquistador, back when the Conky was one of the grand Texas ranches. In the late Forties, after World War II, when the children of the original Scots divided up much of the original spread and began selling it off to pay debts, Malloy's grandfather had bought about two hundred acres. The family had had to sell about fifty of them during some of the bad years, but Malloy had always been proud that they'd been able to hold on to the rest of it.

The air carried a hint of freshness as he turned to enter the house. Last summer had been brutal and blazing, followed by a winter every bit as bitter and frigid as the summer had been hot. The old-timers were saying the drought would continue at least for one more summer, which meant another year of trying to keep the stock tanks filled, finding enough hay, and scrambling to keep the whole place from shriveling up and blowing away.

Spring already was simmering, warming itself toward summer again. He'd have to get after his own cows soon, which meant a lot more weekend work. He should have gone to see Mama before now.

He went through the front door and saw Darla and Colt already at the table, well into their supper. He hung his red gimme cap on the rack by the door and walked into the dining room. His hiking boots echoed on the raised wooden floor in spite of their rubber soles. The table was stocked with a plate of chicken-fried steak, cream gravy, potatoes, pinto beans, and bread. Malloy could smell the pecan pie for dessert hidden somewhere in the kitchen. He realized he hadn't eaten since lunch and it was now after eight o'clock.

"We waited as long as we could, but we got hungry," Darla said, glancing up at him. "I figured you might be awhile."

What she meant was that she knew he probably wouldn't be in much of a mood for conversation when he got home, and as usual, she was right. Darla was a large fireplug of a woman, though she didn't appear overweight so much as stout. Her brownish-blonde hair hung just above her shoulders. As he sat down, Malloy watched his wife's large hands ladle gravy on top of the breaded, pan-fried cube steak she'd put on his plate.

He started to eat without saying anything. Darla stared at him for a moment, and then resumed her meal.

"I got the tiller working again," Colt said, his words seeming to blast through the silence at the table. "I can't promise how much longer I can keep it going, but for now, it'll work."

Malloy nodded in approval. Colt had a serious look on his face, knowing his father had bigger worries, yet still needing to let the older man know he'd done something, however small, to make things run more smoothly around the house. His deep-set brown eyes rested on his father. His dark brown hair was slicked to one side, a style that made him look like a young man instead of a fifteen-year-old boy.

Colt had developed an aptitude for all things mechanical, and he spent his spare time puttering with the bits of machinery that lay around the barn in various stages of disrepair.

"At the rate you're going," Malloy said finally, "there won't be anything left to fix by summer."

Colt smirked. "Something else will break."

Malloy snorted knowingly and chewed a bite of his steak. "How was school?" he said at last, prying his thoughts away from the scene at the homeowners meeting.

"Same old stuff. We're still reading *The Red Badge of Courage*. I don't see why they make us read that. It's all about Yankees and them winning the war. And then Ms. Hawkins said today that Jim Conklin, this character in the book who gets killed, is supposed to be like Jesus—a 'Christ figure' she called him. I don't think that's right. Why would Jesus be a Yankee?"

"I think you're missing the point, son. The book's about the atrocities of war, it's not about choosing sides. Jesus don't take sides in war, especially that one. He just turns his head and looks away in disgust. When war breaks out, it's basically man telling God that even after all these years, we still don't understand what Jesus tried to tell us. War is man thumbing his nose at God."

Malloy hadn't read the book since he was Colt's age, and he realized that about the only thing he remembered of Conklin's character was that he died. Death on the battlefield—an image of Luke flashed in his mind, an involuntary reaction. He forced his attention back to his son.

Colt nodded. "Yeah, I guess." He paused and then added, "I'm not a fan."

"Well," Trace said, "It's no *Man in the Iron Mask,* I'll give you that."

Colt smirked, mopped a final blob of gravy with some bread and stuffed it in his mouth. Then he gathered up his plate and glass and took them in the kitchen. Malloy noticed his son's gait still had a slight hobble to it.

He watched the boy head to his room, and his gaze caught Darla's. She looked at him with a silent smile, and he tried to ignore the inquiry coming from her eyes.

"I wish he wouldn't worry so much about stuff around here. He should take time to be a boy," Malloy said, looking after Colt. It was an old conversation, but Darla played along.

"He's been a boy. He likes helping out. It makes him feel grown up."

"Being grown up doesn't have to mean working around here. He's doing well in math. He could learn something about computers or something. That would give him a future worth working for."

"You know he doesn't want to do that, and there's no point in pushing him. He's still talking about the Air Force."

"That's not any better. He's not going in the military," Malloy said flatly.

"It's just talk. He wants to fly one of those new stealth jets."

"The F-22."

"If he can't do that, he's not interested. It's just fantasy. Besides, with his leg, he probably couldn't even sit in the cockpit."

"Yeah, I hope you're right. Computers would be a better way to go."

"He's not any more interested in studying computers than you are."

"There are days when I'm ready to give it a shot." Malloy shook his head slightly as he shoved a bite under his mustache and chewed furiously. Darla, who had finished eating, cradled her chin on her clasped hands. "Seriously," Malloy said before taking another bite. She kept staring as he chewed.

"You know," he went on, "what was the point of giving the whole town away to AzTech if it doesn't mean boys like him can have another option? If he's just going to stay here and work on the ranch, why did we do it?"

She smiled slightly but didn't say anything, her chin still resting on the bridge made by her hands. Eventually, her stare drew the story of the meeting out of him.

"I know I shouldn't have hit him, but what did he expect talking about my mama like that?" Malloy said as he concluded. "He had it coming."

Darla began gathering dishes together on the table so she could talk without looking directly at Malloy. After almost twenty years of marriage, Darla Malloy knew that confronting her husband with the truth while he was still stewing about it was a little like stepping through a tangled pile of barbed wire—there was no good way to do it.

"Well, well, I never thought I'd see the Devil himself in our little town," she said slowly. "Good thing you were there to pop him in the nose."

Trace stopped chewing and looked at her. He didn't say anything.

"Is that going to take care of it, then?" she went on. "Are they going to pack up and go home? Tear down the houses and spread the dirt back the way it was?"

Trace looked down at his food, scooped up a bite on his fork, and stopped, the cream gravy dripping back to the plate.

"So, I'm supposed to let him say things like that? 'Your mama's bad hygiene?' They get to rewrite the rules of what's polite, too?"

"Busting his nose is polite? In front of a room full of people? Trace, darling, I never expected you to win any charm school contests, but even you can manage a might bit better than that."

He shoved the piece of steak in his mouth and chewed ferociously. He suddenly realized what he wanted to say, and his jaw worked even faster to clear his mouth.

"Those people," he said, pointing in the direction of the subdivision with his empty fork, "don't care about us or our way of life. All the while we were working with AzTech to get them here, we assumed they were going to do all these good things for us. They don't care about us. They don't care about Conquistador or Texas or anybody in it. They have this attitude that now that they're here, they shouldn't be inconvenienced in the slightest, and if we don't like it, too damn bad."

Darla paused and looked down at the empty dishes she'd assembled in front of herself. Her husband was not the kind of man who typically resolved disagreements with his fists, especially not against men who were essentially defenseless. What had been a simple concern about the whole AzTech issue—a concern she could understand—had grown into something that now seemed to border on desperation.

"He's never touched a cow in his life," she said finally. "Never had to head 'em or hoof 'em or drag 'em through the dirt. Never been kicked or gored or butted. From the looks of him, he probably never even spent much time in the sun. Yet here he is, and bringing with him a whole bunch of jobs that pay well and where you don't have to—how did you used to put it?—'shove your arm up the back end of a cow.' Isn't that how you used to describe it back when you were gonna leave and join the—what was it?—the Merchant Marine?"

Trace snorted and went back to his food.

"This is home," he muttered.

They didn't need to say more. He'd known Darla since the first grade. Growing up, she'd heard all his plans about getting out and seeing the world. When they were dating, she'd listened to all his country-boy clichés about leaving and making something of himself away from the smell of manure. Her only response had been polite silence, knowing it wouldn't happen, that he was as bound to this place as his father or her father had been. He'd left, all right, vowing to see the world. He got as far as Kansas.

Trace had to acknowledge that Darla might be right about the fight with Witherspoon. Maybe there'd been just enough lingering resentment to loosen his grip on his temper. Still, he had long since learned that he could be happy here, amid the barren nothingness that to him had the feel of a comfortable chair.

Sure, as a kid he'd wanted out. Everyone did. Age, though, brought with it a sense of acceptance, even pride. That's the nerve that Witherspoon was striking. Witherspoon's presence belittled everything Malloy had worked for, everything he'd *chosen* to do. Everything his father and his grandfather had worked for, too. Witherspoon was the final attack.

Soon, even the day workers at the ranch would be lining up in front of the AzTech plant with job applications, ready to trade in their chaps for a plastic suit that plugged into the wall.

Cowboying had been dying for almost as long as the profession had been in existence. Malloy had no deluded notions about the survival of his trade. He just didn't like being reminded that unlike his father or grandfather, who had fretted about the end, he was likely to be the one who witnessed it. He looked down the hallway toward Colt's bedroom.

Light came through the doorway and spilled into the hall. Over the clanking of dishes from the kitchen, he could hear a song coming from Colt's compact disc player, and he caught a few of the words: "edge of the plateau…" "stone marks the grave…" "old cowboys lie…"

Colt's voice, joining the chorus, drowned out the rest as Darla set a slice of pecan pie on the table in front of her husband. Malloy pulled his gaze from Colt's door.

"I forgot to pray," he said, more to himself than to Darla, and he bowed his head. ✯

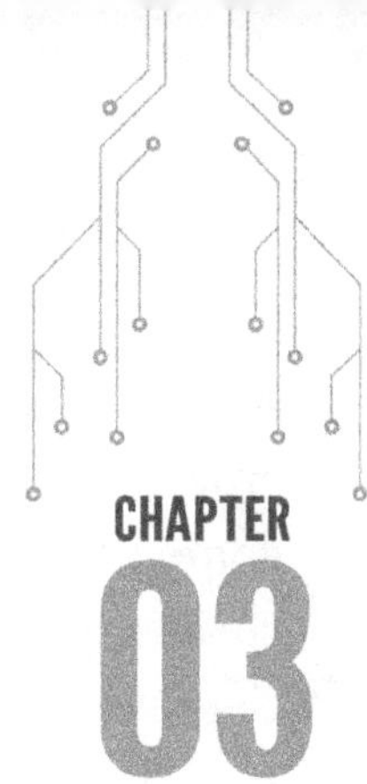

CHAPTER 03

BLAINE WITHERSPOON felt the doctor's cold fingertips cupping his nose, and he winced as she pushed the cotton deeper into his nostrils.

"This is embarrassing," he muttered again. He must have said it twenty times since arriving at the office. His eyes were bloodshot, and his head was abuzz from too little sleep. His nose had throbbed all night, but it was Malloy who kept him awake. The bushy mustache and those deep-set brown eyes bored into what little fits of sleep Witherspoon had managed to coax from the night. The bed felt like a bag of charcoal, dampened by his sweat, as he put one shoulder into it, then the other, turning and stretching, folding and unfolding his legs — a constant shift of positions in a vain attempt to find comfort.

He'd managed to locate the doctor's office, inching the Lexus along, slow as a retiree and squinting over the steering wheel, which added to the ache in his head. He wondered how long it would take to get a new pair of glasses in Conquistador. He'd been unable to rouse Jenna to ask her to drive him. He'd had one scotch the previous evening, after the meeting, to calm his nerves and numb the throbbing in his nose. She'd joined him and presumably continued after he'd gone to bed.

It had been all too typical. He had stumbled home with a broken nose and somehow *she* was angry with *him*. He hadn't done anything other than try to follow the plan that had already been established. The cowboy had no business telling the association how to develop the property.

Call a doctor, she'd said. But there was no one to call. No office was open, no after-hours numbers were published, and there certainly wasn't a hospital within forty miles. So he went to bed, the scotch dulling the pain just enough to fool him into thinking sleep would come.

He'd showed up at the doctor's office the next morning without an appointment, but there was no one waiting in the small reception area, not even a receptionist. The doctor ushered him to the examining room, deflecting his apologies and soothing his humiliation.

The doctor smiled patiently. "I've seen worse," she said gently.

"I'm sure. Around here they probably have bare-knuckles boxing on Friday nights. Saturday mornings must be big business for you."

"Friday nights? No, that would be high school football, which can be equally good for business." She seemed unaffected by the sourness of Witherspoon's mood. He realized that she hadn't asked what caused his injury, and he wondered if the small-town gossip chain had already informed her.

The doctor had olive skin and deep blue eyes that seemed to draw him into their calmness in spite of his pain. Her brown hair cascaded past the collar of her white lab coat in a wave of curls.

"I'll bet," was all he could manage to say.

She leaned back and rolled a few inches away on her stool, her eyes never breaking contact with his. "You'll be fine," she said, emphasizing the last word. "In a few weeks, no one will even be able to tell you were in a fight."

"I wasn't in a fight. I was assaulted."

"I heard there was an argument."

Dr. Diana Lambeau had been expecting Blaine Witherspoon long before she walked down the cracked concrete sidewalk and opened her office around the corner from the propane shop on Main Street. Darla Malloy had called her last night and suggested she might want to be in early. The Malloys had become friends in the year since Trace had burst into her office cradling Colt, the boy's leg hanging to one side like a limp sausage. Practicing medicine in Conquistador had taken patience, and it had meant learning to find wealth in the purity of a good deed. The Malloys couldn't have afforded to pay her for all the work she did on Colt, or the physical therapy that followed. What they couldn't pay in cash they insisted on making up over time with interest shelled out in the form of supper invitations and cookouts at the ranch. It had meant more to her—and to her practice—than money, because it helped her gain acceptance among the ranch hands and farm wives who were her most frequent customers.

She looked at Blaine Witherspoon and wondered if she had been like him when she first came here, filled with as much hope as he now was with anger.

"That Malloy is a thug," he said. "Nothing but a thug. You don't like what somebody says, just punch them. That solves it. No need for enlightened discussion."

"Let me ask you something," Lambeau said slowly. She didn't want to alienate the new wave of homeowners—homies, as Malloy called them—but she felt protective of the patients and the people who had surprised her with the warmth of their welcome. "You ever heard of the term 'fighting words?'"

"Oh, please. That justifies it? It's still an assault."

"I'm serious. Around here, there really is such a thing, and fighting words usually involve land or a woman. You insult somebody's mother, you're probably going to get hit, and you'll have a hard time finding anyone who feels sorry for you."

"I don't care how he feels. Or anyone else. I'm still going to sue that stupid redneck, or file charges or something. Look at me. He can't get away with this."

"Where are you going to find a lawyer? You'd probably have to go all the way to Lubbock to get one that would take a case over a one-sided fistfight, and any judge west of I-35 would probably fine you for filing such a suit."

"I thought the Wild West was over. That's all I heard when we came out here for the site survey. 'We're all about progress. This isn't the Wild West anymore. That's all a myth.'"

"It isn't a movie set, but it isn't Silicon Valley either. It took me a while to figure that out, too. You just found out a little harder than I did." She smiled, and her eyes radiated with a warmth that blunted Witherspoon's anger.

"How long have you been here?" he asked, slightly calmer than before.

"Almost three years. I got out of med school in Boston and thought I'd practice frontier medicine. So, I came down here and set up shop. They hadn't had a doctor in town in about five years, so I figured it was a good opportunity."

"Seems to have worked out."

"Not at first. Most of the folks would have kept on driving fifty miles to Gunyon rather than see a woman doctor, especially a woman of mixed race. Most of them didn't know my heritage, of course. But I'm Creole, and to many folks I look Hispanic. Anyway, even the women in town weren't comfortable with it."

"What changed?"

"Nothing. It just took time. These people aren't Neanderthals, and they aren't Luddites. They're just used to certain things, and they're slower to change than us city folk. After a while, you'll find that quality endearing. I figured when I got here, I'd stay a few years, do my bit, and move on to one of the big hospitals in Houston. I've got family in Louisiana, and I'd promised them I'd be moving back after school. But the 'adventure' of living in a big eastern city didn't...well, it didn't have the appeal that I thought it would. I needed to decompress more than I realized, and Conquistador was just what I needed. I liked a town where I could know everyone. That was the appeal of rural medicine in the first place, but instead of doing it in the bayous, I'm doing it out here on the plains. I'm hooked on this place. I'm not leaving."

"So how many broken noses do I have left to go?"

She smiled.

"Just take it slowly. Realize people like Trace Malloy see you and what you're bringing here as a threat to their way of life. You're taking something away. You've got to learn what's important to them and how they do things. You know, when patients did start coming in here, it was almost worse than when they wouldn't show up at all. Some of the cowboys would bring in their kids with these horrible bruises or broken bones. They'd just stand there in the corner, stone-faced. I even told one of them I was calling Child Protective Services because the kid was battered so bad, it looked like abuse. His father just looked at me and said 'he fell off a damn horse' gathered up his son and walked out shaking his head."

"What did you do?"

"I realized I wasn't in Boston and I needed to understand more about my patients, so I went and spent a day on the ranch."

"Did it help?"

"Yeah, it helped me understand the place. I got to see what started it all, and I got to see how the people around here were living. Once I began to understand that, the injuries I was seeing made more sense.

"Look, everyone who works at the ranch understands the implications of change, but in some ways, you represent a type of change they hadn't counted on. You're as much a shock to the system as a city-girl doctor coming in here and telling old ranch hands they need to take care of their prostate. Eventually, they began to accept me. When Trace Malloy's son got hurt last year, they didn't even think of driving up to Gunyon."

"What happened to his son?"

"He was helping with the spring roundup. They were separating the calves from the mama cows and his horse got spooked. It threw him and pinned him against the fence. He broke his leg in four places."

"Jesus."

"That's just part of growing up in Conquistador. Times are changing though. After that, the company decided the ranch hands' kids couldn't work the roundup. That means less money for a lot of the families around here."

"Well, I'm hoping that AzTech will mean a lot more money for the folks around here."

She paused, staring at him for a moment, her lips pressed tightly together. She was thin, and shorter than he was. Her legs straddled the rolling stool, her tennis shoes serving as brakes on either side of its wheels.

"I hope you realize that just about everybody in town, everybody in the county, wanted the plant. Everybody. Even Malloy."

"He's got an interesting way of showing his support," Witherspoon said. The pain in his nose had developed an itching quality, and he touched it gingerly. The contact hurt and intensified the itching at the same time. He'd broken his wrist playing squash in college and it hadn't been as uncomfortable as this.

"When I first came here, they were trying to get the state to build a prison outside of town," the doctor said. "They'd even talked to Frye about donating some land from the Conquistador. Nobody wanted a prison, but everybody felt they had to do something to keep this place alive. When the Conquistador first started opening some of its pasture for deer and quail hunting, there was talk that it might become a big enough business that somebody would open a few hotels. But Frye made it clear they weren't about to go whole-hog into the resort business, and things fizzled. What I'm trying to say is that AzTech's proposal was a godsend. You've given the town a future. But it also reminds people like Malloy that everything they've done, all the hard work, the suffering of their parents, wasn't enough to secure that future on its own. It's a bitter pill, to use a medical cliché."

Witherspoon didn't look the part of an economic savior, she thought. His nose was swollen into a bulbous mosaic of mauve and gray. He sat with a slump on the edge of the examining table, the white paper crinkling as he shifted his weight to stand. His brownish hair was slicked back, and without his glasses, he looked much older than he should have for someone in his late thirties.

Lambeau decided she had made her point. There was no need to go on about the spirit of hope that had pervaded the town since AzTech announced it plans. There was a good chance things would change for the better. AzTech was bringing in a lot of people, perhaps as many as a thousand. That spawned the belief that the town would not only keep its school, but that it might actually have to build new ones. That many people, with their fancy West Coast tastes, would mean stores and restaurants and maybe even a movie theater. Eventually. It might take years, but it would all be here. And there was the promise of better-paying jobs, of course. Even those who didn't want to give up ranching would be able to supplement their income working part-time at one of the new businesses.

Malloy had his own concerns, of course. He wouldn't give up the lifestyle, but even he had to acknowledge the benefits AzTech could bring. Over one of Lambeau's supper visits last week, he had raised his latest worry — the better paying jobs and new shops would mean a higher cost of living, and that meant everything would be more expensive for people like him. Chain restaurants and Wal-Mart would move in and put the propane shop and the feed store out of business, and locals he'd known all his life would be without jobs.

The price of change, she'd argued. The new stores would hire more people than they'd displace. The alternative was to let AzTech go somewhere else and let Conquistador continue its economic decrescendo of the past fifty years. She'd listened to Malloy's explanations of the cattle industry, how financially unviable it was, and she'd seen his determination that his own son be saved from its doomed struggle. She doubted even his sensitivity to the past would hold out against progress.

Witherspoon was standing now, and he wobbled slightly. They walked out to the reception area, and Lambeau began looking for paperwork. She had no receptionist or assistant or business manager, so she handled everything herself. For most of the residents, she just took their check or cash and shook their hands. If they couldn't pay, she worked it out later.

She considered it one of her concessions to the past — medicine first, business later. They didn't teach you that in med school. Now everything was about "building the practice."

But out here, she could make her own rules, just as her daddy had when he worked the bayous and boondocks of southern Louisiana. She could still remember him packing up his black leather case and heading out on house calls, which sometimes meant paddling a canoe through the swamps. She had sworn to him, even the last time they'd seen each other, that she wasn't going to be doing country medicine. She wanted the action and the challenges of the big city, the chance to move up at a large facility. She had something to prove. She wanted to show all the doubters, all those who'd tried to stand in her way, that this girl from the back woods could succeed on their terms as well as her own.

The past, though, has a way of pulling you back, even when you're determined to fight against it. There'd been too many dinners where she'd listened to her father talking about medicine, too many times when she'd been proud of something he'd done to help someone. When she heard about a group with the ridiculous name Hippocrates in Action that wanted to place eager young physicians in rural settings where they were so desperately needed, she was signing up before her brain had a chance to weigh the arguments. The big city would wait. She would do this thing and feel good about it, and then move on to her dreams. When she arrived in Conquistador, though, she found her past waiting for her. The small town, personal form of practicing medicine, of knowing patients and being a part of the community, cut through all those years in Lafayette, New Orleans, and Boston, overriding all her efforts to remake herself as a city girl bent on success.

Blaine Witherspoon was holding out a plastic card, asking her if she would accept his company's health plan. She chuckled.

"Do I have a choice? It's probably as good a time as any to get it set up." ✯

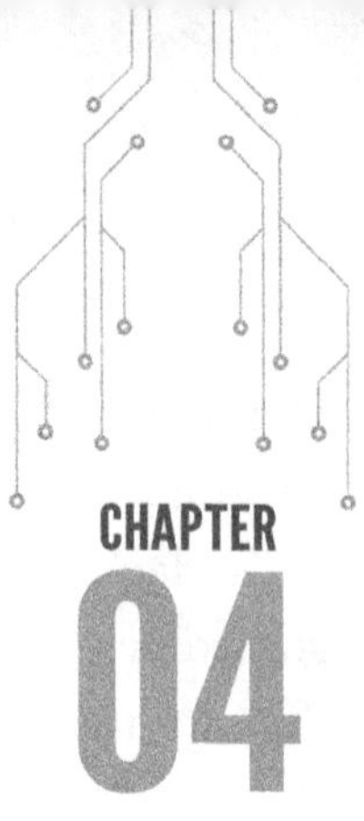

CHAPTER 04

BLAINE WITHERSPOON'S NOSE hurt worse than ever after Lambeau's tinkering. He stepped out of the cool of the doctor's office and into the blazing heat of the day. He still simmered at the loss of time that this whole incident had cost him. He didn't even want to be involved in the homeowners group, but as plant manager, the developers had demanded his presence. They were just pandering to AzTech, of course, but how could he say no? He needed to remain on good terms with them if this project was going to be a success. Employees distracted by construction delays or poorly installed air conditioners or doors that wouldn't close could undermine AzTech's ambitious plans, *his* ambitious plans. It was a two-way street, though. The developers needed him as much as he needed them, and now that symbiosis was costing him physical pain and an increasing drain on his time that he couldn't afford.

He turned the key and the Lexus sedan hummed alive. He headed toward the house, frustrated that his cell phone couldn't pick up a signal anywhere in town. He'd hoped to get a few phone calls out of the way and then go to the plant site. Even after all these months, he couldn't get used to driving without talking, driving without a few business matters juggled on the road. Driving in silence, he felt the moments slip away unused and unproductive.

The sedan's sealed soundlessness allowed his worries to percolate, bubbling to the surface of his mind like gas from a swamp. In four months, production was supposed to begin, and they were falling behind. Every day spawned new problems that were as bizarre as the daily happenings around this barren backwater of humanity. Even simple details ballooned out of control—water, electricity—just getting enough had become a struggle, and as of last night quite literally a physical one. He thought back over the months. His time in the Big Empty had been an endless dance with uncertainty, full of fits and starts, and every time he caught a glimmer of hope, it was snatched away by new despair. Everything felt out of sync, and even straightforward tasks became Sisyphean. He hadn't even been able to turn in the rented moving truck without feeling awkward, embarrassed, and ultimately angry.

He could feel his face flush just thinking about the day—what?—seven months ago now, when he'd gingerly steered that monstrous van into the driveway at Garrison's and brought it to a stop in front of the gas pumps. He instantly knew it wasn't a place that rented a lot of trucks, and a sense of apprehension welled up in him. Garrison's was nothing more than a gas station with a trailer or two for lease around the back.

A man in navy work clothes walked toward him, wiping his hands on an oily rag that had once been red. Witherspoon opened the door and stumbled as he got down from the cab.

"How's it going?" the man said, vigorously chewing on a wad of gum. He wore a greasy gimme cap with "Cat Diesel Power" embroidered on a square yellow patch. The skin on the man's face and forearms was the color of burnished wood.

Witherspoon had nodded slightly, trying not to look as uncomfortable as he felt. He motioned to the van.

"They told me I should turn this in here," he said.

"Not here." The man stared at him without saying anything else. His hands stopped in mid-wipe.

"Umm...isn't this Garrison's?"

"This is Garrison's, all right, but you can't leave that thing parked in front of my pump."

"Oh. Sorry. Where shall I put it?"

"Hell, if I know. I ain't got room for something like that."

Witherspoon took a deep breath and studied the red soil that had blown across the pavement. He looked back up at the man, hoping for a little sympathy.

"Look," he said, "the guy in San Jose told me this was where I turn it in."

"Guy in San Jose? I don't know a guy in San Jose. And he don't know me, either. And he damn sure don't know that I ain't got room for nothing like that."

Witherspoon eyed the station. No one else seemed to be around. A pickup rolled down the street, the first sign of traffic since Witherspoon pulled up. The driver raised two fingers off the steering wheel as he passed, and the man with the rag returned the wave half-heartedly.

"Looks to me," Witherspoon said finally, "like you have a large field out behind your place here. Think you might squeeze it in out there?"

The man—Witherspoon assumed it was Garrison himself—glanced toward the rear of the station, then back at Witherspoon. A deep rolling laugh came up suddenly, and he started wiping and chewing again.

"I guess maybe I could at that. C'mon inside. You can help me figure out how to do all the paperwork on this shit."

Witherspoon gave a sigh and followed the man into the building. The inside of the station was dark and cluttered. Papers raised their edges as if waving when the breeze of the electric fan in the corner passed over them. Every surface seemed to have a film of grime and engine oil.

After twenty minutes of watching the man shaking his head, scratching out information on the forms, throwing them away in frustration, and starting over, Witherspoon finally asked, "Do you have a bathroom I can use?"

The man didn't look up. He pointed over his shoulder with his pen.

"There's forty thousand acres out there. Help yourself."

Witherspoon had just wanted an excuse to step outside anyway. He dialed the cell phone. It shot a blast of static in his ear, then went dead. After three tries, he gave up and went back inside, cursing under his breath.

"You trash that thing out?" the man asked as Witherspoon stepped through the doorway.

"Excuse me?"

"You wreck it or anything?"

"Uhhh..." he could feel beads of sweat breaking out on his scalp. Did this guy know? Had the cowboy already told him? Lie, he told himself. Don't give this jerk any more excuses to mess with you. Just lie and get the hell out of here. He couldn't. He found these sorts of feather-fluffing exchanges of bravado pointless anyway. "I, uh, did hit this guy in a pickup just outside of town."

The man looked at him and stopped chewing again.

"I, uh, I'm pretty sure it didn't do any damage," Witherspoon added, and his voice sounded fainter than he'd intended.

"Yeah? Shit!" the man flung his pen down on the latest half-completed form with a thwack. He rested his hand over the edge of the counter, staring at Witherspoon and chewing with newfound determination.

"Well," Witherspoon fumbled, "I mean it knocked his truck into the ditch, but, really, I don't think it hurt the truck—my truck, I mean. Uh, the van."

"I don't need this shit this morning, you know? I got a tranny to rebuild. I don't need some damned city slicker from San Ho-say showing up with a busted-up van that I don't know what to do with. I'm supposed to collect all these vans. Who am I gonna rent them to? Especially if they're wrecked."

It was the first time Witherspoon had actually heard the term "city slicker" used in serious conversation. He found it made him defensive, even though he had no defense.

The man was still talking. "You better tell all your buddies before they even get here that I don't need this shit," he said, pointing a finger at Witherspoon's chest.

Witherspoon knew he should lean across the counter and stare the man down. He'd lost whatever he'd gained with the comment about the acreage. Instead, he opted for an old management trick.

"Look, I'm sorry for all this. I don't need it either. This guy was a pain in the ass. He said I should tell you that Trace Malloy said he'd make it good if there were any problems, and I wouldn't normally stand for that, but I was trying to get into town, and I really didn't see any damage..."

"Trace? You knocked Trace into the ditch?" The man emitted a loud roaring laugh that seemed to echo off the Formica-covered walls, ricocheting upon itself until Witherspoon thought he would suffocate.

When the outburst subsided, Witherspoon recounted the details of his collision with Malloy, the man interrupting him frequently for details. In all, he spent over an hour in the claustrophobic confines of the shop. The man, who later introduced himself as Terry Garrison, had wound up giving him a Dr Pepper and offering him a seat in the corner of his grimy office. Again, time wasted and for what? To return a rented truck. The process should have taken five minutes.

It was his first experience with the pace of life in Conquistador. Time wasn't money. It was a valueless commodity spent wantonly on the irrelevant.

Witherspoon pulled his mind back to the present as he glided the Lexus into his driveway—just a quick stop for a glass of water to take some of the pain medication Lambeau had given him. The smell of fresh mortar hit his nose, which throbbed with each step. The house next door was just about finished on the outside, the one across the street in frame. Three more down the road already were occupied, Swain had already moved in on the next street over, and more of his lieutenants would be coming soon. In all, more than a dozen AzTech employees were "on site,'" as they liked to say in Milpitas.

Beads of sweat formed at his hair line. It was already—at mid-May—unbelievably hot. He missed the non-summers of the Bay Area, the blissful, perpetual chill of the ocean breeze that chased away the extremes of the seasons. Here, he'd endured a winter that in some ways was worse than anything he'd experienced back East. Less snow had fallen—only a few inches at any one time—but the winds, unfettered on the open plains, cut across the landscape like a scythe. Wind by itself wasn't a problem, but here, wind brought dust. Dust had become his greatest enemy. He would find the water he needed, even if he had to duke it out with Malloy again. He'd get the electricity. The lines were already being strung. If he failed to get the plant running, the dust would be his undoing.

He'd have to go over the engineering schematics again. Had they really planned for heat like this? It must be ninety-five, and it was only midmorning. By late summer, they'd need to cool one hundred and fifty thousand square feet to seventy degrees, taking into account the heat from the machinery running inside. It would probably be over a hundred degrees outside by then. They'd need a cooling plant similar to what they'd set up in Tucson, and he hadn't counted on that. With an average annual temperature of eighty-two, he'd figured he could cut the air conditioning specs a little. Average, sure, but if they stuck to the schedule they'd be starting up at the peak. Had he figured that? That might shave the margin for error, and it was already a hairline. Better run the numbers again, he told himself, and bump them up as much as possible without blowing the entire cost projection to hell.

Another recalibration. Undoubtedly, another upward revision to the operating budget. This was not what he had wanted to tell Soderheim later this week. He'd wanted to have a good report for a change, "All's well, we're right on track." Or better yet, "we're ahead of schedule, and the dust and heat problems turned out to be minor." He wanted to promise that the plant would be contributing to revenue, if not earnings, by year's end — less than eight short months away.

Those were the kind of promises he made to the land the job in the first place. Old Soddy had to know he'd been overly optimistic. That was the nature of the business, and surely Soddy himself had done the same thing back in his day. Things were different now, though. They were building wafers — the dinner plate-sized slices of silicon that contained as many as five hundred chips each — at three hundred millimeters. The electronic "gates" between the components were now a fraction of the width of a human hair. In the near future, manufacture would be limited not by the size of transistors, but by the thickness of light. Soddy, coming up in the business when the idea of a handful of transistors on one slab of silicon made men babble on about the marvels of human achievement, hadn't had to deal with this level of precision.

Years ago, Witherspoon had had a chance to talk to Jack Kilby, the engineer who invented the integrated circuit. Kilby, a towering but easy-going figure, regularly sat down with young engineers over a lunch at Texas Instruments in Dallas, reminiscing about the old days. Witherspoon had been visiting one day and got to join them. Kilby's presence was intimidating, his face scrunched and weathered so that he seemed to be scowling even when he wasn't. But he was an affable and gracious host, patiently taking questions and sharing stories. He had none of Old Soddy's bravado or harshness, even though the two men were contemporaries. Witherspoon took solace in knowing that Kilby, whose personality seemed more like Witherspoon's own, had succeeded without the need for rough elbows and belittling others to get ahead.

Kilby told a story about TI setting up its first clean room. The plant manager, he recalled, had inspected it with a smoldering cigar clenched between his teeth. The engineers at the table shook their heads in disbelief. Now, workers spent twenty minutes washing up, donning bunny suits, going through air showers, covering facial hair with special masks, all to reduce the threat of dust particles. Women couldn't wear makeup into a clean room. If you needed to jot down notes, you had to use a special note pad, each sheet formulated to reduce the fibers that might fly off when you turned the pages.

Witherspoon had known all these difficulties, of course, long before he lobbied for the job of opening the plant in Conquistador. Others thought Soderheim was crazy for trying to build a high-tech wonder in the middle of an unpopulated dust bowl, but Witherspoon, hungry for the chance to run his own shop, brushed aside the concerns and doggedly pursued the spot. Soderheim saw the project as a way of reinvesting in rural America or some such social hokum. But he wouldn't have gone for the location if it hadn't been for the ridiculous tax giveaways and other freebies from the county. Even then, the old man was reluctant. It took Witherspoon months of politicking to win the job. Now, he found himself again wondering what he had done. Was he going to wind up like Harcourt in Tucson? Where would that leave him?

His nose throbbed in a relentless tidal current of pain, washing from the front of his head to the back, where it pooled in a dull ache that grew progressively more debilitating.

As he opened the car door, the heat of the day slammed into him. Sweat came instantly, and he again found himself thinking about the cost of pushing back such intensity on such a large scale.

But it could be done, and as if proof of that, he felt the cool blast of the air conditioning hit him as he entered his house. Cold slammed into him as if he'd plunged into ice water. Yes, he could fight this heat, he *would* fight it, and he would beat it. Somehow, inside the concrete and steel monolith that marked his future, inside the hundreds of thousands of square feet that would spell his success or failure, he would find a way.

Jenna was sitting on a chair in the "formal" living room, her left hand cupped around a gin and tonic, her signature drink of worry and frustration.

In the seven months since they'd arrived in Conquistador, he'd been greeted by this scene far too often. The electricity had gone out. The toilet had backed up. The landscaper had put the holly bushes where she'd wanted the red-tipped photinias.

How long, he wondered, would Jenna stay here with him? He buried the thought as quickly as it had come to him. Jenna understood the importance of this opportunity, and besides, she knew that no assignment was permanent. If she changed her mind about staying here for "years and years," they could be back in Milpitas or anywhere else AzTech had a plant in three years, five at the most. She'd bought into the move, based on his promise that this would be the last before she picked a permanent place for them to settle into their dotage. But as the months wore on, the daily frustrations grew. She had little else to focus on. She'd met a few of the other executive families, but as the plant manager's wife, there was a natural distance, an unspoken sense that she could never truly be a part of their group. After all, her husband was probably the cause of whatever their husbands were complaining about. And yes, it was all husbands. Tech, especially at the executive level, was largely a white male business. Witherspoon believed in diversity, of course, but he would have time to focus on that after he got the plant running. In the meantime, he needed Jenna to figure out some way to deal with the isolation and boredom.

As he approached his wife, she lifted her right hand, the one that wasn't holding the drink, and slowly opened it.

"I found these in Brandon's room today."

Witherspoon didn't have to look to know what she was showing him: two hand-rolled joints, a roach clip, a plastic bag with green flakes, and a package of rolling papers. Witherspoon grabbed the paraphernalia and walked into the kitchen. He found a bottle of the mineral water they had shipped in from the Napa Valley, fished the pain pills the doctor had given him from the pocket of his Khakis and turned back toward his wife, embracing her frustration.

"I'll talk to him again," he said hoarsely.

"I wasn't snooping," Jenna said as he climbed the stairs. "I wasn't checking up on him."

Witherspoon trudged up the steps and slowly swung open the door to his son's room with the back of his hand. Brandon was sprawled on his bed, flicking the remote control on his stereo in disgust. Two long shocks of black hair hung in his face; the rest of his head was shaved almost to the scalp. The ends of the strands were dyed red. Wrap-around sunglasses covered his brown eyes, though they were often so dilated that it was hard to see the color. He was wearing a sleeveless t-shirt and shorts that were so long and baggy, they looked almost like long pants as he lay on his bed. He punched the remote again and the station on the stereo changed.

"Country. Classic rock. Country again. That's all they get here. Christian talk. Four stations and it's all crap. This place sucks."

"Brandon, we have to talk."

"Yeah, Mom found my stash again. Time to talk. See the problem? She's so bored, she's got nothing better to do than rifle through my room."

Witherspoon sat down on the edge of the bed. For a brief moment, he remembered the model rockets they'd built—when?—just three years ago. Pictures of the space shuttle that were packed in Milpitas hadn't made it onto these walls. They'd been replaced by bikini-clad models, the Farrahs of the day, and posters for violent movies that Brandon was theoretically too young to see.

Witherspoon lined up the fingertips of his right hand with their counterparts on his left and looked down at them as he spoke.

"She wasn't going through your stuff. She was cleaning."

"She doesn't clean where the stash was. That's why it was there."

"Brandon, you know how disappointed your mother and I are—"

"Christ, not the 'disappointment' trip. Jesus, Dad—" Brandon stopped in mid-sentence, noticing the swelling and bruises on his father's face for the first time. "Shit, what happened to you?"

"I, uh, had a little problem, a disagreement, last night at the meeting," Witherspoon said, a little embarrassed.

"The *homeowners* meeting? Whoa, Dad, wish I could have been there. Probably the most exciting thing that happened since we got here. What did the rest of them look like? You kick some ass?"

"No, actually, Brandon, that wasn't the goal. I got hit by one of the workers from the ranch. We had invited him to talk about the water situation. He and I had a disagreement and it got out of hand. We both made some bad choices."

"What did you do?"

"Well, nothing at the time. I was bleeding. But it's not over, rest assured. He can't act like that. That kind of behavior isn't tolerated, even here. I may have to take legal action or something. I don't know yet."

"Oh, God, you're so pathetic. You didn't hit him back?"

"This wasn't what I came up here to talk about, Brandon. I'm not here to discuss my choices, I'm here to discuss yours," Witherspoon said, hoping the tone was firm enough to get the conversation back on track.

"My choices?" his son replied, his voice cracking on the question. "You mean that I choose to blow reefer every chance I get? Isn't that the way they said it back when you used to do it?"

Witherspoon sighed and he felt the throbbing in his nose intensifying. They'd done this verbal sparring too many times before. Brandon assumed his father, growing up in the Seventies, had done his share of drugs in high school, just based on the times in which he was living. Witherspoon never felt a need to share the whole truth with his son, who didn't even want to believe the partial truth. In fact, Witherspoon had dabbled, succumbing to peer pressure on occasion—a party here or there where the joints were passing around and he'd taken a few tokes, not wanting to embarrass himself in front of a particular girl. There was the Fleetwood Mac concert his junior year in high school, where the joints flowed down the aisle in a steady stream. Feeling insecure because he'd worn a striped polyester shirt instead of another concert souvenir or some other "cool" attire, he'd puffed away, terrified that each breath would bring the steel grip of a security guard on his shoulder.

No, the truth was he'd done little experimenting. He was too afraid of the consequences. He'd believed all the scare stories. Pot would make you impotent. Acid could blow your mind on the first try. One shot of heroin and you're hooked. And worse, what if he got caught? He couldn't face his parents, and he couldn't live with the shame. Brandon didn't need to know the details. His father's youth had been remarkably drug-free compared to most.

"I've told you before, Brandon, I didn't do it. I never felt the need," he said, trying to adapt the old argument he used on himself then to his son now. "And you shouldn't either."

"Why? Because you moved me to hell on earth and I should welcome the opportunity?"

"Well, think about that. Things are different here. You don't know what opportunities there might be. You might be the smartest kid in school here, without even having to try that hard. Yeah, this could be an opportunity. You just don't know until you give it a chance." Witherspoon could tell from the rise and fall of his son's brow that his eyes were rolling behind the sunglasses. Brandon pounded the remote with his thumb again.

"Brandon, what are we going to do?" Witherspoon went on. "We've tried to help you with this problem before. Quite frankly, I'm shocked we're back to this. And I'm disappointed in you. Terribly disappointed. And now, we've got a real problem. The nearest treatment center must be a hundred miles away, at least."

"Yeah, well whatever. Those were my last two joints from SJ, and it doesn't look like there's anyone around here to sell me more. Hell, these dudes probably light up cowshit."

"We're going to come up with a solution," Witherspoon said. "I don't know what yet, but we're going to solve this. You should think about how we should do that." Empowerment, Witherspoon thought to himself. If he feels like he's got some control, maybe he'll be more willing to make the right decision. "We'll talk about this more later. I'm really not feeling well."

"Yeah, whatever." Frustrated with cycling through the radio stations, Brandon got up from the bed and slid a CD into the changer. He turned on the television and began playing a PlayStation game as the grinding cacophony that sounded like a chorus of kitchen appliances exploded from the stereo speakers. Witherspoon rose to leave, and as he got to the door, Brandon called after him without taking his eyes from the TV screen.

"What the hell were you thinking moving here anyway?" ☆

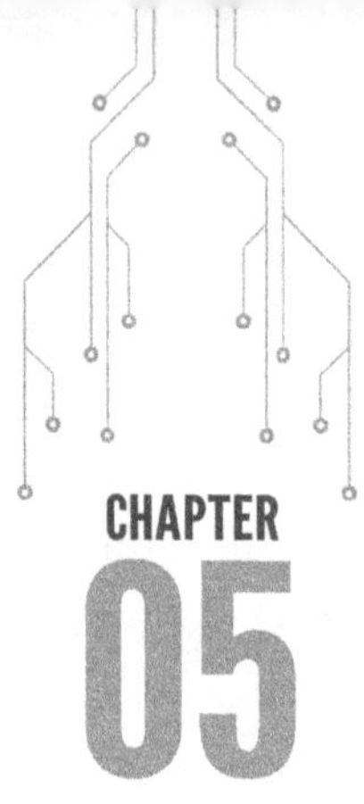

CHAPTER 05

WHEN ROLAND KERR got mad, the ends of his ears turned bright red, and because they stuck almost straight out from his head, they served as warning beacons for his temper.

As soon as Malloy entered Kerr's office, he knew his timing was bad. The beacons were already lit.

Kerr had just set the phone down and was staring straight at the far wall.

"Roy?" Malloy asked hesitantly.

Kerr's glance snapped sideways to Malloy. He didn't say anything.

"Everything okay?" Malloy said, dipping a verbal toe in the waters of his boss's temper to determine how bad his timing really was.

Kerr shook his head slightly. Fringes of white hair still ringed the sides of his head but the top reflected the florescent light like a mirror.

"Just this damned power line," Kerr said finally. "If I'd known the trouble it was gonna be, I never would have pushed the company to let them do it."

"They still want to cut across the cells?"

"Yeah. You'd figure that as far as they've got to string that thing, a few hundred yards wouldn't make that much difference."

Kerr had argued with his bosses at Frye, the company that owned the Conquistador, to let Cap Rock Electric run an electric main across part of the Tie Bow. AzTech needed a lot of power, and the electric company was worried that the additional load would strain the grid. Add in the new subdivision and the prospect of future growth, and the line seemed like a necessity. Kerr thought by donating right-of-way across the ranch, the company could show its support for the town's future and extend a welcoming gesture to AzTech.

Kerr's family had been around the Conquistador from the beginning. The original Scottish investors who set up the ranch just after the Civil War had brought Kerr's great-grandfather along to help manage the new herd. The Kerrs had raised sheep in Scotland, but they quickly took to cattle and cowboying.

The families of the original investors ran the ranch until the mid-1980s. A crippling drought in 1981 forced them to sell off much of the breeding stock, and the herd suffered. The rise of big feedlots drove down prices, and the ranch began losing money. The remaining heirs sold out to Frye International, which rolled the company into its agribusiness unit, officially known as Frye Agricultural Industries. The corporate bosses managed to cut costs and replenish the herd, but it seemed as if Frye were perpetually on the verge of selling. Ranching had always been a business of survival more than profits, and big companies had little use for sentimentality.

Kerr tried to balance his historic ties to the Conquistador with his responsibilities as manager. Technically, his title was Vice President for Ranch Operations, Southern Sector. After

Frye bought the Conquistador, Roy had moved all around the Western Hemisphere, helping the company run its agriculture properties. Now in his early sixties, he'd come back to the Conquistador to work until his retirement.

The last thing he needed was trouble from the company or the town. The community of Conquistador had been built by ranch hands for ranch hands. In fact, the Conquistador had donated much of the land for the town, and at one time, the ranch had surrounded it. In later years, some of the ranch land was sold off to private owners, including Malloy's parents, to pay debts or other costs related to the droughts of the Fifties. Those sales, at bargain prices, only made the bond between the townspeople and the Conquistador grow stronger. There was a sense of symbiosis, each needing and helping the other. The ranch wasn't just an employer, it was the *raison d'etre,* a tap root from which all else sprang. It was the town's soul.

After Frye bought the property, many of the townsfolk felt strangely disconnected. Frye wasn't bad as corporate owners go, but its struggles were its own, and the town was simply a place for employees to live.

To save money, the company cut jobs. Many full-time employees were reduced to day workers, meaning they were hired only when they were needed. Day workers had to provide their own horse and tack and got no health benefits.

Livelihoods that were stable became sporadic. Uncertainty crept in like a slow-moving cold front, seeping into the houses and the minds and the hearts of the locals, creating a numbness of worry. You could see it on their faces, sometimes even now, when you passed them on the street or sat down next to them in church.

Many felt the ranch had abandoned them. And when AzTech arrived with a proposal to bring the future to Conquistador, indeed to the whole surrounding county, it was like the first rays of daylight breaking through storm clouds, a bright shining promise of hope. Maybe the soul of Conquistador wasn't dying. Maybe it wasn't constricted by the past. Maybe, just maybe, there was more than one reason to live here in the midst of so much nothingness. As crazy as it sounded, maybe a high-tech boom would fill up the Big Empty. If all hope needed to blossom was a few million dollars in tax breaks to pay for it, why not? What did they have to lose? And if all AzTech needed to power it was an electric line, why not? And no one asked that question louder and answered it more firmly than Roland Kerr. It wouldn't cost Frye a thing, he'd told the bosses in Chicago, and it might just help the company gain back some of the goodwill it had lost over the years.

After the first two towers were built in the pastures, though, Cap Rock decided it needed to cut across one of the paddocks where the ranch was testing a new cellular grazing method. The program was designed to improve grassland management by concentrating grazing in a few areas, while leaving others to grow back. The space was seeded with buffalo grass, the traditional ground cover of the Big Empty that had been missing from these parts for more than a century. No one knew if it was viable on a large scale, given the soil erosion and the encroachment of parasitic plants like mesquite and juniper. Kerr didn't want construction crews upsetting the balance before the tests were complete.

Malloy knew Kerr felt responsible for the problems with the power line and other complaints that people in town had about the new growth flooding into the county. Kerr had been AzTech's biggest proponent, and his support had swayed a town buoyed by hope, yet frozen by doubt.

Malloy remembered the town meeting where Kerr made an impassioned speech to save Conquistador.

"No one treasures this town's history more than me," he had said, standing in front of almost three hundred people crammed into the high school cafeteria. Folks were sitting on the floor and standing around the edges of the room, one of the largest civic assemblies Conquistador had ever seen. And Kerr was holding court in the middle of it all, casting aside his soft-spoken nature, his voice booming over the group. He turned first this way, then that, speaking so that all could hear. "No one's fought harder to preserve the heritage of Conquistador. My great granddaddy came here with the Scots. You all know that. But I have to tell you I've never been more worried about our future than I am right now. We can't all keep living off of one ranch, no matter how spectacular we think it is.

"Let's face it, most years it loses money. I've had to cut a lot of your wages, cut a lot of you to day labor, and cut back contracts with a lot of your businesses. I can't promise you I won't have to cut more. We've thinned the herd, sold off acreage. We can't afford to underwrite the community like we used to, and the town doesn't have the tax base it needs to support itself.

"What I'm trying to say is the Conquistador isn't growing, and it never will again. Its days of majesty are over. Sure, we're doing better than most. Hell, they sold off the Four Sixes to turn it into hunting leases. We aren't that desperate, but if you ask me will your sons have jobs out at the 'Quistador, I'd have to say most of them won't. That means a lot of them will leave. Hell, they've been leaving, we all know that. They go to college in Lubbock and they don't come back. Why should they? We're down to five hundred people from two thousand and we're going to keep shrinking if we don't do something.

"I serve on the town council, on the school board. You all elected me. And because of my concerns for this town's future, I agreed to lead the economic development commission. This company, this AzTech, is the best option we've got. High tech is the future — computers, cell phones, electronics. The town of Conquistador has to be more than a ranch, and it's up to us to ensure that it is.

"Some of you wonder why we're giving away so much tax money," he went on. "Free land you call it. Well, Texas was founded on giving away free land. It's why we're all here, if you think about it. We need the people more than the taxes. We need them to move here and spend money here and bring new life to this town. The schools will still collect taxes, and we'll use that money to make our kids smarter and our schools better. When a lot of you retire, maybe your kids won't have gone to Lubbock or someplace else. Maybe they'll be right here, working at that high-tech plant, wearing a suit and tie and collecting stock options.

"And maybe there will still be a town here, maybe even after the ranch is just something the old timers talk about and the young ones can only imagine. I'd be sad to see the ranch disappear, and I hope I die before it happens, but if the town survives, I know my great-granddaddy would be damn proud."

Malloy remembered how the speech had moved him and everyone else. Conquistador wasn't used to public oration; it was a town of few words. The townsfolk, many of whom had viewed the tax breaks as one more betrayal, a giveaway demanded of people with nothing left to give, began to talk about investment, about building a future, and in the end, they overwhelmingly voted in favor of the plan. Kerr knew he, more than anyone else, had sold the deal, and if something went wrong, he alone would be blamed for leading them astray.

The power line project, though, pitted Kerr's community concerns against his professional responsibilities to the protecting the ranch. As a community leader, he'd convinced Cap Rock Electric to build the line on the promise of new retail customers from the subdivision and the six hundred kilowatts a day it would be able to sell to the chip plant. As a Frye executive, he'd convinced the ranch's owner to give the electric company access to the land. Now, Cap Rock was trying to cut its own costs at the expense of the Conquistador. Giving into the electric company would get him in trouble with his own company. Standing firm would get him in trouble with the town.

"So, how did things go at the meeting?" Kerr asked after Malloy had stood inside doorway to his boss's office for several minutes. Malloy wondered if Kerr knew the answer already.

"Well," Malloy said more slowly than usual, "I told you I wasn't much of a diplomat. I think I managed to prove that."

He recounted the story of the argument and subsequent fistfight, and Kerr's ears began to light up again. He tapped his front teeth together without opening his mouth, a nervous habit that meant he was considering how to handle the situation. Kerr didn't yell when he got angry, but Malloy could sense the temper building beneath the calm façade. When he spoke, it was from between lips pressed tightly, allowing only the minimal movement necessary to speak.

"I didn't send you over there to whup up on them. And I damn sure didn't need you to start a feud," he said after Malloy had finished his story.

"Well, I hadn't planned on that either. Then again, I also hadn't figured anyone would insult my mama."

"You know these city folk don't think like that. Besides, he couldn't have known about Nelda."

"No excuse," Malloy said flatly.

"Fine. But now we've got a bigger problem," Kerr said, and began tapping his front teeth again.

"We? Hell, Roy, I don't know why you sent me over there in the first place. I really don't want any part of this."

"I sent you because I knew you understood the issue. They don't get the seriousness of the water problems they could cause. If we don't work something out, they'll pump us dry."

"I know that. I said that all along. If you're so worried about it, you should have gone. You could have made another fancy speech and won them over."

Kerr stewed on the comment for a moment. He was more than just Malloy's boss. They were friends, and the comment stung. As more outsiders moved in, as the town began to change, old-timers who voted for the tax plan began to have second thoughts, and they were blaming Kerr. He'd been reminded of his dramatic speech in the high school cafeteria more than once. He was beginning to feel like a snake-oil salesman who hadn't left town fast enough.

"I couldn't go," he said quietly. "I'm on the council. It sends a mixed message. The council doesn't want to mediate this, and I don't want to make it look like I'm using my influence improperly. We can't risk screwing this up because I got careless. You can speak for the ranch. You're the only other person around here who could. At least I thought you were."

"I'm just a damn cow-puncher."

"You're a manager on this ranch. I needed you to act like one."

Malloy hated that title almost as much as he hated Kerr throwing it in his face. It had protected him from being cut to day labor like many of his colleagues, and it paid better than being a regular cowhand, but it made him feel dirty. In a business that valued independence, being a "boss" had certain connotations he wasn't comfortable with. Malloy wondered what his father would have thought, after a lifetime of working the ranch, to know his son was "management." Just working there had been good enough for him.

"I guess I made a management decision, then," Malloy snapped back.

Kerr brushed off the sarcasm. "Not a good one. Listen, Trace, we need these people to work with us. We're losing, you realize that, don't you? Margins have been crushed by the drought. Frye's not going to keep pouring money into this. We don't show a profit this year, it may be the last. I can't have a man-made drought on top of two years of natural ones."

"Maybe it would be better if they did sell. Maybe we could find an owner who wasn't so focused on profits in a business where there aren't any."

"Maybe we get an owner who doesn't want the business at all, just the land. Maybe in five years, you're a tour guide leading around some slickers from New York who stink of sunscreen telling them about the history of the prickly pear."

They both laughed a little at the mental picture, a quick West Texas chuckle that seemed to come from their shoulders. But there was a nervousness in their shared amusement, too, because it was tinged with the realization of truth.

"Look, Trace," Kerr said finally. "You know what's at stake here. We've got to fix this. Don't mention the fistfight, but I need a memo on the status of the talks with the homeowners. Just say it's unresolved and negotiations are ongoing, that'll do for the paperwork, but then I need you to fix it."

Malloy cringed at the idea of memo writing. Memos were the worst part of corporate ranching. He didn't mind having to carry a laptop on horseback to record cattle statistics. He'd adapted to that. But memos were like grade-school assignments:

"Write a page on what you did today." For Malloy, the doing was what mattered, not the documenting.

"How do you propose I fix it?" he asked.

"Make peace with this man."

"I'm not sure I can, Roy. I busted his nose pretty good. He was talking about suing me."

"Really?" Kerr shook his head in disbelief, but Malloy could tell he was concerned at the prospect of having to explain a lawsuit over a broken nose to his bosses in Chicago. "You have to find a way," he said finally. "Hell, invite him out here for the day. The best way to solve a problem is to understand it. This guy's an environmentalist, right? I remember him bragging about how that plant would recycle water and stuff. Play on that. Bring him out here and show him the paddocks, explain the cellular program. Get him to see why the water's so important."

"He already knows water's important; he just doesn't care that it's important for us. We're evil exploiters of the land and cruel abusers of animals."

"So get him out here and show him he's wrong." ✯

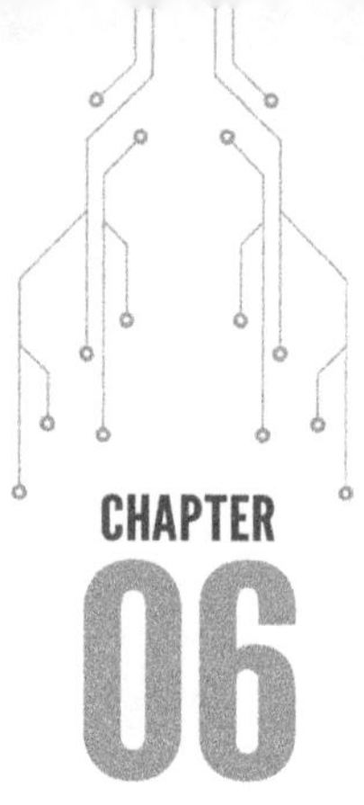

CHAPTER 06

TERRY GARRISON pulled the dirty felt hat off his head by the brim and mopped the sweat from his brow.

"Already a scorcher," he said, making small talk with himself.

Trace Malloy bent over the prostrate calf in front of him, injected the vaccine from the hypo-gun and stood up slowly, taking his time to enjoy the completion of an unpleasant task. He turned to Colt. "You and Manny finish up here."

Malloy and Garrison climbed into their saddles and rode back through the thistles and prickly pear, their horses' hooves slipping occasionally on loose rocks as the animals grew more tired from the sun. By the time the two men pulled themselves up the slight rise from the barn and under the shade of a towering cottonwood in the front yard, they were feeling a little wobbly themselves. Malloy leaned his back against the side of Garrison's blue pickup and looked at the faded tan clapboards of his one-story house. Tan paint set against tan brick rising from the tan ground. Malloy closed his eyes and even the back of his eyelids seemed tan as the sun pressed through them.

Garrison scanned his truck, then flung both arms over the side of the bed and began rummaging.

"Pretty sorry lot again this year," Malloy said as Garrison fished through the cooler in the back of his pickup.

"Well," Garrison replied without looking up, "you don't want a big herd. You ain't got time for it." He chuckled a little as he pulled two beers out of the cooler.

Malloy instinctively looked over his shoulder toward the front door of the house before taking the cold bottle in his gloved hand. Darla had gone to Gunyon to do some shopping and check on his mother. He and Garrison walked up to the porch, eased themselves onto the wooden chairs, and leaned them back on two legs until they touched the wall. Their boots, dusted from the morning's work, hung over the railing as they talked.

"Just wonder if it's worth it," Malloy said finally, picking up the conversation where it left off five minutes earlier. "We culled so many cows last fall, and we got so little to show for it. At the prices we're getting, I can't afford to keep replenishing. What did we have out there? Ten calves? This used to take us all day."

"Yeah, when it was us helping our dads and we had to clean up, and if we decided to screw around and take our time about it, which we usually did. C'mon Trace, you sound like my old man used to. You ever remember your dad saying business was good?"

"I can remember it being better."

Garrison sat silently for a moment, staring at the searing incandescent force of the sun beyond the shade of the cottonwood. "You know," he said finally, "by the time Colt and Manny take over, they'll probably just skip the cows and go right for the beer."

Malloy had to smile in spite of his sullen mood. He slipped off his cowboy boots and aired his sweat-soaked feet on the railing. He wondered if he was the only cowboy who hated boots. Usually, at the end of the day, he kept a pair of hiking shoes under his desk to change in to. Kerr once said it reminded him of the women who worked office jobs in Manhattan and switched their high heels for tennis shoes before walking to the subway.

Malloy had worn boots almost as long as his feet needed covering, but he'd never had a pair that felt comfortable the way they were supposed to. He broke them in properly. He filled them with water and a splash of rubbing alcohol and let them soak. Nothing worked. He'd years ago relegated them to being just another tool, like gloves or a hat—something he needed when he was at work but not something he needed at home.

Malloy sighed and looked out over his property. Most of the one hundred and fifty acres stretched beyond the back of the house, but he enjoyed the front, which drifted slightly downward to the road. Off to the north and across the two-lane blacktop was the Tie Bow, and behind the house, visible only from the back corner of his property, he could see the top of the AzTech factory if he were on a horse. Too close, he thought. Every inch of the land had once belonged to the Scots, who had first started selling parcels to help cover losses from the drought in the Fifties. His father, fresh from his time in Korea, had snapped up a chunk for himself and his new bride. The Conquistador provided the mortgage, and he'd spent most of his life working on the ranch to pay it off. If his dad had ever thought that he might be able to make it raising his own cows on his own land, he'd never mentioned it. But the ranch work was steady, and their own small herd provided a little extra income. They'd managed to get by.

When his father died, Trace managed the property for as long as his mother was able to live on her own. When Nelda Malloy became too confused to care for herself, Trace and Darla took over the house and moved in with her. Darla cared for Nelda as best she could, but Nelda's ailment, later diagnosed as Alzheimer's, progressed rapidly, eating away at her mind, at her consciousness, and even, it seemed to Malloy, at her very soul. Within a few months her condition became too severe for home care. Three years ago, Trace had to put his mother, or what was left of her, in a nursing home in Gunyon. It wasn't really her, he told himself. Not anymore. Just a collection of loose flesh strung over a frail frame, her mind sealed to the world and those who loved her.

Each time he went to visit her, each time his mother failed to recognize him, it became harder for him to make the drive to see her again.

Darla still checked on her when she went to town, and Trace knew his wife might be sitting with his mother at the same moment he and Garrison were sitting on the porch. Malloy's own visits to see Nelda, though, had become infrequent. Torn with guilt, he was still unable to face those blank eyes. He often snapped at people who asked how she was doing.

Animals who were in such a state, he knew how to deal with. It was quick and while it might not be easy, it was efficient and beneficial for all involved. People, though, could just linger for years, suffering, their very souls slipping into oblivion, and nobody did anything. He couldn't bear to see his mother, and he couldn't bear the guilt of not seeing her.

Nelda's deterioration ended Trace's relationship with his only surviving brother, Matthew. Matt, three years older than Trace, had left the Big Empty years ago and started a plumbing business in Dallas. He refused to return, showing up only briefly for their father's funeral. As Nelda's grasp on reality loosened, Matt never bothered to see her, never even called to check on her. He and Trace hadn't spoken since he'd driven his mother to Dallas seeking treatment. She'd managed to muster just enough of herself to stubbornly refuse, demanding that Trace take her home immediately. That had been more than two years ago, and other than that, his only contact with his brother was a brief phone argument that ended badly.

Matt and his mother had both retreated from this place — one willingly, the other dragged away by the specters of time and age — leaving Trace alone with the land he'd grown up on and all the heartache still steeped in its soil. He looked at the fresh calves' blood staining his jeans, at the rip in the left sleeve of his shirt and wondered why it was worth so much to him.

He could move back to the ranch, sell the house, the land, the sorry excuse for a herd that he still tried to keep. With AzTech coming in, land values were supposed to rise. He lived on the edge of town, almost to the Tie Bow, but he still might benefit from the homies' influx.

Even so, there were no guarantees he could sell the place for enough to cover the debts on it. Malloy had never been able to get ahead, and his father hadn't been able to either. Just as the land had passed from his father to him, so had the revolving loans needed to keep the place running. Old notes were paid off with new ones. No sooner had one debt been retired than he'd need to borrow more to cover vaccines or new stock or feed or fencing or any other among a host of unexpected costs.

His world weighed on him. Any year that things seemed to be moving ahead, a drought or some other catastrophe wiped out the gains. He knew that the cycle of ambition, stagnation, and frustration was the nature of small farms. It was why most people gave up and moved.

He and Darla had considered it themselves. They'd talked about relocating to Lubbock and settling into city life. Colt would have better schools and an easier shot at college, which he might even decide he wanted. But Trace couldn't quite accept giving up. Living in Conquistador was a struggle, but one he'd always managed to survive. Every year that ended with him still standing, his land still intact, and his herd still alive, he counted as a victory. Could he find such satisfaction in city life? Did Matthew claim such triumph from an unclogged drain?

He told himself no, but it was a ruse. Dreams of leaving were for the young and the old. Growing up in Conquistador, everyone had a plan for getting out, and some did. Those who didn't buried their dreams in hard work, bringing them out to ponder only as their own children got older. Then it was time to dream again of something better, not for themselves, but for the offspring they'd doomed to the same cycle of hope and despair.

Malloy and Garrison had taken part in the spring ritual, vaccinating and castrating calves, since they were nine years old. Garrison's father used to help Malloy's, which meant the boys were conscripted into service as soon as they had enough bulk to help hold a calf to the ground.

While the Malloys clung to their tiny herd, the Garrisons hadn't been true cattlemen in years. Terry's father was what the locals called a "wild one" in his youth. In truth, he was one of the few who dared to chase the dream and not turn back, at least not all the way. Hank Garrison loved working on cars. Even by rural teenage male standards his interest and his skill were exceptional. He enlisted in the Army during the Korean War and wound up honing his expertise with the 179th Infantry, where he spent most of his time in what was little more than a canvas garage, keeping World War II-era vehicles running longer than they should have. After the war, he returned to

Conquistador but refused to "make a living on anything that eats or shits" as he liked to say. He survived mostly by working on trucks and other service vehicles for the ranch, and from there would fix the cars of ranch hands and their wives. By the 1960s, he'd developed a full-blown auto repair business and was doing well by 'Quistador standards. He was even elected mayor and held the office for more than a decade before he died of a heart attack.

Caleb Malloy and Hank Garrison had been friends since childhood, which meant their sons became friends by default, thrown together by parallel generational cycles. Hank hated ranch work, but he would show up without being asked in the spring and fall when the Malloys needed extra help with their small herd.

Colt and Manny, the third link in this genealogical chain of friendship, walked slowly up to the porch, the sweat making dark splotches in the center of their denim shirts. "All done," Colt said as the two boys stood before their fathers.

"Okay," Garrison said. "Grab yourselves a cold one and have seat." The boys rushed off to the truck and threw their hats in the bed. Their sweat-caked hair—Colt's short and dark brown and Manny's jet black and wavy—was pressed against their skulls, two classic cases of "hat head."

Manny's mother had died giving birth to him. Terry, who inherited his father's unconventional attitude along with his auto repair business, had raised the boy himself. Garrison had been married only about a year and a half at the time. He'd fallen hard for Consuela Eribe. She was the daughter of a day laborer who lived outside of town in a rundown silver Gulfstream trailer that reminded Malloy of a rusted soup can.

Garrison had known the girl for several years, but they got together at a 4-H rodeo in Gunyon two months before high school graduation. Garrison had tagged along with Malloy, who was showing a steer he'd raised. Terry's stated purpose for the trip was "chasing *chicas*," his term for younger girls he could lure behind the goat pens and, as he used to say, "practice his breaststroke."

Consuela, a devout Catholic girl whose father had warned her about the urges of young Anglo boys, was too smart to go near the barns. She wound up leading Garrison around the rodeo grounds, convincing him to buy her a cream soda and a corny dog. By the time he and Malloy drove back to Conquistador, Garrison was love struck. Malloy wrote it off to his friend wanting what he couldn't have, but a week later he asked Consuela to the senior prom, giving rise to a six-month courtship. They married that fall, drawing muted disapproval from many in town who didn't think the former mayor's son should be marrying a Hispanic girl. Garrison had too much of his father in him to care.

For his part, Malloy was happy for his friend. Malloy himself had been working at the ranch since graduation, earning enough to begin his trek west toward San Francisco and the Merchant Marine. He stayed in town long enough to be the best man at the wedding and headed out the next morning.

Connie was beautiful and sweet, and she and Garrison had fun together. Not many men in Conquistador followed their heart, most simply settled for the best among limited options. Trace loved Darla, but looking back, he wasn't sure if he loved her when they got married. They'd been friends so long, marriage had been a logical step, rather than a leap of the heart. He'd often wondered if his infant sister had lived, would he have felt a different kind of love for her than the one he thought he felt for his wife?

As best man at Garrison's wedding, he experienced the emotion that would be absent at his own a few months later when he got back from Kansas. His wedding always seemed less a celebration and more a ritual, a submission to the Big Empty, an acceptance of the limitations it enforced on those who chose to stay. He didn't listen to rock n' roll much; he'd never had a taste for it, but he remembered hearing a song—Springsteen, he was pretty sure—on the trip to Kansas, dozing in a stranger's car on a dark, bleak stretch of unknown highway. "Is a dream a lie if it don't come true?" The dull, husky words rolled out of the speakers and pushed across his half-wakened thoughts. Even now, he couldn't remember the rest of the song, he never knew the name, but those words still welled up and haunted him in the lulling darkness of semi-consciousness just before sleep. The Big Empty had pulled him back, and he accepted that when he said "I do."

When Connie died, Garrison took it hard. Darla watched Manny for a few weeks while Trace helped Terry arrange the funeral and get his head straight. If it hadn't been for the boy, Malloy knew Garrison would have left Conquistador for good. Sometimes, Malloy would lie awake at night, wondering if Garrison at that moment was loading his truck and heading out.

Terry, though, was drawn to the boy, and as the days passed it became clear he wasn't leaving. He'd named his new son Manuel, honoring Connie's wish that their son be named after her paternal grandfather. For the past thirteen years they'd lived first in a trailer behind the auto shop, and later in a small house just behind Main Street that Terry had saved for. Garrison, much to everyone's surprise, became an attentive and caring father. Trace believed he felt a need to honor Connie's memory by making sure the boy turned out right.

Garrison still talked a good game, but in the years since Connie's death, he'd never resumed his *chica* chasing. Terry rarely talked about his wife, and Malloy never pried, but he wondered if his friend was too afraid or too dedicated to seek companionship. Or perhaps it was out of respect for Connie's family. They grew closer after her death, drawn together by the child she'd left behind.

"Guess Colt's taking the football thing pretty hard," Garrison said, watching the boys walk back toward the porch. Colt still had a slight limp.

"Yep. He blames himself for all of it, for there not being a team this year."

"Hey, Dad, I'm gonna show Manny something in the workshop," Colt called as they approached the porch.

"Okay."

The boys headed off toward the barn. Garrison watched them go and smiled.

"Probably pictures of naked girls," he said, slapping Malloy on the arm lightly with the back of his hand.

"Isn't that where we kept them?" Malloy said, chuckling. "I seem to recall you having Playboys rolled up in the cylinder housings of an old V-8 in the back of your dad's shop. I don't think I even knew what a woman looked like until my dad brought the truck in for a tune up."

They both laughed until their guffaws evaporated in the heat.

"God, I'm really worried about the boy," Malloy said after the silence returned.

"What's to worry about? He's a good kid, doesn't cause any major trouble. Helps out around the place."

"Helps out too much, maybe. All he wants to do is this," Malloy said, waving his hands across the landscape, spread like a tablecloth in every direction.

"Nothing wrong with that. It's what he knows. I reckon Manny will take over my business someday, too."

"There's a future in that. You and your dad were smart to stay away from cows. It's a damn stupid way to make a living. You don't have to worry about bad weather, disease, drought."

"No, I have to worry about all that and then some. What hurts my customers hurts the business. And I have to worry about what kinds of parts to stock and how many and whether the tanker truck will decide to show up to fill the gas tanks this week. You have any idea what it's like telling folks around here that you don't have any gas? What are they going to do?"

"He wants to join the Air Force," Malloy said, not allowing Garrison's counterpoint to disrupt his gloom. "He wants to fly the F-22."

"Hell, who wouldn't? I'd like to have a shot at that too."

"He's not going into the damn military."

"You decide for him? He ain't your dad, and he ain't Luke, either. Maybe he wants to serve his country. Nothing wrong with that. It's different now."

Malloy didn't have many memories of his oldest brother. Luke Malloy joined the Air Force in 1969, almost five years after Trace was born, and flew A-6 missions over North Vietnam. His plane was shot down later that year, and although they never found his body, the Air Force declared him dead.

When he was growing up, Trace often kept himself up at night wondering what horrors his brother endured and wondering how he would manage if faced with the same fate. His brother's death, though, was largely an abstraction. Luke existed mostly in postcards and letters and old school pictures. There was the senior yearbook with the lipstick stain where Luke's girlfriend had kissed the page. After Luke shipped out, the girl, Patty Buford, took a job as a cashier at the feed store.

A year later, she met a salesman for a tractor dealership, and they got married and moved to Gunyon. Trace often wondered if Luke ever knew she'd left, or for that matter, if Patty ever new Luke died.

Trace's mother cried on and off for weeks after the word finally came, confirming the fears that had mounted after the letters stopped. Luke was dead.

Malloy remembered the two men with close-cropped hair and crisp uniforms standing on the porch—*this* porch, the same one he was sitting on. He could still hear the heavy footfalls of their polished shoes, shoes that were shinier than any he'd ever seen as he peered out from behind his mother's skirt. "Ma'am," one of the men said, and that was all he heard, all he needed to hear even at such a young age. His mother began crying immediately, and Malloy scampered for his room.

While his mother cried, his father said nothing. He did nothing. He didn't comfort her, he didn't talk, didn't try to help Trace and Matt make sense of the loss. He just sat silently at night, coming home from work and easing into his chair, staring across the room at the crook of the far corner.

Caleb Malloy had his own demons, and his son's death only amplified them. Caleb had been an Army infantryman in Korea, and other than acknowledging his service and giving his rank (private), he never spoke to his children about his military career. While other kids could brag at school about their father's military exploits, Trace sat silent, unable to share stories he would never hear. After his father's death, Trace discovered that even his mother didn't know what had happened in Korea, "But whatever it was, it was the most horrible thing he ever saw, because when we were courting, he used to talk like he had grasshoppers in his pockets," she said. "Once he came back, he'd just sit there, sometimes for hours, lost in thought and not saying a word."

After Luke's death, Caleb became so quiet he never told his family about the times he would awaken in the middle of the night, coughing up blood. He never mentioned how hard it had become to breathe or to do simple chores like lifting a saddle. One day, he came in from the field just before lunch, laid down on the couch and died. Lung cancer, undiagnosed.

As a boy, Trace thought of his father as the Marlboro Man, the rugged cowboy living the American dream. The four packs a day only enhanced the image. Trace wanted to be just like him. Malloy stopped smoking the day of his father's funeral — three packs a day to nothing on sheer anger and stubborn determination. He hadn't had a cigarette since.

"Colt's a fine boy," Garrison said, cutting into Malloy's reverie. "You got nothing to worry about."

Malloy never could understand Garrison's carefree outlook on child-rearing. As a single parent, Garrison should be the one worried about his son, but to Malloy it always seemed that fathering came naturally to Garrison. He had an easy manner, rarely losing his temper, and still had managed to raise a fine son. Malloy, for his part, saw nothing but trouble ahead.

"Besides," Garrison went on, "Everything's going to change now that AzTech's coming in. There'll be a lot more opportunities. He may change his mind about ranching."

Malloy snorted. "He may have to. The homies aren't going to leave much of the ranch by the time they're through."

"According to you, that might not be so bad to give up ranching for computering."

"I don't know. We're giving away so much. It's more than the taxes. These folks have decided they own the place. They get to say where the streets go, who gets how much water, how much electricity we need, they want us to sell bonds, they want this and that. We gave them our heritage, and they don't appreciate it."

"Hogwash. We bought a future. When was the last time you were outside of 'Quistador? All these towns are dying—Gunyon, Carlson, Tysonville, Florence. They're all shrinking, and they have been for years. Nobody's staying out here. There's nothing anymore. They used to call it the Big Empty because of the land. Now, it's a testament to the future. At least we're trying to do something about it."

"What kind of future are we wanting, though? It's like we were just grabbing the first thing that came along. AzTech is just the latest. Remember the prison? All our kids were going to have futures as prison guards. Is that better than cowboying? It made no sense, but we would have done it if the state hadn't backed out. Turns out this place is even too desolate for a prison.

"Now we got AzTech, the great economic savior. Give 'em fifty years without taxes, build roads for them, run power lines. Money? No problem, we can sell bonds. Never mind we don't have the money to repay it. Once AzTech gets here, we'll get more. The tax base will grow like wildfire. Money in the streets. And, oh yeah, give them all the water they want in the middle of a drought, not just to drink or to water their precious flowers, but to fill up their damn pretentious little lake so the poor homies can have it just to look at because that's how they do it in California."

Malloy, realizing he was ranting, turned back to survey the front lot as it flowed down to the road. A white pickup was going by, Brock Peterson, the owner of the feed store, it looked like. Malloy and Garrison instinctively waved, and Peterson raised two fingers from the steering wheel in response.

"All I know is I'm seeing all these fancy new cars," Garrison said, resuming the conversation. "They all want super premium gas. You ever buy super premium? Course not. That hand-me-down truck of yours is still burning buck-fifty-a-gallon regular. Sooner or later, all the red dust around here is going to work its magic and one of them fancy new cars are gonna break down. You know what I can charge to fix a Lexus?"

"Yeah, that's good for you. Like I said, you were smart to stay away from cows."

"From the look of my boots, I can't be doing too good of a job at that. Your problem is you can't handle change. That's why you never left here. That's why Kansas seemed like hell on earth."

"Nothing wrong with a strong sense of place," Malloy said defensively. He knew Garrison was right, and Garrison knew he didn't have to say anything more. Malloy had had his chance. He hadn't taken it.

What he took was a job as a day laborer on ranch in the western part of Kansas with about two hundred head of cattle. He saved enough money from working part time at the Conquistador to fund the first leg of his trip. He planned to work in Kansas for as long as he needed to pay his way to San Francisco.

He saw it as an important step because it got him away from the shadow of the Conquistador. The day after Garrison's wedding, Malloy had hitched his way north, telling himself that in a year, he'd be on a boat in California. He'd enlist in the Merchant Marine and embark on a life opposite from the one he'd known, flush with whatever wonders the world offered him. He would be a counterpoint to the folklore figure Old Stormalong. Rather than an oar on his shoulder walking inland, he would tote a saddle and head toward the coast, not stopping until somebody asked what he was carrying.

Malloy stayed in Kansas through the summer and fall, scratching out about thirty-five dollars a day. He had to pay rent on a horse and tack because he hadn't brought his own with him from Texas. It was hard to hitch a ride with a horse.

By the time winter came, he'd had all he could stand. One morning in December, he went outside to saddle up after breakfast. About four inches of snow had fallen the night before, and the wind sliced through the quilted down of his jacket.

He wasn't used to riding in snow like this. The Conquistador had its share of light dustings every year, but this was thick as freshly sheared wool. He got to the stable and found his saddle encased in ice.

"What the hell am I supposed to do about this?" he asked another cowboy.

The other man didn't respond, he just held out his hand. In it was a plastic ice scraper, the kind used for cleaning off a windshield. Malloy stared at it for a moment, then headed for the foreman's office and barged in.

"I'm going home,"' he said flatly.

He was back in Texas by Christmas, and he and Darla married in the spring.

"I don't know if I've ever been as uncomfortable in my life," Malloy said out loud. Garrison looked over at his friend in silence. He didn't know if he was talking about then or now. ☆

CHAPTER 07

BLAINE WITHERSPOON CRINGED at the sound of the Lexus's oil pan scraping the ground as he turned up the driveway toward the Conquistador's ranch office. His latte, which he'd made at home as he did every morning, splattered out of the hole in the travel mug and onto the faux-wood detail of the dash.

"I must be out of my mind," he said to himself as he pulled under the shade of an old cottonwood. He threw the car in park and touched his nose self-consciously. It was still swollen, but most of the bruising was gone. He didn't relish the idea of again meeting the man who'd done the damage.

Malloy's phone call after dinner about a week ago had taken him by surprise.

"This is Trace Malloy. I'm calling to apologize." The cowboy had let the statement hang there, and Witherspoon himself must have been silent for a full two minutes.

"Did your lawyer put you up to this?" he'd asked finally.

"Lawyer? I don't have a lawyer," Malloy's voice sounded as if he'd swallowed a slug. "My conscience put me up to this."

"Uh huh. Well, okay, I guess your conscience can be clear now."

"That wasn't why I was calling. Truth is, I really don't feel all that bad about busting your nose."

"Why am I not surprised?"

"I called because I realized that you and I can't leave things like this. We both represent business interests vital to this community, and we have to work out our differences."

Was he reading from a script Witherspoon wondered to himself? He was growing more indignant the longer Malloy stayed on the phone.

"So you punch me in the face and now you're appealing to reason?" Witherspoon said, his voice rising. "Mr. Malloy, I think it's best if we settle this in court."

Witherspoon slammed the receiver down so hard that Jenna, who was reading a book on the couch, lost her page. He had stood there, breathing heavily, feeling anger coursing through him. The phone rang again, and he snatched it from the hook.

"What?"

"We aren't going to settle this in court. That's not how we do things here. We solve our own problems."

"Well, there's a new way of doing things. I know my legal rights."

There was a long pause, and Witherspoon thought he could hear a voice—a woman's voice—whispering in the background. Finally, Malloy said slowly, "Don't you think it would help to learn the old ways before you try to change them?"

"This is a pointless conversation," he shot back.

"The point...the point is you may be right. Someday soon folks here may settle every pissing match with lawyers and drain the water table dry to decorate their subdivisions, but wouldn't it help to understand why we're not already doing that?"

"Well, that's obvious. You're living in the past. You've got an antiquated mindset, a macho complex run amok."

There was another pause, and then Malloy's voice seeped through the silence slowly and deliberately, as if his teeth were clenched.

"Maybe, but we've also survived out here for a long time," the cowboy said. "A lot of people who work for me may someday real soon be working for you. I'm not happy about that, but I can't blame them. They're that cheap labor pool you were hoping to tap. Wouldn't it make sense to learn who these men are?"

"I'm not planning on only hiring men."

There was a long sigh. More silence followed by the low whispers in the background. Welcome to the future, Mr. Malloy, Witherspoon thought to himself, and it felt good, as if he'd landed a few punches himself.

"If I were you," Malloy said finally, "I'd start slow. Look, all I'm saying is I want to get past the feuding we've been doing and come to some kind of understanding."

"What did you have in mind?"

"Why don't you come out to the ranch next week and let me show you around?"

"You're not serious."

"Uh, well, that's why I called. Most folks would consider that hospitable."

Eventually, Malloy's persistence wore him down. Witherspoon couldn't rebuff the other man's attempts to make amends. After all, he was hoping to keep the whole matter from drawing attention back in Milpitas, which was the main reason he hadn't filed assault charges in the first place. And Malloy had a point about the labor pool. Witherspoon was still angry about being punched in the nose, but he'd spent enough time in the grade-school tutelage of Sister Mary Elizabeth to know there was a time to forgive.

As he stepped out of the Lexus, Witherspoon wondered if that time had actually arrived. He grabbed his cell phone and bike helmet, closed the door, and clicked the keyless remote. The car chirped in recognition. Witherspoon walked toward the old house of limestone and white wood, a long, one-story structure with pane windows made of thick leaded glass that shimmered in the sunlight. As he stepped up onto the porch, his footsteps echoed on the wooden floorboards, and he debated whether he should just walk in or knock first. The place still looked like a house, but he knew it was now a corporate office.

As he hesitated, the door swung open in front of him and a short, older man with a ring of white hair around the back of his head stepped through. The man held his arms away from his sides as if they were wet. He nodded at Witherspoon and extended a hand at the same time.

"Howdy, Mr. Witherspoon, good to see you again."

"Hello. You can call me Blaine."

Witherspoon had met Roland Kerr several times before, though briefly. There had been the site surveys and endless negotiations with the county, not to mention all the initial preparations to get construction going. Kerr not only ran the ranch, as near as Witherspoon could tell, he seemed to run the town as well.

"Call me Roy," Kerr shot back.

Kerr invited Witherspoon into the ranch house and offered him coffee. Stepping over the threshold, Witherspoon thought they'd passed through some sort of portal. The quaint country surroundings of the outside gave way to a modern corporate office. It wasn't up to AzTech standards, by any means, but it was surprisingly new, from the smell of the low-pile carpet, which was a sort of muted green, to the blond wood of the office furniture. Just inside the hundred-year-old door was a receptionist desk, complete with a personal computer bearing a flat-screen monitor, and Witherspoon saw what appeared to be a high-speed data line running up the side of the desk and into the back of the CPU.

Kerr led him down a hallway to a room that served as his office. Witherspoon imagined that when the house was first built, the space might have been a bedroom or a drawing room. As the two men sat to talk, a secretary brought Kerr a cup of coffee. Witherspoon had declined. After his morning latte, he usually switched to tea.

"I'm sorry we don't have any tea," Kerr said, as he took a sip of his own cup. "At least not hot tea. I'm afraid we don't get much call for it."

"Not a problem."

Kerr got right to business. He told Witherspoon that he would drive him out to meet with Malloy and some other ranch hands shortly. Witherspoon would get to see a crew working the cows, then they'd ride out to one of the paddocks and show him the cellular grazing program.

"Now, I mentioned we were going to be riding," Kerr said. "You ever been on a horse before?"

"Well, not since I was a kid," Witherspoon said sheepishly. "You know, county fair, pony rides…"

Kerr nodded and stared at Witherspoon for a moment before snapping his gaze to the papers on his desk.

"But Malloy had warned me. I did come prepared." He held up the bicycle helmet he'd been carrying since he got out of the car.

Kerr stared at it silently.

"You know, for the horse," Witherspoon said. "For safety. To protect against head injuries."

"Head injuries?" Kerr furrowed his brow. "Not sure I've seen that. Seen busted arms, busted legs, seen boys get bucked and stomped and dragged and kicked. I guess I maybe saw one or two fellas get kicked in the head. Would that count? I mean, most horses, if they kick you in the head, they'd bust a plastic helmet like that in half, or else knock it plum off your head."

"Well, uh, I mean, you're not exactly making me feel more comfortable here." Witherspoon chuckled nervously and he could feel the warm wave of embarrassment wash over his face.

Kerr stared silently again. He appeared to be nibbling on something between his front teeth, like a rabbit, only slower, as if it were part of his thought process.

"Well," Kerr said finally, "then I guess you'll understand why I have to have you sign this." He handed Witherspoon a piece of paper but didn't give him the time to read it before he spoke again. All Witherspoon had time to see was the Frye International logo and the word "waiver."

"It's a release," Kerr went on. "Frye's lawyers—you know the corporate types—something they came up with. I guess they don't want you to sue us if you fall off."

"I'm not surprised," Witherspoon said. He found it refreshing to confront something familiar, even if that something was bureaucracy. "It must be a huge liability."

"Actually, it never made sense to me," Kerr said. "I had to have all the day workers sign it, and they thought I was joking. That was years back, after Frye bought the place."

Witherspoon signed the paper, and Kerr led him back out the front door. They got into a white pickup, and Witherspoon wondered if it was the same one he'd hit with the rental truck when he was moving to town. The windshield had a crack that ran most of its length.

As he turned the truck around, Kerr pointed to an old whitewashed building adjacent to the headquarters. "That's the old bunkhouse," he said. "It's still on the original site where it was built in 1882. The big house, here, replaced the old ranch house in the early 1900s. The original house was all wood, but when they rebuilt it, they decided to use limestone they dug out of the cap rock over near Lubbock. Those windows, though, are the same ones from the old house. They had to bring them in by wagon from Fort Worth. I guess when they rebuilt the house, they decided it was easier to reuse them."

Witherspoon understood he was supposed to find this idle history interesting, so he nodded and said "uh-huh," as if to show he was paying attention. But he really wasn't. His mind was already drifting back to problems at the plant. The air handlers weren't cycling the air in the clean room properly, and the parts per million on the dust counts were higher than they should be. Why? He had no idea, but he'd put Swain on it and demanded answers by tomorrow morning.

Witherspoon didn't trust Swain. He was a climber, but he'd been involved in the Tucson project, and despite the cost overruns and persistent production problems, he knew a thing or two about meeting a startup schedule.

Kerr was still talking about the ranch house and some of the surrounding buildings, where the paint peeled like flecks of dead skin from the crumbling frames, the bare wood underneath bleached from the cycles of a thousand unrelenting suns. What did Witherspoon care? This was the past, and he saw no point in reveling in it. Cowboys and horses and cattle and hardship, they all meant nothing. It was a vicious circle of abuse—abuse of the land, of animals and ultimately of the people themselves.

And now that he was here, it would end, because on the cusp of the new millennium, he had brought with him the promise of something better — the promise of the future.

Kerr began to ease the pickup down the driveway, the gravel crunching under the tires. The truck cleared the small gorge at the bottom of the drive nonchalantly, with greater ease than the Lexus had on the way up.

As he drove, Kerr continued his travelogue:

"Used to be all of this, including everything that's now the town, was part of the Conquistador. A group of Scottish investors bought almost two million acres in the mid 1870s. They paid more than a million dollars, which back then was a lot more money than it is now. One of them had a fascination with Spanish literature and he chose the name 'Conquistador' after the first European explorers who pushed through here looking for gold in Colorado. The Scots didn't know anything about the cattle business, and they did a lot of their learning the hard way.

"They were attracted by the cheap land and the hucksters that were going around Europe at the time talking up big profits that could be made raising cattle in the American West. Of course, a lot of development in the Old West got funded from England and Scotland, but these investors were different. Some of them, the active partners, they actually moved here to be involved in the operations of the ranch.

"My great-grandfather was a part of that first group that came over to run the place. He wasn't an owner, just a hired hand — a sheep herder by trade, actually. Back then, we raised mostly Longhorns. I think they had something like seventy thousand head. They switched to Herefords in the late 1800s. Herefords brought a higher price on the market and were easier to manage.

"The Scots started the town shortly after the turn of the century. By then, with the railroad and all, enough folks moved out here to where it seemed to make sense.

"So the Scots donated the land for the town. At that time, the ranch was at its peak, and you had maybe a thousand people employed in some way or another. We had our own blacksmiths, cooks, you name it. Even lawyers. Even then.

"The town kept growing. They found oil in the Western Fork in 1951, which was about thirty years after they first started looking for it. It was good they found it when they did, because that helped us through the drought. Even so, oil hasn't ever been a big source of income for us. Not too many wells around here. There's been a few natural gas plays over near Gunyon that have worked out okay, but these days, mostly it's just a few stripper wells that pump ten or fifteen barrels a day.

"Anyway, by 1958, the population of the town had hit more than seventeen hundred. Now we're down to about five hundred eighty, and that's on a Sunday when no one's off working jobs in Gunyon or Lubbock or some place. In fact, that was as of the last Census, and I think the number's probably fallen some since then. Folks die and whatnot.

"Some of the early Scots sold out and went home by the late 1800s. Those who stayed bought the remaining interests and the whole thing stayed in family hands until the 1960s. Some of the kids wanted out, which you know happens with things like this. That just wasn't a time when people wanted to be ranchers anymore. Prices had fallen and costs had risen, which pretty much describes the history of the business from the beginning.

"The grandkids and great-grandkids of the original Scots started selling to outsiders—absentee owners mostly, who kept some of the staff like me on hand to make sure things were run right.

"Over the years, some pieces of the ranch were sold off, and then in '84, when Frye bought us, they sold about fifty thousand acres, a decent chunk, to help finance the purchase.

"Frye's a pretty good outfit. Old Quentin Frye, he grew up in the Panhandle, not far from here, and he was real proud to own the Conquistador. He died four years ago, but so far his wishes still prevail, and the company's been willing to keep the place. Frye's private, you know, so they can indulge themselves without answering to stockholders.

"Frye's got about a dozen ranches around the world, but this is the crown jewel. Some of them are just corporate retreats, but a handful like this one are still working operations.

"I mean, Frye does all sorts of stuff—oil and gas, chemicals, agribusiness, pipelines, financial stuff like commodities trading, oh and now they're getting into that high-speed Internet stuff."

"Broadband?" Witherspoon said, his interest suddenly piqued.

"Yeah, I guess. Fiber optics. They run the lines through the pipeline rights-of-way. It's pretty low cost, but they say the potential returns look good."

"Oh yeah," Witherspoon said, a little amazed he was having a discussion about bandwidth demand while riding shotgun in a pickup bouncing down a road from which a telephone pole was the tallest thing to be seen in any direction. "The potential's huge. That's the future. Everyone's getting on the Internet."

"Yep, it's sure changed things for us. Every morning, I log on and check cattle prices. Malloy, he's more into technology than I am. He always looking up weather reports and reading papers from all over the place."

"Well, see?" Witherspoon said cheerfully. "And just think if everyone does what you're doing, they'll need all that fiber you guys have in the ground and more. And people will need the chips we're going to make here to run their modems. Who knows? Conquistador might become a high-tech Mecca, drawing in a new breed, just like the Scots."

Kerr smiled dryly as he turned the pickup off the Main Road and onto a gravel driveway blocked by a metal gate. He threw the truck into park.

Kerr got out, opened the gate, returned to the truck and drove through. He put the transmission in park again, got out, closed the gate and walked back to the pickup. Over Witherspoon's right shoulder, had he turned around and looked, he might have seen the AzTech plant across the paved road, on the horizon, as well as the rooflines of his house and those of his employees.

As they drove on, Kerr continued to relate the history of what to Witherspoon looked like nothing more than a barren expanse of wasteland, dotted with the occasional scrub cedar or thistle.

"This section is called the Tie Bow. Basically, what's now the Conquistador is in three pieces: The Main Ranch, which is the largest, the Western Fork which is out Highway 74 on the other side of the town, and this chunk here. The Scots called it the Tie Bow because up ahead there's a clearing, just over that rise." He pointed without lifting his hand off the wheel.

"When the first Spanish missionaries pushed up from Mexico in the early 1700s, the Comanches used to attack them every chance they got. This was sort of a staging area. Some of the survivors of the attacks claimed that they could see warriors sitting on that ridge, stringing their bows for battle."

Witherspoon looked, but he didn't see anything he would consider a ridge. He saw a slight swelling of the ground, which barely broke the horizontal plane of the landscape. The road ahead turned and veered down into the bowl of a depressed area, although he wouldn't have called it a valley. Still, he supposed that on horseback, the rise might make a good vantage point for Indians waiting to attack. It wasn't hard for Witherspoon to imagine a line of Comanche warriors standing there now, the eagle feathers in their heads blowing in the breeze, their faces painted for war. If they hadn't been bouncing along in a truck, or if he wasn't able to feel his cell phone pressing against his side, he would have had few modern reminders that the twenty-first century was less than a year away.

"Personally," Kerr continued, "I think the Scots probably made the whole thing up. The Comanches probably rode with their bows tied. This may have been some sort of encampment or something. Maybe somebody saw some warriors repairing bows or making new ones. But the story never made sense to me. Not that it really matters. This area's been known as the Tie Bow for over a hundred years."

Kerr pulled the pickup down the other side of the rise and up along a corral in the middle of a vast, unbroken expanse of rocky soil and patches of sparse vegetation. The corral was old. Years of merciless sun had bleached its planks a deathly gray until they resembled ancient bones rising from the ground. In a few places, rusted nails worked their way out of holes they'd been hammered into long ago.

The corral had two holding areas, and one was filled with huge cows and their calves, a mass of flicking tails, moving clumps of brown and beige, and the constant din of mothers calling to their young. In the other area, about a half dozen cows pressed against the fence separating the two sections.

At the gate between the two Witherspoon saw Trace Malloy on horseback. Five other men, two of them mounted, were chasing the cattle around the pen. The bleating and braying rang across the emptiness of the prairie, drowning the voices of the men, who would occasionally yell things at each other that Witherspoon couldn't make out.

Witherspoon grabbed his bike helmet from the front seat of the truck and began to walk over to the fence, on the other side from Malloy and his horse.

Malloy didn't break his gaze. The other men drove the cows toward him, and Malloy's horse wove back and forth under him, bounding left, then right, as if it had springs in its legs. It reminded Witherspoon of a show he'd seen on the Discovery Channel about border collies herding sheep.

A cow ran forward, its bleating calf close behind. Malloy worked his horse between the two in one swift motion, then pulled his horse back. The calf bolted in fear, running back to the middle of the pen. The cow spooked in the other direction and ran through the gate, kicking its back legs in frustration and fear.

Malloy repeated the process several times, twice successfully plying the cow from its calf, once sending the cow in the wrong direction and missing the gate. Even Witherspoon, uninitiated to the ways of the Old West, could appreciate the skill he was witnessing, as man and horse moved in a unified motion with the agility of a wide receiver coming off the line and faking out a defender.

Witherspoon put a foot up on the lowest board of the fence and slung his arm over the top. He knew he wasn't going to like what he was about to see, but he also didn't want to make a fool of himself. After all, part of his job was to learn to get along with these people. Malloy had had a point when they talked earlier on the phone. Some of the men he saw before him might one day be working at AzTech.

Witherspoon had to smile to himself as he stood on the fence. What would the folks back in Milpitas think if they could see him like this, hanging out on the range, scoping out potential recruits? Even old Soddy, with his archive of glory-days tales, couldn't top this. Witherspoon knew he was gathering fodder for a thousand cocktail parties, grand tales of his adventures in taming the Old West, heralding a sea change that would fill up the Big Empty with prosperity. He wasn't just Blaine Witherspoon, plant manager, he was a one-man paradigm shift, one foot on the rotting gray skeletons of the past, one eye on effervescent prospect of the future.

Suddenly, Malloy's voice cut into his thoughts.

"Son, you're in about the worst place you could possibly be."

At first, Witherspoon wasn't sure Malloy had even spoken. Had he imagined it? Had the cowboy just called him "son"? Malloy's gaze was still riveted on the livestock moving toward him. Chagrined, Witherspoon began to back away. He could feel his face flush. The embarrassment and the blaze of the sun, which even at mid-morning was becoming oppressive, made beads of sweat form on his brow as he slunk back toward Kerr and the pickup. As he retreated, trying not to appear dejected at Malloy's rebuke, a bolt of fear shot through him: He'd left his sunscreen in the Lexus. He turned and leaned his back against the pickup, standing next to Kerr. Neither man spoke.

Malloy, atop the brown horse, rhythmically darted one way and then another, a man in complete control. At one with his task, he was perfectly attuned to the unique tempo of the Big Empty. Witherspoon sensed insecurity well up inside him. Would he ever fit in here, or at least find his own comforting cadence? He'd felt this same intense self-doubt almost twenty years ago, when he'd tried to become manager of the high school basketball team. He was never good enough to play, but he wanted desperately to be on the team, or at least to avoid the humiliation of his regular phys ed classes. The manager posts on various teams were hot commodities among the geeks, a popularity contest for the least popular kids, a beauty contest for social lepers.

Witherspoon didn't get selected. None of the players thought he knew enough about sports, or they just didn't want him around.

"Son, you're in the about the worst place you could be." Malloy's voice echoed in his head, and the words throbbed as surely as if Malloy had broken his nose a second time. How could that cowboy be so condescending? Witherspoon asked himself. I have a master's degree, for crying out loud.

The whole tableaux underscored the growing sense of failure that had been overtaking him. For months, he'd been talking up Texas to his friends back in Milpitas. He'd say things like "well, we Texans..." Even though he was joking, a part of him was starting to believe it. He would talk about things "out here" as if he had learned about the land, when in fact, as Malloy had just made utterly clear, he knew nothing. And of course, he hadn't told anyone about the beating Malloy had given him. He was counting on his nose being completely healed before his next trip to the home office.

Witherspoon sulked in the solitude of his embarrassment until Malloy and his colleagues had separated all the cows from their babies. With that part of the job done, Malloy dismounted, climbed over the fence as easily as if he were stepping over a tree root and walked toward Witherspoon and Kerr.

"Sorry I wasn't here to greet you," he said, extending a gloved hand. He seemed oblivious to the damage his earlier comment had inflicted. Did he even remember saying it? Witherspoon took the cowboy's hand and tried not to wince outwardly at Malloy's crushing grip.

"No problem," Witherspoon said, trying to bury his earlier feelings. Put on the manager's mantle, he told himself. He took a deep breath and ran through the little mental exercise his psychoanalyst had taught him back in California: "It's not about you. It's them. You must make sure they get your message. Their message is irrelevant. Their thoughts are irrelevant. You are in charge. They know that, and they expect you to act like it." The words had helped him through his first assignment in management, and he found it comforting now as he stared into the round, reflective sunglasses that hung just below the long arc of Malloy's hat brim.

Sweat was showing along the button line of Malloy's shirt, and the blue and white plaid pattern wouldn't hide it. Focus on that, he's sweating, Witherspoon told himself. He could feel beads rolling down his own scalp, triggered not by the blistering sun, but by his own discomfort.

"I've got to get back to the house," Kerr said abruptly. He shook Witherspoon's hand—another firm grip—and climbed back into the pickup. As the truck bounced back up the road, Malloy surveyed Witherspoon. He stared coldly at the bike helmet in the engineer's left hand, but he didn't say anything.

Witherspoon stood silently and waited. He was expecting a face-to-face apology before the diplomatic mission went any farther. He wished he'd demanded it before Kerr left with the truck. Malloy watched the dust stirred up by his boss's departure and kept staring until the trail dissipated in the air. When he finally spoke, his eyes were still on the faint particles of dust floating after the truck.

"I'm sorry about popping you in the nose," he said, as if the words, caught in his brushy mustache, needed extra force to get out. "I shouldn't have done that. I lost control."

Witherspoon had prepared for the moment for a week, and now that it arrived, he found he didn't know what to say. Saying nothing could be as bad as saying the wrong thing. The pause in the conversation grew to an uncomfortable lull. He didn't want to say something stupid or weak. He almost instinctively blurted out "don't worry about it," but he stopped himself. That wasn't the message he needed to send.

Witherspoon felt choked by the weight of the moment. A lot was riding on his response. He needed these people, but he needed their respect too. Future employees? Surely not Malloy. Not this walking anachronism, this fist-fighting Neanderthal. What could he expect? Brawls in the clean room? Posting signs that outlined the company's no fighting policy?

In the silence, Malloy had shifted his gaze and was staring at Witherspoon, waiting for some sort of response. Was there some other "old way" Witherspoon might trample on? Was there a set amount of time after which a response no longer counted? Be sincere, he told himself, just don't let him off the hook.

"I accept your apology," Witherspoon said finally, closing the chasm of silence. The words came straight from elementary school. Sister Mary Elizabeth would be proud. Then for good measure, he acknowledged his own faults, an act of contrition. "I never should have insulted your mother. That was my mistake."

Malloy looked at his own boots, then shot a glance over his shoulder at the corral. The other cowboys were setting up some equipment. A man was connecting a propane tank to a long metal cylinder while another cowhand walked up with a batch of metal rods. Even Witherspoon, an outsider, a mere interloper in this archaic world, knew what they were. He suddenly longed for the whole day to end. He wanted to skip what he knew was the upcoming theater of animal cruelty and get back home. He could already feel his skin burning from the sun.

Malloy, though, wasn't finished.

"It wasn't your mistake," he said. "Roy sent me to that meeting because he thought I was a good diplomat. That must seem pretty funny to you now. I'm a big enough man that I can take an insult, especially an unintentional one, and not start swinging. I'm afraid I gave you the wrong impression, not just about me, but about a lot of folks out here."

Was he reciting this? Witherspoon wondered. Had Malloy been practicing this little corral-side speech all week? Maybe Kerr even wrote it for him.

"It's funny, in a way," Malloy went on. "My mama would have been furious at what I did. Of all people. I guess the doc or somebody probably told you she's in a bad way. Alzheimer's. She used to always say 'you mess up, you fess up.' That was one of her favorites. So this, I guess, is me owning up."

Witherspoon didn't know what to say. He didn't know about Malloy's mother, of course. Malloy must have realized that. Why would he expect Lambeau to have shared confidential patient information with him? Was this a ploy? Was the aw-shucks cowboy trying to manipulate him with false sympathy? Again, his silence grew into a prolonged pause. Witherspoon's own rehearsal of the conversation hadn't gone at all like this. He was supposed to have been assertive, pressing the advantage that his battered nose clearly gave him. Instead, he'd weakened his position the way he always did. Frustrated by his own verbal inadequacy, he looked up at Malloy.

Witherspoon wondered how old the man was. He guessed they must be about the same age, but it was hard to tell. He knew Malloy's son was about Brandon's age, maybe a year or so younger, yet the boy looked like he was twenty. Malloy's skin was leathery, his hands cracked. The long bushy mustache gave an appearance of seniority, yet the man could easily be ten years younger than he looked.

Malloy seemed to snap to attention, as if he felt awkward at the talk of his mother. "Well, c'mon," he said, turning toward the corral.

Inside the fence, the other ranch hands stared at Witherspoon. He began to feel as if his nose had swelled into a huge, bulbous turnip in the center of his face. Their looks were expressionless, but he could sense the men laughing at him from behind their blank faces.

"Let's get this over with," he said to himself as he stepped through the gate that Malloy held open for him and walked toward the group to introduce himself. As he extended his hand, his left foot slipped. He swung his arms wildly and retained his balance, thankful not to have fallen.

He glanced down and saw the greenish brown pile of dung smeared across the ground and oozing around the sides of his tennis shoe. Instinctively, Witherspoon lifted his foot and inspected the sole. The manure was pressed into to the tread. He could hear the muted laughter of the cowboys rolling across the corral, a stormfront of derision that seemed to grow louder as it washed over him. He put his foot down and tried to smear the stinking goo from the shoe.

"Don't worry," Malloy said over his shoulder. "It won't be the last. We're just getting started." ★

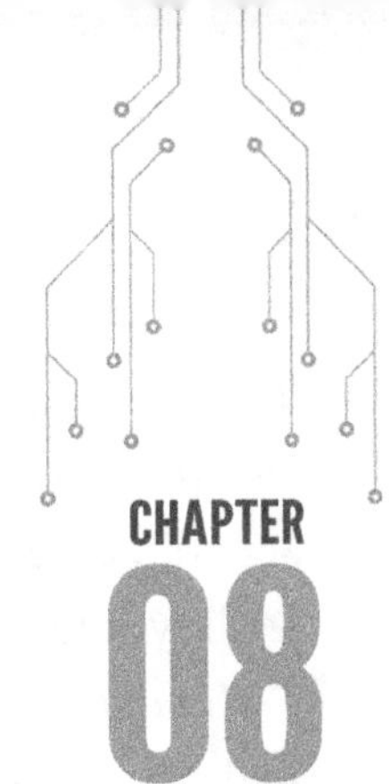

CHAPTER 08

BLAINE WITHERSPOON WALKED behind the pickup parked in the center of the corral. The cattle had dispersed around the perimeter. While the men finished setting up the branding equipment, he discretely wiped his shoe on the front bumper. Trace Malloy saw him from the corner of his eye and smiled to himself. The irons were hot, and the crew was mounting up as Witherspoon returned.

Malloy could feel the other man's nervousness as he stood next to him. The calves were huddled on the far side of the corral, bleating for their mothers, who could only reply helplessly from the other side of the fence. Some of them peered through the slats, their giant eyes bulging from the sides of their heads.

Witherspoon hadn't gotten the best of the show when he arrived. Malloy had had to fill in for Buck MacKenzie today, who'd called in sick for the first time in twelve years. MacKenzie was a master of what Malloy considered the ultimate artistry of ranch work. MacKenzie and his cutting horse, which the man had unimaginatively named Cutter, were a sight to behold weaving and dodging in front of the open gate. The cows, in a mad dash to avoid the lunging horse, slipped into the pen.

Then with a quick jab, MacKenzie and Cutter would spook the calf in the other direction, back into the corral. With the cows separated, the men were ready to move the calves into what Malloy referred to as the "disassembly line."

The roper was a cowhand known mostly as Old Hank. Malloy had heard his last name was Butterworth, but never confirmed it. Hank had worked at the Conquistador for decades. He retired about five years ago but continued to sign on for day work.

Malloy always found Hank delightfully old-fashioned in his approach to cowboying. He didn't worry about the future of the profession, perhaps because he had already retired from it and he had no children to steer away from it. Still, he liked to say that "modern" cowboying had been around for only a hundred and fifty years or so, since Texas independence, and that people had been saying it was in decline for at least half that time.

Hank, like a lot of the older ranch hands, always took his rope with him, even if he didn't plan to use it. Roping was a source of pride, and the men used every spare minute to practice their skill. Malloy had come upon Hank several times eating a sandwich, holding it in one hand while making an idle one-handed toss with the other, snagging fence posts or even a prickly pear.

If Hank hadn't volunteered to work the calves today, he no doubt would be lecturing Witherspoon on the history of roping, the way Malloy had heard him tutor countless other visitors to the ranch.

"You mighta heard of a lasso?" Hank would ask slowly. "Well, lasso comes from the Spanish word *lazo*, which means 'noose.' And lariat? That comes from *la reata*, which means 'the rope.'"

Hank liked to let the slickers in on these terms and let them stew on them for a while, get comfortable with them. After a few hours, the slicker would inevitably compliment Hank on his "lassoing" of a calf. Hank would turn away in disgust and leave it to Malloy or Roland Kerr to explain that "lasso" was never used as a verb.

On this day, Hank moved up slowly on the calves huddled together against the corral fence, and they began to turn their hind quarters, eyeing him warily. He swung the rope in a slow, vertical arc over his head, choosing his target in mid-swing. He slipped the rope under the calf's hind legs as the animal was taking a step forward. The instant both rear hooves were in the loop, he jerked the rope tight and dragged the calf from the group toward the middle of the corral. The entire process took mere seconds, and to the uninitiated it looked as if Hank rode into the herd and plucked a calf the way a little girl might pick a daisy from a field.

Hank backed his horse up, pulling the calf to the corral's center, where the branding crew waited by the small propane stove that held the irons. The calf fought to maintain its balance on its front legs as Hank pulled its bound hind legs backward, making it easier for the "rastlers" to throw the calf to the ground. Another cowboy—Felipe Garza—moved toward the calf, reaching over its back and grabbing two handfuls of skin, one at the foreleg and the other near the flank.

He leaned back, using his weight to bring the disoriented calf over on its side. It hit the ground with a thud and a slight billow of dust. Malloy noticed it was a bull and smirked in spite of himself. The goodwill tour was just about over.

"What you're about to see," he said to Witherspoon without turning his head, "is more efficient than anything you'll see in an auto plant in Detroit. I bet it's even got more precision than you got in that computer chip factory. Time it if you like."

Malloy himself started his mental stopwatch, timing how long it would take Witherspoon to demand to leave.

The branding crew went to work with a dexterity and cooperation that did indeed remind Witherspoon of a manufacturing plant. He had to admit that the speed and efficiency with which the men carried out their duties impressed him.

The cold precision, though, was directed at a living animal and just seeing the calf dragged across the corral was enough to disgust him at the whole operation.

Garza grabbed the calf by its hind leg and pulled it out straight, bracing his boot against the calf's other back leg. The second rastler put his knee on the calf's neck and held its foreleg up. In an instant, the animal was helpless.

Terry Blake and Bobby Ray Cox approached the calf's head, while John Cyrus pulled an iron out of the propane stove and turned toward the hind quarters. Cox brandished a hypo gun in each hand. With his chaps and gauntlet gloves, he reminded Witherspoon of an old TV cowboy stepping out into the street of some dusty ghost town for a shootout. Cox applied one vaccine, then the other, with lighting speed.

As he stepped back, Blake put his boot on the calf's nose to hold its head still, and Witherspoon realized for the first time the cowhand was holding a knife. His gloved thumb extended down the back of the blade, as if he were concealing a weapon. Blake bent down, flicked his wrist, and cut a notch in the calf's ear. Blood welled up and flowed down the calf's head in a widening stream.

Blake stood and turned toward the hind quarters, as Cyrus pulled away the branding iron and waited for the smoke to clear to make sure he'd gotten a clean burn. The calf struggled in vain under the heat of the brand and let out a low moan. Malloy knew Witherspoon didn't appreciate the skill of what he was witnessing. Branding required care. The trick was knowing how much pressure to apply. A hot iron required very little. Push too hard, and the iron would burn right through the hide. Apply too little pressure, though, and the iron was inclined to slip. The "iron man" had to be careful to keep his hand steady to get a clean brand.

The Conquistador brand had been used for more than a century, and the legend was that it was derived from one of the old Mexican brands that had come north with ranching itself. Some guys like Old Hank would even try to say that the brand dated to Cortés, the Spaniard who led the conquest of Mexico in 1519 and planted the seed for the cattle business in what would become the American West. Malloy never believed that story. He thought it was a bunch of public relations hype drummed up by the corporate bosses to maintain the ranch's mystique in case they ever decided to sell.

Either way, the inverted U with two feet had been around for a long time, and everyone from sheriff's deputies to day workers to meat cutters in Chicago knew it. It was supposed to represent the helmet of the Spanish conquistadors, the ranch's namesake, but it always reminded Malloy more of the Greek letter omega.

As Cyrus turned to put the iron back in the propane stove, Blake reached down between the calf's legs and sliced open the scrotum. With his other hand, he scooped out the testicles. The two rastlers let go and the calf jumped to its feet and headed for the far side of the corral. The calf had been on the ground less than thirty seconds.

As the calf rose, Garza, who had been lying almost flat on the ground holding the calf's legs during the cutting, now held on to the tail and let the animal pull him to his feet. It was a dangerous move, especially as the branding crew grew tired. If the cowhand held just a second too long, the calf would kick him with both his hind legs to break free.

Witherspoon, his mouth agape and his face contorted, wasn't watching the calf anymore. He followed Blake as the cowboy walked over and threw the pink, bloody testicles on top of the propane stove. In a few minutes, the stove would be piled high with smoldering organs.

Malloy smiled in spite of himself. Some of the old timers, guys like Hank, still enjoyed the taste of fresh "calf fries." When he was first starting out, Malloy had tried them prepared on top of the branding stove, but it was more because of pressure from the veteran members of the crew than for his own taste. He didn't make it a habit.

That was all Witherspoon needed to push him over the edge.

"Oh my God. That's the most barbaric thing I've ever seen."

Malloy looked at Witherspoon blankly. He quickly dismissed his impulse to suggest a tour of the slaughterhouse. The Conquistador didn't have one, but Witherspoon probably wouldn't know it. Malloy had done enough visitor tours — slicker shows, he liked to call them — that he was pretty well able to telegraph the conversation that followed.

"No anesthetic?" Witherspoon went on. "That's horrible."

Malloy focused on the branding crew, which was now working on a heifer. Instead of castrating it, Blake was using a special tool to dig the roots of the horns from the calf's skull. Before long, calves with bloody legs and bloody foreheads were lining the edges of the corral. They huddled as far away from the branding area as they could and brayed pitifully for their mamas.

"Let me guess," Witherspoon was saying, "anesthetic isn't practical. They're too dumb to feel it. I know the truth — it's too expensive and too much trouble."

"You're probably right," Malloy said slowly. "It isn't practical."

"It's all so unnecessary. And the branding. Jesus Christ, what's the matter with you people?"

"Probably quite a bit, but that don't mean we take the Lord's name in vain. I'd put that up there with insulting my mama."

Witherspoon didn't even acknowledge the comment. "You could use cold branding. That's much more humane. Or even paint. Hell, we use paint to tag bank robbers and criminals, it ought to be good enough for cows."

"Paint?" The sides of Malloy's mouth drew up in a slight chuckle under his mustache. "Paint would last about two weeks out here. You can burn a brand into a calf and it can disappear. The hair can grow over it in the winter, or it can just heal up. Paint wouldn't last one season."

"This is just so cruel."

Yep, Malloy thought, it's always the castration that gets them. "It's necessary. It's one of the most important things to maintain a herd."

"I don't buy that. It's just because that's the way you people have always done it. It's unnecessarily brutal."

Malloy turned to Witherspoon. He felt anger building inside of him, but he spoke calmly.

"You know, mister, if you're going to live out here, you'd best drop this attitude that everything we do is done out of a love for cruelty and suffering. We don't torture these animals. There's a lot of things these guys would rather do than cut balls off a calf for eight hours straight in ninety-five-degree heat, especially for seventy bucks a day.

"And if we could find a better way to do it, we would. Around here, they've tried just about everything, and they're always testing new methods. This is still what works best."

"Sure," Witherspoon shot back, "as long as you don't care about the animals."

"If we didn't care about the animals, we wouldn't spend hundreds of thousands of dollars on vaccines and vet bills. We'd just let 'em run around and fight and screw each other and pretty soon there'd be so many they'd be eating up that fancy sod in your front yard."

"Yeah, the old hunter's argument. If we didn't kill them, they'd overpopulate the earth."

"This isn't about hunting. These are domestic animals, and a lot of what we do comes down to simple economics we don't control. Fact is, most markets pay better for steers than for bulls. There may not be much scientific reason to it, but for some reason people believe steers produce better tasting meat. If you like a good steak, you're as much the reason for all this as any of us."

"I'm a vegetarian."

"No doubt. But it's also for the animals' welfare. Steers are easier to handle. They're downright docile. You can keep them in the same pasture with heifers and not have to worry about them breeding with cows that are too young. Bulls need special handling, and that usually means more grazing land."

"I'm sure on an operation this size, you've rationalized all this," Witherspoon said. He turned for the side of the corral, near the truck that the crew had used to bring the stove and other equipment.

"I'm sure from Silly Cone Valley, it all seems that simple," Malloy called after him.

Malloy had always found the criticism of city slickers as condescending as it was inaccurate. They seemed to think they had all the answers, but they had little understanding of a reality with which they'd had scant first-hand contact. They assumed a ranch was some brutal anachronism that revolved around insensitivity.

The industry had made more than its share of mistakes, and the Conquistador was no different. Witherspoon, though, hadn't seen the biggest problems yet, and he wouldn't understand that the ranch itself paid the highest price for the things it had done wrong.

Malloy had grown to understand the ugly dynamics of this business through a lifetime of living it, and after a childhood of coming to terms with it.

He once read that the biggest problem with raising cattle was that they were alive. They couldn't be crated or stored or shipped easily like steel or computer chips. They had to be fed and maintained daily. Just taking inventory required riding across miles of pasture, rounding up animals, and searching for the ones that got lost or ran away or just plain hid. Even once they were corralled, counting was difficult. He'd seen many roundups where three cowboys came up with three different tallies and they had to keep counting until they could reach a consensus.

The animals did represent latent profit, to the extent it was possible to sell any steer for more than what it cost to raise them anymore. But even the most hardened ranch hand could find himself favoring a cow who had a friendly demeanor even if she had long since passed giving healthy calves.

Malloy remembered his own father, trying to keep their little stock farm afloat, poring over the cattle records, analyzing which cows had to be culled because they'd grown too old for breeding purposes. Malloy always found that the hardest part, the weeding out of the old cows or the young calves that had to be sold simply for reasons as impersonal as drought or disease or the family's need for money.

In his early teens, Malloy had broken his arm when it got twisted under an ornery calf. To pay the medical bills, his father had to sell more of the herd than usual that year, including the cow Malloy had nicknamed Big Bertha. When Malloy came into the pasture, Bertha would seek him out and nuzzle his pockets for sunflower seeds that he sometimes brought to share.

Even now, when he pressed his foot down on a calf's head, a part of him wanted to lean over and say "sorry."

He'd cut his first calf when he was nine. He could still remember staring down at it. His father, leaning over it, was handing him a knife, the blade cupped in the leather glove covering his father's hand.

"C'mon son. We can't hold him forever," his dad said impatiently.

Trace grabbed the knife and moved forward. He felt as if he were sinking deeper into a tar pit with each step. Then, suddenly, he pushed himself to the calf's side, surprised by his own determination. His sympathy for the animal gave way to the desire to make his father proud, to show his dad that he was right to bring him along instead of leaving him back at the house to play. He grabbed the end of the calf's ear and lopped if off.

He stepped back while the other cowboys finished their work. He stood there, looking down at the piece of the severed lobe. It got easier after that. Now, thousands of ears and testicles later, he hardly thought about it. There were days, though, when he was still the little boy, standing alone in the corral, feeling like someone had cut off a part of him as well.

To Witherspoon, it was simple cruelty—a determination to injure or maim. Bringing him here was a waste of time. He couldn't appreciate the efficiency with which the Conquistador's team worked. He wasn't interested in the economic benefits or the needs of the men who worked the herd because they had no choice.

Malloy's family had come to the land around the Conquistador three generations ago, carving a life out of desolation. Everything they were looking at today made Witherspoon's move here possible, but Malloy knew the homie couldn't see that. Witherspoon couldn't make that link because it was clouded by a vision that saw the world beyond his freshly poured streets and antiseptic chip factory only on his own terms. The Big Empty, in its natural state, was chaotic, cruel, and overwhelming. Witherspoon didn't fully recognize the challenge of bringing a modicum of order to it—at least not yet.

Finally, Malloy walked over to Witherspoon, who looked as if he'd been pouting by the truck. "You know, out here, all that," he pointed a gloved thumb over his shoulder, toward the center of the corral, "is a source of pride. You may not agree, but you're going to have a hard time changing folks' opinion. They've been living it for a long time."

"It makes me ashamed to be a human," Witherspoon said slowly, surveying his manure-covered tennis shoes.

Malloy pondered the thought for a moment. "Funny thing," he said finally. "Around here, this life is what makes most people feel that they *are* human."

An hour later, Witherspoon was still standing by the truck, cursing his cell phone because it couldn't grab onto a signal long enough to call for someone—Jenna, Swain, anyone—to come extricate him from the rest of the freak show he was witnessing. This had been a mistake. Malloy wasn't trying to make amends; he was trying to humiliate him again. Last week's phone call had been a set up for this week's joke, and he'd fallen for it, playing the patsy for a cowboy comedian. They'd all have a good laugh about this one around the chuck wagon or the dining hall or wherever it was they ate.

In the corral, calves and cows had been reunited, and the ranch hands were spraying the herd with insecticide before driving the whole group back out to pasture. Malloy came around the front of the truck and stared at Witherspoon without saying anything. Witherspoon found the other man's comfort with silence truly annoying. Sweat lined Witherspoon's brow and dampened the front of his shirt, all just from standing. Without his sunscreen, he could feel his exposed skin, the back of his neck in particular, shriveling and blistering.

Malloy, wearing long sleeves and jeans, didn't seem to notice the heat. Witherspoon guessed it to be well into the nineties.

Cows and calves crowded closer to the truck, wary of the ranch hands and trying to escape the one on horseback who was spraying insecticide from a nozzle like a fireman. The man with the sprayer, Witherspoon thought it was the one Malloy had called Old Hank, held a hose that ran back to the truck, where a generator throbbed, drowning out the wailing of the cows. The livestock were using the truck as a natural shield to escape the spray from Hank's hose. The calves, some bleeding from the sides of their heads, some from their loins, were agitated, their survival instincts heightened.

Witherspoon began to get uncomfortable. A large cow was moving within a few feet, and some of the others were starting to run past him. He could smell the dampness from the insecticide on their coats and feel the heat of their bodies as they pushed by. Witherspoon pressed himself against the pickup, stiffening his back like a board and drawing in his breath. He dropped his cell phone on the ground and emitted a gasp he'd hoped to stifle.

Malloy stepped forward, injecting himself between Witherspoon and the cow. "Yah!" he yelled, flapping his arms upward and making a bold step in the cow's direction. She reversed course and ran back toward the fence.

The two men resumed their silence, and Witherspoon bent down, picked up his phone, and dusted it off. Still no signal.

"They're just about done here," Malloy said. "Why don't we move on."

As if on cue, one of the hands turned off the generator, and they loaded the hose in the back of the truck. Malloy climbed into the driver's seat and motioned for Witherspoon to get in the passenger side. He pulled the truck through the gate, and Cyrus closed it behind them. As they rattled along the road, Malloy looked over at Witherspoon, who was fumbling to connect his seat belt.

"You seem to like noticing our mistakes, how we do things wrong," Malloy said. "Look around, and you'll see the biggest one we ever made."

"What do you mean?"

"These pastures used to be rolling grasslands. Like most ranches, though, it was overgrazed in the late 1800s. Kerr probably told you about the Scots who first put this place together. Well, they knew even less about geology than they did about ranching. The ground under here is all limestone caprock. There's very little topsoil. When the Scots first got here, they saw hundreds of thousands of acres of rich grasses, and they turned the cattle loose on it.

"At one point, they had almost seventy thousand head. It didn't take that many cows long to eat up two million acres of grass. Once the grass was gone, the rains began washing away all the dirt. Soon, no grass would grow. Now, it's mostly prickly pear, thistles and those scrub cedar trees you see. In less than a hundred years, the entire landscape changed completely. There's mesquite, too, like that over there."

He pointed to a dark thorny scrub brush off to Witherspoon's right that came up just shy of the pickup's door handle.

"We cut some of the mesquite and sell it as firewood," Malloy went on. "But it's impossible to remove it completely."

"Isn't it native?" Witherspoon asked. "Can't you just let it be?"

"Mesquite's like a giant weed," Malloy said. "It sucks up water from other plants. Of course, so does most of the other stuff you now see growing here. The ground's so thin that only the most obnoxious vegetation will take hold. As the soil began to disappear, the scrub cedar, or juniper, and the mesquite moved in, hoarded the water, and choked off the native grasses that remained.

"To answer your question, though, no, mesquite isn't native. It came in with the Spanish, with the missionaries who moved deep into this territory from the Gulf. The theory is that they found mesquite beans—which come in these long seed pods, almost like green beans—along the coast when they landed and used them as feed for their horses. They couldn't bring enough regular feed over on the boat to handle such a long journey, and the beans were pretty easy to gather and transport. As they moved into this area in a vain attempt to convert the Indians, the horse droppings spread the seeds all over the plains.

"The Catholics gave up on the Indians and most of the rest of Texas by the early 1700s. Comanches weren't interested in knowing Jesus. There were too many raids, too many friars relieved of their scalps or other body parts. The climate was too inhospitable—blazing hot in the summer, bitter cold in the winter—and the bugs and critters were too nasty, biting and stinging and crawling in boots and beds year-round. The

Catholics abandoned most of their Texas missions, but the mesquite stayed behind."

Despite himself, Witherspoon could imagine the majesty of the scene Malloy was describing. He began to understand the attraction of such a bizarre land. In some ways, the old movies that portrayed a romantic vision of Texas weren't too far off—sweeping, alluring, harsh. Land was everywhere for the taking, but keeping it, living off it, had been almost impossible. For all the romanticism, how had people survived, day to day, out here in a place that even with modern conveniences such as electricity and indoor plumbing could seem barely habitable? Witherspoon couldn't imagine the hardship, but he could appreciate the sense of accomplishment that those who were still here must have felt, just for carrying on for so long.

The truck pulled up to another small corral. This one had horse pens on one side. As they pulled to a stop, Malloy said, "Anyway, we're trying to undo that mistake. I really think if you're interested in the environment, you'll be interested in seeing this."

The horses were already outfitted and waiting for them. The men got out of the truck and Witherspoon retrieved his bike helmet from the seat. Malloy introduced Witherspoon to Sal MacGruder, another old-timer who oversaw what they kept referring to as "the project."

MacGruder zeroed in on Witherspoon's feet. "You're going to ride in those?" he said, pointing to Witherspoon's tennis shoes, the greenish-brown manure still smeared on one side of his left foot.

"Well, they're all I have," Witherspoon said self-consciously.

MacGruder shook his head. "Then don't plan on falling off, or you're gonna get dragged."

"Tennis shoes have a habit of sticking in the stirrups. That would be a problem if you get thrown. You'd go flying off the horse, but your foot would stay stuck there," Malloy explained.

MacGruder helped Witherspoon into the saddle. He may have felt awkward and blistered by the sun, but Witherspoon was in good shape, and his tall frame made it easy to swing his leg over the horse's midsection. He told himself he could have done the maneuver without help. Once he was in the saddle, he popped the helmet on his head, fumbling with the chin strap as he wobbled uncertainly atop the horse. The brown mare clomped the ground with irritation.

"What the hell?" MacGruder muttered, looking from Witherspoon to Malloy and back again.

"For safety," Witherspoon said.

"Uh huh. Ride much?" MacGruder asked.

"Not really."

"For guests, we're pretty careful to give them a tame horse," the old cowhand said. "Company policy."

"Well, I appreciate that. That's probably a good policy," Witherspoon said with a chuckle, trying to diffuse the awkwardness. The old man patted the horses flank.

"This old gal's named Fancy," he said. "She's about fifteen. She won't give you any trouble. She's my granddaughter's horse. My granddaughter's seven." He turned to walk away, then said over his shoulder, "And she doesn't wear a helmet." ✯

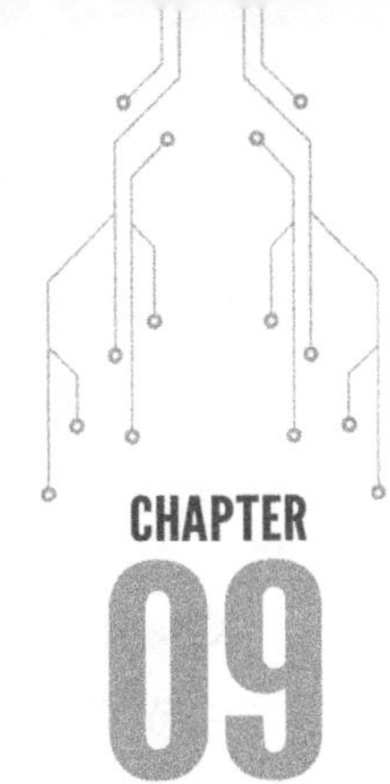

CHAPTER 09

BLAINE WITHERSPOON'S BACK tensed with the rolling motion of his horse's hips. Gradually, he got used to the rhythm of Fancy's lope, but it was an unsettling movement. Sweat built up along the ridge of his helmet where it made contact with his scalp, and the perspiration ran down in beads that coated the inside of his glasses.

The sun was remorseless, and the wind—despite its sudden gusts—wasn't enough to mute the assault of the unbroken rays. He could feel them mercilessly searing his skin, and he shuffled his arms nervously to try to find them some shade. His neck, he knew, was done for. It already hurt where it rubbed the collar of his polo shirt, and by tomorrow morning the pain would be excruciating.

He guessed it must be a little after noon by now. They rode on at a slow walk. Fancy picked her way over the limestone rocks that dotted the dry soil. She seemed oblivious to the brambles that would have lacerated the feet of a man walking through them unprotected. Occasionally, she stopped to nibble at the purple thistle blossoms, and Witherspoon would look around helplessly, unsure what to do.

"Just pull up. Don't let her do that," Malloy said patiently. "She knows better. She's just seeing what she can get away with."

Great, Witherspoon thought, even the horse knew he was an easy mark. At one point, MacGruder's black mare started to trot, and Fancy began to follow. Witherspoon bounced uncontrollably in the saddle, his arms flailing as if grabbing for an invisible handhold in the air. He leaned forward to maintain his balance, and his first instinct was to throw his arms around the horse's neck to keep from falling. His helmet flopped forward, almost covering his eyes.

Suddenly, a gloved hand appeared, grabbing the reins from his hand and pulling them back gently. "Whoa," Malloy muttered. The cowboy had come up alongside Witherspoon, and now was handing the reins back.

"Just like I showed you," he said. "Just pull back, gently. She knows."

Malloy had taken a few minutes before they left the corral to teach Witherspoon the basics of horsemanship, but Witherspoon had found the lesson woefully inadequate. As a practical matter, he found the whole process counterintuitive. It didn't seem natural to pull back with his hands to get the horse to stop, not to a city boy used to slamming brake pedals with his feet. And while he knew to kick the horse to make it go, he still wasn't clear on how hard, or how to regulate the speed once it got going. He wanted something between "stop" and "go," but what he really wanted was to not anger the horse with his confusion. What if the massive creature he was straddling got pissed off? What if it felt the same way about him that Malloy and MacGruder and just about everyone else on this ranch did?

He found the entire idea of riding such a large animal disquieting. It did, after all, have a mind of its own, regardless of how old or docile it was. And no matter how many young children it was used to carrying, it could decide to do something that would wind up inflicting severe and perhaps permanent pain on its unsuspecting rider. Witherspoon felt totally at the horse's mercy.

MacGruder rode up a slight rise and as he got to the top, his horse began to whinny and toss its head. It started to back up, kicking and throwing its head around wildly. MacGruder kicked its side with the stirrups and urged it on, its hooves drumming up dust, as if it were exhaust backfiring from an old car. When it got to the top of the rise, the horse settled down.

Witherspoon felt the sweat making a river down his spine as he and Fancy started up the same hill, plodding along at the only pace at which he felt even mildly comfortable. Please, he thought, let's just go up. Just get me to the top and let me sit here the whole way. He envisioned the horse rearing up, hurling its front legs forward, pawing madly at some unseen danger and casting its hapless rider to the ground. Even with his helmet, he could imagine the impact, the rocks jabbing into his back and limbs as if he were jumping on a bed of nails and broken glass. As he reached the top, he saw the soil was loose, eroded, no doubt by rain that long ago rushed down the barren hillside. He stiffened, expecting Fancy to react as MacGruder's horse had, but she clopped over the loose dirt seemingly without noticing it.

Relieved, Witherspoon gazed around, and he was stunned by the breathless expanse he saw before him. The vastness of the landscape enveloped him, much as it had that first night in Conquistador when he stepped onto his patio. The corral they had left from was nowhere to be seen. Malloy and MacGruder had both stopped and seemed to be discussing the black mare's behavior. Witherspoon turned as best he could in the saddle to take in his surroundings. Nowhere could he find a sign of human habitation.

He suddenly realized he was smack-dab in the middle of a Texas cliché. This was what Hollywood always promised—the open range in all its splendor. He could see the horizon in all directions, a slight line of low hills off to what he imagined was the northwest. Rolling plains tumbled out everywhere he looked, broken only by the occasional juniper or prickly pear. Witherspoon realized he was drawing short, sharp breaths, and he made a conscious effort to breathe deeply and exhale slowly.

Malloy turned his horse, a painted pony, and rode over to Witherspoon. As he spoke, he jerked his head in the direction of MacGruder and the mare.

"We think she might have gotten spooked by a snake," he said casually. "Hard to say. She's a little skittish, but she usually doesn't act like that."

Witherspoon scanned the ground with apprehension, a new worry added to his growing list. Now if Fancy decided to go crazy and throw him, he'd have to contend with getting bit after he hit the ground. He tried to recall the method for treating a snakebite. He dimly remembered seeing something in an old Disney Sunday night movie he'd watched as a child that involved cutting an "X" over the bite and sucking the poison out. He put the thought out of his mind and nodded at Malloy without saying anything.

The cowboy turned the horse around again and the three men rode on, into the blazing curtain of the afternoon sun.

Witherspoon guessed it was almost an hour before they stopped in the shadow of an old windmill that creaked overhead, lethargically pumping water into a metal-sided basin the size of a back-yard swimming pool. The horses lined up and stuck their snouts into the water, gulping it down.

The men dismounted, and Witherspoon popped the strap on his helmet and slid it off his head. His hair was as wet as if he'd dunked it, and it felt as if one of the horses had been licking it for three hours. Malloy studied the windmill, which turned with a weary rhythm, its shaft making a low-pitched moan with each turn.

"We're gonna have to do some work out here by next season," he said, and MacGruder grunted. Witherspoon pulled his glasses off his face and tried to clean them on his shirttail, but the fabric was so damp, it only smeared the sweat around on the lenses.

"Won't be too much farther now," Malloy said, looking directly at him. "I know it's a bit of a ride, but I think you'll be interested to see this little project we got going."

"Okay," was all Witherspoon could manage. His throat was parched, and they hadn't brought any water. He gazed longing at the stock tank, but the water was covered with a layer of algae. The horses continued to drink in loud swallows that echoed deep in their gullets, punctuated by the rhythmic blasts as they exhaled in between. The sunbaked air hung close, enveloping them in its torrid aroma like an electric motor that was overheating. As he spoke, his voice sounded thin and hoarse.

Some of his anger of that morning had faded, evaporated by the heat perhaps. Even so, Witherspoon remained skeptical about the purpose of the visit. After all he'd seen, could Malloy possibly show him anything that would change his feelings? He'd seen men cooking freshly cut testicles and eating them, for crying out loud. It was sheer barbarism. So far, his tour of the ranch had largely reinforced what he already believed—the place was an anachronism, stuck in a past the rest of the world no longer wanted nor needed, except for the nostalgia of it all.

They would remedy this, eventually, he told himself. It might take ten years, or twenty, or even thirty, but eventually the changes that AzTech was bringing to this place would end the cruelty he'd witnessed earlier. He couldn't deny that this expanse was a rarity, unique in its beauty. In time, people would embrace the land for those qualities and enjoy its special allure without profiting from it. He could see this whole area becoming a nature preserve. A few hike-and-bike trails carved through the scrub brush, and just think of the enjoyment for a growing population. Windmills like the one in front of him could fill some quaint lakes, which, with a few picnic tables and shelters, would make a nice little getaway on Sunday afternoons. The thistles and rocks could be cleared away, and lush grasses planted in their place. With proper irrigation, the vegetation would thrive, regardless of Malloy's stories about a lack of topsoil and missionaries' oxen shitting beans all over the land.

Yes, in time, the newly enlightened residents of Conquistador — assuming they chose to keep a name so steeped in the oppressions of the past — would come to think of this place differently. In time, they would bury history and embrace the future, and he, Blaine Witherspoon II, would be the change agent for all of it. It could happen. He knew that cities like Round Rock, right here in Texas, had been transformed by little more than one man's vision into a global hot spot for state-of-the-art personal computers. Where there were once empty fields and small farms, there were now gleaming PC factories, surrounded by shopping malls, huge grocery stores, and massive subdivisions that rose from the cracked prairie with the speed and tenacity of scrub cedar. And it could happen here too — it *would* happen here.

He felt the pain of his blistering skin and told himself it would be worth the suffering he now endured. He licked his cracking lips and cleared his throat. MacGruder had wandered over to the base of the windmill and seemed to inspect the pipe where the water was pumped out.

"There's something I don't understand," Witherspoon said to Malloy, who was sitting on the end of the stock tank.

Malloy turned his head to look at him, his eyes hidden behind his sunglasses. "What's that?"

A breeze kicked up, and though it was as hot as an exhaust fan, it blew across Witherspoon's perspiration with a tingling coolness.

"I know that you were a big supporter of bringing AzTech here," Witherspoon said slowly. "Why? I mean, you don't seem too happy about it now that we're here."

Malloy stared across the openness of the prairie for a full minute before he responded.

"I got a boy, fifteen years old, and more than anything else in the world, he wants to live here and work here. Most boys around these parts, see, they don't think like that. They can't get out fast enough. Colt, he's not that way. He sees it as almost his responsibility to carry on the way I have, and the way my daddy did before me. You got kids?"

"I have a son. He's about the same age as yours."

"I think," Malloy went on, "these days, people don't worry about their kids in the same way." He fell silent.

What the hell is he trying to say? Witherspoon wondered. He grew impatient with the silence, frustrated that Malloy's message was eluding him but not wanting to let the moment slip away.

"All I do is worry," Witherspoon blurted out. "Constantly. Jeez. Out in California, he was always getting into trouble. Too many temptations, I guess, but we're hoping that moving here might be good for him. A chance to start fresh."

Again silence.

"You worry *about* your son. I worry *for* my son," Malloy said flatly. He scrutinized Witherspoon, who had scrunched up his face, partly from confusion and partly to slow the bead of sweat that was sliding down the bridge of his nose. "Oh, sure I worry about him getting into trouble and all that," the cowboy went on. "I don't want anything bad to happen to him, but I also worry, what if he grows up right? Then what? What's his reward? Well, his reward ought to be that he gets to decide what he wants to do with his life. But if he decides to stay here, there is no reward. Me and my daddy, we worked in this business because somewhere along the line, it's supposed to lead to something better. It gets harder each passing year.

"I thought I was preserving something, our way of life." His gloved hands reached into the air, and he made quote marks with his hooked fingers. "It took me a long time to realize ways of life ought to preserve themselves, if they're worth saving.

"So, yeah, I wanted to see AzTech come in. For years, the politicians, guys like Roy, they've been trying to figure ways to keep this place alive. That's hard to do when there's not much in the way of resources. They wanted the state to put in a prison, and then they talked about making a big dump for toxic waste. Prisons and poisons, that seemed to be all this place was good for anymore. AzTech was the best option we'd seen, and I figured, it's probably our only shot."

"And then you turn around and punch it in the nose."

Witherspoon said it before he realized it. His brain, broiled by the heat, failed to check his tongue, and the phrase shot out. He cursed himself. How could he say that? He was, after all, supposed to be making amends. Just when he'd gotten Malloy to start talking about something that seemed to make sense, he'd offended him all over again. He'd taken a cheap shot, a snide retort as unnecessary as it was arrogant. He, Blaine Witherspoon, was the embodiment of this option that would keep Conquistador alive. Blaine Witherspoon, Savior of the Big Empty. He didn't need to give Malloy and the rest of the ranch workers more reasons to find the AzTech transplants condescending. Witherspoon started to apologize. He opened his mouth, but Malloy spoke first.

"My wife would say I've been punching opportunity in the nose all my life," he said, a row of white teeth showing under the bushy edge of his mustache. "I guess wanting change and confronting it are two different things." He paused for a moment, then slapped his leg and stood up. "We better get going, or we won't make it home by suppertime."

Back in their saddles, they followed a narrow path down from the windmill and into a shallow valley. Chunks of limestone dotted the way, and the horses stumbled occasionally. They made their way through the valley, up another rise, and across what seemed to Witherspoon like a plateau, though geologically speaking it probably wasn't. Malloy referred to it as a "cap," a flat table of limestone dotted by tufts of scrub vegetation and rocks. Beyond it, the green-and-brown panorama spread infinitely, as if it were on some unending roll of worn carpet continuously unfurling before them.

The May sun, unforgiving as ever, continued its slow broil of Witherspoon's arms and neck. He again cursed himself for forgetting the sun block, and he realized his burn would be so severe, it would probably make him vomit. He'd hoped he'd make it home before that happened. Each moment he felt the hot rays on his skin intensified his worry. They came to the edge of the cap and paused, staying in the saddle and looking out over the expanse of the Tie Bow. He stared in the direction where he thought the AzTech plant should be, but he couldn't see it. Maybe they were too far away, or maybe he'd lost his sense of direction in this place that appeared the same no matter which way he turned.

Witherspoon could feel the land in his lungs as he scanned the valley beyond. Words like "valley" and "hill" had a muted meaning here, used to describe slight changes in the ever-present flatness of the terrain, but his brain grew accustomed to them out of sheer need for some sort of definition.

He tried to remind himself that this was just one part of the ranch, but its vastness overtook him, and he put the thought out of his mind. His chest grew tight as he drank in the landscape. And yet, this wasn't the suffocating fear he felt that first night on his patio. This was almost a euphoria, both intoxicating and terrifying. They stood amid an ocean of emptiness that was stunningly beautiful not for its features, so much as for its sheer isolation. He felt as if he should whisper, lest he disturb the pristine silence. Had the other two men not been with him, he would have run for the horizon in a desperate hope that there would be something on the other side. Like the chip factory, the town of Conquistador was over there somewhere, too, but it all seemed like it was half a planet away.

Somewhere, far to the west, Silicon Valley bustled, venture capitalists doled out money, and everyone had a business plan, but none of that mattered here. The money, the enthusiasm, the greed, the opportunity that defined the tech world couldn't pierce the Big Empty's protective shroud of nothingness. This thought should have worried him. After all, if the Big Empty was impenetrable, how could he hope to succeed here? And yet, all he felt was a strange calmness. Balky air purifiers seemed little more than a dull memory. His mind wandered, and he found himself *welcoming* the respite. How long had it been since he'd really been able to hear himself in his own head, free of the perpetual worries of his daily life?

Malloy sat silently in the saddle, the afternoon sun shadowing his face and giving his mustache the appearance of drooping even lower. As much as Malloy's comfort with silence unnerved him, Witherspoon found himself afraid to talk, like a Protestant boy attending his first Catholic service. When MacGruder finally spoke, Witherspoon recoiled as if someone had broken a church window with a rock. The solace of the moment dissipated with the sound of his voice.

"I still don't like having to see that," MacGruder said, staring off to his left. Near the horizon—Witherspoon couldn't guess how far because the vastness of the place made assessing distance impossible—was a row of metal towers, their crisscrossing girders making giant Xs that reached toward the sky and sliced into the horizontal dominance of the landscape. The line of towers cut diagonally across the ranch, toward where Witherspoon imagined the town must be.

"Progress, I guess," Witherspoon muttered.

"It's for that factory of yours," MacGruder said. "We got people running all over this place, building towers, stringing lines, tearing up the land. We've had to move part of the herd to a different pasture. It's big a pain in the ass."

Witherspoon didn't say anything.

"Probably not a big deal for you," MacGruder went on. "Out there in Silly Cone Valley they probably got these things all over the place. But I just don't like seeing it going across the ranch. It's not right."

"You know, I feel that way too," Witherspoon said, trying to make light of an increasingly awkward moment.

"Now it's power lines," MacGruder went on, ignoring Witherspoon's comments. "A few years back, it was oil and gas. Oh, we were gonna make lots of money letting them drill wherever they wanted. They came in, made roads all through the West Fork and here, too. They punched holes in the ground. Oh sure, they found a little bit of oil, but it wasn't long before it dried up. Then they came through again to plug everything up. They never did find anything over on this side, just made big mess for nothing.

"Then they were gonna start letting hunters come in. Recreation, that was gonna be the big thing. They were gonna build a big resort over by the main house. Never happened. Too far for most folks to come, they said. We'd need an airstrip. They actually thought about that for a while, as if we hadn't already tore up the place enough. No, I don't figure this factory of yours is gonna amount to much. I figure in a few years, these towers'll all be rusted and falling down and folks around here will be working on the next thing that's gonna save us."

MacGruder's words seemed to float on the emptiness that surrounded the three men. Witherspoon didn't know how to respond. He noticed a wry smile creep across Malloy's face, but the cowboy didn't say anything. Is that what people thought? That AzTech was just some flash in the pan? Didn't they realize that a chip factory meant so much more than a scheme to make the ranch profitable? He remembered what the doctor had said—that the ranch and the town were still in many ways one in the same. MacGruder still thought of the town's prosperity in terms of the ranch. Witherspoon would show him that that cycle was about to be broken. AzTech was a new dynamic, a new economic base for the whole region.

As they rode closer to the towers, Witherspoon could see that most of the construction work was done. Giant spools of cable were on the ground, and on some of the metal arms that stretched outward he could see strands of cable hanging limply from pulleys. Good, he thought. He didn't know exactly what was required for activating a new high-tension line, but he assumed from what he saw the extra juice AzTech needed would be ready by the time the production tests were completed.

He stared at the towers as the group rode past, until he noticed the horses were heading down another small hill. Fancy stumbled on the loose rocks that pocked the trail, and Witherspoon found himself thinking that the landscape could seem almost lunar, even with the scrubby brush. He was becoming increasingly aware of a growing pain in his lower back and the inside of his thighs, and he wondered how much farther they would go. The thought of the ride back only made him more uncomfortable.

They came to a line of barbed wire, broken in front of them by an aluminum gate. MacGruder dismounted and walked forward to open it. Witherspoon could already see the terrain on the other side of the fence was different. The vegetation was thicker and greener, and the rock-dotted landscape gave way to lush fields of swaying grasses.

They rode through the gate, and Witherspoon could sense a new mood overtaking Fancy. It seemed to rise up from her haunches, climbing into his own legs and then spreading upward through his body. A strange sense of ease overtook him. They moved forward, man and horse, and Fancy began to trot. He let her go, suddenly unafraid, unconcerned, unencumbered by his earlier fears. He wanted to toss off his helmet and gallop unrestrained through wisps of green that waved across the ground, caressed by the winds.

The horse moved faster, the long grass swatting gently at her fetlocks. Malloy's horse and MacGruder's mare began to pick up their pace, too, each responding to the other's giddiness. Witherspoon bounced wildly in the saddle, which made him feel like a bowl of Jell-O. The violent shaking restored his caution and he reined in Fancy to slow her down. The other two rode on, and he could feel Fancy's frustration as he pulled tight on the leather in his hands. In a few minutes, he had her back to a walk.

Malloy turned around and rode back toward him. "They love this, you can tell," he said, patting his horse on the neck, just below the mane. "It's almost like they know this is the way the land's supposed to be."

"It's beautiful," Witherspoon said, surveying the undulating ocean of green. It wasn't bright or vibrant in color like a spring field, but a darker, almost grayish green. Yet its stark contrast to the land they'd left on the other side of the fence made it all the more breathtaking.

"It's buffalo grass," Malloy said. "It used to grow all over the high plains of these parts. But the old ranchers who moved into the area a hundred and fifty years ago, they let too many cows loose on it. The animals ate it all up, and like I said earlier, the soil washed away. We've been trying to reintroduce the stuff. It isn't easy, but it works pretty well in smaller areas like this. The trick is to rotate the herd so they graze in different paddocks, that way you keep enough grass to prevent erosion. It's still experimental, but we've been pretty pleased so far. Someday, if this works out, whole chunks of the ranch might look like this. We call it cellular grazing because of the different paddocks, or cells, that we rotate the herd through."

As they talked, Fancy munched loudly on the buffalo grass, as if proving Malloy's point that it tasted better than the thistles and prickly pear blossoms she'd nibbled on the ride out. Witherspoon let her eat until the other two men turned and began to gallop across the field. Fancy, noticing the motion, looked up from her feeding, and Witherspoon could almost sense her eagerness.

He followed after them at a trot. As they rode on, it seemed to Witherspoon as if the soundtrack of the ride had been suddenly unplugged. They were surrounded by a strange silence, the hoof beats of their horses muffled by the soft grass. Even their voices felt stifled by the thickness of the ground cover, and the horses seemed to float effortlessly, marked only by the swishing of the vegetation against their hooves.

"I guess the cows like it better, huh?" Witherspoon asked, speaking in a hushed tone, as if he were talking in a theater during a show.

"Oh, yeah. You may have noticed those big blue drums sitting around the fields as we rode out here. Those are nutritional supplements. The cows come up and lick them. That big wheel turns around and it's got this goo stuck on it that's full of vitamins and nutrients to make up for the lack of good grasses. Plus, we drop feed. Even with the buffalo grass, we'll probably still have to do some of that, but there's no doubt this is better for them nutritionally than what's out there now."

"You keep this up, they're going start calling you an environmentalist," Witherspoon said.

Malloy smiled and his white teeth shone under the bristle of his mustache. "You know," he said, "you'll find this funny, but I always thought I was. I mean, I depend on the land and the environment to make a living, so how could I not be?"

"Well," Witherspoon said slowly, wondering if he should go into it, "you *exploit* the land. So you care about it only as a way to make a living."

Malloy sat stone faced for a moment, and Witherspoon wondered what he was thinking behind the dark sunglasses that hid his eyes. "I reckon," he said finally. "But I'm out here planting and growing grass, and you're the one digging up the ground and putting in a big old concrete building. Maybe environmentalism is in the eye of the beholder."

Witherspoon found himself laughing and wished he wasn't. ✯

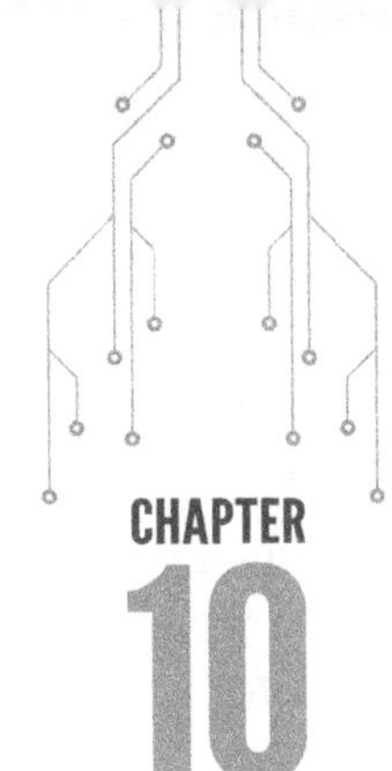

CHAPTER 10

BLAINE WITHERSPOON could barely extend his arm to shake Trace Malloy's hand. The skin on his upper limbs was as red as a strand of Christmas lights and had stiffened and blistered so that it hurt to move them from his side. He now understood why all the cowboys had worn long-sleeved shirts. His legs, traumatized by the interminable ride earlier that day, had adopted an awkward gait, and he worried that the ranch crew would think he was making fun of them.

Witherspoon introduced Jenna and Brandon to Malloy, who pointed at the small cooler Witherspoon was carrying.

"You didn't have to bring anything," Malloy said without a hint of a grin. "We got more food than any of us could possibly eat. C'mon, I'll introduce you to everyone."

Jenna smiled but didn't say anything. She had intended to bring a bottle of gin or at least a few bottles of wine, but at Blaine's suggestion, they left the liquor behind. He just had a feeling it would be somehow inappropriate.

The Witherspoons followed the cowboy around the side of the ranch house. As they walked, Blaine noticed Malloy was wearing canvas hiking boots instead of the traditional cowboy boots he'd worn during their ride. Brandon shuffled along behind the group, the baggy legs of his black parachute pants rustling with every move.

The walk to the back of the house was an agonizing marathon of stilted, awkward steps. Witherspoon had wanted to collapse in his recliner, a scotch in one hand and the TV remote in the other, and channel surf himself into oblivion. But Malloy and Kerr had insisted that he come to supper—as they insisted on referring to the evening meal—and bring his family. They had made big plans, they already had the grill fired up, everyone from the ranch would be there, and it would be a chance for him to "visit" with the cowboys he hadn't gotten to talk to earlier that day. Witherspoon couldn't deny that Malloy had made a sincere effort to patch things up, and although it didn't make up for getting punched in the nose, he appreciated the attempt. Besides, these people seemed to take hospitality seriously, and it made sense for him to be on good terms with the townsfolk. So, he'd forced himself to oblige.

He'd gone home and showered. The water stabbed his burned and tired body like needles shot from a nail gun. He winced with each pass of the bar of soap. Jenna, of course, had resisted the idea, but he'd persuaded her. This was important, he told her. He had to reach out to these people if the plant was going work. "The only way out was through" had become his new motto with her. If she ever wanted to get out of here, she needed to invest in his success—another catch phrase he found himself using frequently. She'd agreed, but her displeasure was branded on her face as surely as the searing of flesh he'd witnessed earlier in the corral. Brandon, of course, recoiled at the very suggestion and had to be threatened with the removal and possible sale of his PlayStation. Witherspoon, his skin throbbing with heat, his head feeling as if it had split open in pain, just didn't have the patience for any nurturing parental skills.

They made a strange trio as they walked toward the gathering of ranch hands behind the main house—Blaine, stiff and sore, hobbling like a beaten dog; Jenna, her every movement pensive and full of hesitation; and Brandon, lagging behind, his disgust and teen apathy exuded in every step.

Four long tables were set under the sprawling awning of an ironwood tree, and Witherspoon estimated there must be almost fifty people, counting kids and wives. Malloy made a few introductions, and Witherspoon recognized some of the ranch hands from the corral that morning: Terry Blake, Bobby Ray Cox, John Cyrus, Felipe Garza and the octogenarian known as Old Hank. He saw MacGruder, who nodded at him with a smirk as he shook his hand.

Witherspoon noticed that the men had gathered around the huge barbecue grills where dozens upon dozens of steaks sizzled, an orchestral hissing that actually drowned out some of the conversation. The women, meanwhile, were fussing over the tables. Young children ran among them, and older kids stood at the far edge of the gathering, pointing toward a stand of white buildings about four hundred yards away. Witherspoon could see the tail of a skunk sticking up from amid the high grass, and he shifted uncomfortably from one foot to the other.

Brandon shuffled in their direction, dragging his feet and staring at the ground, his hands in his pockets. He stopped short of the group, hanging around the periphery, listening to the conversation and waiting to be invited in. The other kids kept talking and looking at the skunk, unaware or unwilling to acknowledge the human interloper.

Meanwhile, Jenna stood next to her husband, transmitting her agitation. Witherspoon knew she didn't want to hang out with the "women folk" setting the tables, yet she clearly didn't want to be with the men, either. Their very appearance repulsed her. They seemed scuffed and dirty and boisterous, drenched in the machismo she found so off-putting. This was definitely not like the cocktail parties back home.

Witherspoon found himself standing alone with his wife, as Malloy and MacGruder headed for the grills. He didn't really want to follow them, but all the other men were watching the smoke rise from the huge metal boxes. He and Jenna stood their ground, unsure which way to turn. He thought of his recliner and the cold scotch he could be nursing. Jenna sighed, a bitter, cutting release that made the hair on the back of his neck stand up.

"Let's um…find a place to set this," he said, patting the cooler with his right hand and strolling toward the base of a massive tree. Anything to be doing something, he thought, rather than standing like a chess club president at the senior prom. Jenna followed a few steps behind, and he could feel her glare boring into his back.

A short, ample woman came toward them, her smile blaring like a loudspeaker at a county fair. She carried a tray with a pitcher of iced tea and some glasses. "Welcome, welcome," she said. "I'm Darla Malloy."

The pitcher was sweating. The condensation trickled down the outside of the base and made a small pool on the tray. Darla set the tray down on a nearby table as the Witherspoons made introductions. Darla meted out the glasses of tea. "Well, this is quite a gathering. Thanks for inviting us," Witherspoon said. The glass in his hand, even though it held only tea, was comforting, a sign that he somehow belonged no matter how awkward he felt. It was his membership card, his official welcome.

"We like to do things when we have special guests," Darla said. "It's not often we all get together like this—at least not anymore." As she spoke, she knotted the fingers of her hands around one another and Witherspoon wondered if she was nervous at confronting the man her husband had pummeled. She couldn't have been more than five foot four, and the only adjective that came to mind was "hefty." Witherspoon wondered how many years of chicken fried steak and cream gravy, of potatoes cooked in butter, of pecan pie, of all the heart-clogging cuisine of this place it had taken to balloon this woman. Had she looked like this when she and Malloy met? Had the dirty blond hair that reached to her shoulders been lighter then? Had it been longer? For all he knew, she may have been the local beauty, the leader of the cheer squad or the homecoming queen.

The sunburn on his neck made his collar feel as if barbed wire were being dragged across his back. The sun was fading but the heat lingered, making his shirt cling and reminding him with every flinch of the exquisite pain that had only just begun. His insides felt tense, as if he were strung by a cord. A pulsating drone reverberated through his skull and rattled the base of his teeth. Into his private concert of agony came Darla Malloy's uninvited cheerfulness. It welled up and pressed into him like the unflinching sun that had chased and cooked him throughout the day, the sun that even now in its retreat still found him. The more she smiled, the more her nervous laugh wafted over him, the more she repulsed him. She was, after all, a fat and uneducated woman, a simpleton in a sea of simpletons.

He immediately hated himself for the thought, and then at the same time, reprimanded himself for being ashamed. It was the truth. Underneath all this claptrap about building bridges, about being good corporate citizens, there was a stark truth:

He was courting dolts. He needed them. He needed their cheap labor. He needed them to make good on the tax abatements and new roads and electricity and water supplies and all the other promises they had made. But that didn't mean fooling himself into seeing these people as something grander than they were. He had tried to admire what they had accomplished, how they had carved out a life, how they had extruded their very survival from amid the harshness and remoteness of the land. Was that spectacular or stupid? They had, in a way, chosen this life of isolation. If they wanted to find some high moral justification for it, that was their choice, not his.

Darla was talking about the heat, about how the hot winds that felt like they emanated from a convection oven were normal this time of year. "The evenings still cool off, though," she said, the smile apparently tattooed to her face. "A nice glass of tea and a shade tree still does wonders."

"Tea," Witherspoon had come to understand, didn't mean Earl Grey or green or Ginseng, it meant just tea, brown and chilled, with a slice of lemon. It didn't mean sweetened unless you put the sugar in yourself. And these people made it and drank it by the gallons per day. In restaurants, not ordering tea drew a glare as if you might be a crazed killer, a leper, or worse, a Yankee. Refusing a glass of tea offered from a friend was an insult on par with spitting in their face, kicking their dog, or calling their mother ugly.

The smile stayed on Darla's face as the conversation sagged, and Witherspoon assumed her expression had now hardened that way, the perky little dimples on either side of her mouth permanent craters. He wondered: Did she smile like that in her sleep?

Witherspoon looked past her for a moment, to one of the tables where several women were setting out glasses and plates and utensils. A wave of brown curls caught his eye, and he found himself almost giddy with recognition.

"Hey," he said to no one in particular. "It's the doctor."

He grabbed Jenna's hand and excused himself from Darla Malloy and her incandescent perkiness. He rounded the table and came up behind Doctor Lambeau. As he said her name, she turned, and he was awash in the soothing blue eyes that had stared out at him through the pain of his broken nose.

"Why, Mr. Witherspoon, I didn't expect to see you here," she said with a broad grin that seemed as genuine as Darla Malloy's had seemed forced.

Witherspoon turned and introduced Jenna, who shook the doctor's hand as she said "I'm Diana Lambeau, nice to meet you. Your husband and I met a few weeks ago, when his mood was a little worse."

Jenna managed a wry smile and nodded at her husband. "I appreciate you taking care of him. I still don't understand how something like that could happen."

Lambeau ignored her comment and reached for Witherspoon's face. "It's looking a lot better," she said, touching his nose gently with the tips of her olive fingers. Her hands were cool from the tea glasses she'd been setting on the table. "The swelling's just about gone."

"Yeah, at least until the sunburn kicks in," Witherspoon replied uncomfortably.

"Oh yeah, today was the big tour. How was it?"

"Excruciating," he said, managing a smile. "I was sweating from places I never knew could sweat."

She laughed, and the whiteness of her teeth seemed to gleam at him. The sun had moved lower and the heat, finally, was starting to break with the advent of the evening. Her smile started to fade into an awkward pause, and they both looked toward their feet. He glanced at Jenna, who was biting her bottom lip the way she did when she was annoyed.

Desperate to escape Darla Malloy, he'd plunged into more treacherous terrain. His eyes darted over the social landscape, seeking an exit. He settled his gaze on Trace Malloy and the horseman, MacGruder, immersed in the smoke that rolled forth from the belly of the massive grill and spiraled upward as the evening breeze caught it.

"I, uh, need to go see about our dinner," Witherspoon said suddenly.

"I'm sure they've got it taken care of," Lambeau said.

Jenna finally broke her silence. "We don't eat meat," she said. "I don't imagine that's zucchini they've got cooking over there."

"Uh, no, probably not," Lambeau said.

"You look awfully trim, doctor, are you a vegetarian?" Jenna said. Witherspoon was already moving away from them, but he caught the barb in his wife's voice. He pretended he didn't hear and kept walking. He felt sorry for the doctor at first, then decided that any woman who made her living giving hernia and prostate exams to weather-hardened cowboys could probably take care of herself. The doctor's response to his wife's question trailed after him.

"Me? No, I was raised in the bayous of Louisiana. I grew up eating just about anything that moved. Stuffed meats, fried turkeys, mudbugs, you name it."

Lambeau began recounting the story of her journey from Lafayette to med school in Boston to the dust-blown wastes of the Big Empty. Witherspoon's exit was too late, though. The damage was done. He started formulating the interrogation he could expect from Jenna about Dr. Lambeau. She'd be mad at him for leaving her to talk to the doctor alone, too. Even at cocktail parties, Jenna liked him by her side to work as a sort of social anchor especially when she was uncertain of the crowd.

Jenna, though, was being unreasonable. Sure, he liked the doctor, and, okay, maybe there was even an attraction, but it was all innocent enough. He was a patient, after all. She was a professional. And so was he for that matter, and he was far too busy for any peccadillos. He tried to remember the last time he and Jenna had had sex and decided it may have been more than a month, maybe two. He seemed to recall it had been a Saturday night. They'd watched a movie, had a few drinks and gone to bed. Practically every night since then he'd fallen asleep in his recliner by nine-thirty, exhausted by the never-ending demands at the plant.

Witherspoon slipped open the cooler that he'd left on the ground, pulled out three frozen veggie burgers and walked on toward the grills.

"Could you just drop these on the grill whenever there's an open spot?" he asked Malloy when he got there.

The cowboy took one of the hockey-puck-sized burgers and turned it over in his hand. "You eat this?" he asked. "Is it food?"

"Yeah," Witherspoon said, an impertinent tone creeping into this voice. His patience had worn to an onion skin. The heat and the sunburn were making him irritable, and he bristled at having to defend his eating habits to these rampaging carnivores. It was like explaining to cannibals that eating human flesh was an aberration. "I told you, we don't eat meat."

"So, what is it?" Malloy said slowly.

"Vegetables, mostly. And soy meal, I guess. They press it into the shape of a burger." Just throw the damn thing on the grill, Witherspoon thought. Just drop it in there among the huge swollen hunks of carcass, dripping and oozing blood. I'm doing you a favor by eating anything that comes off the grate of that grill. How many countless corpses have stained its surface with their vile juices? I don't want to taste the residue of blood, vaporized on the coals and wafting up to infiltrate the purity of my meal. But I'll try to choke it down if you just cook my damn food without interrogation, he thought.

MacGruder was now peering over Malloy's shoulder at the pale-white medallion. "Why?" he asked, confounded. The corner of MacGruder's lip was turned up, as if the burger were made of ground worms.

"Well, it's just a way of having something different. I mean, as a vegetarian—it's just a different way of making a meal."

"But I thought you *liked* vegetables," MacGruder's expression grew more confused with each word. "I thought that's all you wanted to eat. Why wouldn't you just eat them?" He pointed at the burger. "Why would you have that done to them?"

Witherspoon chuckled in spite of himself. "Look, it's not Soylent Green or anything," he said, sure that the reference was lost on them, and surprised when Malloy chuckled. "It's just chopped up vegetables. You know, you eat meat, but you don't always eat steak this way. Maybe you have meat loaf, or you chicken-fry it, or make hash or even eat chicken. The point is, you eat meat in different forms for variety."

"Yeah," Malloy said slowly, "but we don't press it into a shape that looks like a vegetable." He tossed the burgers on the grill and they landed with a clank. "I've never cooked anything like that, but I'll give it a shot," he said. MacGruder walked off, shaking his head.

A few minutes later, they sat down to eat at the long tables, segregated by gender. Darla guided Jenna to a seat near her, at a table made up entirely of women and small children. The men sat at the next table over, and Brandon sat next to his father without speaking. He pulled out his chair and sat down, then stood up again when he realized everyone was still standing.

Roland Kerr, at the head of Witherspoon's table, took off his white straw hat and bowed his head. Everyone else did the same. Witherspoon and his son glanced uncomfortably at the ground as Kerr spoke:

"Dear Lord, we thank you for this food and for the chance to gather together with friends, both old and new. We thank you for bringing our guests to us, and for the opportunity they bring with them. We thank you for all the blessings you have bestowed on us, and we hope that you will guide us in making the right decisions as we embrace the change that we know is coming. We ask this in the name of your son Jesus. Amen."

Witherspoon cleared his throat awkwardly and sat down. Malloy made sure the veggie burgers were distributed to their proper owners. Without buns, they were undisguised, their culinary deviance blatant and unhidden, an alien comestible, stark and alone on the emptiness of the plate. While Witherspoon stared self-consciously at the naked concretion of vegetable meal, Malloy passed a plate of thick T-bones and ribeyes around for everyone else.

Malloy was seated directly across from Witherspoon, and he watched as the homie cut into his food. He'd pulled the veggie burgers off the grill as soon as they'd started turning brown on the outside, but he could see by the way Witherspoon tugged at his fork as he tried to cut it that the burger was still frozen in the middle.

"Sorry," Malloy said, looking across the table at his guest. "I never even cooked a steak frozen."

"It's okay," Witherspoon said, picking at the thawed edges of the burger. He tried to eat slowly, expecting an awkward conversation dominated with talk of cows and ranching and beef prices and other topics that would remind him of his alienation. Instead, the talk quickly turned to broader topics—television, and then movies.

"They're lining up in Lubbock for that new 'Star Wars' movie—'Phantom' something or other—I don't get it," Kerr said. "I wouldn't camp on a city street for Super Bowl tickets. Why would you do that for a movie?"

"Yeah, if they wait a few days, there won't be a line at all. Why do they have to see it the minute it comes out?" MacGruder chimed in.

"Well, I'm not much of a sci-fi fan," John Cyrus said, drawing out the term "sci-fi" as if he were stretching a piece of gum from his mouth. "I mean, them movies are okay, but it's just a movie."

Malloy shook his head. "I can't get too excited about it. I mean, we know how this all turns out—we know Anakin Skywalker becomes Darth Vader, why do we have to wait ten years and sit through three more movies? No, I enjoyed the first three—well, at least the first two—but I think they should have stopped there. It all just seems like a big money grab."

Suddenly, Witherspoon felt like he was running alongside a moving train, wanting to jump on but unsure where or how. He'd had this discussion with friends back in California, almost word for word, but now he seemed unable to speak up.

"I heard the first movie is terrible," he blurted out finally, killing the conversation with the suddenness and tone of his words. "I mean," he stammered, "I mean, the fourth movie, the new movie, but you know, it's supposed to be the first. The first in the series. But I heard from friends back home that it's the worst one." Witherspoon cringed to himself. Great, come work for me, he thought, I can't even make coherent conversation.

"You're right," Malloy said finally. "I read some reviews that weren't good. And I don't reckon this next one will be much better. You know, it's like any other. The first one is good, the second might be better, but after that, it's all downhill. You gotta know when to stop."

After they'd eaten the steaks, and the sides of potatoes grilled in butter, the biscuits, the green beans boiled with ham, and the dessert of peach cobbler with ice cream, the men stood and began to mingle. Witherspoon had eaten little—a few small helpings of potatoes and a plain biscuit to augment his semi-frozen veggie burger. He'd made excuses about not being hungry, about how the heat had sapped his appetite. In truth, he was famished.

Brandon had spent the entire meal staring at his plate and muttering to himself. No one had even tried to speak to him, which probably suited him fine. As they rose after the meal, he noticed the other boys were walking away from the group, and tired of being ignored by the adults, he shuffled after them. He hung back, drifting in the periphery of the other boys as if orbiting around their indifference.

A few of the ranch hands lit cigarettes and stood under the late shade of a huge bois d'arc tree, far removed from the tables. Witherspoon noticed Malloy didn't go with them. The women rose, too, and began clearing the dishes from all the tables.

Witherspoon tried to avoid making eye contact with Jenna. He tried to remember the last time she had cooked or cleaned up after a meal. He did most of the work in the kitchen, often spending a good part of Sunday afternoon preparing meals for the week, then carefully labeling each one in Tupperware and storing it away in chronological order. He washed up, too. He liked his cookware to be put in the designated places, not thrown willy-nilly out of sight in some forgotten cabinet. He wanted to be able to reach for his utensils instinctively, without searching, not fumbling through drawers while the *unagi donburi*—his signature vegetarian "eel" dish that he'd adapted from a traditional Japanese menu—browned its way to disaster, unturned in the skillet.

Malloy and Roland Kerr stood near Witherspoon, and they all watched the women clearing tables. A few younger children began to run and giggle, turning the adults into mere obstacles for dodging and hiding behind. Malloy observed the children in silence, and Kerr looked down the slight hill toward the white outbuildings that had the specter of vacancy about them.

The light was fading, the orb of the sun ballooning into the magnificent orange globe that Witherspoon had found intoxicating in his first days in Conquistador. Now, even with the strength of its rays diminished, he could feel the staccato jabs of their heat on his sunburned face. He turned eastward, the stinging on the back of his neck preferable to the fading sun's frontal assault. The throb in his head continued, unabated. Sun poisoning. He cursed himself again for forgetting the sunblock. He knew by morning—if not later tonight—his overexposure would be causing him to vomit and run a fever.

Malloy spoke suddenly, interrupting Witherspoon's mental flagellation.

"Services start at nine on Sunday morning," the cowboy blurted out. Kerr looked from one man to the other without saying anything.

"Services for what?" Witherspoon said, immediately realizing his gaffe.

Malloy stopped and stared at him for a moment. "The church," he said pointedly, "is on Fifth, just off Main. You're welcome, of course."

"I'm not much of a church-goer."

Malloy turned away briefly, his eye catching one of the children darting under the table. He snapped his gaze back to Witherspoon, and his voice had an edge to it. "Guess out there in Silly Cone Valley you've got so much stuff around you, you've forgotten how you got there. Probably can't hear the call for all the noise."

"Well, my beliefs are really my own business," Witherspoon replied, feeling both annoyed and defensive. It was a line his mother had taught him in grade school to deflect the bullies. He'd grown up in rural Jersey, in a town that was small and Protestant. Bead-squeezer. Cracker eater. Statute worshipper. Mackerel snapper. He'd gone to Catholic elementary school, which, as far as other kids on his street were concerned, made him a stranger in his own neighborhood.

"One good West Texas hailstorm will change your mind," Malloy was saying.

"Strike the fear of God into me, eh?"

"Damn sure make you realize there're things a lot more powerful than you. When the wind rips the roof off your pretty new house, you'll be looking for something. You can't live out here and not believe in a higher power. It's by the Lord's grace you survive, and by His will you don't."

For a minute, Witherspoon felt like he was back at St. Theresa's. He could feel the cut of his collar, the clip-on tie getting in the way of his hand as he tried to write. Malloy was out of his league. No hailstorm could overcome the bitterness he still felt, the needless guilt, the unnecessary psychological trauma.

"So, the weather's bad?" he said, trying to steer the subject onto more comfortable ground. "Worse than we've seen with those bitter cold winds last winter, then all those pounding rainstorms and now this heat?" He'd gotten a good feel for the extremes. The winter had been short compared with what he remembered growing up in New Jersey. In Texas, it didn't start until mid-December really, and by February it had begun to warm up, but the ensuing months were marked by harsh winds from the north that blew unchecked across the vast plains. The fronts lumbered down from Canada with a tall-tale quality that no one would believe unless they experienced it. You could actually see bad weather coming, sometimes for hours before it arrived. With the horizon laid bare, the storms were like gray walls pushing ever closer, until finally the rain plunged down in torrents, battering the ground. And in January, the storms weren't blowing rain, but ice. Not snow, for the most part, but ice that coated the ground with a thick glaze that seemed to freeze everything. Traffic disappeared. Stores and schools closed. No one ventured out. A day or two later it thawed, and everything came back to life, as if the entire Big Empty were a video that had been paused and then restarted. Of course, the storms they'd gotten that year didn't amount to much. The drought had persisted, unabated. By May, they were five inches behind on average rainfall.

"We had it pretty easy this year," Kerr was saying, and Witherspoon welcomed the ranch manager's effort to lighten Malloy's tone. "It can get a lot worse—dust storms, hailstorms, electrical storms, tornadoes, floods that come up without warning, even blizzards sometimes. One way or another, most of our weather is related to the wind. It will blow like crazy sometimes—not a tornado or anything, just strong straight-line winds. The land's so flat, there's nothing to stop it."

Witherspoon nodded and didn't say anything. He hadn't really wanted to talk about the weather, and certainly not about religion. As brutal as the day had been, and as much as his skin ached, and as appalling as the corral display had been, he had intended to carry on the efforts to make peace with Malloy. Now, things were turning against him.

He didn't want to offend Malloy again, and yet, who was the one pushing views on whom? He could imagine Malloy, hatless, his hair slicked down, wearing some sort of outdated suit sitting next to his wife, a floral print draped over her squat frame and her neck lined with fake pearls, clutching a worn leather Bible, and singing "Amazing Grace" *a cappella* from a rigid wooden pew. Witherspoon hadn't been inside a church since high school, and even now the thought of returning made him bristle more than if he'd pulled a wool sweater over his sunburn. No, as he'd told his mother when he graduated, part of being an adult—an adult *in America* were his exact words—was that he got to choose his religion, and if that meant not choosing, that too was his choice. At the time, standing in the foyer of his parents' house, his diploma still sitting on the coffee table from the day before, he realized he was paraphrasing a song by Rush, but the plagiarism was lost on his folks. Ultimately, they'd left him there rather than be late for the service, and with the precedent established, he'd spent the rest his summer Sundays sleeping late before heading off to his freshman year at Purdue and blending into the agnosticism of college life.

"Well, anyway, you're welcome to come if you want," Malloy said, still studying the table under which a blond-haired girl of about seven had disappeared.

"Thanks," Witherspoon said. "By the way, I appreciate you taking the day to show me around. It was definitely... interesting."

Malloy nodded, turning back to the conversation.

"We're still doing production tests," Witherspoon went on, talking cautiously as if each word were drawing him closer to something he might regret. "I mean, the plant is running, but we won't be in full production for a while yet. Still, it's, you know, a good idea of how things work. If you'd like to come out some time and see it, I mean."

He looked up at Malloy, who shot a glance at Kerr. The ranch manager stared at Malloy, his face emotionless, but his eyes fixed on the cowboy as if giving a command. Malloy turned back to Witherspoon and cleared his throat. "Well, sure, I reckon that might be pretty interesting." ✯

CHAPTER 11

TRACE MALLOY wasn't in a good mood. His feet ached, and they'd been hurting more than usual for the past week or so. He had things to do. The windmill they'd seen on the ride with Witherspoon needed to be repaired, two day workers had called in sick, and some of the buffalo grass in the far paddock was dying and nobody knew why. The plant sciences guys were on their way from Lubbock and he should be out there waiting for them. He scowled under the brim of his gimme cap and tapped his fingers on the vinyl arm of the chair. And then, of course, there was his mother. Her condition was getting worse. She couldn't feed herself and most days couldn't even remember her own name. He'd hadn't been to see her in months. He'd intended to go the weekend after he'd punched Witherspoon, but he got busy fixing things around the house, mundane tasks that had suddenly become terribly important.

Witherspoon, too, wasn't helping things. Malloy shook his head at the thought. He had to admit, he liked the guy more than he imagined he would, but he still couldn't say he truly regretted breaking the man's nose. He'd deserved it. He needed to be reminded that you don't just move into town like an occupying army and have everything changed to suit you.

How long was Witherspoon going to keep him waiting anyway? It had been at least twenty minutes already. Maybe it wasn't rude to ignore people in California, but damned if he didn't have things to do. He stood up, and the chair crackled as the vinyl upholstery began to rise with the absence of his weight.

The whole place smelled funny. It was antiseptic. Clean, in a stifling sort of way, not like his mother's nursing home, which stank of disinfectant, medicine, urine, and the decay of life. This place was blaringly new and so spotless he was afraid to touch anything. Even the front door handle gave him pause. As he'd walked in, he'd checked behind him to make sure he wasn't leaving muddy footprints or scuff marks on the shiny white floor.

In fact, most everything in the lobby was white: the walls, the ceiling, the front of the receptionist's desk. Only her desktop was a dull, bluish color and appeared to be made out of Plexiglas.

Malloy knew the receptionist, Sherrie Duncan. Her father had been a manager at the propane store before he retired about five years ago. Her folks still lived out on the road to Tysonville, between the edge of town and the fence line for the West Fork. Sherrie had gone to the junior college in Gunyon after graduation and had come back to help her dad. Even though her father didn't work at the ranch, Sherrie was one of the best horsemen Malloy ever met. She'd entered cutting horse competitions for a while and even won a few belt buckles at the regional level. She was a few years younger than Malloy, but like him, she'd also had big plans to make something of herself. She'd always insisted she was going to college, and Malloy had heard that her cutting horse winnings had been enough to help pay for it. She'd married Colin MacGruder, Sal's son, and they had one child, a daughter. She and Colin had split up a couple of years ago, and she got the kid. AzTech, no doubt, seemed like a great opportunity, especially if Witherspoon made good on his promise of free childcare. Malloy wasn't surprised that Sherrie had been one of the first in line when Witherspoon started accepting applications.

Sherrie smiled at him as he stood up. She was wearing one of those business suits that women wear, which Malloy thought would have been masculine if it hadn't been teal. Her blond hair was tied up in a bun, and she had a new pair of glasses that looked like they were made out of stainless steel. Evidently, the new job had required a shopping spree in Lubbock.

Malloy walked over to her and took his hat off, flipping it idly in his right hand as he spoke. He leaned his left elbow on the edge of the desk.

"Look, Witherspoon's obviously busy," he said, almost whispering for fear his voice would sully the pristine cleanliness of the place. "I reckon something came up. I'll just come back another time."

"Trace, I told you he said he'll be out in a minute. Just have a seat."

"I've been having a seat for twenty minutes already. I know he's a big important guy around here and all, but I'm kind of important over at the ranch, and I got stuff to do too."

"Trace, Mr. Witherspoon is—"

"C'mon Sherrie, I know he's the boss and all, but it isn't right to leave me sitting out here all this time. I'll come back when he gets some manners."

"Trace," she said, leaning forward and staring him down as if he'd just farted in church. "Just be patient." She emphasized each word a little more slowly than the last. "Look, things are a little hectic today."

Malloy sulked back to the chair and slumped into it. He leaned forward and scanned the magazines on the glass coffee table: Electronic News, Interactive Week, Telephony. He chuckled to himself. He wasn't even sure what the last one meant. Was it pronounced "tele-PHONY"? He began to thumb through the magazine, which had articles about new telephone switches, fiber optics, and something called, as near as he could tell, the C++ language. He tossed the magazine back on the table and it landed with a thwack that caused Sherrie to look up from her desk.

"Guess that's their version of the 'Cattleman's Journal.'" he said, pointing at the magazine. Sherrie didn't respond but went back to the computer monitor on her desk as if she were doing something important. He knew she wasn't. He'd seen the green background of the solitaire screen reflected in her glasses when he'd gone up to speak to her.

His thoughts began to wander. Would Colt be able to get a job here someday if he went to college? Would he drive up here to meet his son for lunch? He imagined Colt in a white pressed shirt with a tie and Khaki pants, his hair slicked down and parted on the side. Colt would have a big house among the homies that he'd buy with the big salary he'd make here as an engineer or a designer or something. He'd have a wife, too, no doubt. Some pretty thing from California, blond and tanned and beautiful in the otherworldly sort of way that those kinds of girls seemed when you saw them on TV or in magazines. They'd probably have a hot tub out back and his wife would wear a bikini.

Malloy tried to remember if he'd ever seen his own wife in a bikini and decided he had, when she was nine. Then again, they'd never been to the beach. They'd never been farther east than Dallas, and Conquistador didn't have a proper pool. The ranch hands were known to soak in a muddy stock tank after a long day, but it didn't have the same social enticements as a hot tub.

Colt, though, would have it all. On weekends, Colt and his wife would invite Trace and Darla over for supper, and they'd watch football in the fall, and "the kids"—he and Darla would call them that—would worry about their folks and how they were getting on and did they have enough money. Yes, he could see his son here, happy and successful and untouched by mud and shit and blood. He could see his son's skin white and soft like Witherspoon's, not baked and cracked and scarred by years of wrestling calves and cutting barbed wire and setting fence posts.

Colt, of course, wanted none of it. He kept threatening to join the Air Force, and Trace and Darla would never see their boy again. There'd be some damn fool war—wasn't there always?—and he'd get shot down and killed and they'd get two men in crisp polyester and shiny buttons standing on the doorstep, the same doorstep where they'd stood when they'd given Mama the news about Luke. It had been January, he remembered that. He remembered the men's breath steaming from their mouths as they spoke in hushed tones and Mama, already crying, reluctantly inviting them in. They'd sat on the couch, the bitter chill of their message rolling through the house as if they'd left the door open. How old had he been? Six? He barely remembered his oldest brother. His most vivid memories weren't pleasant ones—that last winter a year before Luke shipped out when he'd teased Trace in the snow.

No, Malloy didn't want that for his son. Yet the alternative—the one Colt seemed most willing to accept—was to stay here, sign up for day work at the ranch, and try to scratch out a living on seventy dollars a day, excluding horse and tack. No house, no hot tub, no bikini-clad wife. And that was in good years, when the ranch needed everybody, beef prices stayed up, and there was no drought.

"Hey! Welcome. Sorry I'm late." Malloy, caught off guard by the sudden interruption of his thoughts, jumped as if he'd been jabbed in the back with a fork. Witherspoon was standing over him, extending his milky hand. Malloy regained his composure and rose. Witherspoon's hand collapsed in his like porridge, and he let go quickly, expecting to hear the bones snap.

They walked toward a set of steel and glass doors on the far side of the receptionist desk. Sherrie Duncan's eyes followed them over the rims of her new glasses, but Witherspoon didn't acknowledge her. He led Malloy to a vinyl-covered bench just to the side of the door.

Next to it was a machine that reminded Malloy of an old shoe-polisher that he'd played with at the barber shop when he was kid. There was no shiny metal ball with a button at the top, but the bottom had a box with an opening for a shoe. The bristles of the brushes stuck out through the slot. Witherspoon stuck his right foot in, and the machine whirred to life. He held his foot there for a second, then switched and jammed his left foot into the hole. He stepped aside and held the machine on for Malloy, who mimicked his actions.

When they were done cleaning their shoes, Witherspoon reached into a bin beside the bench and pulled out two plastic-clad packages. Inside were sock-like coverings made of light blue material.

"We have to put these on out here," he said, handing one of the packages to Malloy.

Malloy sat down on the bench and tore open the package. He understood the concept, but it took him almost five minutes to work the paper booties over his hiking boots. The elastic was too tight, and when he could pull it around his heel, it pinched his finger, and when he removed his finger, the bootie slipped off again. Witherspoon, who'd slid his own booties over his loafers in one fluid move, watched without offering any help. Malloy grew more annoyed with each failed attempt. He could feel Sherrie's eyes on him too, and he could imagine her snapping up the phone and dialing as soon as they were out of sight. Darla would still be laughing by the time he got home.

When he finally got the booties in place, Malloy stood up and tried not to slip. He felt as if a thin layer of ice was coating the floor. Witherspoon held the door and ushered him inside.

They stepped into a windowless conference room, where a round, doughy man was waiting. Malloy recognized him from the homeowners meeting, and for a moment he wondered if the two men were going to gang up on him and extract revenge.

"You remember Howard Swain?" Witherspoon asked as they entered the room.

Malloy shook the man's hand. More porridge.

"We've got a little presentation about the company that we like to show our visitors, and Howard's going to run through that for us."

There was, though, no "us" involved. As Swain turned on a projector, Witherspoon excused himself, telling Swain he'd be back in a few minutes.

Swain flashed a Power Point slide of the company's logo on the screen and Malloy quickly realized this was a standard program for potential customers, not something they'd designed out of hospitality to him. Swain began by talking about the history of AzTech Semiconductor—founded in 1973 in Berkeley, California, and known as Abrams & Zimbalist Electronics. It made calculators and circuit boards for everything from children's toys to microwave ovens. In the 1980s, it tried to build its own personal computers, but abandoned that market and focused on memory chips. The presentation became a blur of acronyms, numbers, and bizarre examples—DRAMs, DSPs, x86, MIPs. "Today we can make semiconductors with components that are eight hundred times smaller than the diameter of a single human hair," Swain said. Malloy found himself stroking his mustache as he tried to comprehend the statement.

When the slide show ended, Swain picked up a round, flat object off the table in front of him. At first, Malloy thought it was a dinner plate. "This is a 300-milimeter wafer," he said proudly, as if he were showing off his latest golfing trophy. "It's the mainstay of what we'll be making here. Of course, production's scalable, so we can retool for the next generation when we get to that point."

Malloy leaned closer and saw row after row of black squares set against the grayish-brown background of the platter. He noticed Swain was perspiring, beads of sweat forming amid the thinning forest of his hair.

Swain explained that the tiny rectangles on the shiny platter, each of which was about the size of the nail on Malloy's pinky, contained one hundred eighty million transistors. Malloy thought back to the transistor radio that sat beside his bed when he was Colt's age. It was the size of a shoebox. He'd taken it apart when it stopped working, and he remembered its lone transistor, rising like a tiny black water tower above the circuit board. Malloy tried to image one hundred and eighty million water towers. He didn't get a chance to mentally shrink them down to his thumbnail before Swain rushed on.

Swain stammered periodically, hurling more numbers so fast that Malloy couldn't absorb their magnitude. There were two thousand pinky-sized squares on each platter, and the plant would make about thirty-five thousand platters each month when it reached full capacity, Swain said. "Our initial production, though, will be somewhere around ten thousand a month, we hope," he added.

The flood of facts bombarded Malloy's brain. He didn't consider himself an ignorant man. He knew how to use a computer, he had cell phones with two-way radios that they used at the ranch. He surfed the Internet every day. It was almost as if Swain were trying to overwhelm him, and yet Malloy didn't think that was the case. This was the standard spiel. Everyone who toured any AzTech plant probably got the same recitation, slightly altered for each specific location. Swain presented it as if he'd been rehearsing for years, and Malloy figured he probably had.

Witherspoon returned to the room just as Swain was talking about future inventions that could come from the company's technology — cars controlled by voice commands, video phones, computers that ran without wires or connections.

"Did we get Mr. Malloy up to speed?" Witherspoon asked with a false laugh. He and Swain exchanged some rehearsed banter, then Swain excused himself, mopping the top of his head as he closed the door behind him.

As if he'd never left, Witherspoon picked up the conversation, firing off specifics about the clean room they would soon enter. The area was one hundred and eighteen thousand square feet in all, although the initial plans called for only about half that space to be used.

"This is what we call a Class One Hundred clean room," Witherspoon said. "It was designed to filter out dust and contaminants down to one hundred parts per cubic foot." The number didn't mean much to Malloy, but he knew it was supposed to, so he grunted in affirmation. Then, Witherspoon added: "A normal cubic foot of air has between three hundred thousand and a million particles. Out here, with all the dust and wind, I'd say we start at a million plus.

"When we first were building this place, I worried about the dust from outside," Witherspoon said. "Now that the building's mostly complete and sealed, we just worry about the conventional stuff. You know what the biggest contaminant for a clean room is?"

"No idea," Malloy said flatly. He'd already had enough, and the tour hadn't started yet.

"Us. Flecks of our skin that slough off and float through the air. Just walking around in there, we'd do a lot of damage if we weren't wearing the bunny suits." Witherspoon didn't miss the irony of his statement, given that his own skin was still peeling from the torturous visit to the ranch.

"Bunny suits?" Malloy felt his mouth getting dry. He knew Witherspoon was referring to the protective gear he'd seen in the materials AzTech had floated around town over the past year and half. Still, for a moment, he flashed on a mental image of himself in a giant rabbit costume, surrounded by the ranch hands laughing hysterically.

"By the way," Witherspoon said, turning off the slide projector, "all of this represents about a three-billion-dollar investment by AzTech over a multi-year period. Our estimate is that employment could top two thousand people when we reach full production."

He turned to head for the door, but the last number hung in the air like a million particles of dust. That was the one number Malloy could appreciate. Two thousand jobs: more than three times the population of the entire town of Conquistador. Two thousand people, and each of them putting kids in the local schools, paying taxes, buying things at Terry Garrison's auto shop, grabbing cups of coffee on their way into work.

Two thousand people, drawn to tiny, dusty old Conquistador because here, among all the dying towns for a hundred miles in any direction, here was where there would be jobs. Malloy imagined Conquistador with rows of new houses, the smell of fresh paint wafting over the town and chasing away the stench of cows and the acrid aroma of feed grain.

Witherspoon continued to talk over his shoulder as he stepped outside the room. "What you'll see in there today isn't as exciting as if we were actually in production. We're still testing equipment and doing the final build-outs, but it'll give you an idea of how things will work."

Witherspoon led Malloy down a frighteningly white hallway and up a flight of stairs. They hadn't seen anyone else since they left the reception area, and their footfalls echoed on the shiny linoleum.

"We're not anywhere near full production yet," Witherspoon was saying as they walked up the stairs. "That's probably a year away. If we were running at top speed, there'd be a lot more people bustling around. But we should be cranking out wafers at a good clip by the time the new century gets here. This, he paused for a few seconds, "is literally where we're building the future."

Malloy tried to think if he'd ever heard someone he knew use the word "bustling." He felt as if he were wandering in a daze. His feet seemed leaden, and the booties slid along the well-buffed floor.

Witherspoon opened another pair of stainless-steel doors with thick glass windows. Inside, a man wearing what appeared to be a shower cap walked by.

They entered, washed their hands in a set of deep sinks, and sat down on low benches. The room was cool, but other than that it reminded Malloy of a high school locker room. There were rows of garments hanging on racks, and what appeared to be lockers and cubicles that held various pieces of apparel he couldn't begin to identify.

Witherspoon disappeared for a few minutes, then came back carrying a bundle of antiseptically clean clothes.

"You'll have to take your hat off," he said.

Malloy set his gimme cap beside him on the bench and looked up at Witherspoon, whose glasses reflected the florescent sheen of the room. He suddenly seemed vaguely malevolent, Malloy thought.

Witherspoon put the bundle on the bench and pulled out one of the shower caps. He snapped it over Malloy's head, touching the sides of his neck to make sure the cowboy's hair was underneath the covering. His fingers felt cold and clammy, and Malloy winced at the contact. Only Darla and his mother had ever run their fingers along his hairline. Witherspoon leaning over him made him uncomfortable, and he wanted to push the other man away. He shifted on the bench.

"Um, you're going to have to wear a mask because of that mustache," Witherspoon said.

Before Malloy could question or protest, Witherspoon produced a surgical mask and began tying it around the back of Malloy's head, the swatch of cloth in the front covering his mouth. He straightened up and handed Malloy a white jumpsuit that seemed to be made of plastic. "This looks about your size," he said.

While Malloy wriggled into the jumpsuit, Witherspoon put on his own set of new booties, shower cap, and jumpsuit. Then he donned a hood fashioned from the same material and pulled on a pair of boots that made the bottoms of his feet ridiculously large, like some sort of cartoon character.

He helped Malloy into the same gear. The hood felt tight on the cowboy's head, and it pulled close on both sides of his face. It reminded him of the snowsuit he'd worn that winter day before Luke left. Running around in the front yard with his brothers after a couple of inches had fallen, young Trace felt the insulated material punctuate every move he'd made with a crunch or a swish. He'd tripped over a rock because he wasn't used to having his vision limited. When he got up, Luke pelted him in the face with a snowball, finding the one vulnerable spot in his little brother's fiber-filled armor. Malloy hadn't been able to see the attack because he had no peripheral vision. Luke and Matt had doubled over in laughter as Trace had run blubbering into the house. It would have been later that year that Luke shipped out, he thought, and instinctively shifted his mind back to the present.

Witherspoon was tucking the bottom of the hood inside the collar of the jumpsuit. He zipped the suit up tight, then knelt to fix the boots. He flashed back to the dung encrusted tennis shoes and sweat-soaked shirt he'd endured during the ranch tour. How could anyone prefer a day like that to this predictable, immaculate environment? He helped Malloy put on a pair of gloves, pulling the sleeves of the jumpsuit over top of them. Malloy felt as if he were being sealed inside the clothes, and they weighed heavily on his chest. He made a conscious effort to breathe.

"You need to take notes for any reason?" Witherspoon asked. "I can get you a small pad. You can't take a regular notebook in there because it'll give off too much dust. We've got some low-fiber paper if you need it."

Malloy didn't think he could speak. He was imprisoned behind his surgical mask. He could sense the sweat beaded up along his forehead, but he didn't know how to wipe it away. He tried to simply shake his head 'no,' but he didn't feel as if he could turn his neck. He ended up moving his entire torso back and forth, his arms sticking out awkwardly because it didn't seem possible to put them against his sides.

Witherspoon smiled and motioned for Malloy to follow him. They pushed past some hanging sheets of clear plastic and immediately were blasted by jets of air from the ceiling. "Air shower," Witherspoon called over his shoulder. "It gets off any remaining free particles."

Malloy grunted in acknowledgement, but his grunt was barely audible, muffled under the mask and the whoosh of the rushing air.

Witherspoon led them through a door at the other end of the air shower and Malloy knew they had finally entered the clean room itself. Giant machinery surrounded them. There were large bays of equipment emblazoned with names like Applied Materials and KLA-Tencor. He could see other workers now, also in bunny suits, moving around some of the bays. Areas off to the left contained ordinary-looking work benches, complete with conventional tools—hammers, pliers, screwdrivers—things Malloy found comfortingly familiar.

Malloy detected movement out of the corner of his eye. A tiny track was suspended about eight feet above their heads and a little square car was moving along it.

Witherspoon followed the line of Malloy's gaze and began to explain what he was seeing. The other man's words were muffled beneath the hood and the hum of the machinery.

"That's our robot distribution system. The less we have people handling the wafers, the less chance there is that someone will drop them. It's not like a CD. If we drop one, it's ruined. So we've got these little robot trains that move the wafers through the production process."

Malloy noticed he was standing on a metal grid. He could see through the floor to the one below it. Witherspoon had explained this was part of the clean room design. Air from above was forced down toward the floor, pushing any remaining dust particles through the floor and into the non-clean area below.

Malloy found the experience unnerving. He didn't even like climbing open-backed staircases. He could feel more sweat building up inside the hood, soaking his hair and tracing a path behind his ears and down his neck.

Witherspoon was still talking, but it was harder to hear. The roar of the machinery seemed to grow more intense. The area of the room they were standing in was bathed in a sharp yellow light, and Malloy felt as if the light made everything around him blur.

"Here's where we use a photomask to imprint the wafer," Witherspoon said, pointing to a large piece of machinery in front of them. Malloy nodded, but he didn't understand. He wasn't sure he was even in the room anymore. He seemed to be watching from behind himself, as if he were standing on the other side of the glass doors they'd come through. The machinery grew louder, and Witherspoon's words began to drift away from him.

The tour was moving forward. Malloy took a step toward Witherspoon, who'd already turned away and was heading toward the next bay. The room lurched and wavered. Malloy's chest heaved, but he couldn't find any air. He opened his mouth, gulping frantically like a goldfish. He tugged at the surgical mask, but he couldn't get the fingers of his glove under it to break it free. Instead, he just pawed uselessly at his face.

Witherspoon was still walking and talking, his voice just a varying murmur that flitted in and out of the drone that surrounded them. Another of the little robot cars drove past overhead.

The room pitched again. Malloy could feel his sweat lining the entire inside of his bunny suit. He reached for a nearby workbench to steady himself, but he was unsure where his hand was. He straightened up, and regained his balance, only to have the room sway in the other direction.

He was gasping. The mask and hood were constricting him. What had Witherspoon done? Was the homie trying to kill him? To suffocate him in this high-tech tomb where there were no witnesses other than a few loyal employees? The sweat cascaded down the front of his face now too. His scalp burned. He was back in his front yard now, in the snowsuit again. He pawed frantically at his head with his mittens, unable to grab anything. There was something in there, he could feel it. Cold and moving, running down his neck. Just snow, melting snow, but his face hurt, and he was sure there was something solid inside his suit, creeping, *crawling*. What was it? "Maybe it's a scorpion," Luke called, and he and Matt laughed. He slapped his head with his hands frantically. "Get it out! Get it out!" he screamed.

He turned and stumbled. He was back inside the clean room, but it rolled like the view in a funhouse mirror. Breathing was impossible. He slapped at his face, but the mask wouldn't come off. His scalp crawled. Something was alive inside his suit. Scorpions. His brother's voice, silenced for thirty years, called back to him. "Maybe it's a scorpion." A vegetarian scorpion. From California.

He lunged forward, flailing for anything solid to hold onto. The glove of his left hand caught the edge of the work bench, but its surface was too slick. His hand shot outward, and he plunged forward. He saw a hammer, a good trusty hammer, lying in front of him as his chin smashed into the tabletop. He felt his head snap back and then he seemed to float down into blackness, enveloped by the roaring moan of the machinery that swallowed him as if he were sliding down into a cave. ✯

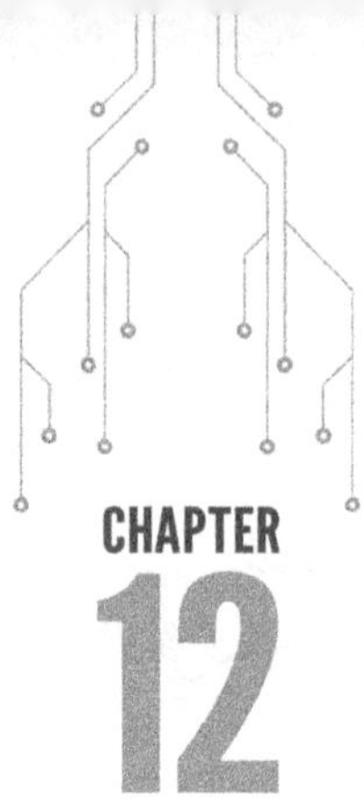

CHAPTER 12

DR. DIANA LAMBEAU'S EYES sliced into Blaine Witherspoon like cool, blue daggers of ice. "You moved him?" she demanded. "He passes out, hits his head, and you drag him all the way down here?"

They were back in the lobby of the AzTech plant. Witherspoon had been almost halfway through the clean room tour before he noticed Malloy was no longer behind him. He'd retraced his steps, returning to the first bay, where he found the cowboy sprawled on the floor in front of a work bench. He could tell Malloy was still breathing, although the blood-soaked mask and hood had alarmed him. Still, there was no point in contaminating the room. Leaving him there would have meant opening the sealed environment to paramedics, shutting down the blowers and the air showers, throwing open the doors to a litany of unwanted particles and contaminants. That would have put them weeks behind on a schedule that was already slipping.

Witherspoon corralled a few workers and they carried the limp cowboy back to the locker room, where they had stripped off his hood, mask, gloves, and boots. Other workers carried

Malloy to the reception area, and then, realizing he didn't know if Conquistador had paramedics, he called the doctor.

"I just thought it would easier," he said feebly.

"Easier? Don't you know you don't move somebody with a potential head injury?" He'd never expected her to be capable of such vitriol. As he'd phoned her office, he'd been almost happy Malloy had collapsed. He'd relished the idea of seeing Dr. Lambeau again. At first, he worried because he hadn't made the cowboy sign any sort of waiver, but then he'd reminded himself that most of the locals were genetically predisposed to tort reform. He quickly put any worries about lawsuits out of his mind.

Witherspoon thought the doctor would be glad to avoid winding her way into the bowels of the plant. He'd saved her time. And her concerns about "head injuries" seemed overblown, too. After all, by the time she'd gotten there, Malloy had started to come around. Even now, sitting in the vinyl chair, his eyes blinking mechanically, Malloy seemed to be getting back to normal. The gash on his chin was still red and moist, but it was no longer gushing blood. The receptionist—what was her name? Susie? Sharon?—was standing behind the doctor, still holding the blood-stained towel they'd used to staunch the flow from Malloy's chin.

"I'll be okay," Malloy kept saying. And Witherspoon was convinced.

The cowboy tried to stand, and Witherspoon welcomed the movement because it diverted Lambeau's anger. "No, Trace, you stay put." She pushed Malloy's shoulders gently back in the chair.

Witherspoon stared at her dark hair, pulled back in a ponytail that stretched midway down her back. She wasn't wearing her lab coat. Instead, she'd come out in a deliciously tight cotton top tucked into jeans. Maybe she had worn it for his benefit, he thought, and he found himself desperately wanting her to repeal the blame she'd directed at him.

But she was so angry. Angry that he'd moved Malloy, angry that he hadn't been able to tell her the details of what happened. Why hadn't he seen Malloy fall, she'd wanted to know. Had he said anything, done anything unusual? Did he seem to be feeling okay before they suited up? Witherspoon really hadn't noticed. After all, he'd been running late. He wanted to get the tour over quickly. He'd been on a conference call with Soderheim most of the morning, running through the latest reports. The old curmudgeon was starting to smell the problems hidden behind the glossy words Witherspoon had sent him. Why hadn't he run a full power test yet? Why was the water filtration not up to spec? Question after question bombarded him from the speaker. He'd turned the early part of the presentation over to Swain, who, caught unprepared had protested mightily. Witherspoon knew he didn't want to be left in a room alone with Malloy, which made his order all the more enjoyable.

Witherspoon reaffirmed his assessment that Swain was a climber, a back stabber. He was sure the little doughboy had been leaking details of the schedule problems back to Milpitas. Witherspoon had intended to scour his subordinate's email, but there simply hadn't been time. There was never time. Time was killing him.

Now, more time was being whisked away, stolen by a semi-conscious cowboy sprawled on his reception area couch. He turned his gaze from the doctor's back to Malloy, slumped uncomfortably, his head resting on the black vinyl arm. The cowboy's dark hair was matted with sweat, pasted against his face. The skin of his cheeks was white and translucent. Only his hands retained their usual leathered appearance. Malloy held one of those hands up, pushing Lambeau's arm aside.

"Diana, I'm fine. I'll be fine. I just need to get out of here," he said. "I need some air, that's all."

"Trace, you need to take it easy."

"I need to go."

There was a pause, and Lambeau cast her gaze at the floor. "You may have a mild concussion." She bit her lip and thought some more before turning to Witherspoon. "Can you help me get him to the car?"

He nodded. They each grabbed Malloy under the shoulders, their hands overlapping behind his back as they carried him. Witherspoon welcomed the contact, but Lambeau seemed not to notice. He could tell she was still furious.

The cowboy reeked like a dead animal. His clothes were so soaked with sweat that he might have worn them swimming. Witherspoon tried to ignore the smell, which seemed to stab at his nostrils as if he were inhaling glass shards. He tried not to think about touching the perspiration-caked back, tried not to retch at coming in contact with the repugnant armpit. He focused on the soft olive skin of the doctor that had brushed against him as he shouldered Malloy's weight.

They loaded Malloy into the front seat of Lambeau's Ford Explorer and closed the door. Witherspoon followed the doctor around the back of the car. The heat reflected from the parking lot and washed over them. As she got in the driver's side, she stared at him, and he saw that her deep blue eyes retained their sharpness.

"Somebody'll get his truck later. I'm going to take him home. Maybe Darla can make him stay put," she said.

Witherspoon nodded and smiled slightly, hoping that the doctor's anger would subside. Any hope of a warming in her soon vanished. "I'm going to want to review your safety policies out here, at least in terms of medical procedures." She slammed the door and started the engine. She backed out furiously, and spun the car forward, heading for the road. Witherspoon half raised his hand, waving her off, then stopped himself.

She couldn't really demand anything of the sort, he thought. She had no authority. She wasn't OSHA, or even the local health department. Still, he wouldn't mind having Dr. Lambeau in his office for what would probably take hours, reviewing policies and procedures. He pulled out his Palm Pilot and made a note to call her the next week. She would have calmed down by then.

He returned to his office and slumped into the high-backed leather chair behind his desk. The skin on his upper back and shoulders was peeling again. It must have been the third layer that had sloughed off since he'd returned from his ranch tour. He rubbed his hand under his collar and felt the rough flakes breaking loose and falling down his back. Frustrated, he scratched furiously until his skin burned.

He perused the stack of monthly reports on the left side of his desk and the little pile of pink phone messages on the right. Each pile represented a different component of the mounting failure he was presiding over. Thumbing through the little pink slips, he could see most were from one department or another in Milpitas: accounting, human resources, corporate communications, and of course, old Soddy himself.

Why was this deadline slipping? When would that equipment be ready? How was the hiring going?

The other stack answered those questions and more, but not in the way Witherspoon had intended. AzTech had planned to spend about three billion dollars on the new plant, and part of that money was designed to grease the startup process, cutting it from the usual two or three years to about eighteen months.

Witherspoon no longer thought they would make it. The new power line had taken months longer than promised, and as he'd just seen on the ranch tour, it still wasn't connected. The power company—an electric cooperative actually—kept saying it would be ready any day. They didn't know he'd just seen the towers, with the lines unstrung, for himself. He made a mental note to call them again. In the meantime, he scanned the latest reports on the plant's operations. Not much had changed from the day before. They would produce the first test wafers "soon." That's all he kept hearing from everyone—"soon." "Soon" wasn't a word that had any meaning in the corporate world. "Soon" was a euphemism for failure. "Soon" meant the plant didn't have all the juice it needed for full production, and couldn't even begin full-scale test runs, let alone start working on the ramp ups.

The water filtration system, a polymer membrane technology, hadn't performed up to spec. It was good, but not as good as he needed to keep the water consumption to a million gallons a day. The plant was going to draw seventeen percent more water than he'd originally predicted. The locals were sure to scream about that. Everyone in the Big Empty was prickly about water. It was, after all, what had caused Malloy to punch him in the nose. As angry as he was about that, he'd gotten the message. He'd simply stopped discussing water all together.

The homeowners association in Rolling Ranch Estates still intended to build a golf course, which, it just so happened, would wrap beautifully behind his own house. He hadn't quashed those discussions, but he hadn't encouraged them either. As mad as the locals had gotten over the little pond at the subdivision entrance, they might just storm the gate in protest if they knew there were plans to irrigate an eighteen-hole championship course.

He wanted it, of course. Every plant manager in the company lived on a golf course. Saturday afternoons his subordinates would be on the greens and they would look over and see him and his family lounging on the back patio, which no longer was an angst-inducing gateway to nothingness but a showcase for his success. Sunday mornings, his preferred tee time, they'd see him in the clubhouse, and they'd jockey week after week to be the lucky ones joining his foursome. Some weeks Jenna would play, freezing out one of the hopefuls, his way of keeping them off guard and hungry, while placating his wife with a few hours' reprieve from the town's simple-minded social scene.

Yes, he needed that golf course, all right. He just had to figure out a way to get it. As for the plant, no one had to know about the additional water consumption. The county would figure it out eventually, but there was no need to invite problems by telling them ahead of time. At this point, he had nothing he could tell them anyway. He had only estimates. The recycling system itself was being shipped in from Kansas, and pieces of it were weeks late. They had little more than a test system in place. But he'd pushed on with the rest of the internal build-out. They were using almost fifty percent more water than he'd expected at this point, and no one had complained. So much for the drought and Malloy's mama not being able to wash.

Then there were the chemicals. He'd secured a contract for ultra-pure sulfuric acid and benzene from a company called ChemPurCo in Bryan. He was particularly proud of the deal. ChemPurCo would ship the stuff in by rail and haul it off again when AzTech was done using it to treat its wafers. Even after AzTech was finished with the acid, it was still pure enough for most industrial uses, and ChemPurCo would simply resell it to another customer whose needs were less demanding than AzTech's. That meant AzTech got a significant discount on the upfront cost, and they essentially got environmentally approved disposal for free. It worked well for everyone involved except that ChemPurCo had recently been acquired by a French conglomerate. The new owners intended to renegotiate the contract, a move that would cost him eight percent more. They knew he'd have to agree to the revised terms. ChemPurCo was one of the few producers of ultra-pure sulfuric acid, and its proximity, less than five hundred miles from the plant, made it convenient and cost-effective. Even with the price increase, it was cheaper to buy from them than from one of their competitors. Witherspoon knew he might be able to haggle the eight percent down to six, but there was little he could do to keep his chemical costs from going up.

The employment issue was even less encouraging. He'd transferred about a hundred and fifty workers from other AzTech operations, and he'd predicted that would be enough to get the plant off the ground. The rest they'd planned to hire locally. AzTech prided itself on having the lowest labor costs in the industry because it sought out areas of high unemployment or low-wage pockets and offered good jobs. It had developed extensive training programs to make up for the lack of a skilled labor pool. The strategy had worked in New Mexico, in Arizona, in upstate New York, and in northern Kentucky, but so far, it wasn't working in the Big Empty.

This place was just too spread out. In Conquistador, there weren't enough people to make a full shift, even if every man, woman and child in town went to work at the plant. Witherspoon had hoped to draw workers from neighboring cities, but the distance was proving to be a major impediment. Gunyon, for example, was almost forty miles away, which meant an eighty-mile commute each day. He had assumed this wouldn't be a problem. In California, a lot of people did that, in heavy traffic. Two-hour commutes were common. Even in Dallas and Houston long travel times weren't unheard of. And out here, forty miles was no more than a thirty-minute drive, and he'd been assured by all the local economic development types that people would drive a lot farther than that for a good job. They would come from throughout the county and beyond. Roland Kerr had even told him how he drove over an hour each way to take his date to supper the night of his senior prom.

But it wasn't happening. Maybe it was because they didn't understand the opportunity, or they didn't trust a big out-of-state company, or they didn't think they'd be qualified for the work. For whatever reason, the applications were coming in slowly.

Education wasn't as big a problem as he'd anticipated. He'd had a few applicants with degrees from Texas Tech, several others with associate's diplomas from the community college in Gunyon. And of course, a handful of high school graduates. He could make it work, given AzTech's prowess at training workers in-house, regardless of their educational background. All he had to do was say the word and the training team would be on the next flight out of the Bay Area.

But it was still, to use a local term, slim pickings. So far, his local employment was less than two dozen people. He didn't even have enough to schedule a training class, and Milpitas was getting antsy. They wanted ten thousand platters a month by year's end, as if they were building a bridge to the future. Even now, six months out, Witherspoon knew that it was impossible.

He figured he had maybe three months before he had to start fighting for his job. He could stall and evade and fudge the numbers at least that long, but sooner or later, headquarters would start looking for someone else. God, after all the sacrifices, all the promising and cajoling with Jenna, all the schmoozing and politicking in Milpitas, after everything, it could still amount to nothing. His plan, his dreams, his carefully crafted future were all crumbling before his eyes.

He pulled the computer keyboard closer to him, called up the website for CBS Marketwatch and tapped in "AZTK." He waited for the latest price and cursed under his breath. AzTech's stock had fallen another seventy-two cents while he'd been out dealing with Malloy. It was down thirty-five percent just this month alone and had been sliding for more than a year. In a way, the decline bought him time. Milpitas was fraught with worry over the stock price. It coincided with a decline in chip prices, and AzTech's attempts to calm the market's fears hadn't worked. Its strategy, when it announced the Conquistador plant, was to invest in the downturn, to boost its capacity so that when the market picked up, it would be able to churn out more chips than any of its competitors.

But the investment—the debt load—had been so huge, and the decline in chip prices so persistent, that investors doubted the strategy's chances for success. Changing plant managers now would only exacerbate those fears and drive the stock even further in the tank. He had to smile as he charted the slow plunge of the price graph on the screen. It had cost him personally, of course. His options were underwater, and his 401(k) plan had taken a beating, but those losses he could recover from. He felt a perverse sense of satisfaction the longer he stared at the jagged southeasterly tack of the graph. It meant job security, at least for the short-term.

There was only one real immediate drawback to the stock's slide. Three months ago, AzTech's chief financial officer had been in town, visiting the plant as part of some executive-level junket. In the interest of community relations, Witherspoon had arranged for him to speak to the Kiwanis Club, which happened to have its monthly luncheon that week.

The meeting had drawn a crowd. People were standing around the back wall of the Church of Christ Fellowship Hall as the CFO, Jack Watley, had talked up AzTech's big plans for the Big Empty. Watley had given the speech a hundred times—it was his standard spiel on Wall Street roadshows, in investor meetings, at civic functions—but it was falling flat in Conquistador. The crowd didn't seem to fathom his lofty predictions for global semiconductor demand in an era of PCs, cellphones, and untold new devices that would come as they crossed into the twenty-first century. Nor did they appreciate the cost benefits for 300-millimeter wafer production. Witherspoon detected a touch of nervousness in Watley's eyes as he scanned the crowd. Cowboy boots shuffled impatiently on the linoleum. Women coughed with a touch of ambivalence. Children squirmed and ran down the aisle to play outside.

Witherspoon noticed moisture on Watley's forehead, reflected in the light at the lectern. He had chuckled to himself. Watley had been grilled by shareholders at AzTech's annual meetings, he'd been peppered with questions from financial analysts and interrogated by fund managers, and he'd never broken a sweat. But faced with the stony silence of a room full of granite-faced Marlboro Men, he was perspiring like a triathlete in August. There must have been more than a hundred people in all, sitting politely yet apathetically on folding metal chairs or standing against the wall with their arms crossed.

"What this means," Watley said, raising his voice in a preacher-like crescendo, "is opportunity for each and every one of you. Does that mean I'm saying you should all come to work for AzTech? Of course not, though Blaine would welcome your applications. What I'm saying is that now AzTech is a part of your town, a part of your future, and you can participate in that whether you work directly for the company or not. Our stock is at a ten-year low. The market doesn't understand and doesn't appreciate what we're doing. But you do. You see it every day, just up the street. You see our future rising on the horizon. When the market rebounds, chips made in Conquistador will be shipped to OEMs all over the world and put into all kinds of electronics." Witherspoon winced. No one in the audience knew what an original equipment manufacturer was. It didn't matter, Watley built to his conclusion. "There aren't any sure bets in the marketplace of course, but knowledge is the key to any successful investment, and you now have the knowledge. You see AzTech's success. And you have a chance to profit from it, because the stock only goes up from here."

The speech had ended to polite applause, and afterwards, dozens had come forward to ask Watley how to buy the stock. Some were ready to write him a check on the spot.

What Watley had done was borderline illegal, of course, but Witherspoon knew that the chance of the SEC finding out about a Kiwanis Club meeting in Conquistador, Texas, was less than slim. You'd have better luck picking a grain of sugar from a white sand beach.

The problem, of course, was that many of those people did buy AzTech shares and had watched as the stock that "only goes up" had gone nowhere but down. Cowhands who had drained their savings accounts were now giving Witherspoon dirty looks in the grocery store.

Watley had been shameless in his promotion, but he didn't realize how well he had connected with the crowd. This was a company town. It had been built by the Conquistador Ranch, and for more than a hundred years, it had tied its fortunes to the property. No one could buy stock in the ranch, of course, but they believed in the ranch because it was their livelihood, either directly or indirectly. They knew the men who worked there, they knew the Scotsmen who'd bought the place and stayed to run it. They trusted them, and in return, the Conquistador and its managers took care of them.

Now, there was a new company in this company town. Many people here didn't understand exactly what AzTech did, but they understood how to treat a company that meant as much to their future as the Conquistador meant to their past. They *had* to believe in AzTech, just as they'd believed in the ranch. They *had* to trust Blaine Witherspoon and Jack Watley and all the faceless executives out in California.

This time, their trust would be betrayed. That was always what happened when people unaccustomed to the market bought into a "sure thing." First, it's too good to be true, then it's too good to pass up, and then it turns out to be too bad to be an accident. It didn't matter if Watley had conned them. With each day the stock fell, more people in town grew suspicious.

They would start to question if this new company would be the caretaker that the Conquistador had been. They would wonder if this company with its fast-talking city slickers had deceived them. They would see the declining value of their investment and feel a sense of dread like a cold dark hole growing inside them. And Witherspoon was AzTech's public face in the Big Empty, and that made him personally responsible for the stock performance. The only thing that was keeping the furious mob from his doorstep was the overarching sense of decorum and fair play that permeated this place. No one wanted to be rude, even if they'd lost a lot of money. He might be safe at least as long as their manners held out, and he didn't provide any personal animosity, and he didn't cross any unseen lines like he apparently had with Malloy.

He needed the town on his side, but he was walking a dangerous line, with angry locals on one side, and uneasy superiors on the other. He was running out of time. ✯

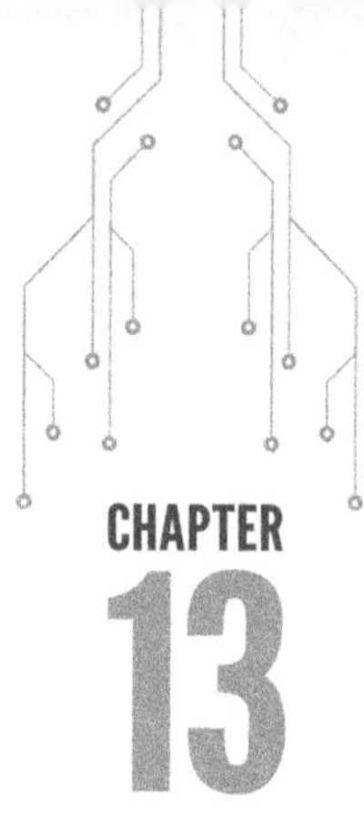

CHAPTER 13

COLT MALLOY KNEW his grandmother was dying. He could tell by the icy silence that wrapped itself around the cab of his father's pickup as they drove past the ranch house and southwest toward Gunyon. He could tell because his mother wasn't pointing out the red-tailed hawks or the jackrabbits or any other items of interest that she always found as they drove. She stared out the window, her unseeing eyes bleary and reddened.

He knew the night before, when the phone had rung late, and his parents talked into the early hours of the morning in tones too hushed for him to hear but laced with an anxiety that floated down the hall and into his room, keeping him awake.

They had taken him out of school. They had never done that before. He hadn't seen his grandmother in at least six months, but his last visit had been more than he could bear.

He wondered if she would remember him this time. Would she again wallow in the depths of her own delusions? Would she implore him to carry her out of the home and free her from the nurses who, she insisted, were working for the North Koreans? Her husband, after all, had fought them and now they wanted her to reveal his secrets.

"Please, young man, you have to help me," she'd begged. She didn't remember his name, yet somehow, she knew he was on her side, the bonds of family, the link of generations not completely broken by the disease assaulting her mind.

Would it be different this time? Would she recognize him, her own grandson? Her *only* grandson?

Her mind, though, wasn't the only problem. This time, it was pneumonia, the latest in a series of infections to take advantage of her weakened state. Colt's mother had told him that the antibiotics weren't working, and her breathing had become more strained. Last night, she'd had a stroke.

Come as soon as you can, the doctors had implored. It may be your last chance.

He hoped his grandmother hadn't forgotten him. He hoped she'd understand why he hadn't come more often when his mother visited her. He hoped she still remembered the Saturday mornings when he would charge into her kitchen to embrace the smells of freshly cooked cherry pie or other treats she always seemed to be preparing.

Colt hadn't known how to handle his grandmother's illness, and he hadn't asked to go see her in the nursing home, waiting instead for his parents to suggest it. In many ways, she was already dead to him, and he preferred to savor the memories of the days when they would sit on the porch and sip lemonade and talk about books. She had loved to read, and she taught him to love books, too, though he could never keep pace with her voracious habits, plowing through several volumes a week.

Out here, amid all this vast nothingness, they would sit and stare at the flat line of the horizon and talk about Dickens and Twain and Melville and his favorite, Dumas, and hers, the Bible. She had helped him understand words that were too complicated for his young mind, given them context, and taught him to search for meaning.

But then he had gotten older, and he had less time for porch-sitting. He started helping his father at the ranch and playing six-man football. He still tried to stop by on Saturdays when he could, but their visits became less frequent and for a while he didn't notice that she was getting confused more often, that she forgot some of those big words she used to explain to him, or that later, she would forget where she put her keys.

He barely noticed the day she put her pajamas on over her clothes. It took him awhile, staring at her, before he realized what she'd done, and had gone home and told his mother. He'd laughed. It was kind of funny, wasn't it? But his mother hadn't thought so, and immediately, he knew what seemed like the simple confusion of an aged mind was a harbinger of life-sapping illness.

He looked over at his father, whose gaze was fixed on the two-lane blacktop that scrolled out in front of them. The gash on his chin was now a dark red line that pointed down toward his sternum like war paint. What must it be like for him, to drive forty miles to watch his own mother die?

Colt felt sorry for his father, a rare emotion that made him uncomfortable. Mostly, he envied his dad. He didn't want to admit it—and he hadn't acknowledged it to anyone but Manny—but he knew he would never make it into the Air Force now, not with his leg the way it was. And if he couldn't be a pilot, then his father was the model of man he most wanted to be. He wondered what the kid from California—that Brandon kid with the pierced ears and long black hair that hung in his face like a dog's—would think about that. Brandon hated his own father. He'd said as much even though Colt was a total stranger.

He'd seen the Witherspoon kid around school, of course. You couldn't miss him. But they'd never talked. No one talked to him, not even, it seemed, the few other kids from California. Colt had purposely stayed away. At the cookout by the ranch house, though, Brandon had wandered over to talk with Colt and Manny. They'd ignored him for a long time, but after a while, they'd acknowledged his presence and managed to make tense, disconnected conversation.

"Can't believe the old man dragged me to this. He's such a whore, kissing up to these cowdudes. It's just so lame, know what I'm sayin'? Pretty funny, too, considering the way your dad bitch slapped him. That's word, yo."

Colt and Manny had just stared at him, unsure how to respond. He'd never heard anyone refer to their father as a "whore," nor was he sure what to make of Brandon's delight at his own father's beating. His whole way of speaking, let alone thinking, was alien.

Colt, squeezed between his mother and father, shifted in the seat. His bad leg was starting to hurt, and he could feel it cramping. He winced, uttering a mental curse, which had become his involuntary reaction to the pain. Doctor Lambeau had told him the pain might never go away completely. The hobble in his walk would be with him the rest of his life.

He could live with the pain. His father always said you weren't really alive unless you felt some sort of pain. He knew his father was feeling it now as each rotation of the wheels brought them closer to the death in his grandmother's eyes. Still, the pain Colt felt was different. Without meaning to, he replayed the accident from the previous summer. He felt the panic in the horse under him — what had triggered it? A rattlesnake, maybe? No one had ever told him. He felt the pain shoot through his left leg as the horse slammed against the corral fence. Then he was lunging forward and sideways, trying to bring the animal under control. He could hear the apathetic bleating of cows all around him. Then he was flung backward, his leg hitting the fence again. He felt his grip on the reins loosen and could feel himself coming out of the saddle.

He knew he was going over the fence, yet he knew, too, that inexplicably his left foot was still in the stirrup, pinned between the horse's flank and the fence slat, and he could still remember questioning how different parts of his body could be two places at once in the split second he remained conscious. He heard the resounding snap, which he was sure had to be the fence board giving way. Only later did he realize it was the sound of his own tibia fracturing in four places. His final memory was of hanging upside down, peering back across the fence and still seeing his own foot on the other side. Then his head hit the fence post and saved him from the blinding pain that followed.

He knew the rest by what he'd been told. His father, working the cows nearby, jumped off his horse, vaulted over the fence and scooped Colt up in one fluid motion, moving with an urgency and conviction that made him look as if he were borne by the wind itself. His father loaded him into a pickup and drove him to Doc Lambeau's office, where she watched over him through the night. His mother had arrived, bearing food. It was her form of therapy. When she worried, she cooked. He regained consciousness the next day and the reality of his accident overtook him in a flood of pain and despair.

He could still hear the doctor's words echoing in his mind: "No more football. Not this year, not ever. One wrong tackle and there's a good chance you'll never walk again." The azure of her eyes bored into him, reinforcing the point. She held his gaze for a full minute before she turned to do the same to his father and mother.

Doc Lambeau knew the gravity of what she was saying. She wasn't just depriving him of a sport he loved. She was robbing the whole town of a team that everyone expected could go on to win regional or even state championships, if not in the coming year, then in the one after that.

There were only six of them, that was all the town could muster, but it was enough in the Big Empty. They'd been playing in cow pastures since they were old enough to run. As they grew, the boys adopted rules that became more formal, and when they hit high school, the friends became an official team, playing offense and defense—every down, every play, every minute.

Colt never wanted to play on an eleven-man team. Six-man football was fast and exciting, like ice hockey on dirt. Everyone was a receiver, and the scores were always high, more like basketball than traditional football. If Colt got open, he was gone. It was that simple. That was their playbook, their Packers Sweep, their unstoppable offensive onslaught. Get open and get the ball. Colt the Bolt, Manny Garrison would call him on the field. Manny was the quarterback, and if he wasn't running the ball himself, he was usually throwing it or pitching it out to Colt the Bolt.

And now, Colt would never get the ball again. No more racing down the eighty-yard field, no more tackling an opponent in the mud puddle that always developed near the thirty-five yard-line on the Carlson County High field after a good rain. No chance to play under the lights on Friday nights in the coming years.

In fact, everyone in town was worried that the lights would go dark permanently by the time Colt's class reached their senior year. With only five boys left to play, they'd scrapped the junior varsity team this year. So far, the AzTech plant hadn't attracted anyone who could handle Texas-style Six-Man. All they'd gotten was a few bleached-blond pretty boys and one pierced pothead.

Colt studied his father, whose eyes were still fixed on the black ribbon of asphalt strung out in front of the truck. What must he be thinking? How do you deal with the death of a parent when you know it's coming? He turned toward his mother. Her eyes, blood-shot and moist, were staring straight ahead, but he could tell she wasn't seeing anything. His parents had known each other since their first day of school. His father's mother might as well have been his mother's mother, too. A death in the family in Conquistador cut deeply, because everyone either was family or felt like they were.

Neither of his parents was speaking, but Colt knew they were playing out their own private conversations in their mind. Did his father feel guilty? Why had he not come to see her more?

Colt knew the answer, and it shamed him. Not for his father, but for himself. He'd watched his grandmother's slow deterioration, and he couldn't bear to see her in the nursing home. With each visit, there was a little less of her there, her personality retreating deeper inside the frail exterior of her mind. It was as if her soul had fallen in a pit that was slowly being filled with sand, a little more of it obscured every day. A retreat into a personal nothingness — a Big Empty of the mind.

He knew at times they had her strapped down. Sometimes she would wake up terrorized by the North Koreans or some other secret demons, and she would rush for the door, finding remarkable agility in eighty-two-year-old legs. They never had her restrained when family came to visit, of course, but Colt knew it happened.

In some of her more lucid moments, his grandmother had told him during one of his visits, and somehow, he knew that for that moment, she was herself, fully cognizant of her surroundings.

Who wants to see their loved ones like that? He wanted to remember his grandmother sitting on her porch, a pitcher of iced tea sweating on the low table beside her, her finger marking a page in the big leather-bound volume of Melville. He wanted to talk to her about the *Red Badge of Courage.* She would help him see the book in a new light, or at least explain the Jesus thing. He didn't want his father's terse explanations; he wanted his grandmother's insights. He wanted her to pull the tattered old volume off one of her cluttered shelves and flip knowingly through its pages, pointing out passages that supported what she was saying.

Her living room, the same one his own family now used, had been a haven, an escape, a dimension removed from the perpetual emptiness that surrounded them. Those books, hundreds of them, had been his grandmother's way of coping with a life that had so little else in it to fill the time. It was how she found her own definition of meaning, and how she inspired others. It was how she gained the education she couldn't afford and the experiences that the Big Empty had denied her.

When Colt's parents moved into the house, they'd put most of the books in boxes and stored them at the back of what had been the garage. His father had converted the space into a room for his grandmother, but he'd left an area at the back for storage. Colt was about ten then, but he'd made sure all the books were boxed up, and sometimes at night, when his parents were asleep, he would sneak into the back room and pull out a volume at random. He'd read the entire *Count of Monte Cristo* by the dim overhead, sitting on the floor while the Big Empty slept in unbroken silence. His grandmother was still clear-headed enough to help him keep all the characters straight.

He didn't understand everything that had happened to her. He hadn't even heard of Alzheimer's when they'd first found out. His parents had explained it to him, but it didn't seem real. After all, his grandmother was simply getting old, getting a little confused as old people do. Sure, she was having problems putting her clothes on right, but how could that be a disease? When Charlie Weeks almost hit her coming back from Tysonville, when she'd been driving on the wrong side of the road, they'd taken her big Buick away.

Then they'd found out she'd stopped eating. Colt and his mother had gone over one Saturday morning and found groceries rotting in a sack on the kitchen table. Stinking juices soaked through the brown paper of the bags, lettuce turned to putrid goop inside. Tomatoes had formed little pools of mush, their insides no longer contained by the flimsy outer skin. Milk, thick as wet cement, sat moldering in the bottle.

It had been a week since they'd taken her for groceries, and she'd left them on the table, not noticing their demise and oblivious to her own hunger. After that, Colt's father had decided she couldn't live alone, and he, Colt, Manny, and Manny's father turned the garage of her own house into a room for her, a place to keep her safe, a place with one window and no books.

He'd gone with his father on some of the trips, taking his grandmother first to Gunyon, then to Lubbock, and finally all the way to Dallas. The doctors had poked and prodded, talked and tested, scowled and crossed their arms, done scans and X-rays until Colt wondered if they were trying to confirm a diagnosis or disprove it.

The good news was that Alzheimer's alone wasn't fatal, not in a physical sense. It killed the mind, devoured the soul, but it left the body intact. His grandmother could live for years, the doctors told them. "Every day is a gift from God," his grandmother used to say.

Except he didn't see how it could be a gift to live like that. Soon, she couldn't tell one day from another, each just another unanchored moment in a blur of perpetual confusion. Colt felt sure that people treated animals better than their own. A sick cow would be put out of its misery, but not his grandmother.

She'd stayed in the house for a few months, but it soon became clear that it was more than any of them could handle. She needed help eating, going to the bathroom, getting dressed. The slightest distraction and his grandmother might be out the door, heading for the gate, throwing rocks at the cows. All of that was before Doc Lambeau had moved to town, and every infection, every bout of pneumonia meant a trip to Gunyon, often with her fighting their attempts to get her in the car. They'd had to accept that they couldn't provide round-the-clock care. It had been a bitter realization. The woman who had taken care of them, who'd raised Colt's father, who'd considered Darla as her own daughter, who doted on Colt, was now too much for them, her gifts to them overshadowed by the demands of her disease.

They all felt like failures when they'd sent her away to the place in Gunyon, with its wretched smells and bedsores and patients howling with their sundry pains. That had been five years ago.

He'd seen a hint of moisture in his father's eyes that day, the only time Colt could ever remember seeing his old man close to tears. Colt's grandfather had died before he was born, but he doubted that was as wrenching. Sure, his grandfather had died of lung cancer, but from everything Colt had heard, he'd kept the ailment to himself. No one was aware that his humanity was rotting away until it was gone.

He stared out the truck window at a cluster of live oaks as his family sped past and wondered what it must be like. How must it feel to lose a little more of yourself every day? And once it's gone, what's left? What are you if you don't have your memories and dreams? His mind was wandering now, moving gently away from the cruel reality of his grandmother's fate. He wanted to believe that her soul was safe, that what the Bible said — what she herself had told him years ago — was true, that God would sort out the shards of her soul amid the broken pieces of her mind. But what happened when the mind was too broken to be the warren for the soul, yet the body wasn't ready to set it free?

Colt shifted his weight again and the vinyl of the truck seat squawked in protest. He'd always thought about himself in terms of things that defined him: football, the ranch, his family. What if all those were somehow swept from his mind? Who would he be? Would he be anyone at all?

Ever since he'd damaged his leg, he'd found his mind, in times of idleness, swirling around these questions of self-awareness. It wasn't something he'd thought about before, but without football, he'd realized how quickly he could lose a part of himself. He loved the game, and he and Manny Garrison sometimes would sneak a junker from the service station and drive out to the Tie Bow and sit on the hood, gazing at the stars and dreaming of their future in football.

That was the way it was going to be. He and Manny and 'The Plan:' After high school, they'd enroll in the Air Force, play football for the academy, learn to fly the F-22, and get assigned to some exotic locale as officers, and catch the eye of some foreign girls who'd never eaten chicken fried steak or knew how to saddle a horse.

Then it was gone in one buck of a horse, one tumble over a fence. He and Manny still talked about joining the Air Force, but the recurring pain in his leg made Colt doubt his chances of passing the physical. Colt's father had hated the idea all along. It was one of their few sources of conflict. His dad hated anything to do with the military, a bitterness wrapped up in the changes he'd seen in his own father after Korea and the unhealed wounds of a long-dead brother still rotting somewhere in the jungles of Vietnam.

Since the accident, Colt began to become more and more certain that he'd never see Colorado Springs, never march on the parade grounds at the Air Force Academy or slide into the cockpit of the F-22, never pull back on the stick and feel the g-forces slam him against the seat as the futuristic stealth machine shot toward the stratosphere. Now, it hurt just to walk most days. He knew his Air Force dreams were done. Lying in an old truck bed, staring at the sky, the stars of the Tie Bow seemed to shine down on him with the weight of truth.

He scanned the roadside as the outlying buildings of Gunyon moved toward them. No, he was of this place, and he didn't intend to hide from that. He glanced at his father, stone-faced, his hands in a drivers-ed-perfect ten-and-two position on the wheel. It would be an honor to emulate this man. His father was honest and hardworking, a man who took care of his family, a man who'd scooped up his broken son and wasn't afraid to ask a woman doctor for help in his moment of desperation. Trace Malloy commanded a quiet respect. He was the kind of man that you didn't want to disappoint, and Colt had tried to live up to that responsibility. He knew many of his friends, including Manny, didn't feel this way about their fathers, but Colt had always felt his father was different.

Why, then, did his dad find his plans to stay in Conquistador and work on the ranch almost as revolting as his dream of joining the Air Force? In recent weeks, they'd stopped talking about it, even at supper, which was when they usually handled the weighty matters of the day.

"You need to go to college, son, and study something with a future, like computers," his father had insisted the last time they'd discussed what Colt wanted to do with his life. And do what? Colt had wondered. Work at AzTech? He looked at the coagulated maroon stripe on his father's chin. Just visiting the plant had damn near killed him. Colt knew he couldn't work there. That wasn't the life he knew or wanted. He wanted to be outside, to be able to move around and breathe the air, not anchored to some ergonomic chair, walled off in a little cloth box staring at a screen all day.

"Most parents would be proud of their sons for carrying on the family traditions," he'd countered.

"What traditions? Ranching? Hell, son, it's been dying for the past hundred years," his father had snapped. "It's been dying almost since the day it got started. You damn near got your leg torn off and you aren't even old enough to drive. There's no future. I ought to know because there's hardly any present. And hell, most of the past is just made up, made to look all fancy for the movies and to sit around and tell stories."

"It was good enough for you," Colt had said. "You never made it to the Merchant Marine. You came back from Kansas in an all-fired hurry."

That had pretty much ended it. Colt knew his father wanted something better for him. He knew his father was invoking the old 'do as I say, not as I do' clause that parents so often used on their children. But he also knew what had happened during those frozen days in Kansas. His father had a chance to get out, a chance to do something different somewhere else, and he'd turned around and headed home. Uncle Matthew had left, but Colt's father felt the strange call of the Big Empty, the beckoning of a home where God never intended anyone to live. It was a desolation so complete that its emptiness—the big overturned fruit bowl of never-ending sky, the land unfurling toward the horizon drawn ruler-straight just at the edge of sight—became its beauty. It was, in simple terms, home. And it called to them, Colt and his father alike, a siren wail from oblivion, evoking both a physical place and, perhaps even more powerful, a state of mind.

But what if...he hesitated, unsure he wanted to let the thought finish forming...what if it was something else that held them there? What if it was...fear? What if his father, in the face of overwhelming change, had decided on that frozen Kansas morning that it was all just too much and retreated back to the empty comfort of the only place he'd ever known? What if his ambition simply hadn't been enough to override the battering tide of the familiar, a tide that bound him to the place like a castaway from the larger world? What if he, Colt, felt the same thing? What if the pain in his leg, the constant reminder of the dreams he'd lost, had become an anchor. Did he really want to be like his father, or was he just embracing the pain that would keep him tethered to this place for the rest of his life, like his father and grandfather before him?

He whisked the thought from his mind. His grandmother always told him God had a plan for him, and his job was to figure out what it was. Now, he knew it wasn't the Air Force, so why wasn't it to stay here and carry on the way his family had for generations? Besides, the future was on the doorstep. Change was on the horizon—literally—as the gleaming new chip plant rose from the empty plains. By the time he graduated from high school, Conquistador would be a different place. Everyone was talking about it. There would be three times as many people, from all over the country if not the world. There'd be new streets and schools, probably an eleven-man football team and fancy foreign cars. His father knew the change was necessary, but he struggled to make peace with it. For Colt, it seemed less intimidating. He could embrace the new Conquistador, he would welcome the world it would bring, but he could also hold on to the soul of this place.

Trace turned the wheel of the truck and eased it into the parking lot. Colt saw the stained beige brick of the nursing home with the long, covered roof leading to the double-glass doors at the entrance. The truck stopped and his mother and father opened the doors and stepped out. He eased across the seat, feeling the warmth where his mother had sat silently for the entire trip. She held the door and helped him out. The day had clouded up, and even though it was hot, there was a dampness that hinted of a rare rainstorm, making his leg ache.

He stepped down from the truck, a movement that was still awkward to him, and he felt a jolt of pain run up his leg and into his hip. He turned and followed his parents toward the building, steeling himself to say a final farewell to the woman who'd helped define his life and introduced him to the vast and unfathomable universe beyond the void of West Texas. He'd read somewhere, in one of his grandmother's books, that life was about finding the simple truths and embracing them. In spite of the adventures that lured fictional heroes to faraway lands, Colt knew he'd found his own truth: He was going to be a cowboy, just like his father and his father before him. ✯

CHAPTER 14

BLAINE WITHERSPOON STARED at the message on the computer screen in disbelief. Fear washed over him, rising from the base of his spine, moving upward toward his skull. This was it. He was done for. Finished before he'd really gotten started. He could feel tears starting to well up and he pulled off his glasses and pinched the bridge of his nose. He needed to think. He needed a plan. How had things gotten this out of control?

He knew the answer. He'd been distracted — no, immersed in — the unending litany of crises that needed his attention. The thousand interruptions in his time had finally sunk him. Today had been no different. He'd gotten in early and settled at his desk ready to listen to the conference call that Jack Watley, the AzTech CFO, was scheduled to hold with Wall Street analysts. It was part of the public company routine. Every quarter, Watley walked analysts through the chipmaker's income statement and they asked questions, digging for clues that might help them recommend whether investors should buy or sell AzTech's stock.

Actually, it was a cozier relationship than that. Tech was the darling of Wall Street. A company with few assets other than a sock puppet could rocket to a billion dollars in market value overnight. AzTech had been in business for decades, and its chips were helping to fuel the booming demand for computers and other high-tech gear as more consumers found their way onto the World Wide Web. All the analysts were telling investors to buy — the only question was how much money the company would make and how long its rise would persist. Witherspoon had tuned in and listened to Watley's dull monotone. Then the questions started, with one analyst after another congratulating the CFO on another "great quarter."

They had reason to be upbeat. Most of them had bought the stock for their personal accounts before they told investors to, giving their personal investments an added boost.

By the time the questions started, Witherspoon was studying the latest report on the filtration system, which still didn't seem to be functioning right. He muted the phone so he could concentrate. After about ten minutes, the other line on his phone lit up. He ignored it. Then, his email notification dinged. Then again. And again. Another ding. Then a staccato burst of dings. The phone fell silent, then rang again.

He realized the conference call had ended, but he hadn't heard anything that was said. His voicemail light flashed. He clicked the mouse button, bringing the PC on his desk out of sleep mode. He opened his mailbox and a series of unopened emails poured down the screen. The subject line of the first one was "what the fuck????"

It was from Tom Bledsoe, head of the main wafer fab — the chip factory — in Milpitas. Witherspoon opened the message; it had one line: "I can't believe you'd screw us all like this."

He glanced over at the stock ticker that was permanently updating in the corner of his screen and saw that AzTech shares had plunged four dollars and fifty cents in the past fifteen minutes. He opened another message. "I knew you'd fuck that up. As stupid as it was to build a plant in the middle of nowhere, putting you in charge was even dumber."

One after another, other plant managers and mid-level execs across the company were launching profanity-laden fusillades at him. What the hell was going on? What had he done, or more important, what did they *think* he'd done? Witherspoon logged onto the company website and went to the investor relations page. The replay of the conference call wasn't available yet.

He picked up the phone and listened to the first voicemail message. "Blaine, it's Bill Tomlinson up in Fishkill. I gotta say I'm just stunned that you would hide something like this. If you were having problems, why didn't you call? Jesus. This is going to hurt a lot of people."

He opened the next one: "Goddammit Witherspoon! You know the rules. No surprises! Fifty percent? You're cutting production estimates by fifty fucking percent and you didn't tell anyone?"

Witherspoon squinted at the phone. He hadn't cut the production estimates. He'd come to doubt them, given the delays and difficulties they'd been having, and he was afraid he might *have* to cut them, but it was too early for that. He'd sent the progress report to Milpitas just the week before, and he'd been clear: They were still on track to meet the first-year operating goals.

He cycled through several more messages, all berating him for his apparent deception. He glanced at the stock. It was down more than seven dollars. Even as the panic welled up inside him like some alien spawn, and he felt as if at any moment his chest might explode, he noticed one thing that was odd: No call from Soderheim. Old Soddy didn't suffer fools. If Witherspoon had screwed up as badly as his colleagues thought, why hadn't there been a blistering termination call? Where was the declaration of dismissal carried on such a torrent of profanity that even the target of the tirade had to take a moment to marvel at its creative obscenity? When Soddy had fired the Tucson plant manager, it was rumored that the invectives went on for a full twenty minutes without him even taking a breath.

And yet, he'd gotten no call. Soddy wouldn't resort to email or voicemail. He'd call directly, and if he didn't get through, he'd call the receptionist—Susie? Cindy? Whatever the hell her name was—and tell her to get him on the phone in twenty seconds or she'd be fired too.

But there was nothing. He realized Soderheim hadn't been on the conference call, either. While he usually let Watley run them, he typically was in the room, just in case someone had a question that only the CEO could answer—or in case he wanted to berate an analyst for a question he found particularly insulting. But there was no call from Watley, either, which was even more curious since Watley must have been the one who gave the response that sparked the selloff in the stock. He'd gathered that Watley had said something about the production forecast for the plant. But what? And why? If Watley questioned Witherspoon's forecast numbers, why hadn't the CFO said anything last week when he first saw them?

Witherspoon's voicemail light was still blinking, and he realized he had one final message. "Blaine," the voice was almost a whisper. "It's Craig McAlister. I'm not sure we've met, but I'm the guy who took over Tucson. Call me on my cell. It's urgent." Witherspoon dialed the number.

"Craig, it's Blaine Witherspoon. What the hell is going on?"

"You've seen the stock, right?"

"Yeah." Witherspoon pondered the screen. It was down almost eight dollars. It seemed to be stabilizing, but it had plunged almost thirty percent. He did a quick calculation and estimated the company had lost more than a billion dollars in market value in the past hour. "I missed the end of the call. I had a, um, meeting, but apparently something happened, and everyone thinks it's my fault"

"Yeah, I know," McAlister replied. "Did you put anything in your numbers that indicated you were coming up short on the production forecasts?"

"No," Witherspoon said, a little more emphatically than he would have liked. "Absolutely not. Everything here is, uh, right on track. I have no reason to doubt the forecast."

"Well, that Merrill analyst, Loudermilk, you know how he scours the production stuff."

"Yeah," Witherspoon cut in. "Bledsoe calls him a 'wafer chaser' because he's so obsessed with the output at every plant."

"Right," McAlister said. "Well, he started out praising what we'd done here in Tucson, saying he was impressed that we'd been able to boost wafer production by thirty percent. Then he asked if production for the Conquistador plant was still in line with the forecasts, and Watley said 'Well, the plant's still in startup mode, but we think we're probably going to revise the initial forecast down a bit.' And Loudermilk asks if Watley can provide any guidance on what 'a bit' meant. So Watley—and this is just unbelievable—but Watley says, 'well, it's still early but it could be as much as fifty percent for the first year.'"

"What?" Witherspoon was stunned. Watley had just thrown that out on the call? Without talking to him? "That makes no sense," Witherspoon protested. "He didn't even talk to me. He has no idea…." He didn't finish the sentence.

"Honestly," McAlister said, "I don't know what your situation is there. It's a startup plant, it's an initial forecast, I mean, the stock will recover. The only reason the market is reacting like this is because, well, to be honest, everyone on Wall Street thought your plant was a dumb idea, and Soderheim kept talking it up. The more they doubted him, the more he pushed it."

Witherspoon knew that was true, and it wasn't just investors who hated the idea of a wafer fab in West Texas. Most of the other company executives did, too. But Old Soddy had come from the Midwest and wanted to see the economic prosperity of Silicon Valley shared with "flyover country" as he called it. It was his pet project—bringing the tech boom to the middle of nowhere. He was now almost seventy years old, and this would be the exclamation mark on his legacy. As for Witherspoon, he'd been happy to ride on Old Soddy's quest for public relations glory. He might have had to wait another decade to run a plant. So he took the job no one else wanted. The Big Empty, for all the potential pitfalls, was his fast-track to the most sought-after currency of the tech world—stock options. AzTech showered them out to plant managers like zookeepers dished out peanuts to elephants.

Witherspoon checked the share price again. The stock's plunge seemed to have halted just above eight dollars, but his beloved options had been obliterated in a matter of hours.

"This is crazy, Craig," Witherspoon said. "I didn't change the forecast, and I don't know why Watley would say that."

"Yeah. Well, it gets crazier."

"What do you mean?"

"Look," McAlister said, "I haven't even been in this job a year. And you know this place was a mess when I got here. We'd never hit the numbers, all kinds of fits and starts on the line, we kept losing the recipe, cost overruns constantly, just one disaster after another. The weird thing was, I kept going over the old reports, and it didn't make sense."

"What do you mean?" Witherspoon asked, though he wasn't sure he cared. Couldn't McAlister see he had bigger problems at the moment?

"I couldn't figure out some of the expense lines in the budget. There were things like "HVAC upgrade."

Witherspoon frowned, suddenly more interested. "That doesn't make sense," he said. "That air conditioning system was brand new, and it was built specifically to handle that environment. I know because we based our design here on it."

"Yeah, well, the weird thing is that I couldn't find any record of upgrades actually being made."

"What are you saying?"

"I'm not sure. Just like everything else, the records here are in a bit of a shambles, and I'm still piecing stuff together. But one thing I found was that the production problems were actually worse than I'd been led to believe."

"How's that possible?" Witherspoon asked. By all accounts, the Tucson startup had been an unmitigated disaster, and after Soddy's blistering termination of Harcourt, the previous manager, McAlister had been hired from tech giant Intel to clean it up and bring some credibility to the operation.

"Well, all I know is that I went over everything with my finance guy," McAlister said. "As near as we could tell, they've been overstating chip production since the beginning."

"But how? Corporate would catch that."

"Yeah, but here's the weird part. Once we found the error, we adjusted it in this quarter's report that we sent to Corporate last week."

"Wait, but you just said on the call that Watley said your production..."

"Went up, yeah, but it didn't. The actual numbers were about twenty percent *below* what had been reported. We told

Watley we needed to restate the production figure back to the beginning."

"What did he say?"

"Oh, he acted very concerned," McAlister said. "But he didn't change it. He rewrote my report and inflated the numbers even higher, so it looks like we had this great turnaround."

Witherspoon's mind raced. How could a CFO ignore a material misstatement—to use accounting lingo—of that magnitude? He'd never heard of an executive just basically erasing one set of numbers and writing in another. There had to be more to it. But even so, how did all this relate to him?

"So," McAlister continued, "I couldn't figure out how they could get away with this until I heard what Watley said about Conquistador. Something is very, very wrong here Blaine."

"They're pulling down my numbers so they can make yours look better," Witherspoon said, as if he were in a trance. His breathing had become short and shallow, and the room seemed to flutter.

"That's what it seems like," McAlister said. "You couldn't tell if you looked at the overall numbers, so no one noticed except for Loudermilk because he's such a chip nerd. I guess Corporate's taken so much shit from the Street over the situation here, they needed to show improvement. When I found out things were worse than anyone thought, well, they weren't about to let that get out."

"But," Witherspoon said feebly, "this is…."

"Illegal as shit. Yeah."

"What are you going to do?"

"I haven't decided," McAlister said. "I've copied all the files and brought them home. I never thought of myself a whistleblower, but Jesus, it sure as hell looks like accounting fraud. I really should take it to the SEC, but of course, that'd be the end of my career." No one liked a rat, especially in Corporate America.

And maybe my career, too, Witherspoon thought. He and McAlister agreed to stay in touch, but by the time Witherspoon hung up the phone, he was in a daze. His phone kept ringing, and his emails kept dinging, but he sat staring blankly at the floor of his office, gazing into the pattern on the shallow pile of the carpet squares.

He tried to unpack the situation, but his mind was a swirl of emotion and worry. What would he tell Jenna? If he lost his job out here in this unforgiving void, cut off from everything, what would they do? He had expected to bring the modern world here, to make this place livable. Now, he saw the world that he knew receding, as if he were trapped in some dungeon of his own shattered ambition.

It still didn't make sense. Why would a top executive of a Fortune 500 company cook the books? That's what they were talking about, after all. Watley had manipulated the company's financial reports and misled analysts—which in the eye of the Securities and Exchange Commission meant he had bilked investors. If the press got ahold of this, AzTech would be portrayed as, essentially, stealing from little old ladies.

Whatever Witherspoon was caught up in, it had started in Tucson. McAlister had said the first thing he spotted was unusual expenses. Finance. The finance guy would have been in a position to enter line items on the books. And the finance guy in Tucson had been…"

Witherspoon cursed under his breath as he grabbed the computer mouse. I should have done this months ago, he said to himself. He'd forgotten the first rule of corporate survival. He'd been so focused on keeping the plant on schedule—on keeping Soddy on his side—that he'd failed to protect his flank.

Everyone assumed the problems in Tucson had ended when Soddy profanely dispatched the plant manager, Darren Harcourt. Harcourt may have been inept or simply overwhelmed, but he didn't strike Witherspoon as the kind of guy who would do something criminal. No, this was the work of someone far more insidious, someone who was a manipulator and corporate climber. Someone with a shrewd eye for finance yet lacking a moral compass.

Witherspoon tapped furiously on the keyboard and soon he was paging through Howard Swain's emails. There were thousands, a never-ending stream documenting the electronic detritus of life—grocery lists, off-color jokes, bawdy comments about the receptionist, meetings, conference calls, requests for memos, receipts of memos. He searched on the name "Watley."

He flipped through more memos sent to all the finance managers, an exchange about an annual golf outing that Swain and Watley apparently planned to take in Scotland, a message labeled "haha" with an inappropriate, and dated, quip about First Lady Hillary Clinton and health care. Then, he found it: A message from Watley, but it was sent to and from what Witherspoon gathered was a personal email account. It didn't have an "aztech.com" address. It was written about three weeks earlier with the message line "Tucson." Witherspoon opened the thread, scrolled to the bottom and the read the messages in the order they were written and answered.

WATLEY: We have a problem. The new guy is poking around the accounting.

SWAIN: He won't find anything.

WATLEY: He already did. He wants to adjust the production numbers down. We need them to go up.

SWAIN: That's not on me.

WATLEY: Maybe not, but I need you to fix it.

SWAIN (four hours later): We can take the numbers down here in Texas. I don't trust the forecasts anyway. The purification system's not up to spec, internal temperatures are too high, dust is a bigger problem. I don't see how we'll hit the numbers. We'll be lucky to get any production at all in the next year.

WATLEY: What about Witherspoon?

SWAIN: He's in over his head. This whole operation was a stupid idea, and the only reason he thinks it can work is because he's sucking up to Soddy.

WATLEY: He'll never sign off on a new forecast.

SWAIN: He doesn't need to know. McAlister either. You'll get the reports next week. You've got to compile all the regionals, right?

WATLEY: You do it. You want the job.

SWAIN: Fuck you. I don't have the final signoff here anyway. Can't be me.

WATLEY: Jesus.

SWAIN: No need to draw attention to it unless anyone asks, but it could cover Tucson. What about Soddy?

WATLEY: I'll tell him. He's going to be disappointed in his golden boy.

SWAIN: Withy's toast. :-(.

WATLEY: Almost feel bad for him. Hope you can turn the place around.

SWAIN: I'm a miracle worker, baby! Just remember. Two years, corner office, Bloomberg machine, hot secretary.

WATLEY: If Withy gets canned, what happens to the stock?

SWAIN: Who gives a shit?

WATLEY: Can't have margin calls.

SWAIN: Oh yeah, forgot, Mr. Leverage. Should be fine. The Street hates this place. Stock'll drop and bounce back. Buying opp!!!

Witherspoon stared at the message for several minutes before he hit print. He felt numb, not just at the betrayal, but at the realization that everything he had done, or tried to do, had been futile. This plant was never going to succeed. He didn't know exactly what Swain and Watley were doing, but it seemed pretty clear that Swain planned to step into Witherspoon's job, restore the numbers he'd fudged, look like a hero, and get a cushy corporate gig back in Milpitas. Given the "Mr. Leverage" comment, Witherspoon assumed that Watley had been borrowing money against his corporate stock. He'd heard that the board offered low-interest loans to some execs, but that was way above his pay grade—and now he was certain it always would be.

Obviously, the plan had been to ignore the Conquistador forecast and make it appear as if Tucson was turning around. That would boost the stock, and no one would notice because Witherspoon's plant wasn't in production yet and wasn't adding to earnings. If Loudermilk, the wafer chaser, hadn't raised the issue, Witherspoon might not have realized what was happening until Swain made his move.

Of course, the analyst's question had forced their hand. He didn't know what to do. If McAlister went to the SEC, should he join him? Should he share the email exchange he just printed? God, how had it come to this? If he went to the feds, he'd never work in tech again. There'd be no grand plan, no rise through the corporate ranks, no golden boy status. It was all slipping away—the house, the golf course, the Sunday morning tee times, the congratulatory trips back to Milpitas to join Old Soddy on his yacht.

The phone rang again, and Witherspoon ignored it. This sort of thing just didn't happen. Watley was a top executive at a major company. People like that didn't manipulate earnings. Swain was smarmy as hell, and he might have been a thief, maybe even an embezzler—but Watley? The CFO? A senior executive? This just didn't happen at major corporations. That's the sort of thing that you found in too-good-to-be-true penny stocks.

Witherspoon felt paralyzed with fear and mired in uncertainty all at once. What was his next move? How could he salvage his career? He thought about quitting, but quickly discounted it. That would make him look guilty, and Swain would still win. No, he would take this email, and he would show it to Soderheim himself. Soddy liked him, and he'd listen to him. He *had* to listen to him. He'd want to know that his CFO was a crook, wouldn't he? Surely, he wouldn't believe that Witherspoon had botched the start up.

His mind raced. No, that's exactly what he would think. Why wouldn't he? It was a far more plausible explanation than anything Witherspoon could offer. Failing at a successful startup, especially under the conditions in Conquistador, was entirely believable, even likely. Soddy would simply assume he'd put his trust in the wrong person and move on.

Witherspoon walked over to the printer in his office, picked up the email thread and read it again. Swain, that sniveling bastard. But would an outsider see a conspiracy? Really, all Swain was suggesting was that the forecasts in Conquistador were inaccurate. "It could cover Tucson" didn't mean Watley was manipulating those numbers, although Witherspoon was sure that's exactly what happened. The email, though, wasn't really proof of anything. It *looked* bad, but it didn't really prove anything. At best, it might support whatever McAlister had found, but Witherspoon had no idea what that might be.

No, if he tried to take the email to Soddy, Witherspoon would come across as a pathetic and desperate fool who was trying to cover his own shortcomings by blaming others. It was exactly the kind of behavior that Soddy hated.

He could confront Swain. Hell, maybe he should borrow a page from Malloy's playbook and walk down the hall and punch him in the nose. But anything he did would just make him look more guilty, as if by professing his innocence he was merely inviting blame.

He couldn't prove Swain had changed the numbers. After all, the CFO was the one saying his numbers were wrong. He was trapped. He'd been outmaneuvered and now everything he'd worked for would come to an end. All that was left was waiting to find out when and how. He checked his watch. It was almost noon. He had to go. At least it was a Friday. He'd have the weekend to think about his next move.

He began gathering his things, shoving the printed email thread into his backpack, the receptionist—Sallie?—knocked quietly on the door, eased it open and leaned her head in.

"Mr. Witherspoon?"

"Yes."

"I just got a call from Corporate. They asked me to make sure you knew that Mr. Soderheim is sailing back from his vacation early and wants to talk to you first thing Monday. ✯

CHAPTER 15

"YOU SHOULDN'T BE HERE," Roland Kerr said as he shoved the gleaming dome of his head into the doorway of Trace Malloy's tiny office.

"I'm just checking the markets, catching up on some paperwork," Malloy said without taking his eyes off the computer screen in front of him.

"Go home, Trace. Spend some time with Darla and Colt. How's he holding up?"

"Fine. He's a tough kid."

"Like his old man." Kerr patted the doorframe and disappeared. Everything Malloy had said was a lie, of course. He'd been in the office for an hour and hadn't accomplished anything. His mind spun like a flywheel. He'd been sitting, staring at the screen yet unaware of the cattle auction prices flickering in front of him. He couldn't get his brain to focus on anything.

He leaned back in the plastic typist's chair that was the only seat in his office and rubbed his eyes. He'd had to get out of the house—*her* house, his parents' house. Everywhere he'd looked, he was reminded of his mother, and when he wasn't, when his mind found a sliver of peace, Darla would start sobbing. He moved his hands away from his eyes and stared at the ceiling.

The florescent lights were exactly the same as those that had illuminated his mother's room in the nursing home. His mind flashed to a picture of her lifeless body, pale and vacant, lying in the bed. She'd passed before they arrived. He hadn't gotten to say goodbye. He hadn't been able to ask her to forgive him for any number of things he felt needed forgiving, not the least of which was not visiting her for months.

He forced his mind back to the present. Why had they done this to the old ranch house anyway? What did they need florescent lighting for? The place had been standing for a hundred years. Couldn't they have left its guts alone? Did Frye have to rip out the old cedar planks and plaster and replace them with wallboard and drop ceilings and that brilliant, unforgiving light?

He slumped forward and brought his gaze back to his desk. He made a half-hearted grab for a stack of papers piled near the monitor. It was the latest report from the county water commission that someone had left there while he was over in Gunyon. He scanned the pages and a grin unfurled under his mustache. The commission recommended against the homies' plans for building a golf course, which they'd been awfully quiet about lately, and it also proposed draining their little lake during the driest summer months and restricting lawn watering. It was a water conservation plan just like big cities used.

The influx of new residents, the demands of the ranch and the AzTech plant, and the "water amenities" of Rolling Ranch Estates — the evaporation pool, as Malloy liked to call the fountain and pond at the front of the subdivision — "presented serious constraints on the available water supply of the region, especially in times of drought," the report said. The analysis stopped short of addressing the real monster, the water usage by the AzTech plant. That didn't surprise Malloy. The county had too much invested in AzTech. No point in biting the hand that feeds, he thought with a twinge of disgust.

The recommendation wasn't law, of course, but it gave the county commissioners something to point to if they decided to get tough with the homies.

Malloy realized he'd been reviewing the report for almost a full five minutes without thinking about his mother's death. Even so, the two were related. The water dispute had provoked the conversation with Blaine Witherspoon, and his insults about Malloy's mother had prompted Malloy to break Witherspoon's nose.

As he ran through the relationship, the hollowness returned, an unrelenting undertow on his heart. God, how he missed her. His father's death hadn't been like this. He and his father had loved each other, but there had been a comfortable distance built on years of respect and obedience.

His mother had been his lifeline, his confidant and consoler. His father's death had been sad and difficult. His mother's seemed insurmountable. Each new day seemed like a hole in the world that he was stepping through, leaving her further behind each time.

He wondered if the insignificance of his life could ever mitigate the void that now seemed to engulf his soul. His mother had wanted something better for him, and he had stubbornly rejected it. When he left for the Merchant Marine, she had kissed him and wished good luck upon him. His father had merely grunted goodbye and shook his hand. His father hadn't criticized his decision, but Malloy could see that the older man expected his son to be back in Conquistador in time to help birth the next round of calves.

His father had been right. Malloy had come back just a few months later. Even after all these years he wasn't sure he knew why. His mind flashed back to that lonely, cold afternoon hitchhiking through Oklahoma and the Springsteen song on the radio. "Is a dream a lie if it don't come true?"

That line from that damned song haunted him still. He did, in fact, know why he'd come back, but he didn't like to admit it, even in the solitude of his own mind. He'd come back because he was scared. The closer he'd moved toward the unknown, the more afraid he'd become.

So he'd come back, settled into the comfort of marriage and responsible adulthood, removing forever the temptation of leaving. It was the life he knew he could lead. His family needed stability, certainty, the kind of comfort that comes with putting down roots. And where better to sink those roots than in Conquistador, the very land he knew better than any other, an engulfing emptiness from which he couldn't break free, but that he could fill with the familiar? He loved Darla and Colt immensely. He had no regrets, except that he hadn't had the courage in his youth to confront his fears, and that cowardice created a question he could never answer. What if?

His mother had wanted him to know that answer, even if it meant he never came back. She knew the cost of staying and the torment of a question unanswered. Had she answered the question for herself? Had she found relief in all those books that filled the house until it seemed some days as if the mustiness from their pages would stifle them all? He and his mother had never talked about her dreams.

Later that day, he would watch as they put her in the ground next to his father. Caleb and Nelda, together again for eternity. One plot over, they were saving a spot for him and Darla. Maybe Colt, too. Dammit. That boy had to get out. He had to find the courage Trace couldn't.

He looked at the water commission report again. He had no right to smirk. Like it or not, Blaine Witherspoon and the rest of his homies *were* the way out—not just for him or Colt, but for everyone in the Big Empty.

This time, it would take more than a little frost on the saddle to make him give up. If Colt wanted to stay here, sink down roots like the three generations of Malloys before him, then let the boy make that choice, he told himself. Just let there be something worth staying for beyond long-dead grandeur and the pitiful prospects of a business that existed at the whim of Nature and a brainless collection of cows.

Malloy finally gave up pretending to work and decided to return to the house. Colt had gone to school in hopes of taking his mind off his grandmother's death. Darla was coping the way she always did when she was distraught—by cooking. Malloy walked in just before lunch to find the table lined with a stuffed chicken dinner, cornbread, mashed potatoes and gravy, glazed carrots, and pecan pie.

Darla smiled, her face lined with red stripes from the intermittent showers from her eyes. "I thought you might want some lunch," she said, as he stared in disbelief. Then she laughed in spite of herself, and so did he.

Neither of them, though, felt like eating, and they contemplated their food in silence until the warm vapors faded and even the potatoes grew cold. Suddenly, Darla began to sob again.

Malloy got up and rounded the table, cradling his wife's head against his chest to comfort her.

"I'm sorry," she said. "I just can't help it. I've been like this all day."

"It's okay," Malloy said, and he bent down and kissed her forehead. Her skin felt clammy.

"No, I don't mean to, I just miss her so much."

"I know. Me too." His voice was coming out in little more than a whisper.

He bent down and lifted her head up and kissed her on the lips. Her face was damp, almost soggy, and her lips tasted salty from tears.

He had always found Darla attractive. When they were in elementary school, she was the only girl he knew who wasn't afraid of snakes and frogs, and they became fast friends, tromping through creeks and scooping critters and muck out of stock tanks.

Later, it was her smile and her sense of humor that did it for him. Then, along about high school, he began to realize that Darla had what his mother called "just darn good sense." When he had left after graduation, she never told him not to go. She had simply said that they would find each other later, when he figured out what he wanted to do. She wasn't angry or even terribly upset. She would wait tables at the diner, the one that closed four years later, and save her money and join him wherever he was.

And later still, after he'd come back and they'd gotten married, it became even more clear: marriage and motherhood suited her. They had tried for years to have Colt, and his delivery was difficult. They had to go all the way to Lubbock to have the baby, and the doctors advised against more children. But she had rejoiced in Colt. That, for her, was good enough.

For as long as Malloy had adored her, he couldn't bear to see her cry. The wonderful smile would crumble. Her eyes would cloud with despair. All happiness drained from her face in a single flood, leaving reddened streaks in its path.

When they were eight, they'd been playing in Darla's yard. The game, to her, was "house." Malloy had agreed to play the husband only if she allowed him to have the occupation of international spy. He returned from a particularly long mission to the far side of her father's hay bales in the lower pasture to find Darla sitting on an old tricycle with the front wheel turned backwards, so that the handlebars pointed away from her.

"This is my super-vac'm machine," she'd said, punctuating the announcement with a "vroom vroom." As a spy, young Trace could appreciate such innovative gadgets, but Darla was missing something. She was rocking back and forth, but the super-vacuum wasn't moving.

"What you need now is a little push," he'd said, giving the trike a shove from behind. She'd screamed "no" but by then the tricycle had already lunged forward, and Darla wailed in pain. She held out her foot, and blood poured down her heel from a gash just above her ankle. She'd held her leg there, extended sideways, and Malloy had seen a hunk of skin dangling like a piece of deli meat that had gotten stuck halfway through the slicer.

To this day, Malloy didn't know exactly what had happened. Her foot must have been lodged between the pedal and the front axle, and when he pushed, the pedal turned and stripped the skin.

Screaming, Darla hobbled into the house, leaving Malloy alone in the yard. He hadn't known what to do. He didn't want to go home and tell his parents, and he didn't want to wait for Darla's parents to come out and scold him. He'd simply squatted down in the yard, too terrified to move, like some small animal hoping not to be noticed on the flat open expanse. He must have looked like a rabbit trying to hide on top of a kitchen table.

After a ten-minute eternity, Darla's mother had emerged, carrying the girl in her arms. Darla's ankle had a big round bandage on it, ringed by the orange tinge of mercurochrome.

"Trace Malloy!" his future wife had screamed. "Don't you ever do that again! You stupid head!"

For a moment, Malloy was paralyzed. Then, Darla's mother had smiled in way that told him all would be forgiven. She'd set the child down on the porch and went back inside without saying a word. Darla had sulked for half an hour and Malloy canceled the rest of his spy missions until he eventually won her over and made her smile again. Ever since, though, the sight of her crying filled him with a desire to make her stop.

As she sobbed against him now in the dining room, he leaned forward and kissed her again, longer and more passionately than before. Then again. His wife's lips were wet and salty, and he could feel the resistance in them. With the third kiss, he felt the reluctance snap and give way. They stood up and backed toward the bedroom, and as they moved down the hallway her hesitation returned.

"Trace, we can't..."

"Of course we can." He kissed her again, an unrelenting embrace that melted her defenses.

They made love without even closing the curtains, ignoring the unnecessary habit of seeking privacy in the middle of nowhere. Afterwards, as they lay on the bed – what had once been his parents' bed—Darla began to cry again.

"I can't believe we did that on the day of your mother's funeral."

"She'd probably get a kick out of it," Malloy said, half whispering. There was a long pause, and then he added: "You know, she always wanted us to be happy."

"She was a good woman."

Malloy nodded.

"I know the Lord needs her," Darla went on. "But it's just so hard to let go."

Malloy lay on the bed in silence. Darla hadn't said whether she was happy, and Malloy didn't press the point. Mourning aside, he had no idea whether his wife truly was happy. Was this the life she wanted? He knew it was the life she'd always envisioned, even back in the days when he'd maimed her with the tricycle. But that wasn't the same thing. What if she really wanted to meet up with him in San Francisco? He'd always thought of Darla as too pragmatic to dream of a different life. He always figured she'd say there was no point, that you live the life God prescribes for you.

What if she had had dreams of escape every bit as wild as his had been and she'd just never told anyone? He wondered, for the first time since they'd known each other, what was her Merchant Marine?

The post-coital exhaustion overtaking him, Malloy began to doze. His mother drifted in and out of his semi-dream state. He saw her driving her big Buick down the road to Gunyon, dressed up for a day of shopping. He saw her, shotgun pulled to her shoulder, taking aim at a rattlesnake that had slithered near the chicken coop. He saw her chopping wood in the winter and patiently helping him snap up the dreaded snowsuit. He felt her cool hand on his forehead as he lay sick with a fever.

Then, suddenly, she was old and jabbing a finger at him, her face contorted in anger. "How could you not come to say goodbye, Trace? How could you?"

He jolted awake and lay there in desperate silence as his mind grabbed for realization amid the shards of sleep. He rose slowly and swung his legs over the side of the bed, staring at his knees as he let reality push back the squall line of his dreams. He forced himself toward the bathroom to shower. When he got out, he dug to the back of his closet for his suit. He'd already tried it on twice, and he knew it still fit, even though it had been the same one he'd bought for his father's funeral a decade earlier. Many of the people at the service wouldn't have suits at all. There wasn't much call for them in the Big Empty except when people were getting married or dying.

After he dressed, he climbed into the pickup and sped down the road toward the small lodge that Frye maintained over the propane store. Back when the company had thought about opening the ranch to hunters, they'd outfitted the building with four sleeping rooms of various sizes, a kitchen, dining area, and a front lounge. When they abandoned the hunting plans, they kept the lodge as accommodations for visiting company officials or — since there hadn't been a hotel in town in thirty-seven years — guests and out-of-town family members of employees. Malloy's brother Matthew fit the description of the latter, and Malloy decided he'd put off seeing him long enough.

Malloy's footsteps echoed on the hollow wooden steps leading to the lodge, each footfall reverberating like some war drum, warning his brother he was coming. His dress shoes cut his feet and their unworn soles felt slick, as if the stairs were covered with ice. His feet felt heavier with each "clump" on the stairs until he reached the landing at the top. He rounded the corner and saw his brother sitting on the couch, his shoeless feet propped up on the old wooden trunk that served as a coffee table. He was watching daytime television — Oprah Winfrey, it looked like, though Malloy had never seen her show.

He took a moment to study the room even though he knew it well. A stone fireplace had been built in the corner. It ran on gas supplied by the store below, an arrangement that proved easier than hauling mesquite in from the ranch. The walls of the room sprouted heads and antlers in all directions — mostly deer and antelope, a few bobcats, and one jackalope, the mythical jackrabbit with horns that was such a mainstay of Texas kitsch that Malloy had insisted on it. He and Roland Kerr had bought all the "trophies" at a taxidermist's going-out-of-business sale in Tysonville a few years back.

On the far wall was a long rectangular hat rack with "Conquistador" written in red letters on a white background. It used to hang in the old dining hall near the main ranch house, back when the ranch employed enough full-time hands to warrant a dining hall. Now, it was a decoration, a photo op for rich businessmen who'd never come. A faded orange cowboy hat hung from one of the pegs. Malloy had no idea how it got there.

Several old upholstered chairs were positioned around the room and the big-screen TV sat straight across from the couch where his brother sprawled. On the screen, women were screaming and cheering as the camera panned the audience.

Finally, when Malloy had stared down everything in the room, he turned his gaze to his brother, who hadn't turned his glance from the television. Matt Malloy was slightly shorter than his younger brother, but stretched out on the couch, it was hard to tell it. He had black hair with more of a natural wave than Trace's. Seeing him now, Trace realized his brother was developing a paunch, a testimony to too many nights cradling a beer mug and too many days with no more physical activity than squatting under a sink.

Matt was three years older than Trace, which Trace realized meant his brother must have turned thirty-eight the previous April. He hadn't seen Matthew in three years, and that visit had been brief and marred by their mother's deteriorating health. He'd taken her to Dallas for more tests and Matt had managed to find time to pull himself away from his plumbing business and stop by the hospital. They'd sat in silence in the waiting room, then argued when it was time to go about how their mother should be treated. Trace wanted her to stay in

Dallas, to stay with Matt, so she could get the best care. His mother, of course, refused, wanting to return home.

"I ain't no city gal, and I don't want to die surrounded by concrete and glass," she'd squawked in one of her more lucid moments. Matt had been all too happy to support her wishes, and Trace had been furious with him. He didn't remember Matt appearing any different then, but staring at him now, he was stunned by his brother's pasty appearance. Red blotches dotted his face, as if he'd been scrubbing with steel wool. Matt hadn't heard his brother come in.

"I see you found everything okay," Trace said, as if they'd just seen each other the day before.

Matt looked up with a start, then stood, pointing the remote at the TV to silence it.

"Well, Trace, how are you?" He swung his big hand around and offered it to his brother, who shook it formally.

It had been—what?—six months since they'd spoken, and that had been a short phone conversation. They'd argued bitterly. Mama's insurance was running out. She needed more and more care to fight the recurring infections, she needed round-the-clock supervision, and he didn't know where they were going to get the money, Trace had said. Matt didn't want to hear it. Why couldn't Trace and Darla simply take care of her? How could they keep her in a place like that? Come see for yourself, Trace had countered. Matt responded with the usual flood of excuses about the demands of his business and his inability to get away.

"Some things are more important than money," Trace had said. "This is Mama we're talking about. We don't know how long she's got."

"I'll be there when I can, Trace," Matt had said. Enraged, Trace had slammed the phone down, and they hadn't talked since. Thinking about the conversation again, Trace wanted to grab his brother by the shirt and say, "I'm glad you could finally make it out, now that she's gone." Malloy found his brother's attitude infuriating. He'd assumed that Trace and Darla would shoulder the burden of their mother's supervision just because they lived in Conquistador with her. It was as if Trace, the last brother, the one who'd stayed behind, automatically inherited sole responsibility of caring for her.

Matt, of course, had always been too busy to visit. His reasons oscillated between fortune and adversity, both of which prevented him from making the drive from Dallas. His company was doing well, or he'd met a girl and it was pretty serious, or his business was struggling and needed his attention, or he'd broken up with a girl and just couldn't handle seeing Mama right then—the excuses were recycled so often Trace could number them.

Although they were close in age, he and Matt had never been buddies growing up. Matt had been the local hell-raiser, climbing on pumpjacks and riding them like a bronco, flushing cherry bombs down the commodes at school, setting fire to just about anything that would burn. Trace had actually been embarrassed to claim him as a relative.

Matt had never paid much attention to his younger brother anyway. He had been closer to Luke, and after Luke was classified as MIA, Matt stopped talking to just about everybody for a few years. Quiet and withdrawn, he'd made good grades and had kept to himself. He helped their father with the family herd and rarely complained. Then, he hit the final years of high school and rebellion erupted from him with the force of soda erupting from a bottle that had rolled down the stairs.

After that, he was gone. Two weeks after graduation he'd loaded up the old pickup he'd bought for a few hundred dollars at Garrison's and headed east. He'd worked at odd jobs around Dallas for years — night club bouncer, restaurant manager, security guard, construction, lawn care. He'd been fired from each one, his transience drawing their mother's scorn. Through it all, Matt remained determined to stay in the city and not return to the dust, shit, searing heat, and overwhelming nothingness of Conquistador. His problem was always the same — he couldn't take orders. It was as if he were on the run, fleeing the gaping maw of the Big Empty that always seemed to be on his heels. There would be no frozen morning revelations for Matt, no quiet acquiescence to the anchors of his past. All that mattered, it seemed, was staying away.

Finally, he'd scratched together enough money and enough maturity to start his own company and make it work. Plumbing, he used to tell Trace, was the future. Nobody likes dealing with clogged drains or backed up toilets, but the rich and self-absorbed in north Dallas viewed bad plumbing as a disease — a leprosy to be addressed by someone — anyone — but them. They would pay any price to make their problems go away. "Everybody needs water, and everybody has to take a dump," Matt used to say.

Matt had built what he claimed was a profitable business. If it weren't for his past antics, Trace would have had no reason to doubt him. He had about ten employees now, and he'd moved from repair work to new construction, which let him capitalize on the housing boom in the ever-expanding Dallas suburbs. Maybe, if he saw what was going on in Rolling Ranch Estates, he'd move his business back to Conquistador, Trace thought, smiling to himself at the absurdity.

No, Matthew Malloy had left Conquistador in a busted-up truck without a rearview mirror. He'd been home only twice since, when their father died, and now. As he followed his brother down the wooden stairs of the lodge, Malloy wondered if Matt would come home to bury him when his time came. Or was his obligation to the specter of death finally paid, sealed with the last clod of dirt that would be thrown on their mother's grave in a few hours? Now that she and their father and Luke were gone, would Matt finally be free of this place?

They reached the landing and Matt fumbled in his pockets for his keys. He pulled out a ring and squeezed the black keyless entry tag. A gold bauble of an automobile a few spaces up the street chirped in response.

"Check it out," Matt said, seemingly oblivious to the fact they were about to attend his mother's funeral. "It's an Audi A6. Just got it. Sweet ride, brother. How about if I drive?"

Trace agreed, sliding into the leather seat on the passenger side. As they drove, Matt pointed out the in-dash six CD changer, the dual climate controls, the burnished wood trim, the cockpit-styled dashboard. His brother's cheerfulness rubbed like sandpaper on Trace's brain. Their mother was dead, dammit, and Matt was bragging about his car.

"Beats the hell outta some clunky old pickup, huh?" Matt said, ending the sales pitch.

Trace nodded toward the back seat.

"Can't haul much," he said flatly. His brother gave a long guffaw, drawn out like an air raid siren, and sped out the two-lane blacktop road toward Trace and Darla's house.

By the time they got there, Colt was home from school, still brooding. He was polite to his uncle, but said little as Matt shook his hand, patted him on the back, and made comments about how big he'd gotten. Matt didn't ask about the leg. Trace watched as his brother embraced Darla, lifting her off the ground and swinging her back and forth. Darla, surprised, hung limp like a rag doll.

Matt insisted on driving to the funeral, and Trace again agreed, though it meant he and Colt had to squeeze into the back of the Audi. Darla marveled politely over the interior, and Matt gave the travelogue of its features again. Trace worried what people in town would think when they pulled up in the thing.

For Trace, the funeral itself moved forward in a fog. The service was handled by the Reverend Ezekiel Bass, whom everyone knew as "Sandy" since he'd gone to the beach when he was five and insisted on bringing bucketsful home with him. He'd kept them for months, seeming to appreciate even at a young age how rare it was for anyone from the Big Empty to find tidewater. He'd get his buckets out after school and plunge his hands into them, letting the grains pour through his fingers. Sandy said all the usual words—ashes to ashes—and spoke fondly of Nelda Malloy, whom he'd known since before his beach-combing days. He had, in fact, offered to share his sand with her and no one else. His comments were punctuated by sobs from Darla and a few other women, who dabbed their eyes with handkerchiefs.

Afterward, a parade of people shook Trace's hand, but they were a mélange of faces and conversations that had no meaning and were quickly forgotten—niceties and sympathies offered, accepted, and dispersed as if by the wind that kicked up from the north. Roland Kerr and his wife, Dorothy, were there, of course, as well as Terry Garrison and Manny, Doc Lambeau, the ranch hands—Buck MacKenzie, Old Hank, Terry Blake, Bobby Ray Cox and John Cyrus, Sal MacGruder, Felipe Garza—and Charlie Weeks, the lawyer, and Sherrie Duncan. Malloy was, however, surprised to see Blaine Witherspoon with his wife and gloomy son standing at the edge of the graveside service.

Malloy thanked them for coming.

"I felt like it was the least I could do," Witherspoon said. "I'm terribly sorry for your loss." A moment of silence hung awkwardly between the two men, then Witherspoon said slowly, "You know, I had no idea of your mom's condition when I...." Malloy nodded. Nothing more needed to be said.

The cemetery was on a slight rise, about a mile from the main ranch house on the other side of the Gunyon Road. Technically, the land belonged to Frye, but the company wasn't about to quibble with the locals over a half-acre graveyard. They stood near Nelda's freshly dug grave, catching the wind, which blew harder now, making Malloy notice it was coming from the north, which was odd for this time of year. It battered them like a pioneer woman beating a dirty rug. It was hard and forceful, yet it did little to ease the heat of the day. Instead, it carried the hotness like the breath of some unseen dragon. With it came a cover of gray clouds, but to Malloy it only felt like rain in the hollow pit of his stomach, where the anguish of his loss roiled and churned like a spring hailstorm. The wind whipped up, gusting even harder as the last of the sympathies were expressed, and the last of the hands were dutifully shaken.

Off to one side, Matt greeted everyone as if he'd missed them terribly since he'd left town, slapping men on the back, kissing women on the cheek. It was as if he'd mistaken his mother's funeral for a high school reunion. Malloy turned away from his brother and faced the wind, which blasted at him, then receded, like some invisible tide crashing across the plains. Without a hat, he felt the tentacles of the warm air tousling his hair.

Another gust threatened to invert the skirts of Sherrie Duncan and several other women—members of Darla's Thursday night bunko group, he thought—and they scurried for their cars like chickens scattering before a mischievous dog.

Darla looked around, holding her hat in place with her hand. "Where's Colt?" she asked.

They couldn't find the boy, and Malloy decided he must have gotten a ride home with the Garrisons, taking the fastest exit to escape the flood of other people's expressions of sorrow. In a way, Malloy envied him.

When everyone else had left, the three of them — Trace, Darla and Matthew — stood alone in the graveyard, staring down at the headstone, Nelda now chiseled in next to Caleb, another generation that had tried to tame the land of the Big Empty and had been claimed by it.

They piled into Matt's Audi and headed back to the house. Before they even got out of the car, Matt began the overture of his goodbye.

"You're going back tonight?" Darla said, stunned.

"I gotta get back. We're behind on a big job. I'm gonna have crews working around the clock through next weekend," Matt said. "I'm not complaining, though. Too much business is a happy problem."

"You want to sit and have a beer before you go?" Trace asked. "I could sure use one."

"Nah, I need to stay awake. Long drive."

He hugged Darla and she went inside. The brothers lingered for a while in the driveway. Trace tried half-heartedly to convince Matt to stay, knowing he wouldn't succeed. The gap between them had become a bitter chasm, a barrier that kept Matt from staying even one night. They punctuated their farewell with a wooden handshake, and as Matt glided into the driver's seat of the still-running car, Trace climbed the three stairs to the porch as if they were a mountain switchback. He sat down, ignoring the creak of the wooden chair as he watched his brother head down the gravel path, then turn right on the paved road. The wind howled at him, angry, like a banshee.

Darla brought him a beer and went back inside, respectful of his need to grieve alone. He pulled a mouthful from the bottle's long, brown neck and watched the last red glimmer of Matt's taillights fade to the east, rushing back toward the city four hundred miles away and the life that called him there.

Trace Malloy knew that he would never see his brother again. ✯

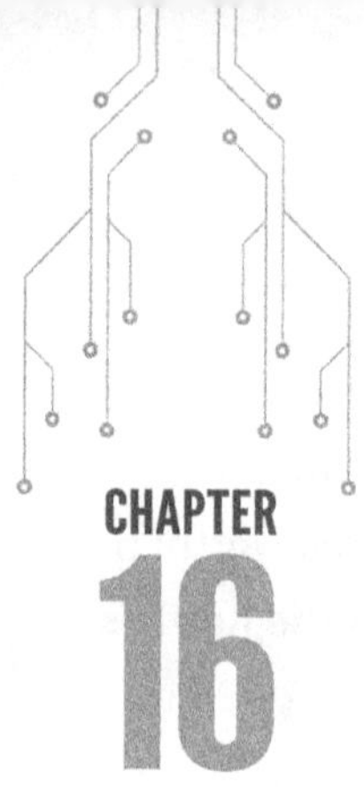

CHAPTER 16

BRANDON WITHERSPOON took in the scene in disgust. Why had his old man dragged him here? Wasn't this whole place depressing enough? Now he had to stand here and watch the yokels put some old lady in the ground. For this he was supposed to miss his online session with his old gaming buddies from San Jose?

The wind whipped up and blew the long tassels of his hair in front of his face. He imagined a striking image: the dark and brooding goth figure standing at the edge of the funeral, looking on ominously. He had wandered to the periphery of the small cemetery, his back to the proceedings. He peered over his shoulder now, making sure no one was paying attention. They weren't.

His parents were shaking the hand of the cowboy whose mom they were burying, offering some totally fake sympathy designed to ingratiate themselves with the shitkicker, for whatever reason. Brandon felt a wave of bile wash up inside him, like water sloshing around inside a fishbowl. He hated his father. He hated the milquetoast mannerisms, the constant sucking up to anyone and everyone. He watched as his father talked to the cowboy, and he knew his father didn't care about these people. They were just jobs, just pawns to be wooed to make himself look good. He would get them and use them and then, when he reached whatever benchmarks he had to make, he'd leave. He didn't care what happened to them.

Really, his father didn't care what happened to anybody. How many times had Brandon heard the lecture? "I know it's difficult, Brandon, but this is a good opportunity, not just for me, but for our whole family." Okay, he'd give him Milpitas. That place had rocked, and Brandon loved it. Lots of gamers, the chicks were hot, and the pot was primo. It didn't last, though, and they'd wound up here. This place was just the opposite. He'd been trying to figure a way out of this hell hole, but so far, it was impossible. There were no buses, no taxis, no exit unless he stole a car, which he didn't know how to do. For that matter, he didn't know how to drive, either.

He'd have to wait it out. That had always worked before. They'd move on in a couple of years, and any place had to be better than this. Still, he didn't know if he could survive this time. This place was worse than any they'd been before. Sometimes, he found it hard to even breathe.

He turned eastward. The land spread before him like a vast tablecloth, a wrinkle here or there, but mostly flat as plywood. You could imagine you were in another world. He did that sometimes, to pass a few hours. He'd sit on the back patio, look out at the barrenness that had swallowed him, and pretend he'd been marooned on an alien planet. It was almost too real. There were no aliens, no man-eating monsters to chase him, no vicious plots to uncover, no way to save the galaxy. There was, simply, nothing. He wound up hating it even more.

He had to find an escape. There had to be some way to get back to the Bay Area. He could live with his collection of gaming partners, someone from his online group, the Warheads. Some were his friends from school. Others he hadn't met, but he was sure one of them would take him in. All he needed was a place to crash and a little food. He'd take his PlayStation with him. He could carry that in his backpack, or just get another one. Once he was safe, his parents would probably send him money. He'd tell them he was checking into a treatment program. That would work. The whole oppressive blanket of boredom that enveloped this god-forsaken place had finally gotten to him. "Mom, there was no way I could lay off the weed in a place like that. I needed to get help." Yeah, she'd go for that. He'd throw in a pitiful whimper or maybe even a tear. His dad wouldn't care. It would get him out of the way for a while. All he needed was a way out.

Brandon turned around and saw the miserable little funeral was finally breaking up. People were milling about, heading to their cars. The wind had begun to gust, licking at the women's dresses like an invisible pervert. A few hundred feet away, he saw a couple of the shitkicker kids, huddled with their backs to him. They were staring at the ground, and one of them was poking the dirt with the tip of the boot on his left foot.

Brandon ambled toward them, a plan gelling in his mind. They'd talked a little bit after that awkward cookout or whatever it was at the ranch. They were rigid and straight, as if they were already adults. But one thing he'd learned during the pathetic months in Conquistador was that these farm kids did stuff you could never get away with in the city. They had guns. They knew how to build shit. And they knew *how to drive.* Brandon didn't think it could be that hard, but he'd only done it in video games. These cowkids drove all the time. Hell, some of them drove themselves to middle school.

Be cool, he told himself as he shuffled toward the shitkickers. The old man ain't the only one who can play this game. He moved closer, but kept his back to them, staring out toward the north and east, as if searching for the source of the battering gusts of wind. In a way, the land reminded him of standing on the beach back on the West Coast, looking out at a huge unmoving sea of earth.

He waited until he was a few feet away from the other boys, then casually glanced over as if he were surprised to see them. The two boys met his gaze. He remembered the one with the greased down brown hair, parted as neatly as Beaver Cleaver's, was the Malloy kid. It was his granny that croaked. The other one was his best buddy. He didn't know the kid's name. Brandon looked over at them and jutted his chin in recognition.

"S'up?"

They stared at him for a minute, then at each other, and started to turn away.

"I'm, uh, sorry about the old lady, dude."

The Malloy kid hesitated for a minute, then began to walk away. Brandon realized his attempt at a greeting wasn't going any better than the first time they'd met out at the ranch. That time, the Malloy kid had offered to shake his hand the way old men do. The kids around here were whacked, no doubt about it. They were all serious and dressed like their parents. They listened to all that "it's-been-lonely-in-the-saddle-since-my-horse-died" country bullshit music.

He took a step after the retreating cowkids. "So, this is pretty depressing. What do you yokes do for fun?"

The two stopped and the Malloy kid wheeled around, fist clenched. The other one grabbed his arm.

"Colt, you can't fight at your grandmother's funeral," he said.

The kid was wearing a grease-covered red baseball cap with a "C" on it, which even Brandon found off for a funeral.

Brandon raised his palms in front of him. "Hey, chill, dude," he said. "Just seein' if you guys, you know, wanna blow this drag and go hang out." As he spoke, he noticed his parents heading toward their Lexus. The wind blew hard against the side of his head, and his hair blocked his vision for a moment. When it cleared, his parents were motioning him to come on. He flashed a quick sign, pointing to the other two boys. "I'm going with them," it said. His parents would be thrilled. He was finally making friends. His father waved him off and his parents got in the car. Good, he thought. They're off to their scotch and martinis, and they'd probably be fucking like rabbits until after midnight. That gnarly scene he preferred to miss anyway.

He turned his attention back to the cowkids. "Hey, dudes, I know this whole scene is bogus. Let's just go chill somewhere, maybe have a beer?" Beer. That should work. These guys had never blown reefer. He was pretty sure of that. But they couldn't be such Cleavers that they hadn't even swigged a beer.

The two boys looked at each other for minute. "Well," the Malloy kid said finally, "we were thinking of going out to the Tie Bow. I guess you could come with us. You're right. I gotta get out of here."

"Excellent," Brandon replied. He had no idea what the Tie Bow was, but it didn't matter. The boys started walking down the hill toward the road, and Brandon followed them. The wind was blowing harder now, whipping the baggy legs of his pants like sheets of canvas in a gale. They walked along the road for about five minutes, the two young cowboys side by side, moving with purpose, and Brandon shuffling along behind them, staring at the ground. The two younger boys swung their arms wide around their sides, Brandon kept his hands shoved deep in his oversized pockets.

They walked to Main Street and Brandon followed the cowkids into a rundown auto repair shop with a red-lettered sign that read "Garrison's Garage." It reminded him of the old "Sanford & Son" TV show he'd watched on afternoon reruns. Rusted pieces of cars littered the sides of the building and spilled into the front. The two cowboys started looking around wildly, making sure no one saw them, Brandon guessed. Not likely, he thought. Planet Boredom was still abandoned. What few yokes were around had all been at the funeral, and now that it was getting dark, they'd all be heading home to their pot roasts and nine o'clock bedtimes, no doubt. The other boys ducked around behind the building, and Brandon followed them.

"There it is," the kid in the red hat said. "I got it running just last week." He pointed to a faded green Ford pickup. Streams of rust poured down the side of the cab and fenders. The hood was missing. A crack divided the windshield lengthwise, and the mirror on the drivers' side hung broken and limp against the side of the door. The Malloy kid got in the passenger side and motioned for Brandon to follow him. The other one got behind the wheel. As he squeezed into the cab next to the other boy, Brandon heard the ignition grinding. After four tries, the engine turned over with a sputtering roar, like a chain smoker clearing his throat in the morning.

"This ride's a piece, yo," Brandon said.

"You got a better one?" the kid behind the wheel said.

Brandon let the comment go without answering. No point in provoking them any more than necessary, he thought. The kid yanked on the gear shift and the truck lunged forward, easing out onto the road. Brandon could sense a hesitation in the way the kid was driving, but it seemed more from a fear of what they were doing than a lack of driving skills. He knew kids in this place learned to drive as young as ten, bouncing through fields hauling hay or whatever the hell it was they did around here.

They drove through town, heading east for several minutes. Then the kid in the red cap turned left into what Brandon first thought was an empty field. Instead, they were on a gravel road that seemed to rise up from nowhere. The truck rolled to a stop in front of a big metal gate. The Malloy kid nudged him in the ribs, and Brandon opened the door and got out. Malloy followed him, walked over to the gate and opened it. He held it while the other kid pulled the truck through, leaving Brandon standing on the other side. He trotted after the truck and waited for Malloy to close the gate. These yokes need some remote controls, he thought to himself.

The giant orange fireball of the sun was beginning to melt along the small rise to their left, and even Brandon knew it would be dark soon. The truck sputtered along, stalling out once when they hit a large gully in the so-called road they were following. After what seemed like twenty minutes, they came to a slight rise, facing the massive sunset. The colors were so vivid that Brandon recalled a memory from his first elementary school, back in New Jersey. It was ancient—built in the early 1900s—and heated by steam radiators that lined the sides of the classroom like an iron fence. He and his third-grade friends would melt crayons on them during the winter, creating psychedelic streams that ran down to the floor. Now, he saw those same colors in the sky—oranges, reds, pinks and yellows smeared across the bluish-purple expanse of sky. As much as he hated this place, he had to admit the display was impressive.

The kid backed the truck around, so the bed was facing the sunset and they all got out. In the distance, the fresh metal of new high-tension towers caught the fading light and shimmered. Brandon imagined for a minute that the structures were alien robots. The Malloy kid lowered the tailgate and raised himself into the bed. Brandon and the boy in the red cap hopped in after him, and they all sat with their backs against the cab. The other kid—Malloy kept calling him Manny—flipped open a cooler that the boys had already put in the bed and handed out beers to each of them. The Cleavers had been planning this all along.

They stared silently at the sun until it was almost gone. Brandon had never really watched a sunset before. He'd never had such a view of one, even in California. He could literally see the giant globe receding below the flat line of the horizon. None of them said anything until the sun was just a faint red lip above the horizon and the twilight had wrapped itself around them.

"I just really can't believe she's gone," Malloy said. "I mean, I've known it would happen, but…"

The wind was still blowing hot and hard, even without the sun. Neither Brandon nor Manny responded to the comment. It was as if it had been swept away by the gusts. Brandon took a sip of his beer before speaking.

"You know," the Malloy kid said, turning toward him, "I guess I should apologize for my dad punching your dad in the nose. I know my dad feels bad about it."

Brandon snorted. "Like I care, yo. I've wanted to do that for years. So, I'm like, 'way to go, cowdude. Hit him harder, next time.' I told you that the other day at that hoedown dinner or whatever it was."

Malloy looked at him, puzzled, and didn't respond.

"I mean, my dad's such a total doink, you know? He gets in a fight and doesn't even fight back. 'Oh, I'm gonna sue.' He's just totally lame. The old man's, like, an embarrassment. You know how it is."

"Not really," the Malloy kid replied.

"My dad's all I got," the other one said. "At least you got two parents."

"Just twice the trouble, yo. The old lady, when she's sober and all, she's always digging around in my room hunting for my stash."

"Stash?" Malloy asked.

"Reefer. Primo weed. You need some, let me know, dudes, cuz I still got the contacts out on the Peninsula." He paused for a moment, but the only response was another blast of wind that whipped his hair across his face. He brushed it aside and went on. "She's raided me twice since we've been here. And they're all, like, 'Oh, Brandon, you need treatment again.' Ain't going back to no detox mansion, yo."

"You know," Malloy said slowly, "If my dad caught me doing drugs, he'd probably whup my ass and throw me outta the house."

"Yeah, at least. I'd consider that getting off easy," the other kid said.

"Dudes, they can't do that. There's laws and shit. That's like child abuse. They can like go to jail and shit. You just call the cops, and it's like 'yo, Dad, have a nice time in the wrought-iron jungle and don't drop the soap in the shower,' know what I'm sayin'? That's word."

"Well, there's laws against smoking pot, too," the Malloy kid said, and Brandon decided the whole Cleaver routine was wearing thin.

"So, what? You yokes don't do nuthin' then? You just little altar boys and honor students out here among the cow turds?"

"Well, we just stole a truck, we're trespassing and we're drinking beer," the other kid said. The wind kicked up again, and this time Brandon felt the truck rock underneath them. The kid kept talking: "I mean, my old man raised hell in his time, and Colt's did too. But I guess people in different places raise hell on their own terms."

"Whatever, yo." He flashed an "L" with his thumb and forefinger, and they stared at it blankly. They all turned back to their beers and the silence returned.

This was a stupid idea, Brandon told himself. He leaned his head back against the cab of the truck, the glass of the rear window smooth and hard against his skull. He stared at the halo of the vanishing sun, now only a faint glow to the west. He closed his eyes. He could feel his exhaustion starting to pull him down. He could feel the drag. He'd been up until two in the morning on the PlayStation, and he hadn't caught his usual nap in fourth period English. He began to drift away, wondering if the cowkids would do something to him if he fell asleep. Would they leave him out here, all alone, enveloped in the darkness that was deepening by the minute?

When he opened his eyes again, he could tell he'd been asleep for a while. He was surrounded by a thick blanket of night, interrupted only by the theater of stars overhead, a vast dome of lights the likes of which he'd never seen. It scared him at first, and he sat up with a start. The cowkids were still sitting beside him, nursing their beers. Six empty cans lay scattered around the truck bed.

Another blast of wind bombarded them, rocking the truck from side to side like an amusement park ride.

"Jesus," Brandon muttered, staring into the darkness as if he expected to see what was causing the turbulence

As the wind died down and his hair cleared from his face, Brandon heard a low, guttural sound coming from off to his right. At first, he thought it was some sort of animal, a panther or leopard preparing to leap from the darkness and devour him. The cowkids heard it too, and they bolted upright. The moan rose in a crescendo of pitch and volume, rolling at them from the expanse of the shallow valley below. He looked at the other boys for some reassurance, some sign that they knew the source of sound. On their faces, he found only confusion that mimicked his own.

"Whaaa?" was all he could say, and Malloy, seeming to understand, simply shook his head slowly.

The sound continued to build until it was crisp and metallic. Brandon's mind, unaccustomed to the outdoors, tapped some deep-rooted instinct and clung it to for comfort: It wasn't an animal. It wasn't a natural sound. It was something distinctly manmade, that much became clear even as the sound itself grew louder and deeper, a groan that shot toward them from the blackness.

Then, lights flashed, followed by a resounding pop and an explosion. Sparks flew in a maelstrom of light, as if a plague of fireflies had suddenly been unleashed. In a burst of brilliance, Brandon could see off in the distance the illuminated outline of a metal tower, the kind used to run power lines. He could see the tower buckling, the top bending slowly down toward its base. The groan of the failing metal gave way to a resounding "Clank!" The two pieces of the structure slammed into each other, followed by a "boom" and the top piece bent completely over and hit the ground.

The power lines that had been attached to it whipped around like angry snakes from the severed head of Medusa, tossing off flurries of sparks when they came in contact with metal or each other.

Just as suddenly as the noise had erupted, the silence of the night returned, punctuated only by a faint buzzing sound. The other boys stared in disbelief. All three were stunned to silence. A faint glow emanated from the scene, and as he stared in shock, Brandon began to realize that the light was getting brighter. The grass at the base of the tower was starting to burn.

"Hoo-lee shee-it," Manny said at last, drawing the expression out until there were no more syllables left to stretch.

Brandon's brain clicked back on and began sending messages, like some old teletype after a power outage.

"Dudes," he said with a newfound sense of purpose, "we gotta blow. We're…we're gonna get blamed, yo. Ev-everyone'll think we did this."

He started to scramble out of the truck bed, and the other two boys instinctively followed him. The Malloy kid stood for a minute on the tailgate, watching the fire that was building around the fallen tower. Then he hobbled down and followed Brandon into the cab. Brandon noticed he was having trouble running.

Brandon leaped into the cab, sitting between the other boys now. He could feel their nervousness on each side of him. It was hot, and they were all sweating.

Manny ground the ignition, but the truck didn't start. Again, then silence. Brandon stared at the keys, as if the sheer force of his will would bring the old battered engine to life. Again. Nothing. Manny gave the key two more twists in rapid succession, and the truck sounded like an electric can opener before falling silent. Manny cursed and pounded the wheel.

Brandon and Colt were leaning forward, if only because that was the direction they wanted the car to move in.

Colt looked over his shoulder toward the tower. Brandon could feel the other boy's arm, hot and damp against his own, and he could feel the sweat running like a river down the back of his own neck.

"C'mon, dude, get this shitwagon moving," he said, feeling the desperation welling in his bowels. What would they bust them for? Arson? Criminal trespass? That was serious shit—an extended stay in juvie for sure.

Again, Manny ground the keys, and the engine turned over, gunned by Manny's foot pressing the accelerator to the floor. He threw it in gear and the truck lunged forward violently, but Manny maintained control. The tires spun wildly, growling at the gravel and dirt beneath them. They sped along the unpaved road, tossed about by each rut and turn.

"It's bad, Manny, it's really bad," the Malloy kid said. "It's gonna spread fast. There's been no rain."

Manny didn't say anything. The dashboard light showed the fear on his face. The fire, Brandon thought to himself, is the least of our problems. Then he noticed that Manny's cap was missing.

"Shit, dude, we gotta go back," he said, grabbing Manny's arm.

"What?" Manny screamed. "Are you nuts? We gotta get help."

"Dude, listen. I'm bailing your ass here. Your cap's gone, dude. It's probably laying on the ground back there."

"So? Who gives a shit?" Manny said, shooting Brandon a desperate look.

"That's evidence, yo. Puts you at the scene and all that shit."

"I don't care about a damn cap, the ranch is on fire," Manny said, getting the pitch of his voice under control.

Okay, Brandon thought, that's enough from the Cleavers. Timmy and Lassie could go get help on their own. He knew where this was going to lead.

"Listen, cow chunks," he said, his voice quavering with the bouncing of the truck. "I ain't taking the rap for this, yo. We go back, get the cap, and get outta here. There's time. No yokes around for miles. No one'll see us. Just be cool and no one will know we were here."

Manny started to speak but the Malloy kid cut his friend off, his voice tinged with exasperation. "We didn't do anything. We can't just let the ranch burn and act like we don't know it's happening." Brandon sensed a touch of fear in his voice.

"Dudes, listen," Brandon said, trying to act calm. "I know how this shit works. They find out we were out there, it'll be 'what were you youngsters up to?'" he said, deepening his voice and bobbling his head in mock adulthood. "And soon, it's our fault. That's word. So be cool, and we can still get outta this. We just need to go back and snag the hat."

"We're not going back," Manny yelled, and as if to punctuate his point, the truck slammed into a deep gully, the same one, Brandon figured, that had caused it to stall on the way out. Their heads hit the roof of the cab, and the truck engine sputtered violently, but Manny, expecting the problem, pumped the accelerator and the engine fought back to life. Manny downshifted and the truck lurched on.

Brandon looked over his shoulder and out the rear window. A glow was rising from the valley.

"It's spreading fast," the Malloy kid said. "All that grass is as dry as straw."

Brandon could feel the panic, a giant bubble of fear that started at the base of his spine and pushed upward, constricting him until his chest ached like it was clamped in a vise. The cowkids were so scared, they obviously didn't realize what was happening. Couldn't they see this was all going to get dumped on them? He'd been in worse scrapes — tagging cars out in San Jose had almost gotten him busted — but he'd always hung with kids who knew what to do. They'd always gotten away, and they would now, too, if these stupid shitkickers would just listen to him.

They stopped at the gate and the Malloy kid jumped out to open it.

"Last chance," Brandon said. "We can still work this, dude."

"Shut up," Manny said, gunning the engine and pulling the truck through the now-open gate. Before Brandon could move, Malloy was back in the seat beside him.

The truck reached the main road, and Manny pulled the wheel hard, throwing them all to the left. Brandon could feel the other boy's sweat as he leaned against him. He saw the cloud of dust behind the truck, and then the shimmer of amber rising behind that. Suddenly, another wave of panic hit him. The beer cooler was gone. It must have bounced out when they hit the gully. More evidence. Now the cops would know they'd been drinking. Between Timmy and Lassie wanting to save the world and their utter carelessness in covering their tracks, Brandon knew they were all toast.

The truck sped down the road with Manny hunched over the wheel, coaxing the old heap forward. The engine, nestled in its hoodless compartment in front of them, shook violently, and the vibration carried through the entire vehicle. Brandon looked at the speedometer — fifty miles an hour. It felt like they were fleeing a crime scene in a steamroller. They were heading back to the west, toward town. On the horizon to their right they could see the glow from the burgeoning flames.

"Go to my place, it's the closest," Colt said.

Brandon couldn't believe them. They'd all wind up in juvie and these yokes didn't seem to care.

"Dudes, I'm telling ya," he urged, "let's just take this piece back to Sanford's garage and sneak back home. No one will ever know. All the yokes are probably in bed already. Even if they're not, no one will be able to prove anything. I'm mean, okay, dudes, I was wrong about the hat. That's word. I'm sure it's already burned up by now. Our tracks are clear, yo, let's just blow."

"Just shut your mouth, you damn pothead!" The Malloy kid was glaring at him, and Brandon could see the panic in his eyes. Sweat beaded on the white slope of his forehead. Brandon remembered the image of his father after the elder Malloy had worked him over. He shook his head and turned his gaze back to the road. Juvie might actually not be so bad. At least in the joint they understand how things work.

Manny turned the truck onto a gravel driveway. They stopped again and the Malloy kid hobbled out to open the gate. Brandon again thought about bolting out the open door, but where would he run to? And Timmy and Lassie would no doubt turn him in. His only hope was to stick with them and make sure they didn't sell him out. At least he'd make sure the shitkickers went down with him.

This time, the Malloy kid left the gate open, hopping in the truck as it drove by. They bounced up toward a small wooden house. Manny slammed on the brakes and the truck slid three feet on the loose stones.

The old cow dude was sitting on the porch, cradling a beer. As the truck ground to a stop, he leaned forward. The cowkids jumped out. Brandon started to move toward the door, but Colt slammed it shut. Brandon sat alone in the cab, instinctively sliding down in his seat.

As Malloy ran toward his father he started shouting. "Dad! The Tie Bow! It's burning!"

"What?" The older man was standing now and trying to make sense of what his son was saying. "Where the hell you been, son? What are you talking about?"

"We were out at the Tie Bow. One of them new towers, the big electric towers, just plum fell over—blew over, I guess. All the power lines snapped, and there were all these sparks and all, and then it lit the grass on fire. It's spreading fast."

The old man hesitated for a moment. "Good God Almighty," he said. "You boys wait here." He darted through the door to the house. The two boys looked at each other for a moment and followed him. Brandon sat in silence, the cyclical sputter of the engine the only sound.

So this was it. The old man was on the phone right now, and by morning, Brandon knew he'd be busted. Yeah, he hadn't thought this through. The cowkids weren't stupid. They didn't care because they already had a good alibi—him. They were in there selling him out right now. 'Father dear, the pothead made us go out there. He threatened us. He said he'd have drug dealers come from California and kill our families if we didn't do what he said. Oh, Father, it was terrible!'

And that was it. He'd wind up in Stripe City while Timmy and Lassie got a lecture about the dangers of under-age drinking. No way, cow dudes, he thought, as he scooted behind the wheel.

Quietly, he closed the driver's side door that Manny had left open. He fumbled with the transmission, grinding it into reverse. The truck lurched backward, throwing him against the wheel, and the truck spun wildly. The force of his chest hitting the wheel set off the horn.

Panicked, he stepped on the gas, and the truck intensified its backward circle. Suddenly, he was thrown back into the seat with a thud. Behind him the trunk of an oak tree was cradled in the crumpled rear of the truck bed. Great, he thought, the only tree in a three-mile area and I hit it. How hard can this be, dude? I rule at Gran Turismo, he thought to himself.

He threw the transmission into drive. The older Malloy, the boys, and a short squatty woman were all standing on the porch now. Manny was shouting something at him, but he couldn't hear it. He tramped on the accelerator and the truck hovered for a moment, spitting gravel from under its tires, then sped forward down the driveway. Brandon flailed furiously at the steering wheel, and finally brought it under control. The driveway was a straight shot, and he steadied the wheel as he went forward. He could hear the cowkids yelling after him, but he didn't heed their calls.

He turned left at the Main Road, heading west, the truck weaving like it was driven by a drunken cowboy. Wait until the Warheads hear about this, he thought. He let out a yell as he sped forward into the night, embracing the darkness like a shroud. ✯

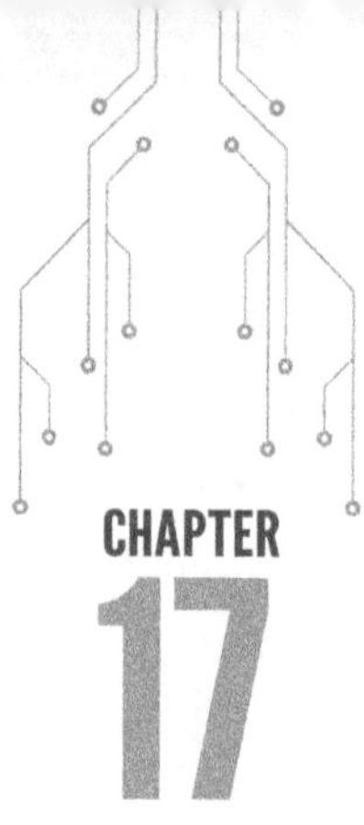

CHAPTER 17

SOMETHING HOT AND LOUD hit Trace Malloy in the side of the head, and he staggered, more from surprise than the force of the impact. He felt the heat blowing against his face and he instinctively turned toward the source.

A juniper tree five feet away had erupted in flame. Junipers, laden with oily, combustible sap, sounded like a small bomb when they ignited, like someone throwing an aerosol can into a fire. Malloy had been dodging the blasts since before daybreak, but he still reacted with surprise at each explosion.

He stumbled to one side, bracing himself with a hand on the ground. Even through his gloves, he could feel the heat of the soil. His head throbbed. He was disoriented.

His lungs were coated with ash and dust. His throat felt like it was filled with sand. His body, worn down by the heat, had stopped trying to sweat. The blaze was burning his mind, too, and he twice had to jolt himself back from hallucinations. Once, he imagined he was with his brother, pulling Luke's broken body from the wreckage of his A-6, mortar fire showering the jungle with flame as he desperately tried to drag his brother from the inferno. Explosions and flame. Had that been the last thing Luke had seen, his last vision of life on earth? Had he died in the crash or ejected safely only to meet death on the field below? Had he spun around in confusion, wondering where the enemy was, where he was supposed to go, only to be cut down by gunfire? Malloy saw his brother, lying on that foreign ground, burned and bleeding and anonymous, another name on a wall for the future. Even standing above him, looking down on the corpse with his mind's eye, Malloy couldn't answer the questions that had dogged him since childhood. Why did Luke have to die? Why did God take him then, and why like this?

He forced the image from his mind, his brother's body spinning away in front of him. He stumbled forward and fell back to one knee. New visions took over. His surroundings morphed into a plain of hell itself, with Satan staring from one of the mesas and laughing at him.

He knew his mind was tricking him. He shook his head violently to dispel the vision, causing him to stumble again and grab the baked earth for balance. No, even if he were in hell, he wouldn't have felt the desperation that consumed him now. If damnation were eternal, there was no rush, no need to hurry out of harm's way, no reason to race against destruction. But now, more of the Conquistador died every minute as the fire chewed its way across the flattened bowl of the ranch.

He said a prayer, partially to chase away the hellish image, but mostly he prayed for the land. He thought he was speaking out loud, but he couldn't tell. The rawness of his throat made his voice little more than a raspy whisper, and the roar of the flames drowned out any sound that came forth.

He kept praying as he kicked dirt toward the flames with the side of his foot. He spun around, trying to get his bearings, but the flames seemed to surround him. He tried to peer through the smoke. Stragglers, he'd been searching for straggling cows. He'd seen a few earlier, through the waves of smoke.

Most of the herd, or at least as many as the ranch workers could gather ahead of the advancing onslaught of flame, had been moved to safety. The animals were being trucked over to the West Fork. Some, though, were still out here.

Malloy had been searching with three other ranch hands, moving as close to the fire line as they dared. The horses, though, had grown harder to control as the flames surged toward them. He'd told the rest of the crew to turn back, but as he pulled on the reins of his own horse, he'd heard the plaintive bleating of a calf. Through the smoke, he could see it standing on wobbly feet near the fallen body of what Malloy could only assume was its mother.

He'd wheeled his horse around, ignoring the retreat of the rest of the men. When he reached the calf, it was clear the mama cow was already dead, the hair scorched from most of her body. He'd managed to chase the baby forward, but in its terror, it ran erratically, and he had to double back several times. He'd focused on the calf and tried to keep his eye on the direction of the road, heading the young animal away from the advance of the fire.

The wind incited a constant swirl of smoke around them, and after what must have been fifteen minutes of good progress, he'd lost the calf in the haze. He made a quick circle, but the cloud was choking him, and he gave up. A gust of wind pushed the flames past him on one side. He turned in the other direction, but fire shot forward, like a hand swatting him from the saddle.

He'd fallen backward, landing hard. The impact added to his confusion. As he tumbled, his mare bolted from the fire, only to run into flames coming from the other direction. The horse turned and reared, and he could see her hooves black against the light of the fire. As she came back to all fours, her back was aflame, her tail and part of her mane singed away. She ran in the other direction and collapsed as the fire consumed her. For a moment, Trace saw her body writhing on the burning ground, then the fire and smoke swept her away as it advanced toward him.

The image of his horse, twisting unnaturally as the fire enveloped her, snapped him back to the present. He forced the visions of his brother and the devil from his head and staggered to his feet. He knew the fire was walling him in. Between the wind and the flames, even a few steps could lead to sudden isolation and death.

As the smoke engulfed him, he realized the futility of his situation, the pointlessness should he die out here among the flames. He kicked vainly at the burning brush again, a hollow gesture against the massive blaze. His search for stray cows was a fool's errand, like looking for a lucky charm in a mine field. He could see Darla, hands on her hips, shaking her head at him. "Stubborn as a two-headed mule," she was saying.

He stumbled forward, feeling dizzy again. A wave of smoke blocked his vision and forced itself into his lungs. He gasped, desperate for any molecules of air in the acrid cloud. His body convulsed and he gagged violently, tumbling to the ground. He felt the earth, hard as concrete and hot as an oven door, under his hands and knees. The smoke, brushed away briefly by the wind, cleared just long enough for him to realize he was kneeling amid the fire, the flames circling behind him and threatening to cut off his escape. He tried to stand and stumbled forward again. Fire shot up on all sides, continuing its relentless march. Looking upward at the heads of the flames licking at the sky like angry snakes, he realized his eyesight was blurring.

He coughed uncontrollably. Each breath he inhaled only filled his chest with more smoke and dust. Even in his cigarette days, he'd never been so suffocated by his own lungs. He felt himself pitching forward and the gash on his chin throbbed as if preparing for another impact.

It didn't happen. A hand reached under his arm, pulling him up. He tried to use his legs to help, but it was like pushing string.

"Trace, dammit, I told you—frequent breaks, lots of fluids."

He couldn't see with his blurry vision, but he knew the voice: Diana Lambeau.

"Doc," he croaked, but he could barely hear himself, as if he were talking through a pillow. "Aren't you supposed to be back at the tent?"

"So are you," she snapped. She spun him around and began pulling him away from the flames. They staggered through the smoke and heat, scarves covering their mouths but doing little to block the undulating blackness that washed over them like acrid waves of night. Malloy realized his neckerchief was so dry, it might ignite from the ambient heat. The smoke flowed through it and into his lungs, unfettered.

Lambeau had arrived soon after the ranch hands and insisted on setting up a first aid station. They had agreed on the condition that she stay there. The last thing they needed, the county fire chief told her, was someone becoming lost in the blaze—particularly the area's only doctor. As devastating as the fire was, they didn't have to worry about getting people out—at least for now. The wind was blowing the flames in the direction of Rolling Ranch Estates, but it had miles to go before that became a concern. As long as the firefighters—mostly volunteers from town and other parts of the county—stayed safe, the damages were likely to be limited to money and land.

Lambeau, of course, couldn't remain in the tent any more than Malloy could fall back and let the fire run its course. She had taken it upon herself to keep a head count and make sure no one got lost as the flames advanced. When the rest of the crew returned without Malloy, she saw it as a call to action, as if one stupid act could undo another.

She staggered under Malloy's weight, his legs moving loosely like a mannequin with broken joints. She managed to find the way back toward the first aid tent, and as they left the front lines of the fire, Malloy felt his head begin to clear. He wondered how much of the ranch could be saved. By the time the sun had come up, he could see through the wafts of smoke that much of the buffalo grass paddocks had already burned.

The wind was driving the fire to the south and east, toward Rolling Ranch Estates and the chip factory, but at least it was blowing away from town. It chewed up the dried grass like locusts. He suspected most of the Tie Bow would be blackened by noontime. They were having no luck stopping the devouring flames. They simply didn't have enough people — thirty-five or forty at most. Terry Garrison was out there somewhere and so was the lawyer Charlie Weeks, and all the ranch hands, of course. It didn't matter. They couldn't dig the trenches or light the backfires or even pile dirt on top of the flames fast enough. All they could do was move the herd and pray.

Malloy sat on a cot, inhaling oxygen through a plastic mask that pulled the hairs of his mustache. Lambeau, coughing frantically herself, checked his vital signs.

He rested for probably a good half hour, his impatience growing as his strength returned. He alternated between the oxygen and cups of water, until his lungs felt clearer, and he pushed the mask away. His throat was so raw, every swallow produced a volcano of pain, rising up along the back of his neck and washing against the base of his jaw.

He heard a sound on the horizon, low at first, then escalating into a steady thumping that reminded him of his mother beating blankets on the clothesline when he was a child.

The noise grew louder and sharper as the Chinook helicopters of the Texas Air National Guard came into view. He could see three of them, sporting huge buckets, like giant soup ladles suspended from their underbellies.

He rushed from beneath the awning, staggered slightly and regained his footing. Lambeau should have protested, but she was watching, too, as the choppers zoomed over the tent, buffeting the canvas with the wash of their dual blades. The Chinooks beat a path toward the fire line and Malloy could see the mist of the water as the huge buckets suspended under the aircraft released their load. They circled overhead and flew back the way they'd come.

Just then, he heard Roland Kerr.

"Trace! I've been looking all over for you. Get over here!"

He followed his boss through the maze of pickups and firefighting trucks, their water tanks already depleted, to a makeshift command center. They spotted the emergency set-up by the cheap awning the town had bought at Wal-Mart in Lubbock for a picnic several years ago. Underneath it, a couple of folding tables were littered with maps held in place against the wind with rocks.

Stepping under the cover, Malloy recognized Ed Scott, the county fire marshal. Malloy didn't know Scott well, but they were acquainted enough that Malloy could read the worry on the other man's face. Scott always had a sad, sunken appearance, even back when Conquistador still had six-man football and Scott had coached the team to a victory. Now his sullen visage was amplified by the soot smeared under his eyes and on the sides of his cheeks.

His face was round and fleshy, with jowls that oozed down toward his collar. His glasses were fogged and dirty, and what was left of his gray hair was covered by a red fire district cap.

Malloy nodded at Scott. Scott motioned toward the other man who was standing beside him wearing an olive-drab jumpsuit and sunglasses.

"Trace, this is Major DeFillippo with the Guard out of Abilene. They've been kind enough to lend us three choppers to fight this thing. That's not a great solution. Fixed-wing aircraft would be better, because in this wind, choppers may just fan the fire, but we don't have a lot of options.

"I talked to the Forest Service command post in Granbury. All the available tankers are either grounded for repairs, too far away, or already fighting other fires. So, we'll make do with what the major can get us.

"Now, we're trying to figure out the best source of water. As I see it, that's Carlson Reservoir."

Trace nodded. Carlson Reservoir was over halfway to Lubbock.

"The problem," the major began in a clipped military tone that reminded Trace of the soldiers who'd come to their house all those years ago to tell his parents of Luke's death, "is that it's too far away. The birds aren't that fast. The way this thing's moving, we need to get more water on it ASAP. With three choppers, the travel time's going to kill us, even if we stagger the runs."

Trace nodded again. His thoughts were slow to form, as if his brain were floating in molasses. He winced to try to clear his head, and and an unlikely solution suddenly materialized.

Blaine Witherspoon came into view.

"Hey! Hey Malloy!" Witherspoon was walking determinedly toward them, stumbling slightly. How could that be possible? Was this another hallucination? Malloy pinched the brim of his hat between his thumb and forefinger and lifted it off his head, scratching his scalp with his remaining fingers. His hair was wet and matted.

Witherspoon looked disheveled, as if he'd been shocked while using a fork to fish a stubborn bagel out of the toaster. Malloy imagined he and the others probably looked worse, but Witherspoon was different. He didn't have any sign of soot, no black smudges from the smoke that swirled around them.

Malloy knew Witherspoon hadn't joined the firefighting effort. None of the homies had. They were all still sitting in their sunny breakfast rooms, sipping cappuccinos and reading *The Wall Street Journal.* He could imagine their conversations: "Oh, dear, I do hope they get that dreadful fire out soon. I just washed the BMW and it's going to get ashes all over it."

Why was Witherspoon here?

Malloy stood silently, letting his eyes bore into Witherspoon without responding to his call. Take the hint, he telegraphed with his stare. Once again, just like that day at the corral, this was about the worst place he could possibly be.

Sweat ran down the sides of Witherspoon's face. The skin was peeling along the ridge of his nose and under his eyes, giving a splotchy, red tone to his otherwise milky complexion.

"Have you seen Brandon?" he asked breathlessly as he reached the point where Malloy and the other men were standing.

"Who?" Malloy said instinctively, realizing the second he said it that he knew the answer. His mind was still fogged from the smoke and heat, and Witherspoon's kid was the farthest thing from his mind.

"My…"

Malloy cut Witherspoon off before he could complete his sentence. Suddenly, an idea popped into Malloy's smoke-addled brain. Ignoring Witherspoon, he turned back to the other men. "What if we got a million gallons or so?" he asked the major.

Kerr, Scott, and DeFillippo all stared at him in silence.

"The AzTech plant," Malloy said. "Roy, remember all those bonds the county sold?" He could feel his throat beginning to bind as he spoke. "Remember all that infrastructure? They ran those big water mains out there because the plant needed a million gallons a day, right?" He turned back toward Witherspoon and tapped him in the chest with the back of his hand.

"Wha?" Witherspoon said, confused.

"Trace, this ain't the time…" Kerr said.

Malloy's throat was still raw, as if he'd been swallowing bits of glass. The vibrations of his voice caused him to cough uncontrollably. He raised a hand to cut Kerr off, then croaked a reply.

"It's exactly the time. That plant isn't even fully running yet, but all that water's sitting there in those pipes."

"Water in pipes doesn't do us much good if we don't have any way to divert it out here," the major said.

Witherspoon stared at the fire and back at Malloy, who had moved a few steps from the group and was looking in the direction of the plant—and the subdivision. Witherspoon had spent enough time in California that he understood the threat of wildfires. He'd witnessed thousands of acres turned to cinder; people's homes reduced to smoldering ash heaps. He'd seen some of the other AzTech employees leaving town earlier in the day. But he'd been so worried about Brandon, he'd been oblivious to the potential consequences of what was happening—to the firestorm raging in front of him.

DeFillippo, Scott, and Kerr had followed Malloy, and Witherspoon found himself walking after them. Malloy pointed to the horizon off to the southeast.

"Right over there is the homies' subdivision," he said.

"The what?" Witherspoon asked.

Malloy coughed again. His throat felt as if it were bleeding on the inside. He tried to summon some saliva and swallowed hard. His words came out in broken bits.

"...over there," he gasped, pointing at the houses in the distance. "AzTech plant. See"—*hack, hack*—"rooflines?"

The major nodded and looked at Scott, who raised his eyebrows in consideration. Witherspoon turned from one man to the other, confused. This was his home they were talking about, but he couldn't grasp what Malloy was saying.

"The water main comes in"—*cough*—"west." Malloy moved his hand again and traced the imaginary line. "... runs ... through...neighborhood." Malloy sucked in air, trying to make himself understood, and coughed again violently. "...out to plant." His voice was becoming little more than a guttural whisper.

Kerr had disappeared for a moment and returned with another water bottle. As Malloy gulped the liquid, Witherspoon began to realize what he was saying.

"Wait! Wait!" he shouted. "The water! It's all connected. We buy it from private landowners to the west and pump it past the subdivision and to the plant. It's all the same lines!"

Malloy nodded as he swallowed, but everyone else still seemed confused.

"Right there," Malloy said pointing back to the southeast, "at the entrance of the estates...the lake." His voice came easier now, but each word still seemed to slice into the back of his throat. "They're pumping water into it. It collects there. It'll probably fill three or four of those buckets on the helicopters."

"And," Witherspoon added, "when the lake level runs low, it's automatically replenished from the mains. We planned it that way so the lake wouldn't dry up."

The major looked at Scott and thought for a moment.

Malloy had hated that feature from the time he first learned of it. In a drought, the last thing anyone wanted was the water table to be depleted for a damn show lake. But he had to admit, that stupid, wasteful lake might just save the whole goddamned town.

"It's designed to fight evaporation, so the refill mechanism might be slow, but it ought to work if the water level of the lake was drawn down," Malloy said, as the water from the bottle Kerr brought him soothed his throat enough to make it possible to speak in complete sentences again.

Witherspoon was running through the old schematics in his mind. It had been a few months since he'd seen those plans. He had bigger problems with the water system *inside* the plant, but he remembered an important detail.

"There's a manual override valve," he said slowly. "If you close it, it will cut off all the water to the plant. The refill valve for the lake is too small. It won't allow enough water to replenish the lake fast enough for the helicopters, but…." He trailed off, his thoughts racing.

"Break it," Malloy said.

The two men stared at each other for a moment. "Yeah," Witherspoon said slowly. "If you could bypass the refill valve, basically just knock a hole in the main, with the cutoff valve at the plant closed, everything would flow into the lake." The last few words came off his lips slowly, and no one noticed the wry smile that swept across his face. It would create havoc inside the plant, but what the hell did he care? By Monday, it wouldn't be his worry anyway.

DeFillippo shot looks between Malloy, Kerr, and Scott.

"It might work," Scott said slowly. "I mean, it's at least worth a try. Even if we only get one run, it'll be that much more water we pour out there."

The major pondered the point for a few seconds, then he turned to Malloy, grinning.

"It's like filling up from our sink," he said. He slapped Malloy on the back and reached for his walkie-talkie.

Malloy looked at Kerr, who had a quizzical smile on his face. "And the best part," Malloy said with a chuckle as he turned to Witherspoon, "is you get the bill." His laugh triggered another coughing spell.

"I'm going to get more than that," Witherspoon said, as the thought of the fudged numbers and the email exchange between Swain and Watley flashed through his mind. "I'm probably going to get a pink slip. We're behind on our testing schedule, and this could take us out of commission indefinitely. But what the hell."

Malloy's smile quickly faded. He nodded but didn't know what to say.

"On the other hand," Witherspoon said, "it'll be a good excuse for a whole lot of problems I haven't wanted to tell anyone about." He smiled faintly and nodded toward the inferno now incinerating the land where he had ridden with Malloy not long ago. "Besides, we have to do something to stop this. I just hope it works."

Malloy nodded again. "By the way," he said. "What are you doing out here in the first place?"

Witherspoon winced. "Brandon," he said. "He disappeared. I was actually looking for the doctor. I thought if he'd gotten hurt, she might know."

"Haven't seen him since last night," Malloy said.

"Last night? Where was he last night? Why would you have seen him last night?" Witherspoon asked.

"He was with Colt and Garrison's boy. They were the ones who first spotted the fire. He took off, though, after they got to my place."

Malloy tried to turn back to Kerr, who had started to follow DeFillippo and Scott back toward the command tent. Witherspoon grabbed Malloy's arm and pulled him back.

"Dropped off? What do you mean?" he implored.

"He had some old pickup."

"Pickup? You mean he was *driving*?"

"If you could call it that."

"But he's not supposed to drive for another year. Oh my God. How could you let him do that?"

"I didn't have much say. The boys got out and he took off. Headed west, I think. By that point, I had bigger worries."

He nodded in the direction of the oncoming flames, but Witherspoon wasn't watching. He was staring straight at Malloy as if he were searching for an explanation. A Chinook roared overhead on its route back toward Carlson.

"Look," Malloy said, as the sound of the chopper began to soften, "he's kind of a hero."

He didn't actually think Brandon was a hero. He thought he was a spoiled and obnoxious example of everything that was wrong with city kids — their entitlement, their incessant video game playing, their rampant drug use. He thought the younger Witherspoon was a punk, overprivileged and under worked, with no concept of responsibility and completely lacking in maturity. He knew, too, that this wasn't the time to say what he thought. Regardless of their differences, Malloy could appreciate the concern that comes with being a parent. Besides, they needed Witherspoon's help, and that meant getting him to stop worrying about his kid, at least until they got the water flowing.

"Colt and Manny were the ones who told me about the fire," Malloy went on. "They were out here with your boy last night. They were the first ones to see it. If they hadn't gotten to me, we might have lost most of the herd."

"Oh God!" Witherspoon shouted, his face moist with tears and sweat. A wall of flame was moving toward them, still about a half mile off. Thick smoke poured skyward, like some infinite black fabric being unfurled into the heavens.

"Not this too," Witherspoon muttered, and returned his head to his hands.

Malloy didn't know what he was talking about. Did Witherspoon believe the boys had started the fire? No, the Witherspoon kid didn't do this. If he'd been alone, Malloy may have wanted to believe that, but Colt and Manny wouldn't have been a part of setting a fire like this. They wouldn't have lied about the electric line snapping.

He looked back at Witherspoon. "He did make off with one of Garrison's trucks. Terry won't be too happy about that, even if it was a clunker." He paused, and then said, "But I'm sure he's fine. Where's he gonna go?"

He stepped around Witherspoon and walked toward the tent to rejoin Kerr and the others.

"What have I done?" he heard Witherspoon wail behind him.

As Malloy neared the command tent, Doc Lambeau sauntered up to him, hands on her hips.

"You should be resting," she said, poking a finger into Malloy's chest.

"No time, Diana, you can see that. Don't get in my way."

"If you drop dead, Darla will never forgive me."

"Look at it this way, you'll never have to cook for yourself again."

Lambeau didn't budge. When he tried to walk around her, she stepped in front of him again. Her hair was pulled back and her face was blackened and sweaty. A stray brown lock hung down over her left eye. She wore a sleeveless shirt, but it was soaked on the sides and around her waist. She reminded him of a contestant in a TV reality show gone terribly wrong.

"Diana, I really don't have time for this," Malloy insisted. He took a long draw from the water bottle and swallowed hard. "I appreciate your help, but I've got work to do. Why don't you go see what you can do for him?"

As Malloy pointed his thumb over his shoulder in Witherspoon's direction, Lambeau saw the other man, broken and hunched over, silhouetted against the flickering flames in the distance.

"Blaine?" she said in disbelief. "What the hell is he doing here? Is the whole damned town determined to run into this fire?"

She didn't wait for an answer. She pushed past Malloy, muttering something about the whole damn town going crazy, and marched up the hill. She crouched near Witherspoon and gently put her hand on his back. In her boots and khaki shorts, she reminded Malloy a little of Jane Goodall comforting a forlorn chimp.

Malloy complimented himself on his own ingenuity. He was grateful for the doctor's presence. Some of the guys had needed first aid — hell, he had to be honest with himself, *he* had needed it — and more people would before things calmed down. The heat, blowing in waves, was almost unbearable. It seemed to pull the air out of his lungs, and the smoke that replaced it made every breath sting as if he were swallowing bees.

He admired Lambeau's guts and commitment. No one had asked her to be here. But this wasn't the time for medical precautions. He knew Witherspoon, whatever his problems, would keep Diana occupied until they really needed her again.

"He's gone! He's gone!" he heard Witherspoon scream.

Malloy allowed himself one last glance at Witherspoon's quivering form and then turned back to Kerr, who was listening to the major bark more orders into his walkie-talkie.

He contemplated the black wave rolling toward them, the orange highlights shimmering below the cap of smoke. It was an unstoppable Armageddon, doomsday inching their way, unrelenting, fed by the grasses and dryness and wind. Ironic, Malloy thought, how all those rocks and thistles and cactuses that made this place so bad for farming provided the fire with a hearty smorgasbord, an all-it-could-eat buffet for devastation.

The wind had shifted farther to the northwest, a strange direction for this time of year. It wasn't helping. The fire line was advancing, a flaming blitzkrieg charring its way across the prairie.

As the wind pushed harder, the small band of firefighters had fallen back to the area around the tent.

"Fighter" was a generous term anyway. With such a vast area and so few combatants, they were basically letting the fire burn, and just trying to retain some minimal semblance of control. They were hoping to save what structures they could, but the open land would just burn.

The paddocks of the cellular grazing program already were just a twisted blackened blot, the fried stalks of grass, charred and shriveled in the fire's wake.

The open grazing areas were gone, too, although those were less troublesome. They were mostly thistles and prickly pear anyway. The Conquistador largely used feeders for its herd, so assuming enough of the cows had been saved, restoring the Tie Bow wouldn't take more than a few years, Malloy guessed.

They'd spent most of the morning rounding up cattle, herding them into trailers and moving them out to the West Fork. It was a hurried operation, and keeping a headcount proved impossible.

"Just get them out of here and we'll sort them out later," Malloy had told Sal MacGruder, who was overseeing the load out. Getting an accurate count might take weeks, and even then, they may never know exactly how many head they'd lost. But every cow that burned up meant one more nick in Frye's profit margin, and Malloy already was worried that the fire, on top of three years of drought and weak beef prices, meant the end of the Conquistador.

How much had they saved? He had no idea. The land would bounce back, but the ranch might never recover. Insurance wouldn't shoulder all the costs. It never did. And once the premiums were raised again, as they inevitably would be, Frye might decide that was it, the last straw on an ever-growing pile that would prompt them to sell.

Any sale would be piecemeal. No one wanted ranches this size anymore, unless it was some Hollywood actor with delusions of grandeur and more money than brains. No, Malloy had seen the same outcome too many times, all across the West—grand old ranches, victims of their own economics, sliced up and sold off like lunch meat at the butcher's counter.

He kept his worries to himself as he milled among the ranch hands, beaten back by the fire line and awaiting instructions for what to do next. He patted a few on the back as he walked by. They looked like a team of coal miners coming off a shift. Their faces were smeared with black, their clothes torn and dirty. Bandanas hung around their necks, stiff with dirt and sweat.

Outside Doc Lambeau's first aid canopy, Charlie Weeks was sitting on a crate, an oxygen mask strapped to his face. Charlie peered at Malloy through the clear plastic of the device and shook his head. Charlie, Malloy recalled, had high blood pressure.

Malloy scanned the area for Terry Garrison but didn't see him. He hadn't seen Colt and Manny in several hours, either, he realized. They'd been helping to load trailers, a clear violation of Frye corporate policy against underaged labor that Malloy himself had endorsed. He assumed they'd gone over to the West Fork with the last load of stragglers.

They'd chosen this site for the command center because there was a small pen nearby that worked as a makeshift corral. It was used to isolate individual cows from the herd for veterinary attention, and it had a narrow chute for loading the animals onto trailers. Now it had become a temporary holding pen for the entire herd. They'd squeezed in as many as they could, moving them through as quickly as possible.

If there'd been any luck at all this morning, Malloy thought, it was that the fire had started behind most of the herd and driven them forward toward the road. They'd gotten many of the cows out before the flames moved in.

A lot would be lost, of course. Once the ground cooled, he and Kerr would ride out through the acrid-smelling fields and count carcasses. It would be a miserable task, following the smell of rotting death until they came upon the burned and blackened remnants, eyes cooked out of their sockets by the heat, flesh seared to brittle bone. He and Kerr might spend days wandering from one such scene to another, dutifully logging the results and pretending it was all just part of the job.

Malloy saw Ed Scott walking toward Lambeau and Witherspoon. She helped Witherspoon to his feet. Scott had a long-handled axe slung over his shoulder. "This is all I got to work on that valve with," he said. "It'll have to do. But I'm gonna need your help getting access to the cutoff at the plant."

Witherspoon nodded, sniffed back his tears, and said "of course." The two men turned and headed off.

The smoke was moving in, and the area around the tents seemed shrouded in fog. Were it not for the blistering sunlight commingling with the blast furnace pushing toward them, the scene would have given off a chill.

Malloy knew the fog-like effect meant the fire line was moving closer. They'd have to evacuate the command area before long, retreating as the flames advanced toward Rolling Ranch Estates. Even a slight change in wind direction, though, and the inferno could turn toward town—burning through his own house on the way.

He guessed the fire was a quarter mile away. A juniper in the distance popped and erupted, and he used it as a marker. He turned toward the ranch hands, who seemed dazed, as if the lull in their activity had caused their brains to go dormant.

Two of the Chinooks roared past in formation, water sloshing from their buckets.

Kerr put a hand on Malloy's shoulder.

"We're gonna have to fall back, Trace. It's moving in too fast. The major and I have decided to retreat to the road and try to set up a defense there. Your idea is a good one, though. Those boys there are bringing in the first round, but it may be too little too late. The water's slowing it some, but not enough."

Malloy nodded, and then paused. "It's really Witherspoon who deserves the credit. I didn't know about the cutoff valve. Without that, I don't think we'd have a chance." Then, without waiting for Kerr's reaction, he turned to the crew.

"Listen up!" he shouted, his words slicing like razor blades into the rawness of his throat. "We need to start breaking this area down and getting ready to pull out. Whatever cows are left out there are now officially barbeque. I don't want anyone else leaving this point. Let's get moving!"

The workers snapped awake and began breaking down the tents and stacking equipment. Horses, what few were still being used, were led down the road, away from the fire, to await their own trailers.

The third Chinook roared overhead as the first two headed back toward Carlson Reservoir, and Malloy followed their arc with his eyes. The bucket under the belly of the inbound aircraft sloshed water from the sides as it flew. It released its contents near the exploding juniper, then angled its blunt nose westward for a slow lumbering turn back to complete its circuit.

Malloy knew the road itself wasn't wide enough to provide a good fire break, not with the way the winds had kicked up. Their only hope was to beat the flames down enough that the road could serve as the final barricade. If they could stall the fire until nightfall, they might have some luck. Winds typically die down at night, and the humidity rises, both of which could help combat the advance of the blaze. If the weather didn't cooperate, it was just a quick open field of tall grass before the wall of flames would jump the road and roar on toward the subdivision.

Malloy pushed his way among the ranch hands and found the major and Kerr in the command tent packing up maps and radios. "I just got off the blower with the Forest Service in Granbury," the major told the men "They're going to send us some more people to help on the ground. And reinforcements from at least two other county fire districts are on the way."

The two dozers from the ranch were already tearing up wide swaths of dirt on both sides of the road, essentially making the bar ditches wider and deeper, trying to create a barrier that would starve the fire.

Malloy nodded. "We probably need to start evacuating people. If we don't stop this thing here, it won't take it long to reach that row of houses over yonder." He pointed toward Rolling Ranch Estates. ✯

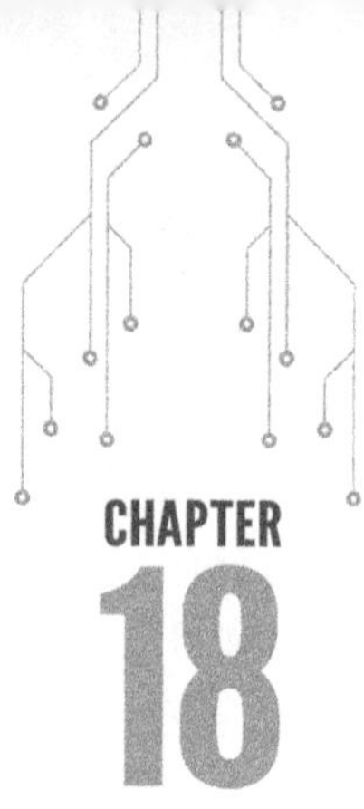

CHAPTER 18

THE AZTECH PLANT came into view, gleaming white in the sun and seemingly unblemished from the flames a few miles away. Ed Scott drove the pickup into the parking lot and pulled up near the front door. Witherspoon told Scott to wait in the truck, then ran inside. He darted through the lobby, past the inner doors and down the hallway to his office. Frantically, he opened and closed the drawers of his desk until he found the set of master keys, then he ran back outside.

As he jumped in the truck, he pointed to a spit of gravel off to one side of the parking lot.

"That's the service road," he told Scott. "Take that around the side of the building. The valve is near the water management system controls." He tried to put his worries about Brandon out of his mind. He had to focus on the job at hand. He'd deal with his son—and the consequences of what he was about to do—later. In the meantime, he'd take some satisfaction in his ingenuity and leadership, something he could think about as Old Soddy's profanities rolled over him Monday morning. Even better—the cleanup, no doubt, would be Swain's problem.

The truck bounced along until it came to an area surrounded by a chain link fence. Witherspoon told Scott to pull up next to it. He jumped out, fumbled with his keys and finally found the one that opened the gate. He searched inside the fence for the valve. Scott stood behind him. Witherspoon saw the control panel for the water system, the pipes coming from the wall of the building, and the ones that ran from the panel into the ground. He knew it was there, but he'd never actually needed it. He whirled around. On the other side of the panel, near the far wall, a large pipe shot up from the ground, made an upside-down "U" and went back in the dirt. In the middle of the "U" was a steel valve and a wheel the size of hubcap. It, too, had a lock on it.

He fumbled with the keys again, trying several before he found the one that worked. He threw off the lock and tugged on the wheel. He couldn't budge it. Scott came up to help him. The radio on the fire marshal's belt crackled.

"Any luck Ed?" It was Kerr.

Scott tugged on the valve and didn't answer. "I thought this stuff was all new?" he said to no one in particular.

Witherspoon didn't acknowledge the comment. "We need leverage," he said.

Scott straightened and stared at him for a moment, then headed back to the truck. He returned with a four-foot length of steel pipe. He fed it through the spokes of the wheel, then standing to one side, began to push upward. Witherspoon grabbed the other end of the pipe and pushed down. Slowly the wheel began to inch forward. Then it stopped again.

The two men let go, sighing.

"Crap. The tests." Witherspoon had forgotten they were doing another test of the water purification system that day. Even though no one was in the building because of the fire, they must have let the test continue. He ran back to the control panel, found yet another key to unlock it, and opened the cover. He was staring at a line of buttons. He had no idea what they did. He didn't know every mundane operation in the plant. Finally, he spotted one labeled "system" and he punched it. A red light began flashing. He could hear alarms inside the building. He'd cut off the flow of water, but the equipment inside was still running. In a few minutes, it would heat up and seize, like a lawn mower without oil in the crankcase. That one action alone may have cost hundreds of thousands of dollars. He went back to the valve and grabbed his end of the pipe.

With the system shut down, the pressure on the valve eased, and the two men were able to turn it with little effort. They wouldn't have needed the pipe.

Scott plucked the radio from his belt. "Roland, we've got the main shut off at the plant. We're headed over to the subdivision."

"Roger that. The choppers are coming your way."

They hopped back in the pickup. Scott spun the truck around in the grass and rushed back to the parking lot. In five minutes, they were at the entrance to Rolling Ranch Estates. They could hear the pounding of a Chinook's dual rotors as the chopper headed for the ranch. The lake was already low, and the normally submerged pipes under the base of the fountain were exposed. The huge helicopters had taken their first drink.

As the men clambered out of the pickup, Scott reached in the bed and pulled out the axe. They walked over to the edge of the lake. Witherspoon had no idea where the lake pumps were. Unlike his role building the plant, he had no real involvement with the construction of the subdivision, and no idea what he was trying to find.

"It's over here," Scott said, walking around the circumference of the retreating lake. "The county actually had to inspect this system, because the plan was to use the lake sort of like a fire hydrant for your neighborhood. I should have thought of this before Trace did."

Witherspoon nodded and followed behind Scott, who was almost a foot shorter than he was. With the axe slung over his shoulder, he looked like a dwarf from *The Lord of the Rings*. They came to a small panel in the ground, and Scott pulled it up. Witherspoon could see a smaller pipe that split off from two larger ones and angled toward the lake. Scott set the head of the axe on the ground, cupping the handle in his right hand, and motioning with his left for Witherspoon to stand back. He hefted the axe over his head and brought it down on the pipe. Nothing happened.

In the distance, Witherspoon could hear the sound of the helicopters growing closer. Scott took two more swings, then stopped to catch his breath.

"If this doesn't work, the choppers might be able to get one more bucketload from here before they have to start heading back to Carlson Reservoir. Once that happens, I'm not sure how we stop the damn fire."

He raised the axe and took two more swings. Each time, the blade bounced off the pipes as if they were made of rubber. Scott raised the axe again and brought it down. And again. And again. Suddenly, a thin geyser erupted from a hole, spraying straight up in the air.

"It's…" Swing. "Starting…" Swing. "To go…" Swing. The stream of water grew heavier, and Witherspoon stepped closer so he could see. With a final slam of the blade, the pipe joint gave way. Water shot up from the ground, spilling over the lip and running toward the bank of the lake. Scott wedged the head of the axe under the smaller pipe and pried it upward. A torrent blasted from the main and flowed into the lake. As Witherspoon watched, he was sure he could see the lake beginning to refill.

"That oughta do it," Scott said, stepping back and watching the rivulet he'd created spew from the underground main, down through the channel for the pipes, and into the lake. The first of the Chinooks was soon overhead, lowering its giant metal bucket into the lake. The helicopter rose, the bucket closing as it did, and veered off, a string of water spilling from the seam of the bucket as the aircraft turned toward the ranch. Witherspoon and Scott ducked as the chop wash from the rotors hit them.

Scott picked up the radio again. "Roland, the first copter's on its way. We got water flowing here at a pretty good rate. This might just work. I'm headed your way."

"Roger that."

For the first time that day, Ed Scott had hope. He turned to Witherspoon.

"I'd like you to stay here, just to keep an eye on things. You shouldn't have to do much, but just in case. Call if there's a problem." He pushed the radio into Witherspoon's chest.

The second chopper was coming in low and loud.

"I have to find my son," Witherspoon protested.

Scott couldn't hear him, and he assumed Witherspoon was agreeing. Scott nodded at him and slapped him on the shoulder, giving him a thumbs up, and sprinted back to the truck.

Witherspoon ducked as the other chopper arrived, took a deep gulp from the lake, and flew off. For a moment, he was left in near silence. He stared at the blackness on the horizon, and the fiery doom that seemed determined, even at this distance, to find him.

He should have been worried about his house. He should have been paralyzed thinking about the damage he'd done to the plant, the still unbelievable events unleashed by Friday's conference call, and the fate awaiting him on Monday. But he couldn't get the image of Brandon driving into the shroud of the night in a stolen pickup out of his mind.

From his post in the Tie Bow, Major DeFillippo watched the first helicopter zoom toward the fire line. Their sorties were now only minutes apart. The second chopper already was rising above the pond at Rolling Ranch Estates, water spilling from its bucket.

Kerr and Malloy nodded to each other but didn't speak. Their eyes watered from the smoke. After pulling back, the command center had reestablished itself as a string of trucks along the Main Road.

The crew spread maps on the hood of the pickup Malloy had wrecked the day Witherspoon came to town.

Every so often a Jaguar or Saab or Porsche would zip past. One more homie fleeing the scene, Malloy thought. This hadn't really worked out, this disposable town they'd tried to create to keep the stifling emptiness at bay. Time to find a more docile location.

The sun was receding, but it still pounded on them. The choppers had doused the fire line with water for hours, but the wind was still pushing the flames forward. They had slowed the advance, but not stopped it.

The water from the subdivision was a godsend, but even with Ed Scott's handiwork, the lake took longer to refill than they'd anticipated. After about six drops the planes had to leave in shifts for refueling. The less-than-furious assault allowed the flames to flicker along the ridge where the command center had been, orange laughter that danced without shame.

Two more tanker trucks were attacking the flames on the ground but weren't the boon they'd first seemed. One of the county vehicles had broken down and sat useless beside the road. The department was, after all, volunteer, and survived largely on donations from the ranch and an annual fried chicken dinner. The meager funding meant there wasn't a fire truck on the scene that was less than twenty years old.

Old Hank and one of the other ranch hands had been overcome by the heat. Doc Lambeau had driven them each home with instructions to soak in a cold bath and drink lots of fluids.

Water remained the biggest concern. With Witherspoon's help, the fire marshal had arranged for the tankers to fill up from a hydrant near the AzTech plant that had been installed specifically for fire suppression. So they had water, but Malloy fretted that they might actually drain the water table. He didn't know what that would take, but he figured they'd be giving it a good test.

Darla had come by with food. She told Malloy that the water pressure in town was weak. He'd give Witherspoon credit for one thing: The homie had certainly figured out a way to get a helluva lot of water out here in the middle of a drought.

Colt and Manny had showed up at the house about an hour earlier, Darla said. They were exhausted. They'd gone to the West Fork as Malloy had assumed. When they'd returned, they'd saddled up and driven the Malloys' small herd to the southwestern corner of the property. That would be the safest place should the fire veer due west. Colt's leg was hurting, and he'd collapsed on the couch an hour ago.

Darla had hosed down the roof of the house and the barn, a process she'd continued at regular intervals to give herself something to do. Between times, she'd cooked biscuits and gravy, sliced some brisket they'd saved in the freezer, and baked about five dozen chocolate chip cookies. She distributed the feast among the crews at the roadside.

There was little more his wife or his son could do at this point. There was little any of them could do.

"How the hell do we tell if any of this is doing any good?" Malloy muttered as he and Terry Garrison stared across the hood of the truck at the mocking flames. He'd found Garrison when they'd moved out to the roadside.

"No telling," Garrison replied. "Just spray and pray, that's all there is."

"Yeah, pray," Malloy said. "I've been doing that every spare moment since I got here. 'Don't let it all die,' I keep saying. This really could be the end."

"The end? Of what? The ranch?"

"Yep. The ranch, Conquistador. Everything."

"We've had fires out here before."

"This isn't like before."

Garrison didn't respond, and they stood in silence, each man with his hands clasped in front of him resting on the pickup's hood.

"Could be we're being punished," Malloy said finally. It was a thought he hadn't fully intended to voice, but it had been gnawing at him since Colt and Manny burst into the house the previous night with news of the fire.

"Jesus, Trace, you're such a fatalist."

"When you get right down to it, it's all about money isn't it? Greed. We want jobs, we want a big company coming in here, we want the place to change. But maybe we wanted all that because we're greedy, because we couldn't be satisfied with what we had."

Garrison laughed a short, staccato kind of cackle. "Wanting a better future ain't greed. Building a town ain't about greed. When the Scots first came here, they set up this ranch and created this town. It's here for a reason that's about more than just money. Wanting to keep it alive ain't greed, Trace. It's just survival, that's all."

"Maybe our time has passed, and we're supposed to accept that."

"I thought that's what we were doing. There's lots of ways of accepting things that don't mean giving up."

Malloy stared at the hood of the truck. The white paint reflected the sun's heat, and for a moment he felt light-headed, as he had earlier when Diana Lambeau pulled him from the smoke.

Garrison didn't understand. They'd had this discussion a thousand times growing up, and it wasn't about the town or the ranch or the Big Empty. It was about them — their futures, their lives. What, Malloy kept asking, did it matter?

One day his brother was tormenting him, and Malloy was so angry he hated him, and then there were soldiers on the doorstep in their crisp uniforms, saying he was dead. What was the difference if you died on the battlefield or burned up in a wildfire or just rotted away slowly in a long, agonizing disease-ridden slide toward oblivion? What was the true and final measure of a life?

Across the street, the flames churned forward, devouring more and more of the Tie Bow.

Garrison didn't dwell on things like that. For him, life was linear, a string of events you had to accept. If your wife dies, you bury her and go on. If the ranch burns, you put the fire out and then go on. He was blissfully unencumbered by existential angst. Malloy pondered how the two friends could see life so differently as he sank into sleep.

A few hours later, Roland Kerr shook Malloy's shoulder, startling him awake. Malloy was sitting on the running board of a company pickup, his head leaning against the hard metal of the door. He was exhausted. He needed a break from the sun, and Doc Lambeau was now ordering the ranch hands into shifts, requiring them to rest. The sun still broiled from the west, but it was sliding toward the lip of the horizon. They had moved to the far side of the road, parking trucks, trailers and equipment in the bar ditch. The tankers had dumped water on the blacktop, adding another deterrent to the flames' advance.

The fire had slowed, but it burned on. Black smoke billowed southward, over Rolling Ranch Estates, filtering the sun's descent through a haze.

Malloy was unsure how long he'd been dozing. There were no dreams, just the deep all-embracing release of exhaustion. Kerr shook his shoulder again.

"Trace, the major's offering us a ride in the next chopper, after they make their dump. I figured we should go up and inspect the damage."

Malloy hesitated. "We shouldn't slow them down. Let them keep making runs."

His thoughts, bogged down by fatigue, were slow to assemble. Kerr chuckled slightly.

"It's okay. They think we've got this thing about licked. You can see it's dying down on the front lines."

Malloy stood up, blinking his eyes furiously to clear sleep and smoke from his vision. Across the road he could see the flames were lower than they had been; the smoke was still billowing but with less intensity. The winds had subsided, and the smoke coming off the smoldering fields rose almost straight toward the gaping maw of the sky.

Locals, guardsmen, and firefighters from three counties had made double trenches along the Main Road, and the dozers had pushed back the grasses and underbrush. The flames seemed to be stalled several hundred feet away. They hadn't moved much from the last time Malloy had looked at them, the first time all day they didn't seem to be chewing their way forward. The winds had settled down, too, Malloy noticed.

"They're going to attempt a few more runs, but then they'll be ready for us in an hour or so," Kerr went on. "In the meantime, I was thinking you could go with Ed and help him fix the damage he did over at the subdivision. After all, it was your idea," Kerr ribbed him.

Malloy milled through the small crowd until he found Ed Scott, and together they climbed into his pickup. Neither man said much. As they pulled up to Rolling Ranch Estates, they saw that the automatic gate was open. Witherspoon was sitting cross-legged on the ground, near the edge of the lake. Ed stopped the truck and they walked over to him.

"We're about done," Ed said, looking back and forth between Witherspoon and Malloy before starting toward the truck. "This idea you guys had, I think it really saved the day." He hesitated a moment, then said, "Well, I'm going to try to find a way to bypass the damage to the pipes so we don't waste any more water. Either that, or we'll have to cut it off."

Witherspoon stood up, and he and Malloy stared at each other for a moment in silence. Then Malloy stuck out his hand.

"I want to thank you for what you did today. I know all of this," he motioned over his shoulder toward the curtain of black smoke still wafting up from the ranch, "isn't really your concern. I can appreciate how much what you did will cost you."

"Well, all of Conquistador was at stake—your ranch, my plant, and the town," Witherspoon said. "And, after all, it's my town too, isn't it?" He smiled sheepishly.

Malloy turned toward the smoke again.

"It's bad. I'm not sure how we'll come back from this."

"Yeah," Witherspoon said, following his gaze, "I've seen this happen in California. You'll manage to come back somehow.

But both our workplaces took a lot of damage today, that's for sure. I burned up a pretty expensive water recycler and set back the opening probably by a couple of months. Still, it's nothing compared with what you're facing. We did what we had to do, I guess."

Malloy turned back to Witherspoon, and a smile spread from under his mustache.

"That we did," he said. "And again, I thank you for it. And I hope you find your boy."

He patted the side of Witherspoon's arm and strode over to where Scott was working to fix the pipe he'd ruptured, leaving Witherspoon heading slowly in the direction of his house.

Malloy was back on the road outside the Tie Bow in less than an hour. Some of the cars that had made up the command post were beginning to disperse. One of the big Chinooks landed in the nearby pasture.

Major DeFillippo motioned for Malloy and Kerr to follow him as they ducked low and trotted toward the door. The twin rotors idled above them in a whirling canopy of metal.

They climbed inside and strapped themselves into seats near the open hatch. The helicopter lifted off with a lurch and then they were airborne, climbing straight up, the vast panorama of the land unfolding before them.

The smoke, though still thick, had dissipated even more than just a few hours earlier. From their elevation, Malloy could see through the blackness, and forms began to take shape beyond the haze.

Orange borders of flame still ringed the area, as the fire line continued to press outward from the downed electrical tower that sparked the blaze. They had fought the fire on one side, leaving the other edges to burn with abandon. There was nothing for miles in those directions except more of the Tie Bow.

The helicopter swung to the west and then turned northward. They swept along a path that would take them over the cellular grazing experiment and the collapsed tower that had sparked the carnage around them less than twenty-four hours ago.

The Tie Bow was a huge smoldering crater, like some devastated world, a computer-generated image in a documentary about Venus, perhaps. Junipers and mesquite had been reduced to jumbles of darkened sticks. The ground itself was scorched, dotted with skeletons of prickly pear, seared rocks, and ash piles that had once been Johnsongrass or thistles.

In the distance, the high-tension towers sagged and buckled. Their scorched girders reached skyward in gnarled and twisted futility. Even from his vantage point, Malloy could see that one tower had broken and crumpled to the ground.

The buffalo grass pastures were a field of fine ash, whipped up by the wind. The earth lay naked and exposed, years of work stripped away.

The soil underneath, relieved of the grass to hold it in place, was already beginning to be scattered in the wash of the helicopter's powerful blades. With the first good rain, Malloy knew, it would be swept away, just as it had a century ago when ranchers ignorant of land maintenance had first encroached on these parts.

Nature's destruction had been far swifter than man's, but no less fatal.

Malloy stared through the portal on the other side of the chopper. They'd stopped the fire at the Main Road. He knew their heroics had saved his own home, the house his father had built. The thick glass of the helicopter window, though, obscured its faded clapboards and the acreage where he'd played as a child and still worked as a man. He couldn't see the roofline under which his father had died silently, where he and Darla ministered to his ailing mother, and where his son now rested, exhausted. From his own window, on the other side of the chopper, all he could see were the patchwork yards and vaulted roofs of Rolling Ranch Estates. Their freshly laid shingles seemed to shimmer unblemished in the advancing twilight.✯

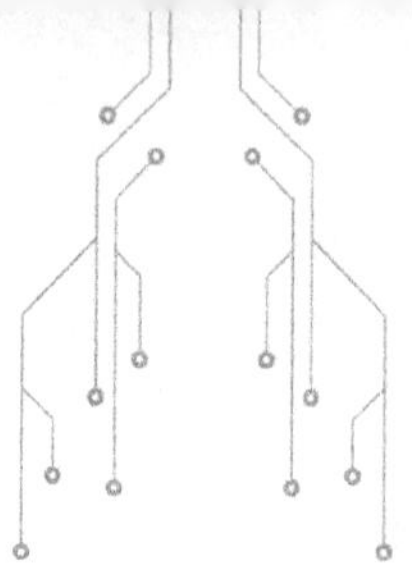

EPILOGUE

TRACE MALLOY TUGGED on the door handle at AzTech Semiconductor Manufacturing. As usual, it didn't budge.

He put a hand up to the window and peered in. The lobby looked as it always did. Clear plastic tarps covered the receptionist's desk where Sherrie Duncan once sat. The room was dimly lit by the natural light that shone through the glass doors.

Sherrie hadn't been in her seat in years. She was now the accounting manager at the Conquistador Country & Golf Club, where Roland Kerr and Charlie Weeks were the local members. Kerr had tried to convince Malloy to join, but he had declined. He couldn't see himself playing golf. Although he'd walked and ridden over what were now the greens for most of his life, the closest he'd ever come to a country club was renting a video of "Caddyshack." He didn't understand the allure of the game. He never could bring himself to sacrifice hours upon hours just to say he'd hit a little ball in a hole. And he wouldn't be caught dead in those clothes.

The vinyl chairs in the reception area were covered in a thin coating of dust. Malloy savored the irony of that for a moment—a layer of dust in a building designed to filter out even the smallest airborne particles.

He turned from the door and completed his circuit of the building. It was a routine by now, a well-worn habit. Once in the morning, once at night. Walk the perimeter, check the doors, report anything suspicious.

Nothing suspicious, of course, ever happened in Conquistador, so his job largely involved just showing up. And show up he did. Faithfully. It was the only way his conscience would allow him to cash the four-hundred-dollar checks that AzTech mailed him every two weeks, denoting his services as a "security consultant."

Malloy took a sip of coffee from the Thermos he carried on his appointed rounds. The sun was inching over the flat rim of the eastern horizon. The heat from the drink caused his breath to be visible, spewing forth like the morning yawn of a dragon.

He walked to the front of the truck, and, ignoring the crack that seemed to split the windshield in half, clambered up on the hood. The engine was still warm beneath him and it felt good against the harsh chill of the morning. He knew he should be getting to the office, but he decided to take a moment and savor the sunrise.

Roland Kerr had retired two years ago, and Malloy was in charge. Whatever that meant, it damn sure allowed him to linger a few moments over a pristine winter sunrise, the kind that the Big Empty served up without equal.

He gazed down the slope from the parking lot, across the broad expanse as the burgeoning sunlight spilled westward over the land like paint oozing out of an overturned can. He could barely see the back edge of his of his own property. He looked beyond the Main Road, straight as a pencil mark below the horizon, to what used to be the Tie Bow. The white splotches of the sand traps seemed almost illuminated against the dark green of the grass.

They'd completed the eighteen-hole "championship" course over a year ago. As yet, they had no championship to go with it. Malloy wasn't happy about it, and not just because it had consumed part of the ranch, as if some of his own life had been lopped off and given away. No, it was, once again, the water. He was still fighting people from far away who didn't understand the unslakable thirst of the Big Empty. A golf course took less water than a wafer fab, but it was still a waste.

Malloy's job was running the small ranching operation that was left. Frye had sold or was in the process of selling about eighty percent of the old Conquistador. Most had been bought by private investors—New York City money managers, Internet tycoons, sports stars, foreign billionaires. In addition to the golf course, which was managed by a real estate investment trust out of Dallas, several of the new owners were trying their hand at tourism. Over on the old West Fork there was even a lodge where city slickers could hire Ed Scott to teach them to hunt quail.

The quail hunters had a big fancy dinner once a year in Dallas—the kind of swanky affair that only Dallas could host. Well-made women in cocktail dresses mingled among the vendors, who held semi-automatic weapons that may or may not have been necessary for quail hunting. It didn't matter. They raised several million dollars in a single night in the name of conservation. Quail had largely been wiped out east of the Mississippi, so now, rich people whose only connection to the land was a hunting lease and a love of long-dead myths raised gobs of money to protect little birds from extinction so they could kill them later.

For Malloy, there was now just the main ranch to keep track of. The old bunkhouse had been renovated into a series of small rooms. Malloy called it a dude ranch, though Frye didn't like that term. They called it the Conquistador Ranch Resort. For $300 a night, you could sleep in the newly refurbished bunkhouse, have Darla cook you a real cowboy breakfast, and then saddle up and ride the range with John Cyrus and Bobby Ray Cox. At night, they'd make a big fire and Old Hank, who had to be well into his nineties by now, would tell stories and sing cowboy songs.

Frye marketed the CRR as a getaway from the hectic pressures of city life. No phones, no TV, just plenty of relaxation. Malloy still laughed at the thought.

He refused, he told Frye corporate, to be a damn innkeeper. So they'd hired a thirty-one-year-old kid from Indiana with an MBA from the University of Wisconsin to come down and handle "the business."

Malloy was officially Vice President for Ranch Operations—basically Kerr's old job. He still punched cows and ran the crews just like always, except now there were far fewer—cows and crew alike.

But with Kerr's retirement, he'd gotten a raise—they actually paid him more to stay and keep doing the only job he'd ever known. Combined with the money for keeping tabs on AzTech, he was making more than he ever had in his life. He and Darla had enough savings to enroll Colt at Texas A&M, where he'd started three months earlier to study agricultural economics. Malloy had even taken some time off and the couple had driven their son all the way down to College Station. Then, they'd turned southward and spent the weekend in Galveston, the first time either of them had seen the sea. They'd walked barefoot on the beach, eaten fresh oysters plucked from the

Gulf of Mexico, and lingered in shops on the Strand. By Sunday afternoon, he'd begun to feel guilty about so much leisure, and they'd headed northwest, through the choked interchanges of Houston, past Waco and on up toward the familiar vast nothingness of the Big Empty.

He resisted the urge to swing through College Station again to make sure Colt was really there and not sneaking off to the Air Force Academy. But the dreams of flying the F-22 were as dead to his son as the Merchant Marine was to him. Maturity had brought clarity as it often does, but not the clarity Malloy had hoped for. Colt had no interest in studying computer science or some other career that seemed to offer a future. He was still planning to come back to Conquistador, to build a life with new theories dreamed up by some tweed-suited professors safely wrapped in the blankets of tenure.

The Conquistador's demise made his son more resolute than ever to follow the family business, determined to find a better way of ranching. Malloy decided not to argue. Besides, four years can do a lot to change a young man's heart.

Even with tuition costs—Colt insisted on getting a job and paying for most of his other expenses—they were still doing well enough that Trace began to think they might actually clear the debts on their land, wiping away two generations of financial hardship.

It was a bittersweet achievement. His good fortune had come as so many others in town had lost the savings they'd plunged foolishly into AzTech stock at the behest of Jack Watley, the former finance officer. Watley had turned out to be a crook. He and Howard Swain had been manipulating AzTech's earnings reports, buying shares for themselves when the stock fell, then selling it when it went back up. Another plant manager apparently figured it out and turned them in. Witherspoon was called to testify in a civil case brought by the Securities and Exchange Commission, which resulted in Watley getting fined $450,000 and Swain $200,000. Neither of them "admitted nor denied wrongdoing," a phrase that Malloy simply couldn't fathom. Rich people's punishment is different from what the rest of us receive, he guessed. He tried to imagine how Nelda would have responded if, when she caught him in one of his many boyhood transgressions, he had used that line.

Despite AzTech's collapse and the added hardship it brought to Conquistador, folks were making the best of it, as they always did. Malloy had run into Ed Scott at Terry Garrison's garage two weeks ago. Scott told him that even between the hunting business and his stipend as fire marshal, he was barely keeping money in the bank. The school wanted to hire him back as a coach. The incoming freshman class was big enough to restore the football team, at least for one year. After that, who knew? The money for his position had been cut years ago, soon after the fire. Now, he was in his mid-fifties with no health insurance and his family's nest egg shattered by AzTech's decline.

Hardship was nothing new in the Big Empty, though, and Malloy was careful to never talk about his own improved financial condition. It just proved what his mother used to say about God's will being a mystery. Somehow, punching a man in the nose had led to prosperity for him, while those who took another man at his word were suffering.

The sun was now a gaping red maw, yawning at him as it pulled itself up from the horizon. He took a sip of his coffee and hopped down from the truck. The AzTech plant loomed dark and silent across the parking lot. Weeds poked through the cracks in the pavement. Off beyond the golf course a coyote wailed, a final howl before ending his nocturnal shift. The sound drifted across the plains, floating lazily on the thick, cold air.

AzTech had discovered that the Big Empty lived up to its name far too well. Witherspoon had never been able to meet the cost projections for the project, nor could he find enough local labor to fill all the positions the company needed. Witherspoon's plan for diverting the water to fight the fire had damaged a bunch of expensive equipment inside the plant, adding to the costs and delays. The power lines had to be restrung, and Cap Rock Electric had to wait for its insurance money to come through. By then, it didn't matter. The plant never did open. The founder of the company, an old guy named Soder-something, had been forced to "retire," which was a nice way of saying he been kicked out of his own company. Apparently, the board came to its senses and realized his idea to build a chip plant in the middle of the Big Empty was insanity. Malloy still wished they'd figured that out in time to save the Tie Bow.

The new millennium hadn't dawned as the golden era for technology after all. The "new economy" everyone had been talking about in 1999 had turned out to be the same economy as ever, and the market for the company's chips collapsed along with most everything else related to the Internet. From what he'd read in *The Wall Street Journal,* most investors still thought the company would survive. AzTech was a hardware maker, after all, not some dot-com daydream. Even so, no one had ever seen anything like the scandal that erupted around the company's accounting—Fortune 500 executives caught cooking the books like a bunch of penny stock hucksters.

AzTech filed for Chapter 11 bankruptcy soon after the turn of the new millennium. It reorganized as a far smaller company, and the new equity owners had no intention of keeping the factory in Conquistador. They needed fewer—and cheaper—facilities, they'd told the county commissioners. The company had never gotten close to the three billion dollars it had once promised to invest. All the same, Conquistador had been a costly failure.

AzTech still owned the building. Technically, it was for sale, but no one expected a buyer to come forward. The county hoped to find one that would revive the dream of economic salvation, but nobody believed it would happen. In the meantime, the company paid Malloy to make sure its asset wasn't ransacked, although to Malloy's knowledge, nothing other than the porta-potties at the 4-H rodeo had ever been ransacked in Conquistador. The company's demise had been swift and brutal, and laid off workers fled the town as fast as they'd arrived.

Malloy pondered the irony and shook his head. He'd never considered a job at AzTech for himself. In fact, from the time the deal was signed he'd weighed whether the costs of the plant would outstrip the benefits. But he saw a future for Colt and a rescue for Conquistador and largely held his tongue.

Colt quickly made it clear he had no interest in a Silicon Valley lifestyle. Conquistador was still struggling to put the mistake behind it. But he, Trace Malloy, the dyed-in-the-wool cowboy and inveterate corporate doubter, was collecting a regular paycheck bearing the AzTech logo. He'd wound up as the chipmaker's only employee in the Big Empty, if not the entire state. Go figure.

Malloy's contacts at AzTech had helped him piece together bits of the internal power struggle that had contributed to the company's downfall. Witherspoon had testified in the SEC's accounting investigation and Malloy picked up snippets of how Swain and Watley had duped the homie. Now Malloy understood why Witherspoon had been so willing to damage his own plant to fight the fire that weekend. It almost made him forgive the guy for all his other quirks and transgressions.

He'd heard some talk that Swain and Watley might face criminal charges from the Justice Department, although nothing had happened.

As for Witherspoon, shortly after the bankruptcy, he'd been "let go."

"That's Californian for shit-canned," he told Malloy before he left, which had given them both a chuckle. Malloy guessed they'd parted as friends, or at least on good enough terms that Witherspoon had recommended him for the security job. He still didn't know how he felt about the other man. He didn't really dislike him, and yet, he couldn't say he was sorry he and most of the other homies were gone, either.

Brandon had turned up three days after the fire. The old clunker from Terry Garrison's garage had broken down in Clayton, New Mexico. Apparently, Brandon's mother had given him a credit card for "emergencies," and he'd tried to use it to fix the truck. A suspicious mechanic pulled up the vehicle registration and noticed it didn't match the name on the credit card. He tracked down Garrison by phone, who told the guy to keep the truck.

The Witherspoons had collected their son and, after Blaine's firing, they packed up and moved to New Jersey. That was the last Malloy had heard of them. By the time they'd left for the East Coast, they had already found what they were sure would be a terrific counseling program for Brandon. The odd part, Malloy always thought, was that they never offered to pay Terry for the truck. Never even apologized.

Malloy drove past the entrance to Rolling Ranch Estates. The gate was open permanently, its hinges streaked with rust. The pond was bone dry. After the last resident pulled out, the county had cut off water to the whole area as a "conservation measure," although he suspected they'd simply diverted it to the golf course. The houses now were falling into disrepair. Paint peeled, screens hung loosely, lawns were overgrown. Some still sat in frame, unfinished, their wood graying from exposure. In a few places, there were only concrete slabs. The whole high-end development would have been declared a blight if anybody other than Malloy were around to see it.

He turned left onto the familiar Main Road. At this early hour, though, he often felt like a character in one of those post-Doomsday sci-fi movies. The last man on earth. The Omega Cowboy.

Roland Kerr sought refuge in retirement, bearing the guilt for the financial hardship that had been inflicted on just about everyone he knew in town. They'd listened to him, after all, and he'd led them into ruin. Folks in Conquistador had plenty of criticism for AzTech, but Malloy had never heard anybody blame Kerr—other than Kerr himself. "We all got sucked into this thing together," Charlie Weeks had said soon after the bankruptcy filing.

That had been more than two years ago. Now, few people ever spoke of the high-tech dreams that once blew across the Big Empty.

But Conquistador was more alive than ever, and people were hoping their financial hardships would begin to ease. Tourism was bringing money to the area. The Dallas real estate company financed a small airstrip behind the new ranch "resort" in the Tie Bow, making the whole place accessible to corporate aircraft. The hunting lodge over on the West Fork and the golf course offered jobs that suited the locals a lot better than being sealed into a clean room. The Big Empty, it seemed, was filling up with visitors savoring an authentic "West Texas experience" and a weekend of peace and isolation that offered a reprieve from urban sprawl and bustle.

The remoteness that had worked against the Big Empty from the time of the Spaniards was now an attraction. It was becoming a premier getaway for wealthy city people. For those who had everything, vacationing where there was nothing was the ultimate luxury.

The locals mostly lived off outsiders now, who came with the same impunity as the homies had. The difference, Malloy thought, is that now they don't just come, they also go. And they leave their money behind. It seemed a much better arrangement for everyone.

Maybe the residents of Conquistador had learned that if economic salvation were coming, it would come from outside. But he hoped they'd also learned to be a little more skeptical of plans that seemed too good to be true and a little less eager to embrace the promises of people they didn't know.

Malloy turned left onto the Gunyon Road. He'd intended to head to the ranch offices, but he kept driving, embracing the solitude of the morning. He drove on, bumping over the dormant railroad tracks, then suddenly hung a hard left, surprising himself. He instinctively put his hand on his coffee mug, which sloshed violently as he hit a rut at the turnoff.

He bounced along the dirt road until he pulled up the little rise and into the open area at the top. The lone ironwood tree stood defiantly off to the side. Malloy slid out of the truck, the gravel crunching under his hiking boots. He wandered to the small cluster of graves, the only reminder of those who, for a few short years, held their own against the unforgiving expanse that had once called to them like a siren, only to grind them, ultimately, to dust. The emerging day cast a golden glow on the headstones. The Big Empty spread itself around him, a vast blanket of nothingness, a barren land embraced only by the equally cold and unfeeling sky.

A harsh wind cut down from the north, much like the one that had triggered the fire. This time it was bitter cold and brought an omen: Snow was coming. Malloy could tell by the feel of the air, by the psychological warning it carried.

He stopped and stood by what he guessed would be the family plot if frontier cemeteries were ever that formal. Caleb and Nelda and Lucas laid straight and proper beneath their granite markers. Loving father and husband. Loving mother and wife. Beloved son. Luke wasn't really there, of course. He'd escaped the Big Empty and never came back.

The sun cast its light on the granite of the headstones, and for a moment it appeared to glow. Malloy stared down at the monuments of his past. Then he looked at the ground under his feet, and back across the boundless carpet of land. Still plenty of room, he thought.✯

THE BIG EMPTY: REAL-WORLD RELEVANCE

In 2022, podcaster Tom Fox interviewed Loren Steffy about the issues and themes in his debut novel, *The Big Empty*. As Fox saw it, the book may have been set in 1999, but many of the issues at the heart of the story are even more relevant today than they were then.

The result was a five-part podcast series, *The Big Empty and Economic Issues Facing 21st Century Texas*. The series looked at key issues that the book examines: Water, power, land investment, housing, and of course, the clash of cultures. It won Communicators Awards for Excellence in a Limited Series and Distinction in Business.

What follows is a transcript of those discussion. It has been edited for length and clarity.

INTRODUCTION

I'm Tom Fox. As much as I enjoyed *The Big Empty*, it struck me that it touched upon many of the current economic and cultural issues facing Texas, its governments, and its citizens, circa 2022.

The Big Empty is set in 1999, and it's a tale about the sense of place, telling the story of a fictional company, AzTech, which builds a semiconductor plant in the dying west Texas town of Conquistador. This attempt is beset by the clash of culture and bringing in Silicon Valley tech entrepreneurs to rural Texas. The book also raises multiple economic issues facing Texas as we move toward the mid-21st century.

We'll consider important issues facing Texas today—water, power, land investment, housing, and of course the clash of cultures. But first, I talked with the author, Loren Steffy, who spent most of his career as a journalist and nonfiction author, about what made him want to write the novel.

—~—

Tom: What motivated you to write *The Big Empty*?

Loren: I was fascinated by this idea of the sense of place and what happens when that sense of place starts to change. If human history is basically change over time, then every place that we know changes—and especially when some change more than others. That was really what I was trying to get at. This was a small rural community that was facing extinction, really, and they were trying to come up with a way to preserve their future, which they thought they had done. But then the question becomes what's the price of that future? And do you have to give up everything that you know, your way of life? And caught up in that is this idea that people live a certain way in certain places based on the environment that they know better than anybody else. And so when outsiders come in, it may seem, "Oh, this is stupid. Why are you doing that?" But in fact, there's a good reason for it. If you show up in West Texas and think that you should have a golf course and a decorative fountain in your neighborhood, somebody may tell you that's not how we use water in West Texas.

Tom: You took that sense of place literally back to about the 1840s, with the original settlers from the geographic area that encompassed the Big Empty and brought the issues that they faced in the nineteenth century forward to the 20th century—and then forward into the 21st century. One of the things that struck me was many of the issues from the 1840s, the 1870s, are still facing those parts of Texas today.

Loren: It's really true, the past informs the future. And not only is it true from what happened in the 1840s, 1800s forward, but the book itself is set at 1999, at the cusp of the new millennium. And at the time I wrote this, I thought one of the things I might get called out for is the idea that we're going to build a chip plant in a small town. Is that really going to happen? And then you look at what's going on now, and a lot of these themes have actually become more prominent since I started writing the book, or since I got the idea for the book. It's really been inter-esting to me to watch some of these things come to pass. And of course part of the reason we're talking today is because these issues are still very current.

I. WATER

"I think we all understand the need for water," Witherspoon said, in a tone so condescending it immediately reminded Malloy of the first ranch supervisor he'd worked for in Kansas. "If you understood it, you turn off that fountain," Malloy fired back. "Mr. Malloy, the people here are trying to build homes. We want to build a community. We moved here to get away from the city, the crime. We want our community to be safe and attractive, and that lake is a big part of that."

– From *The Big Empty*

Tom: So let's start with the issue of water. You mentioned the golf course but tell us about the lake. The lake ends up playing a very big part in the resolution of this story as well. So in many ways the lake becomes a hero near the end of the book. What did the lake mean to the newcomers and equally importantly, what did the lake mean to the towns folk?

Loren: The term "lake" is somewhat... It would be in dispute, depending on what your sense of a lake is. This is more of a pond, or perhaps even a water feature. But basically, when the workers from the chip plant begin to move into the town of Conquistador, they want to build a neighborhood, they want to build a gated community, and it has to have a decorative fountain in the front. Why wouldn't you do that? As we've seen all over the whole country, developers are like, "Oh yeah, great. What's the problem? We'll just do it." The locals are very concerned about water use, and keep in mind that semiconductor manufacturing requires a lot of water, too. So an underlying theme of the book is the scarcity of water and the drain on resources that these kinds of developments take.

Tom: I can't think of a worse insult to say than, "Your neighborhood has a water feature." That may be the ultimate Texas insult. Not a lake, not even a pond, but a water feature. I'll have to remember that one.

Let's use that to explore some of the issues around water in Texas. You obviously touched on the most important one right now: do we have enough? But there's a lot of other issues involved here, such as transportation of water, water treatment, desalinization, and pipelines. Where do you see some of the big issues right now around water and aquifers in Texas?

Loren: Obviously here in the Hill Country, it's a huge issue. The issue of development, you're seeing in all the areas west of Austin, for example, where they're building high-density housing developments without a whole lot of regard for where the water's going to come from for these neighborhoods—not just in the first year or two, but ten to twenty years down the road. The developers will be long gone by then. They don't care. But there's a sustainability issue in terms of whether we will have enough water for drinking and things like that. And you have seen some communities, Dripping Springs, for example, put a moratorium on new development. They've now lifted it, but they were studying the water use issue. A lot of other communities are buying water from elsewhere and shipping it in, and that raises all kinds of problems because it's getting pumped from somewhere, and usually from a ranch or something.

Our water laws in Texas are unique in the United States. They're based on something called rule of capture, which is drawn from England back in the 1600s or something. Basically, it means that if you own the land, you can pump out as much water as you want from under that land and do whatever you want with it. Part of the reason we have that law is because, of course, if you're irrigating cotton fields or other farmland, that's a good thing to have. But if you're living in a water sensitive area and you suddenly have hundreds and hundreds of houses being built all over the place, it's not necessarily a good thing.

There's a lot of conflict coming over water. We see the same thing playing out in Corpus Christi. They're having issues. They had a water plan that involved building desalinization plants. But they have attracted a lot of heavy industry that uses a lot of water. The desalinization plants haven't been built, so they're in a crisis. And what happens in these situations, by the way, is the individuals are the ones that wind up bearing the restrictions, and Corpus Christi was a great example. There were restrictions on who could water their lawn, but you've got an industrial plant that's sucking up millions of gallons of water.

We've seen that here in the Hill Country. There are communities, there are cities that are watering their municipal golf courses at the same time people aren't allowed to water their lawns. And what tends to happen is the residents are the ones that have to deal with the restrictions. They're the ones that bear the burden, and in most cases, they do what they need to do. But you're almost getting punished for it because somebody else is going to come in and build more.

I live in Wimberley, and we have a situation here where they just approved a big RV park, which of course has to have a swimming pool. They requested and received permission for four and a half million gallons of water a year so that people who don't even live here can swim in a pool in an area that really shouldn't have any swimming pools. And it's the rest of us, we're all trying to use as little water as possible, putting in rainwater collection systems and things like that. But those guys show up and, on a whim, they get granted this permit.

So there's a lot of injustice around water. And while that wasn't necessarily the theme I was trying to hit in the book, I think it does touch on that. This idea that water's a shared resource and if we don't figure out a smart way to use it better, we're going to have big problems.

Tom: Let's touch on the flip side—too much water. We both lived in Houston, which has had massive development. What about all those houses built on the Katy flatlands west of Houston? It was lowland that was rice farms for time immemorial. It was designed to have a lot of water in it. Now it's cemented over—streets, houses, et cetera. What about too much water and flood control? Is there any sort of coordination from that, or do residents of West Harris County or counties west of Houston just build without regard for the consequences?

Loren: Well, I think we've saw the answer to that after Hurricane Harvey. If you live down below the Addicks Reservoir, you got the answer to that. Your neighborhood had to be flooded because developers were allowed to go in and build in an area in which they knew, if there was a problem, water was going to have to be released from that reservoir. Those areas were designed to be flooded, a lot of people living there didn't know that.

We moved to Houston from Dallas, where you don't have the same kind of water issues. Somebody told us, "You have to make sure your house isn't in a floodplain." So, when we would look at houses, we would always ask, "Is this in a floodplain?" And I remember one builder saying, "Not really." What does that mean?

They go in, they build retention ponds, and they do all these things that are designed to pull that land off the flood maps. It gets it out of the fl oodplain. But if they don't do it right, then you have problems later, and in a lot of cases it could be years before anyone knows if they did it right. Harvey was a pretty good test, but this is going to continue to be an issue because the need for development, the need for housing, and certainly in a city like Houston, finding a place that's close in, that's affordable, and doesn't flood h as g otten i ncreasingly difficult. And so there's a lot of pressure on development just from a conceptual standpoint. People want to live closer to where they work, and at the same time, you have all these flooding issues. If you're a homeowner or a home buyer, you have to juggle this. Do I want to buy this house? Will it *probably* be okay? Can we put it up on stilts? These are the kind of things you have to go through, and it makes it really tough.

Tom: I lived in one of those neighborhoods that flooded out after Harvey. But let me go to the end of the book where, I won't say water becomes a protagonist, but water plays a very big part in how the story resolves itself. Did that just occur to you? Did you have that in mind? Because I thought it was a great way to tie in this theme of water in the book, where it goes from a scarce resource to something that water has been used for since time immemorial, which is to put out a fire.

Loren: One of the challenges in writing fiction is you have to plan where the story's going to go. So, yes, I did think that through—because of this theme about water. But I think it really forces the idea that water was the saving grace in a dire situation. That was a point I was trying to hammer home. That's what Trace Malloy, the main character in the book, was trying to get the plant manager, Blaine Witherspoon, to understand from the beginning. His whole warning was, "You don't understand what could happen."

II. POWER

What if they couldn't get the power they needed? The company had put up money to run new power lines, but there had been some problems getting the right of way. He was estimating they'd need 60 watts a square foot, far more than anything ever built in this region. What if that number was low? Or what if the infrastructure simply couldn't deliver?

– From *The Big Empty*

Tom: Loren, I'm almost reluctant to raise the topic of power with you, number one, because it seems like you spent a large portion of your professional career writing, talking, and thinking about this. Number two, it is as relevant and probably as divisive today as it was when the book took place, back in 1999. But power plays a huge part in this. Obviously if you have a chip plant, the power needed to air condition the plant is beyond almost anything.

Texas now is a large area for Bitcoin mining, which takes huge power consumption. That was not part of the story, but the chip manufacturing was, and the part that I wanted to focus on is regardless of the power demands and consumption, you have to get power to the plant, and that led to a near catastrophe and the setup for the end of the book. What were you trying to get us to think about with those areas of the book?

Loren: That whole power situation started because I was thinking through the issues of trying to build a plant of that size and that capacity in a place like that, and I realized like there's not going to be any electric infrastructure to make that happen. They'd have to build it, and that would be part of the incentive that the county would offer to get the plant there. They would have to run new power lines directly to this plant or to this area. That led to the question, "What would that entail?" They'd have to get right of way. The more I thought through it, the more it became this theme that was going to really form the centerpiece of the book. The power lines are in the background until the end, when they cause a problem, and it grew out of that necessity in the plot. It just seemed to me like you had to figure out how they were going to power this.

Tom: So if we turn to the great state of Texas, I think you wrote about the first major blackout in 2010 or 2011, you wrote about it again in 2016, and you wrote about it in 2021. Take us through that part of your professional journey, the issues you saw ten years ago, and the resolution, or more importantly, the non-resolution that led to 2021 and even today.

Loren: When I started writing *The Big Empty*, Texas still had a regulated power market, and the issues that I might have brought up had it been set at a later time really aren't in the book. In fact, if the events in *The Big Empty* were happening now, they'd probably be using wind power and getting electricity really cheap out there. I came to the Houston Chronicle soon after the market had been deregulated. It wasn't even fully up and running yet, and as a columnist, I looked at it from a consumer perspective: "What is the benefit of all this?" There's all this confusion, all this complexity, and certainly at that time, power rates were going up, residential rates were going up because natural gas prices were rising and electric prices in Texas are basically pegged to the price of natural gas.

From a consumer standpoint, there was a lot of cost, and there was no benefit. There was a tremendous amount of confusion because they did a very poor job of explaining how the market worked. And that was partly because it's not an easy thing to understand, and that has carried forward over the past twenty years. We've seen it with all the power outages, the blackout situations that you mentioned. People still have a hard time understanding how this market works, what's happening, why these crises are occurring. Fundamentally, it's because we built a grid that is designed to operate right now but has no backup. So when unexpected events occur, the grid's strained, and there's very little that we can do. We trot out some dirty old coal plants in East Texas to try to fill the gaps.

In fact, we pretty much are doing that every year now, but it's not a long-term plan. And actually the Public Utility Commission just came out with a new report looking at this issue of grid reliability and what they can do to enhance things. In Texas, we love the idea of free markets, and we have convinced ourselves that we have a free market for electricity. We really don't, as we saw in 2021 when the regulators intervened in the market at a critical time. We'll be paying for that for a long time. I've made the point that my granddaughter, who was not even born at the time of that crisis, when she becomes an adult, will be paying for the cost of the mistakes that were made in 2021. So it's a very, very convoluted and inefficient system. It benefits a small group of people at the expense of everybody else, and it's a big mess that's going to be very hard to fix.

Tom: Let me touch on one of the topics you raised, which is alternative forms of power. And you specifically mentioned wind farms. If you drive anywhere west of the Hill Country, you're going to see massive wind farms. Texas is uniquely situated to capture wind. I see a huge economic advantage to having wind farms in places that make sense because every one of those wind farms has rotating parts. They have to be oiled, so somebody's got to crawl up there and oil them, and that means a job. But the current administration in the state of Texas often very strongly attacks alternative forms of energy. Are alternative forms of energy viable option if a plant such as the one you wrote about was being built today? So for instance in Taylor, Texas, or any other place where they may need massive amounts of power, could a company really try to self-power themselves through alternative energy, perhaps even solar energy?

Loren: You're seeing more and more onsite generation for large plants, and yes, if it's onsite, it usually is solar because that's a little easier to do. You can put the panels on the rooftops or on carports and things like that. The wind power situation is interesting. We tend to gloss over the fact that Texas is the largest producer of wind energy in North America. It's a major industry for the state, and the big challenge is getting that power from West Texas eastward. For a long time, and I think this is still true, Occidental Petroleum was one of the biggest producers of oil and gas in West Texas, and they were basically buying electricity dirt cheap from these wind farms and using it to power all their rig equipment throughout the Permian Basin. So you had cheap wind energy being used to produce oil and gas, which I guess some people would find ironic, but it was a very efficient use of that resource.

You mentioned Bitcoin mining. You can use wind power, set up a Bitcoin mining operation on an old well site or something, and you can buy large amounts of power for very little money. When the politicians start talking about this—and let's face it, the politicians that talk about it are usually the governor and the railroad commission, and they both get a lot of money from the oil and gas industry—they rush to blame wind power any time there's a problem. Wayne Christensen, the railroad commission chairman, had a very contorted op-ed in *The Wall Street Journal* after the 2021 blackouts in which he desperately tried to find a way to blame wind power. He even took a piece I wrote in *Texas Monthly* and used it to support his argument, which was not at all what I was getting at.

But it's interesting that they're happy for the economic benefits of wind power when everything's working, and the minute there's a problem, they rush to find a way to blame it. Honestly, wind power had very little to do with the crisis in 2021. It's going to play an increasingly important role going forward because, as we talked about in our last episode, water's also an issue. It takes a lot of water to generate electricity through a combined-cycle natural gas plant or a nuclear plant. And so we need to find ways to generate electricity without using water. Wind and solar are probably our best options.

Tom: Loren, you touched on another issue I wanted to explore, which is transportation of power. How do we get electricity from West Texas to East Texas or how can we transport it out to the rest of North America?

Loren: That's a big issue. In Texas, we spent billions building very large transmission lines from West Texas to the eastern parts of the state. That part of the process is actually working relatively well. The big challenge now is getting the interconnects. So if you want to build a solar array in West Texas, how do you get that connected to these power lines? And who pays for that? Which is of course always the big question when it comes to electrification anywhere. It's a national problem. We need a better grid nationally. We need more grid capacity on a national level. I mentioned earlier a piece I wrote for *Texas Monthly* that Wayne Christensen brought up in *The Wall Street Journal*. That story was about Texas being an isolated grid.

The point I was making was that there's this archaic reason for why we're an isolated grid, but there are certain benefits to it. One is that we have been able to build and site wind farms much more quickly because we do that all within the state. We don't have to get permits from anywhere else, and we don't have to get into power-sharing agreements. If we were connected, for example, to the Midwestern grid, there might be situations where they could basically call on Texas to send power to other states, and we don't have to do that. After 2021, of course, most other states are looking at the situation in Texas and saying, "We don't want to connect to that mess. Yes, please just stay down there and solve your own problems." But there are certain factors that come with interconnections that may not necessarily be advantageous to Texas, at least until we get the market functioning better here.

And Texas is a big state with a lot of very unique situations when it comes to power. We also are a state where we have a lot of fuel resources. We produce more oil and gas than any other state. We have more wind energy than any other state. We have more uranium than most other states. We have a lot of fuel sources. We do hydropower. We're looking at offshore wind and things like that. And I think the stereotype of Texas as this haven for oil and gas is increasingly outdated because there's a lot of innovation going on around the state when it comes to some of these issues.

Tom: Could we end with a few words about solar power and where you see the solar power industry currently in the state of Texas and its potential for growth?

Loren: We're seeing some large-scale solar projects, especially in West Texas. Obviously, we have a lot of sun in Texas, and we could be putting it to use, but I think that where you're going to really start to see much more interest in solar is in what they call distributed generation, which is onsite generation. You're seeing more and more innovative technology coming into that space. Your roof tiles can have solar panels in them now. You can build carports with solar panels, and you can't tell they're there. Given the grid insecurity that we have in Texas, more and more residents are looking at solar installations for their homes and businesses. The math is a little tricky. I would caution anybody that's going to do that to look closely at the rate that the installation company or power provider pays you for the power that you generate and upload to the grid. Oftentimes that's a very low number because they want to be able to turn around and sell it into the market at a profit.

But there's some interesting economic models that are emerging there. Certainly on the business side of things, it's becoming something that more companies are looking at. If you're building new a building, a high-rise office building or something, there's a lot more effort to look at the energy consumption and how you manage that and how much you can generate yourself. The technology just continues to improve and get cheaper, and it's going to open up a lot more possibilities there.

III. LAND & DEVELOPMENT

"From the time the first slabs were poured, the big city developers brought in by the homies had controlled everything about the subdivision. Even that term, subdivision, was ludicrous, yet they held onto it. Yet the homes behind him were the newest and nicest for 100 miles or more. Wasn't this going to create jobs? Wouldn't this lead to greater economic prosperity?"

– From *The Big Empty*

Tom: One of the major topics of conversation in Texas has always been commercial investment, and you've really hit that directly on the head in this book. I wanted to use how the town got the company to actually move there as the setup and use that to explore the myriad of ways the state of Texas primarily helps companies relocate to Texas, the cost of that, and who pays for it, although I think we all know the answer to that. But so how did Conquistador get the plant to move there?

Loren: Through series of tax incentives. I didn't go into a lot of detail in the book because quite frankly, as a work of fiction, that would probably be rather boring and tedious for most readers, especially those outside of Texas. But I do reference the fact that there were tax breaks given. And one of the things that some of the characters worry about is all the building that comes with it—a big new plant, new neighborhood, very nice houses. If you're not collecting tax revenue from some of that or all of that, do you have a drain on resources without a revenue increase that matches it? It puts the community in a difficult spot.

Tom: We had something in Texas called Chapter 313 incentives, which allowed counties to discount property taxes. How does the school district make up that revenue? Could they increase residential property taxes? Do they have to go for additional bond issues? Obviously, I'm fascinated by these topics, and I know you are too, and we could probably geek out, but how does a county, particularly a rural county, plug in or get funds to plug in those lost revenues?

Loren: The theory behind it is if you give the tax break to the company, then it comes in, creates all these jobs, and the people filling those jobs will buy houses and pay the taxes. It might work better in a rural area where people are likely to locate in the same town. But in urban areas where we offer these big tax breaks, people may not be living in the same place, or they may not buy homes at all. There's a lot of variables there. You're betting that you're going to make up the tax losses over time with growth in the community.

Of course, it's not just about that one plant. There are all the related jobs that come in and as more people move to town, then you have more small businesses open, and it's this wonderful, prosperous thing that all works out in the end. But we've seen that really isn't the case. Take school districts. The amount of tax incentives that are being given or the tax subsidies that are given away to these companies is disproportionate to the benefits that come back. The tax breaks are so large that it makes it very hard for these communities to earn it back.

We had a situation in Taylor, Texas, north of Austin, where Samsung is building a big plant. At one point, the tax incentives were over $300 million. The plant was supposed to bring in 1,800 jobs. That about $174,000 a job. I don't know that communities look at this and ask themselves, "Is it worth it?" Because what's happened is economic development has really become a game. Every community does this. Every county does this. Every state does this. And I remember years ago, sitting in the governor's office arguing this point with his chief of staff. "Can't we just stop?" And he said, "We would all love to stop. The problem is you can't because you will immediately lose."

Everybody's playing this game, and there's really no way to get off the merry-go-round. And it's costly. If you're a large employer and you're coming into a community, you ought to want to invest in that community. You ought to pay school taxes to make sure that the schools are the best that they can be, because after all, that's where your employees' kids are going to school. And maybe your next generation of employees are going to come from that school. It's just nonsensical that these companies, to save a few million bucks on the front end, are willing to roll the dice on the future of education in their communities.

Tom: This story is, as we have said several times, set in a very rural area, but the problems you've just discussed occur in large metropolitan areas. Austin, which has a massive Tesla plant on the east side of town now, and Corpus Christi has a large industrial port. But what I've seen is companies are beginning to move to the next county over because they get even better deals. So Robstown was able to get an Exxon plant that might have been in the port of Corpus Christi or nearby. So we even have these county-by-county competitions.

In Austin, when I drove by the plant, the first thought I had was, "Who's going to pay for the in infrastructure to be able to get the cars, the employees, and the products over to the plant and to and from the plant?" How do we think about the infrastructure?

Loren: It's a really good point. There's always a debate. Will the company pay for the roads around the plant? I think that's one debate they're having in Taylor right now. But more importantly, beyond that, if you've got two-lane country roads and suddenly, you're having supply trucks rolling down there every week, who pays to widen those roads? Who pays to maintain those roads that are getting a lot more traffic? Ultimately the county taxpayers do. And it's the same thing I was talking about with the school districts. You have to ask yourself, "Is the benefit of the tax break going to cover all of these things?" In most cases, the answer is no.

The other thing is these companies come in and make big promises about who they're going to hire and how many jobs they're going to create. But in many cases, those promises are not fulfilled. It's not anything nefar-ious on the part of the companies. Business climates change. Product demand changes. You're building a chip plant, and it looks great and the government's offering incentives. But by the time the plant's finished, the chip market is in the tank. Is Samsung still going to hire 1,800 people in Taylor? [illegible] that really have no basis in fact. They're just an idea. But the bigger problem is how do you stop it. You still need to grow, and we've created this system. It's almost like a drug. We are so dependent on these tax giveaways for economic growth that we can't stop.

Tom: And let me use the Corpus Christi and Robstown example to explore another issue, which is the cost of land. If Exxon wanted to upgrade their Baytown facility, if Exxon wanted to put a new plant along the Houston Ship Channel, the land cost would be extraordinarily high. In a place like Robstown, Texas, it's going to be considerably lower. And the same in Conquistador. I would assume the land costs were pretty low. How does land cost kind of factor into this, perhaps separate and apart from the tax incentives?

Loren: That's what I call the resort effect. You see it a lot in small, isolated communities. Aspen, Colorado, is a great example of this. Aspen used to be a small mining town, and it became a place where, increasingly, as more and more investment came in, the joke became the millionaires got pushed out by the billionaires. That's great if you want to have a multi-million-dollar house in the hills outside of Aspen, but when you go to the restaurant, you still expect a waiter or waitress to bring you your food and a bartender to fix you a drink. Where do those people live?

Colorado has a lot of examples of this—ski towns where affordable housing is a huge struggle. We love Crested Butte, and outside of town, there's the Rocky Mountain Biological Laboratory. Every summer they bring in grad students and scientists from all over the world. They have some housing on site in this little town called Gothic, but there's never enough housing for everybody. How do you find a place where grad students can afford to live? How do you find a place for your full-time staff to live in a community where an old miner's shack in town is now selling for two or three million dollars?

I'm working on the sequel to *The Big Empty*, and this is going to be a factor. If you remember, there were some changes that occurred in the town of Conquistador at the end of the book. I'll be exploring how those changes play out. It becomes much more of a leisure market, and that has an impact on land prices. And so this idea that the locals basically get forced out as places become more popular is a real problem. That is also happening on what I guess what you'd call the industrial side of the equation. The more development there is, the more people want to live there, then obviously the higher the land prices go and the more difficult that makes it for average folks.

IV. CULTURE CLASH

Trace Malloy's fist landed firmly in the middle of the other man's nose. He could feel the bridge give under the force of his knuckles, and he knew he'd broken it. It wasn't much of a punch, just a quick jab that he pulled back instantly, as if to say, "I'm sorry."

– From *The Big Empty*

Tom: This entire book was about culture clashes. You really made that the centerpiece of this book. And you didn't wait very long to give us a culture clash—I'll call it "The Punch." Give us the setup to the punch and why that really illustrated this clash of cultures that permeates the book.

Loren: It ties back into one of the earlier themes: water. Trace Malloy, who's the main character in the book and represents the Conquistador Ranch, goes to a meeting of the homeowners' association for the new subdivision that's been built for the chip workers. They're talking about water use, and they're really talking about the water feature, the pond at the front of the neighborhood. An argument ensues in which the plant manager, Blaine Witherspoon, without fully realizing what he's saying, insults Malloy's mother. That gets him punched in the nose. Both the incident itself and the reaction to it, was where the culture clash really took off.

Blaine's response is he's going to sue Trace for assault, and Trace is driving home stewing about this and realizing that the only lawyer in town is a guy that he got into a fight with in elementary school. It just shows how their whole view of even something as simple as that one moment are just completely different.

Tom: I really liked the comment that Blaine made, which I'm just going to say is, "Yo Mama," because growing up, even in high school, that was the one thing you couldn't say. Whatever it may have been, whatever you followed that phrase with, I saw a few punches thrown when something was said around that. So what really struck me is, in Texas, you can't criticize someone's mother in that way. And Blaine really had no idea.

Loren: Exactly. It's something I noticed, being born in Pennsylvania and spending some of my childhood there and then moving to Texas. In Texas, there's more of an innate reverence for parents. I remember in Pennsylvania, and again, I was born in a very, very small town in Pennsylvania, and everybody knew everybody. And you knew your friends' parents, you saw them all the time. It was a much more casual relationship. I moved to Texas, and everybody's calling adults "sir" and "ma'am." It was very different.

In some ways, that informed part of this idea in the book. Blaine doesn't say, "Yo Mama" directly. Malloy is referring to a time in the Fifties when we had one of the worst droughts in state history. The aquifers got so low that the sulfur in the water would come out, and it would make the water stink. People were not washing clothes so that the cattle could have water.

Malloy's telling Witherspoon this, about his mom not being able to wash the clothes to save water. Witherspoon says, "Well, your mother's bad hygiene isn't my problem." And part of the backstory, which we find out later, is that Malloy's mother has Alzheimer's and is in bad health. She's dying, and he's having a hard time coming to terms with that. So it was really the worst possible thing Witherspoon could have said.

Tom: There was also another episode later in the book that also struck me as absolutely exemplar of the differences in culture. It was when the company CFO came down to Conquistador to talk to the people. And he turns out to be quite an interesting character in the book in his own right. The townspeople had that ethos that they respected people and authority; they respected their elders. If someone in one of those positions of authority said something to you, you assumed it was the truth to the point where they were literally brought checkbooks and were ready to invest in the company. And many did, which turned out to be a not very good financial investment. So I was wondering if you could talk about that dynamic of a culture clash or differences in culture as well.

Loren: That scene evolved from this idea that, despite all the cultural issues that the locals may have had with the new people coming in, fundamentally they still believe this plant was going to save the town and this was the future. If you think about that, especially in a small town, what happens? Everybody pulls together. Everybody does what needs to be done. I remember, again, going back to my hometown in Pennsylvania, there was a guy who mowed the city park every week for decades. I remember him doing that from the time I was a child. And I found out years later that he was never paid for that. He just did it as a community service.

That's the kind of thing that happens in small towns. You do what has to be done, you invest in your community in whatever way you can. And for these folks, they're thinking, "Wow, this company's coming to town, and it's publicly traded, and we can invest in that, we can participate in that." And of course, the flip side is that the CFO just saw mullets. He was thinking, "This is a great way to help boost the stock price." The townspeople really wanted to believe in the company, and in some ways, they wanted to believe in the company more than the people who actually worked there who just saw it as a job or a means to get somewhere else.

Tom: There's another scene that illustrates the difference in cultures as strongly as the first two we discussed, and that's the roundup. Blaine goes on a roundup, and he's wearing tennis shoes. That tells you all you need to know about that situation. But do you really think that would happen?

Loren: The roundup scene was more autobiographical than you might realize. That scene was formative to the book, after I experienced something similar. I found myself realizing that I was in a whole different world. I'd been in Texas for decades, but that was not anything I'd experienced, and I was just so lost. The practices in ranching have been around and been perfected over a long period of time. There's a reason they do all the things that they do. But if you haven't been in that world, it's just very eye-opening and very alarming in a lot of ways. And again, that was really the essence of what I was trying to capture.

To me, the idea that a high-tech executive would be standing in that place at that time would just seem like the ultimate fish-out-of-water experience. In the book, he's there to make amends, so it was a bread-breaking exercise. People that work on ranches like that, they love to show off what they do. And they think it's, "Hey, this is something you should see." You can go on a ranch tour; you can experience that. But it's a very different thing than touring an art museum.

But it's a glimpse into this culture that has existed for a hundred, almost two hundred years. I really wanted to capture that. Once I did, then I realized the flip side would be having Malloy, the cowboy, go to the wafer fab and go through a clean room, which is also a cultural experience. Those two juxtapositions were really the centerpiece of the book. It all grew out from those.

Tom: When I read about the trip to the wafer fab, it struck me that it wasn't a difference in culture; it was a difference in planets. He was on Mars. And you really did a great job of setting up what he had to put on, a breathing appara-tus, and the instructions he received just to be able to go into the room. Having done that once, I really felt like I was on a different planet.

The way that scene spoke to me was how different for everyone that environment is. But you use that as the culture clash. Is going into one of those clean rooms so different that it's not even a culture clash, it's an inter-planetary experience?

Loren: For Malloy it certainly was. It became surreal. He almost had an out-of-body experience. For you and me it's tough. And I'm a bigger guy, so anytime that I had to go into a clean room, they always had a hard time finding a bunny suit that was big enough for me. It always felt a little constrained, a little tight. It really enhanced the sense of claustrophobia.

Then I thought about what it would be like for a guy who works outside all the time, who's riding horses and looking at this vast landscape. How would he react to being stuffed in a bunny suit? He can barely see anything. Everything's covered except for your eyes. How would he react to that? Obviously, he had never experienced anything like that in his life, and it was problematic.

Tom: Going back to the roundup, the first and only time I did a six-hour horse ride, I never did it again. I can still remember my thighs hurting, and you got that part just spot on. Spot on.

Loren: Again, that was rather autobiographical. You don't forget that kind of pain.

Tom: As the book progresses, despite these cultural clashes, the two protagonists really come together at the end of the book because of a disaster or catastrophe. How you were able to bring them together?

Loren: There had to be resolution to the story. Something had to happen. The whole book was about change, and so something had to change. I wanted it to be uplifting in a sense, or at least hopeful. This is what communities are all about ultimately. The book is about a sense of place, and that's what I'm talking about. This is what you do in communities. You pull together for the greater good. Despite all their differences, at the end, everyone saw their way of life threatened, even if those lifestyles were very different. So they find a way to pull together.

Today, more than ever, that's something that we should be thinking about.

I purposely kept politics out of the book, but there's a message for them, especially the local ones. I see county politicians arguing about federal policy and that's not their job. Tell me how you're going to fix the roads. Tell me how you're going to preserve the water. Tell me how we're going to keep the lights on. These are the things we worry about at the community level, and our national politics really don't matter that much when it comes to those things.

I was glad that it was set in 1999 because it didn't get dragged into the political divisions that would probably exist in that world today. I didn't want that to be a distraction. But the most important point of the book is that when people have a shared sense of place, a sense of community, they pull together in times of need. They set aside their differences and help each other.

V. HOUSING

What if for some reason, cultural or otherwise, the locals did not want to take jobs at the plant? What if they couldn't find enough qualified people in the area to get up to full staffing? When they'd made the deal, the county commissioners had promised drawing workers from nearby towns. Out here driving an hour for supper was routine. Folks would do so for a good job, but what if they were wrong?

– From *The Big Empty*

Tom: When you have a massive, new infrastructure project bringing a plant or a Bitcoin mining operation or something in which you are going to have new people come into the community, housing is going to be an issue. Housing is becoming a hugely important issue across the state of Texas. I think many politicians are recognizing now that a lack of affordable housing could have a negative impact on the state of Texas. The housing that you brought up in the book was equally interesting because it was a gated community in a rural west Texas town, which is probably their first gated community.

The gated nature of the community sets it apart. Did that engender resentment within the town? And when you put in a multimillion-dollar development, what does that do to housing prices?

Loren: One of the themes of the book is that as the people move to a new place, they're often not trying to understand the land, they're not trying to understand what it means to live in the town. They don't have a sense of being a part of the community. The gated community just underscores that. You're literally building a gate to cut yourself off from everybody else. I've lived in neighborhoods where there's been discussion about, "Should we gate the community?" "Oh, we had a car burglary, we should build a gate on the community." Well I didn't move there to put myself in prison. The whole concept, to me, is not really what a community should be about, everybody building their own little walled off areas.

The other thing that you see happening in *The Big Empty* with regards to housing—and there's a much bigger theme here—is you have this grand Texas ranch, the Conquistador, which had been one of the largest ranches in the state's history. Little by little, it's getting sold off. And who's buying it? It's not other ranchers in most cases. And that's a theme that we have seen play out across Texas for decades. I wrote a piece for *Texas Monthly's* 50th anniversary issue about this very thing. I spoke with a ranch broker about what he's seeing in terms of buying trends. Recreational ranching has become a much bigger thing. We talked earlier about the resort effect, and that applies to ranching too.

As these ranches get chopped up, sold off to people that are buying them, not for economic productivity or something like that, but just for leisure. Land values go up and it's harder and harder to afford land. If you're a young person starting out and you didn't inherit land and you want to start a farm or a ranch, it's a lot more expensive to do it than it used to be, obviously.

Tom: One of the issues in Kerrville is affordable housing. And even the term "affordable" housing is now a divisive term because it has certain connotations to certain groups.

But in Kerrville, for instance, and I think in other similar sized communities across the state of Texas, a schoolteacher cannot afford to buy a house in Kerrville, a firefighter cannot afford to buy a house, a policeman cannot afford to buy a house, a city employee cannot afford to buy a house. And when the city leaders talk about trying to bring in businesses and industry to Kerrville, that's one of the first questions is, "Where can our workers be housed?" And sometimes the answer is, "There's a town twenty miles away. It's not a bad commute." That's not the right answer, but how do we address this type of housing crisis in a town such as Kerrville that really doesn't have homes less than $400,000, and there's a solid 30 percent of the community that simply doesn't want change?

How do we start to think through those issues? Because I know in Wimberley, that's also an issue.

Loren: Yes, and in a lot of other communities as well. It's a huge challenge, and you're right, it's not a popular thing with most voters. It's not just that they don't want change, the idea that you're going to do anything to, in any way, subsidize housing, give anyone some sort of a handout or something, is not a popular idea. That's especially true in rural parts of the state where people have carved out a hard scrabble existence for generations and nobody helped them. It's hard to understand how significantly these issues have changed. I think that companies themselves need to be doing more when they look at locating in a community. It's not just about plopping down a plant and seeing how many tax breaks you can get, it's about, are you going to be a part of that community? Are you going to support the community? Do you want your people living in the community in which you built this plant and made an investment?

We're starting to see this trend, at what they call the C-suite level. There is a lot more discussion about communities and a business's responsibility to them. Those are good and important discussions to have, and I hope that they move beyond just the feel-good corporate speak kind of things and actually result in action. You don't want to build a plant so your employees can live twenty miles away in a different town. And by the way, that's not why the town, whether it's Kerrville or wherever, wants your company there. As we talked about earlier, part of the rationale behind these tax breaks is that companies will come in and their employees are going to live in the community because that's where the additional tax revenue's going to come to support the tax breaks. If they're living twenty miles away, that money's going somewhere else, or at least some of the money's going somewhere else.

Companies have to take a more active role in this and really think it through. How do they encourage people to live in these communities? If they're unaffordable, what can we do to help out? I'm not saying we should go back to the days of the company housing, a company store and script and all that kind of stuff, but I think there are things that companies can do to help communities with this effort.

Tom: I don't want to suggest this is a small town or rural Texas problem, because the city of Houston has the same problem in terms of affordability for many workers to live in the city. Earlier, you mentioned Aspen, and you used the example that no matter how much money I have, if I go to a restaurant, I want somebody there to serve me food or mix me a drink. Waiters and bartenders can't afford to live in the city of Houston. Now, Houston, for better or worse, has basically unlimited land and unlimited ability to expand. So you can get a house, probably, within a hundred miles of Houston, but it's the same situation as San Francisco or Seattle. There's no housing in those towns, and you have to live a two-hour commute away, so your lifestyle is significantly reduced. How do you see those issues in major metropolitan area areas, someplace as large as the city of Houston?

Loren: I'm reminded of the old joke that "Houston's an hour away from Houston." It's really true. The big issue there, it's not that you can't find affordable housing, it's just you can't find it in a reasonable proximity to where you need to work in a lot of cases. I hoped that the response to COVID, the fact that a lot of companies have embraced remote work, and many are going to continue using a remote working model in some form, will help with some of this. First of all, remote work could be good for smaller communities because many people like the laid-back lifestyle of smaller towns. The big problem is you got to have a job. I've been saying for years, if I were the mayor of a small town in West Texas, like Conquistador, (I did not have a mayor character in the book and so this did not happen), I would scrape together whatever tax dollars or money I could find and build high-speed internet because that's a big factor.

If you move from a city to a rural area and you're trying to work from home, you've got to have good internet. It will be interesting to see how the remote work mindset plays out, but it seems like it's here to stay, and it may help address some of these housing issues. On the other hand, if you look at housing trends, the average cost of new homes, for example, has gone up, and part of the reason for that is people want bigger homes because they need home offices. It's a double-edged sword. But we're seeing a shift in a lot of these issues and a lot of these characteristics.

Tom: I'd like to come back to the issue of selling off of ranches. As these ranches are sold off, we're losing a part of Texas. Some people may see land just as an asset to be exploited, to be used appropriately by the owner. Others see land as our life or our heritage. We have to acknowledge that change is inevitable, but is there a way for us to retain our heritage as Texans, whatever that may be to you personally, and still use assets that make this state so great to continue that growth into the 21st century?

Loren: Land is very much baked into our state's DNA. The idea of the grand Texas ranch is pretty much what most people think of when they think of Texas. As these places go away, it's difficult. They get sold into smaller pieces and in many cases. Now in some cases, the recreational ranchers that are buying these properties want to preserve them and even make them better. Ranching is not great for the environment, and if somebody wants to buy a thousand acres and turn it back to its natural state, that can be a good thing. But there is some part of the Texas myth that's getting lost in that. It's not all negative. It's an evolution. The economics of ranching are not good, and they haven't been good for a long time, and they're getting worse.

For example, the 6666 Ranch was sold to Tyler Sheridan, the guy behind Yellowstone. He's got an investment group, but he's the lead investor. They want to keep the ranching operations going. They're doing some branding. You can buy 6666 merch, but then he's also going to use part of the property for a film studio, which could be a great idea. I get really annoyed at seeing a lot of movies about Texas that are clearly not filmed in Texas. The point is that the new owners still care about the land.

They're not Blaine Witherspoon's coming in, buying up the Conquistador Ranch and turning it into a waterpark or something. In a lot of cases, the new buyers do want to preserve the land and do appreciate it for what it is, but at the same time, if ranches are becoming smaller, we are also losing something. There's a part of our state identity that, I guess, is going away.

Tom: So that seems, I don't want to say a melancholy way for us to end, but I think really a great way for us to end this series. I wanted to thank you again for not only writing the book that was a great read, but exploring these, I think, important issues.

LISTEN TO THE ORIGINAL PODCAST SERIES

LOREN C. STEFFY is the author of five nonfiction books. He is a writer at large for *Texas Monthly*, and his work has appeared in newspapers and magazines nationwide. He has previously worked for news organizations including Bloomberg and the Houston Chronicle, and he is a managing director for 30 Point Strategies, where he leads the 30 Point Press publishing imprint. His is a frequent guest on radio and television programs and podcasts. *The Big Empty* is his first novel. Steffy holds a bachelor's degree in journalism from Texas A&M University. He lives in Wimberley, Texas, with his wife, three dogs and an ungrateful cat.

Printed in the USA
CPSIA information can be obtained
at www.ICGtesting.com
JSHW021100270823
47091JS00002B/2